Only His Kiss

Other books in the **Promises** series:
Mr. Francis' Wife by Sandy Gills
Best Friends by Debra White Smith
Freedom's Promise by Suzanne D. Hellman
Airwaves by Sherrie Lord

Here's what readers are saying about *Airwaves*, Sherrie Lord's first novel . . .

"One of the very best Christian books I've read."

"A great Christian romance with a happy ending. I recommend *Airwaves* to teenagers and women alike."

"[Sherrie] has a knack for combing romance with serious subjects."

"The faith aspect reminded me of myself twenty-two years ago. I wish I would have had it then to read."

PROMISES
A ROMANCE

Only His Kiss

SHERRIE LORD

Chariot Victor Publishing
A Division of Cook Communications

Chariot Victor Publishing,
a division of Cook Communications, Colorado Springs, Colorado 80918
Cook Communications, Paris, Ontario
Kingsway Communications, Eastbourne, England

ONLY HIS KISS

Editor: L.B. Norton
Design: Bill Gray
Cover Illustration: Matthew Archambault

1 2 3 4 5 6 7 8 9 10 Printing/Year 03 02 01 00 99

Published in association with the literary agency of Alive Communications, Inc., 1465 Kelly Johnson Blvd., Suite 320, Colorado Springs, CO 80920.

Library of Congress Cataloging-in-Publication Data

Lord, Sherrie.
      Only his kiss/by Sherrie Lord.
          p.   cm. -- (Promises, a romance)
     ISBN 1-56476-707-8
     I. Title.   II. Series.
PS3562.0728055   1999   99-18696
813'.54--dc21   CIP

Thank yous

I marvel at those authors whose acknowledgments are so brief. One line? Ha! I struggle to get it onto one page. And since I'm either neglecting people or pestering them to death, hugs of deep appreciation to . . .

. . . my heroes, Harry, Mike, and Erik. There's so much in you to regard. And I do.

. . . my professional support—agent Kathy Yanni, Chariot Victor vice president Randy Scott, managing editor Julie Smith, editor L.B. Norton, and cover artist Matthew Archambault. The sales reps for bragging my up, their families for managing without them while they travel, and the many tireless staff at Chariot Victor for their talents and attention to detail.

. . . my volunteer support—Barbara Campbell, Debbie Samson, and Jonnie Landis. The many who pray, particularly Virginia Bonne, Vickie Gonzales, Wanda Pierren, Linda Waag, and Scott Larkin. And Deb Edgerton for a particular afternoon when we brainstormed on the porch—What if we named him Noble. . . ?

. . . my aunt, Sophia Williams; you will always have your own room in my heart.

. . . Dr. Sara Cifrese for equipping a frontier physician with knowledge and skill. Otto Wiersholm for sharing your first language with Magnus so he could speak endearments to his daughter. Allen McCrady, who loves all things Norwegian. Joanne Bates, who helped the Santa Feins speak Spanish. And Scott Benson, who was born in the wrong century. Some rich and famous author should buy you a museum or wagon train or something.

. . . my precious encouragers, who are never stingy with themselves. Christian bookstore workers for providing a safe place for those who need a gentle moment. And those who give their "free" time to volunteer where Jesus wouldn't otherwise be. Stay in the race, for the gravest sorrow is discovering you gave up one second too soon.

. . . my Daddy; the patience in Your hand is surpassed only by the love in Your heart.

One

The Santa Fe Trail, May, 1858

*I*t's a girl, sir."

The wagon master's shoulders collapsed in exasperation. "I can see that," he said, eyes flashing ominously. "What I mean is, what's she doing here and where in the . . . blazes did you find her?" His jaw clung to the "b" of "blazes" as though it held back more energetic words.

Sonja glanced from the train's commander to her captor, then searched each bullwhacker's grimy face as they straggled in to see what had stopped the train. Her heart fell. He wasn't here, the man with the brown eyes; no chance for another gallant rescue. She tested the prickly rope sawing holes through her wrists; no room for escape either.

"I found her a couple miles back, Captain," the rope's owner continued from where he stood, the mule's reins in his hand. "She wasn't as wily in trailing us as she thought she was. I don't think she counted on me sneaking up behind her, either."

Sonja glared at him. The evil man. Scared her half to death, and for no reason. She wasn't hurting anyone.

The wagon master's right eyebrow arched dangerously, making her heart trip. Her arms, tied behind her, threatened to rip from their sockets, her captor's sweat tasted like gritty salt in his kerchief stretched taut across her mouth, and her right leg hurt like the dickens, but she barely paused to blink. She had to be ready.

"Benton! Saxton! Untie her from that mule," the captain barked with a jerk of his head. Then he stepped back, waiting implacably while two of the bullwhackers snapped to life and approached from either side.

Terror shot through her. No telling what he intended to do with—or to—her. She screamed through the gag and lurched, kicking at the bullwhackers reaching for her. The men jumped back.

"Careful," the man at the reins warned. "I didn't tie her up for my own entertainment. She isn't very big, but she kicks like a shot of sour mash."

The audience laughed, prompting Sonja to scan their faces again. Where was he? Surely this wasn't the wrong train.

Please, Lord, make this the right train.

It was a whole-hearted request, even if spoken from a shadowed conscience. Wouldn't need God's rescue now if she'd sought His advice earlier.

Her brain spun, aggravated by the mule's restless hoofing beneath her. The May sun stared clammy sweat to a trickle between her breasts and pasted her shirt to her back, but her arms prickled with cold and her stomach roiled.

"You can fight all you want to," the captain said with deadly calm, fixing Sonja in the paralyzing beam of his stare. "It won't do any good. I'm going to get some answers out of you, young lady, and we're going to start with what you're doing, all by yourself, two weeks' ride from Independence."

Fingers jerked at the line binding Sonja's ankles under the mule's belly and tugged at the rope around her wrists.

The cord pulled tighter just before it fell free, then clumsy hands pinched around her waist, hauled her off the saddle, and dropped her on her feet. She clawed at the bandanna slicing her mouth as she spun around to face the captain—

A shaft of white-hot pain seared her knee. She tried to breathe, but the agony spread its angry tendrils into her throat. Behind her eyes it burst, swallowing her in a wave of dizziness and drenching her vision with star showers and black.

TWO

*V*oices rumbled . . . unintelligible . . . and from a distance.

Sonja opened her eyes. Blinked. The voices were close—and they belonged to men. Panic tingled through her. She shot for freedom.

"It's all right. You're safe," one of them said, cupping her shoulders and pressing her down again.

Her gaze found his face. It was him, the man with the brown eyes.

"Where do you hurt?" he asked.

Yes, the voice had the same soothing tone, and the eyes behind the round, silver-rimmed spectacles were just as she remembered them, the color reminding her of . . . of nothing she could recall at the moment.

"I'm more interested in knowing where the rest of her party is and why she's holding up my train," the captain growled from where he hunched behind the man from Independence.

Sonja's stomach flipped. She shrank back.

"Would you let me take care of this?" Brown Eyes asked over his shoulder.

The wagon master's brows met in the middle before he rose to a staggering height. "Might as well break for breakfast. Mason! Corral the wagons and unhitch the oxen," he called. His bellow faded with his steps into the distant activity.

"What's your name?" Sonja asked of Brown Eyes, the question tumbling from her lips seemingly on its own, though she'd pondered the answer continually ever since she saw him in Independence.

His eyebrows twitched in puzzlement. "Dr. Staley. Now, where do you—?"

"You're a doctor?"

With a wagon and team of his own, he looked like a bull-whacker, though he would make a noble profession of doctoring—unlike Chas Alexander, Lafayette, Indiana's best barber and worst healer, who answered every complaint with a thorough purging. One dose of his calomel was enough to convince Sonja; her infirmities were never quite that serious again.

"Where do you hurt?" Dr. Staley asked once more.

"My . . . knee," she stammered, deciding it was okay to discuss such specifics with a man who was also a doctor. "What's your given name?"

"Thaddeus."

Thaddeus? Ugh. Didn't suit him at all.

He flipped open a gray wool blanket, let it billow over her, then turned to the knapsack tied to the stick she'd been dragging behind her. Before she could protest—everything moved alarmingly fast—he handed her her own blue calico skirt.

"Let's get you out of those trousers; they won't allow for swelling," he said.

The trousers looked pretty roomy to her. They should be. They came from the wardrobe of a fairly sizable man.

Now Thaddeus was unlacing her boots! Sonja could

only stare at him. He expected her to undress right here? In front of him? Why, Papa would—

"Would you prefer I split the seam?" Thaddeus asked, already reaching to the long-bladed knife in the leather sheath on his right hip.

"Cut my britches!" Sonja winced at the clamor's sharp blow inside her head. He thought he was being helpful. He'd see it her way if he knew how precious the trousers were. Papa didn't have that many pairs to start with . . . and they were all she had of him now.

"I can't examine your knee with them on," he explained.

She raised up on her elbows, tumbling a cloth from her forehead to her nose. She batted at it irritably—hadn't even known it was there—as another pain shot through her knee, a twin to the one in her head. But it was the wave of nausea that took the fight out of her, dropping her shoulders to the twig-poked blanket beneath her. What could possibly happen next? Oh, and what did it matter, anyway?

With clumsy fingers and under the cover of the blanket, she untied the rope that cinched the trousers around her waist—no need to unbutton what was already generous— and scooted them over her hips. The energy she spent bought more misery than speed, but Thaddeus waited patiently, then helped by pulling off the other boot. He stood the pair beside him, then his hands dived under the blanket, his fingers walking up her calves in search of the trousers' waistband. Sonja tensed, wanting to jump out of the skin he touched so casually. No doubt about it, Papa would consider this a killing-violation. But Thaddeus simply pulled her trousers from her legs and folded back the blanket. "Which knee, please?"

"My right."

Immediately he pushed the loose hem of her pantalets above her right knee, while relief washed over her. She'd answered him correctly and quickly enough, so he might not think her simpleminded after all. But he was making himself alarmingly familiar with her limb. She glanced through the fan of wheel spokes to the tumult on the other side of the wagon.

"No one can see us."

She turned back and flinched when Thaddeus pressed his fingers—cool and soft but intruding—into her knee. Then she guarded her expression. If he knew how bad her leg hurt or her head throbbed, he would know she was too ill to travel. She distracted herself watching through the red spokes of the wheels at the men unhitching their teams inside the corral of the wagons. They'd cook breakfast now, though the thought made her want to throw up. She looked to the printing on the side of the blue wagon. "J. Murphy"; could never get close enough to read it before. That wretched rag that had been clamped between her teeth now lay at her shoulder, and it was filthy—

"You fell?" Thaddeus asked.

"That man chased me. There were gopher holes." She tried not to wince. Held her breath instead.

Thaddeus slid his hand under her thigh, making her gasp for that air she'd been denying herself. If the pain weren't bad enough, he was touching her in very intimate places; doctor or not, he was still a man.

He simply went about his business. "Bend your leg for me," then, "Does this hurt?" and "How about this?"

Sonja gave him only tiny shakes of her head—lies of necessity—until his cool fingers probed on either side of her knee. "Do you have to do that?"

"I'm sorry," he replied. "I don't want to hurt you, but the pain tells me more about your injury than you do."

"All right, my whole limb hurts," Sonja snapped. "Are you satisfied?"

"You don't have to be brave with me," he told her quietly.

Not true. And he shouldn't do that. Gentle words only jeopardized her self-control, for there was no reach long enough to bring her comfort, and nerve was all she had left—except for him, and he was finally near again.

He wasn't wearing his brown felt hat with the broad and flat brim that she'd seen on him in Independence. The band had pressed its impression into the hair that fell in an intriguing blend of blonds—the yellow of straw, the silver of moonlight, and the beige of Papa's pulpit. In careful waves and feathery layers, it swept around his ears and collar.

He wasn't as clean as he'd been in Independence, either. His brown britches and blue flannel shirt looked as though he'd slept in them, but three of the four front buttons—whose placket ended four inches above his waist—were loose. The billowy sleeves were rolled back to his elbows, brown suspenders arced over his shoulders, and a navy bandanna ringed his neck. A sidearm hung, handle-forward, from his left hip, where he could draw the long-barreled weapon across his stomach with a right-handed reach, and sunburned skin was peeling on his nose. The lips below it were leveled in a serious line.

But it was his eyes that made her wait for the next time they might turn her direction. The hue was unusual, its brown somewhere between the deep gold of burnt amber and the rich warmth of fertile earth—

"Does your hip hurt?" he asked.

When she shook her head in reply, his brows lifted sardonically.

"Honest," Sonja assured him. She wasn't a liar. At least, not by choice.

Thaddeus sat back on his heels as if he'd reached a decision. "Where's your family?"

"I don't have one." God would have to overlook one more half-truth.

"Then where is the rest of your party?"

She sat up and flipped the blanket over her bare leg, tucking it around her waist and gritting her teeth against the inevitable barrage of questions. "I'm traveling to Santa Fe alone."

"You expect me to believe that?" a third voice demanded.

Sonja and Thaddeus' heads swiveled to the captain as he rounded the wagon. She glanced at her skirt and britches. They were lying in full view, though the wagon master didn't appear to notice.

"Both my parents are dead," Sonja said. "I have an aunt in Santa Fe. I'm going to live with her."

Thou shalt not bear false witness, Moses admonished in her head, speaking in her father's accent. Someone laughed in the distance, as if they knew how ridiculous her fabrication was, but she couldn't help it. What else was she to do? Let them send her back? She'd had a good reason for leaving; finding the man from Independence was a good reason to stay.

Thaddeus was suddenly setting his hat in place, while blood rushed like a waterfall in Sonja's ears. What horrid timing to have to face this inquisition when she was at her worst. There were bees in her head, yet her entire future depended on the next few minutes.

"The knee is stable; nothing's broken or torn as far as I can tell," the physician told the captain. "But she'll be laid up for several days. She's badly bruised."

A smirk tilted the captain's mustache, and he nodded slowly. "Isn't that just like an addlepated girl, to set off by herself behind a freight train full of men she doesn't even know?"

"I do, too!" Sonja snapped.

Triumph glinted in the captain's eyes. It was a trap, and she'd leaped right into it. She set her attention where she wouldn't get in trouble—smoothing her blanket—while the captain crossed his brawny arms.

"Very well," he said calmly. "Why don't you tell me which of my men you felt compelled to follow?"

Sonja fidgeted.

"Now, young lady," he ordered softly and as if his authority were as comfortable as an old hat.

Sonja jumped. "I had to get to Santa Fe, and . . . I'd seen Thaddeus in Independence. He helped me when—"

"What?" Thaddeus asked, his jaw dropping far enough for the word to fall out.

"Well . . . those men were harassing me. You made them leave me alone." And the reasoning sounded so pathetic now, under Thaddeus'—and the captain's—stares. "When I saw you put your things in one of the wagons, I knew you worked with the train. . . ."

Her voice faded into silence—which wore out before it was old.

"That was you?" Thaddeus said. "Those weren't men, they were boys. And they were just teasing you. I merely shooed them away and helped you with your packages. Why would you—"

"I didn't know what else to do!"

The wagon master snorted. "That's too absurd to be a lie. Is there anyone with you, or did you really set out on an eight-hundred-mile trek into this nothingness alone?"

"Seven hundred and eighty miles, and there's no one with me," Sonja told a tiny blade of new grass clinging to the blanket. "It wasn't my intention to inconvenience you— or even join you. I just wanted to follow behind. You knew the way . . . and . . ."

"—Provided some measure of protection," the captain finished for her. "Are you from Independence?"

"No."

When she volunteered nothing further, he filled the

silence. "You're not going to tell me where you live, are you?"

"No."

When neither of the men said anything, she looked up. Thaddeus was glaring at her, his eyes a steady combination of bewilderment and profound annoyance. He tipped his hat back on his head while the captain studied her through narrowed eyes, his finger worrying the right half of his dusky mustache.

The captain shook his head. "That does it, then. She's your responsibility, Thad."

Three

*T*haddeus sprang to his feet, snapping Sonja's head back to follow him. Her vision slid about—and hurt like crazy behind her eyes when it skidded to a stop.

"Now wait just a minute," Thaddeus said. "Why me? I don't even know her."

"You know her better than any of the rest of us," the wagon master replied. "Besides, she's injured, and you're the doctor."

"Oh sure, Harley, old friend. Hang me with my own Hippocratic oath."

The wagon master—Harley—only grinned as he walked away.

Thaddeus marched after him. "Why don't we send her back to Council Grove—or even Diamond Spring? There's a stage station there."

Nearly the last bit of civilization until Santa Fe.

"It's only a few miles back," Thaddeus continued. "We can rig up a travois or something—"

Harley stopped. "Too slow, and I can't spare the help. You know that. This outfit has only as many men as it needs to get this freight to Santa Fe, no more, no less. One stage already passed us, and I can't just leave her here on the road waiting for the next one."

Thaddeus glared at him.

Harley's brows nearly grew together. "Blast it all, this is a Russell, Majors, and Waddell outfit. The freighting company that issues Bibles to its teamsters. You know the rules—not even foul language or a deck of cards, much less a female— so I'm not taking her along to advance my career. Just do us all a favor. Keep her out of the way. We have work to do." Then he shot Sonja a glance of frustration and stalked away.

Thaddeus watched Harley's retreat for a long moment before he swiveled around. His burnt-amber eyes looked as though they'd been fired in a furnace.

In Independence, Magnus Thorseth and his apprentice, Karl, rode the perimeter of another wagon encampment preparing to join the teeming mass of families, animals, and conveyances rattling over the ruts to the Oregon Territory. Most trains had already jangled into the throng, now that the grass was tall enough for the thick-lipped oxen to eat. This one would roll out tomorrow.

Magnus scanned quickly, his eyes not lingering as they searched for one who was familiar—though she might not be so, dressed in his own trousers and shirt she'd taken. They weren't even certain she was missing until well past supper on their own train. That was the fourth day on the trail to Oregon and, even pushing hard, it took that many to double back to Independence. But the travelers they passed had seen someone walking the other way—a young boy dragging a stick with a knapsack tied to its middle. Magnus was sure of it; that young "boy" was his Sonja, who'd helped pack the wagon, then run away from it.

His heart seized in pain. So many days and so far; she could be anywhere.

Thaddeus eyed the left rear wheel of the mess wagon and considered kicking it, except he'd probably break his foot. He stepped to the side instead, medicine cup in one hand and a plate of breakfast in the other.

"Here. Drink this," he said, offering her the cup.

The girl lying inside simply stared at it. The silly fool. Out here by herself, of all things, and making him out to be her physician. *And* guardian. *And* mother, since she'd obviously wondered from home.

"It's laudanum for your pain," he said of the cloudy syrup—and wouldn't she be glad for the opium-alcohol tincture when this wagon started moving. Just the jostling to get her settled inside had stolen her breath. She still hadn't gotten her color back.

The trouble was, Russell, Majors, and Waddell built nothing to accommodate passengers, much less patients. Even if she were able to sit all day with that leg down where it could swell to new proportions, the only wagon with a seat was Jackson's Conestoga. Bullwhackers walked, cracking their whips to keep six yoke of oxen interested in chasing the horizon. So he'd fashioned her a bed of wool blankets and comforters layered over sacks of dried beans, then passed her between the wagon's ribs, since the tailgate was blocked by Jackson's wooden cupboard of spices and utensils. The memory made Thaddeus bite back caustic words. Any patient deserved his mercy, but this one certainly made a burden of herself. If he'd wanted to take anything extra to Santa Fe, it hadn't been a foolish girl.

She stared into the cup, curled her lip, and glanced up

uncertainly, which raised a war in his conscience.

"Come on. The sooner you drink it, the sooner you'll feel better," he said more gently.

Her next hesitation was followed by a rush of decision that lifted the cup to her lips for a hasty draining. She grimaced and shuddered, giving him a moment of revenge. He hadn't promised it would taste good.

"Where are my things?" she asked.

"With mine. What's your name? And tell me the truth."

"Sonja Thorseth."

"Thorseth?" he asked, practicing the pronunciation.

She nodded. "It's Norwegian."

And fit well enough. Her braids were very blond and her complexion fair, despite what the open sun had done to it.

He traded her the cup for a plate of beans and bacon and a biscuit, which got him more mumbled gratitude and a long stare. Her gaze seemed to say things. He looked away. It was a little late for "I'm sorry."

When he returned from another trip to his medical wallets, she was bent over her plate and stuffing bread in as if she were chinking a wall. The sight tugged at his heart. No telling when she'd last eaten a full meal. The only provisions in her knapsack were hardtack and dried apples. Even so, she sure couldn't wolf her food like that and get away with it.

"Slow down," he warned.

Her head popped up, eyes wide and very blue.

"The laudanum could upset your stomach, and I'd hate to see it come back up. It may be rare where we're going."

She straightened and chucked her biscuit into the plate. "Forgive me. I wouldn't want to waste your precious medicine. I never asked for it, you know."

Acid-base reactions aside, the only thing more explosive than a female was a female backed into a corner, and this one was walled on all sides. "I didn't mean it that way. You can have all you need. I just don't want you to get sick on top of everything else, that's all."

From between the wagon ribs, Sonja stared at him, her eye-level boosted above his by the sacks of provisions under her. Despite her strategic advantage, the fight left her eyes, and her chin lowered slightly. She looked almost contrite.

A female, penitent? Naw.

The conversation around Jackson's fire had died, and the world listed a little with the weight of every ear in their mess unit tipped their direction. The men wanted to know about her? Let one of them step around here and pry the secrets out of her—and she had a passel of them. The only thing he was interested in was her injury.

It was going to be a long trip to Santa Fe.

"I've brought some cloths to put on your knee," Thaddeus told her, motioning with the stack. "They'll draw heat from the injury as the water evaporates, maybe put down some of that swelling."

Her nod was a tiny one, but it gave permission for him to set his boot on the wheel hub and climb into the wagon. The interior shrank around him, and it was no graceful dance crawling around Sonja's legs, then jockeying for position on the uneven pack of boxes and barrels beside her. He'd visited roomier privies. He looked to the tin plate in her lap and the breakfast she never did go back to.

"I don't want anymore," she said, chin jerking ever so slightly.

Probably sick—and too stubborn to admit it. Then the whole effect of her defiance was ruined by the slow blink of thickened eyelids. Good. The drug was working, and sleep would serve her best at this point. He reached across her, pulled out the stick wedging the canvas open, and let the tarp flap close, casting them in deeper shadow.

"Why don't you lie down, Sonja?" he suggested, using

her name to calm her further.

The question sank into a dull gaze, so Thaddeus set her plate aside and helped her decide, pressing her shoulders gently to her bed.

He folded back her skirt and slipped the lacy edge of her pantalets past her knee. Shades of blue and purple were beginning to rise in her flesh, and swelling had doubled its size. It was a miracle she hadn't broken a bone or torn the soft tissue. As it was, she'd be shuffling slow for a while.

She gasped when he draped the first strip of cold damp cotton over her knee. Then her eyes fell closed. "Mmm . . . feels better already," she mumbled.

Thaddeus nodded his own satisfaction and draped another cloth, stealing the opportunity for an unguarded study of his patient. She looked very young, lying there with her braids trailing over her shoulders and down her arms. Too young to be so desperate as to follow a stranger over 160 miles on foot. She conversed as if she were intelligent enough and didn't act as if anyone were chasing her, so there was more to this than her simple explanation. No doubt it would be what she'd packed in her knapsack that would give the most honest clues.

He set the last cloth, adjusted her pantalets and skirt, and climbed carefully out of the wagon. He had the edge of the tarp in hand, ready to fasten the grommet, when she asked him a garbled question.

"What?" he asked.

She was supposed to be asleep, though her eyes were open now.

"The gold monogram on your medicine cup—N. T. S.," she said with an odd combination of urgency and sluggish tongue. "What does the 'N' stand for?"

People always asked about that first initial. Mama hadn't been in her right mind, and Dad had surely drowned in her infectious enthusiasm to go along with it.

Sonja simply waited, her sleepy gaze luminous and steady. Even pale, she was a pretty little thing. Her features would form becoming lines on paper, a crayon of pastel stroked into a pert nose, proud cheekbones, a delicate jaw, a softly buttoned chin, whispered brows . . . and eyes like the sky faceted into crystal. In Independence, she'd looked like a harassed little sister. Out cold in the brush, she'd looked like a female patient. Here, lying inside the soft shadow of the wagon, she looked as if a hairbrush and basin of water might uncover a face that would turn a man's head.

Except his.

"Nothing," Thaddeus told her.

"The 'N' stands for something. I was just curious."

"You misunderstand. It does. It stands for 'Nothing.' "

"Nothing Thaddeus Staley?" she repeated skeptically.

"That's right. Now go to sleep."

In Independence, Magnus reined his rented horse to a stop beside yet another wagon encampment and stared ahead, not really seeing. Wasn't anything he could explain. He just knew, just as he'd known not to waste time searching the brush for Sonja along the trail, for he knew she wasn't the victim of mishap. She'd walked away deliberately. And the road had any number of stopping places, but only two end-points—Oregon and home.

He looked to Karl and shook his head. "We can't find her because she's not here. Sonja is not in Independence."

"What in the blue blazes is holding us up now?" Harley

asked. "The oxen will die of old age if we don't pull foot, Thad."

Sonja would have followed the voice over Thaddeus' shoulder, except her stomach lurched again, hurling the rest of her breakfast into the bucket he held under her chin. If the Lord had any mercy, the smelly puddle beneath her nose contained all of that vicious medicine. The only thing near a fair trade for losing the nourishment was that her knee didn't hurt anymore. In fact, the most prominent sensation in her body was the heaviness in her limbs, oddly opposed to the lightness in her head.

"It couldn't be helped," Thaddeus replied to the wagon master. "She's ill, and I don't think she arranged this simply to inconvenience Russell, Majors, and Waddell . . . or you."

Sonja glanced at Thaddeus, adding another rescue to his tally. One more, and he'd deserve a hero's medal.

He hooked a tarp grommet on the end of the stick and jammed it against the wagon to hold the flap open. His stroke on her arm was gentle. "How do you feel?" he asked from where he stood under the tent of canvas.

Sonja spit into the bucket. "Don't ask."

"Are you finished?"

"There's nothing left."

Harley turned, bellowing orders to everyone within miles as he walked away.

"There's been folks unhappy with my cookin' before, but I can't say as anybody's ever throwed it back up." Jackson, the camp's cook, accepted the hateful bucket from Thaddeus' hand. He cast it a dubious glance, humor in his rusty-brown eyes. "I ain't rightly sure, but I reckon I just been insulted."

Sonja sent Jackson an apologetic gaze and God a prayer of thanks. Jackson had been so kind, chatting amiably over his shoulder as the wagon jolted over the trail, while her head swam and her stomach churned with increasing intensity. When she'd finally called to him, he hauled the team to a halt mid-sentence, then sprang from his perch, calling to Thaddeus who was leading the wagon ahead of them. Seconds later, and just in time, Thaddeus all but tore her canvas roof from its moorings in his haste to reach her. He already had the bucket in hand.

"Somethin' I can do to help, Doc?" Jackson asked now.

"You could bring me a wet cloth and a cup of water," Thaddeus replied, setting his boot on the hub of the wheel to climb into the wagon.

Jackson's hat bobbed out of sight. When he returned, he handed up the cup and rag, then watched as Sonja drank and Thaddeus mopped the blessed coolness over her face and the back of her neck.

"Better now?" Thaddeus asked softly.

"I think so." She swallowed; despite the water, her mouth tasted awful.

"How's your knee?"

She grinned. "What knee?" She'd forgotten all about it—which was amusing, for some reason. Jackson certainly chuckled.

"You better lie down," Thaddeus told her, helping her to her pillow and the comforter that was lumpy but cozy.

Jackson closed the canvas, and Thaddeus peeled back layers, baring her leg as if it were his own. He looked so much the serious physician, with his eyebrows drawn together in careful study, and so much a little boy, with his eyelashes brushing his cheek. And oh, his touch was so gentle.

He glanced at her, his expression one of concentration, though his gaze was kind. It always was. Even angry, he couldn't conceal the calling in his eyes, the mission to reach into others' pain with unhurried compassion and a confident knowledge of the healing arts. He sure seemed smart. He must have gone to school a long time, though he didn't look old. . . . Perhaps his father was a doctor. Perhaps they lived in Santa Fe . . . the 'N' of his first name couldn't stand for 'Nothing'. He was teasing her . . . And certainly the desire to heal must have sprung from a well in his soul, some depth of his noble . . . noble . . . heart. . . .

Four

S urreptitiously, Thaddeus watched Sonja's eyelids fall closed; they stayed there. No wonder she surrendered to the laudanum so easily in the middle of the day. By all accounts, she'd walked from Independence, all by herself and with no night watch to lend her deep sleep. Even in Independence, she had a cautious awareness about her, so opposed to her delicate features and youthful braids.

The canvas wall lifted, letting in a spray of midday light. It was Harley MacGregor who held the lifted tarp. "How much longer, Thad?"

Thaddeus shook his head vigorously in a signal for quiet, prompting Harley to glance quickly at Sonja. His voice rumbled just above a whisper as he said, "I didn't get a chance to talk to you before we rolled on after breakfast. Did you find out anything about her?"

"Not much," Thaddeus replied. "I looked more closely in her knapsack. She has a few clothes, traveling food, and a Bible with her name inside, but that's all. Was she even carrying a weapon?"

"An old Colt revolver, but I doubt she could fire it without propping it on a rock."

Thaddeus paused in layering wet cloths on her knee. "She's a little wisp of a thing. How old do you think she is?"

Harley crossed his forearms on the top of the wheel, eyes narrowing in thought. "I don't know. Seventeen. Eighteen, maybe."

"Naw. Closer to sixteen, I think."

A grin pulled at the corners of Harley's mouth. "Older than that, Thad. That's not the leg of a girl. Looks pretty—"

"You aren't supposed to be looking."

"You think I'm stupid? Besides, you are."

"I'm a doctor."

"And I ought to be," Harley replied good-naturedly. "By virtue of association, if nothing else. You'd never have made it through doctor school without me."

"That doctor school, as you so glibly call it, is the oldest school of medicine in the country and, as I recall, you hindered more than helped, keeping me out all hours and in plenty of trouble when I should have been studying."

"You make up for it now—your face always in a book. Besides, you didn't complain."

Thaddeus positioned the final cloth and rearranged Sonja's skirt, leaving her leg exposed to the heat-absorbing air. "So this is how you reward a childhood friendship—saddle me with this impetuous girl?"

"You're the one she followed."

Thaddeus glared at him.

Harley shrugged. "She needs a guardian; I don't have the time, and I trust you. Anyone else in this outfit would thank me, you know." Mirth danced beneath his mustache. "I'm beginning to worry about you, Thad. You don't seem to like women anymore."

The wagon creaked and rocked as Thaddeus crawled over Sonja's legs and jumped down. "Don't do me any favors, Harley. I'm not looking to replace Amanda." He combed his fingers through his hair and set his hat. "I'm working my way to Santa Fe, where I intend to start a new life and a new medical practice. If I want companionship, I'll get a pet. A barn cat would be more loyal—and loving—than the best I've enjoyed in the past."

Harley opened his mouth to reply but lost the chance to the cook.

"How's the little missy?" Jackson asked. He hunkered into his shirt when both men shushed him.

"Sleeping," Thaddeus told him.

With exaggerated stealth, Jackson hung the bucket on its hook at the side of the wagon. Thaddeus fastened the canvas top, hooking the grommets strung along its hem, and worked his fingers into the leather gloves he pulled from the back of his waistband.

"She should rest for the next few hours, but call me if she fusses."

"You got it, Doc." Jackson spun and headed for the front of the wagon, where his team of mules waited with flapping ears.

Thaddeus and Harley passed him to reach Thaddeus' own conveyance, the last of those carrying freight. The most experienced teamsters led this outfit of twenty-five freight wagons, with the progressively less experienced behind. Thaddeus could crack whip two or three spots ahead of where he was—he at least had experience leading oxen— except his patient was in the mess wagon behind him; he ate all the others' dust.

As wagon master, Harley usually rode ahead of the train to scout the trail, selecting the best places to ford streams and camp for the night. Now he looked to the back of the train and raised his arm at a distant rider.

A moment later Mason, his lieutenant, drew his mule to a halt beside them and swung out of the saddle, a gesture of respect and courtesy. "There isn't anyone back there, Captain—at least no one she belongs to."

Harley nodded as if the news made him weary. "Thanks, Lieutenant. Let me know if anything changes."

They watched as the lieutenant mounted and rode back to his position at the rear of the train, near the calf yard of a few dozen spare oxen, their herders, and the reserve teamsters.

Harley folded his arms. His forefinger smoothed one wing of his mustache, then the other. "I don't know why, but that girl's out here all by herself." He gave Thaddeus a glance. "She would have died long before she ever reached Santa Fe, you know."

Thaddeus looked to the mess wagon, where Sonja lay with her secrets. "My guess is, she left in a hurry, before she had time to think it through."

"Sounds desperate, Thad."

Thaddeus nodded. "It does, at that."

Pain and commotion woke her. The pain was everywhere inside her, driving from her knee to her hip and throbbing in her head. The commotion was everywhere around her, the bellow and bawl of steers being freed from their heavy wooden collars.

Sonja shifted and blinked several times. She looked around her. It was evening, and she was in a wagon she didn't recall climbing into. She groaned. She hadn't; she'd been carried, because some overzealous scout had chased her—he on hoof and she on foot—until she fell. Papa was on his way to Oregon, she was all bunged up in a freight train full of dusty strangers, her knee hurt, her stomach felt strange, it was hot in this wagon, she had to visit the privy—

"You're awake."

Sonja's attention darted to the lifted edge of the canvas. It was Thaddeus, who valiantly held—

The bucket!

Her gaze faltered. For eight days she had set one foot in front of the other, following a memory. Now they were finally face-to-face, and she'd been captured a dirty mess in men's trousers, she was surely crippled, and *this man had seen her throw up!*

Things weren't going the way she'd planned.

"How do you feel?" he asked.

"Fine enough," she told the ceiling.

"How's your knee?"

"It hurts a little," she lied. It hurt a lot.

"You can have more laudanum if you need it." He paused. "We're at Lost Spring camp. I'll bring you some supper as soon as it's ready." Then he dropped the tarp, leaving disappointment in his wake.

He'd been so nice to her in Independence, scattering those boys as if he'd stepped into a flock of chickens, then bending to retrieve her provisions where they landed. His grin was softly shy, and his burnt-amber eyes bid welcome; indeed, she tried to follow him, but couldn't keep up.

She didn't need to; he walked right by her the next Monday, leading one of the teams in the wagon train that pulled onto the trail ahead of her own. If he was a teamster, of course it would be for Russell, Majors, and Waddell, the most practiced operation hauling freight between its offices in Leavenworth, Kansas, and Santa Fe. Everyone heading into the unknown themselves knew that.

She watched the road far ahead for just a glimpse of his train, remembering the kindness in his brown eyes . . . while the trust in Papa's blue ones made her avoid their gaze. She couldn't hurt Papa. But she would. So she couldn't stay.

The solution fell together with frightening speed, carrying her away with it until she was packing food and clothes—her own and some of Papa's—into a knapsack she'd hidden in the brush. Even the lying had come as if it were habit.

"I've found another girl my age, and I'm going to ride with her family," she told Papa, committing herself to the awesome step she was about to take.

Strangely divided, she was; the thinking-Sonja watching the desperate-Sonja change her life.

Papa patted her shoulder, but his smile was a weak memory of the one that must have gotten buried with Mama six months ago. "Do not make a bother of yourself, *lille venn.*"

"I won't," she promised, then paused, etching him into her memory. He sat in the wagon, reins in hand, but it was his Bible, mauled to a state of friendliness, she saw cradled in his palm. Could almost hear his thick accent echoing from his Sunday pulpit and the heavy ping of his hammer ringing from his weekday smithy. She missed him already. In fact, she almost backed out . . . except for the shame. It would stay only if she did.

"I'll see you at supper," she called over her shoulder, guaranteeing herself the rounding of the clock before Papa had a chance to even wonder where she was.

The last wagon in their train rolled away while she watched, then she turned around and walked, safe in Papa's shirt and trousers—no one would question a young boy by himself. By noon she'd doubled back to where the Oregon Trail forked to the north and the Santa Fe to the south; she turned to the south . . . and caught up to the Russell, Majors, and Waddell train three days later. They caught her five days after that.

Sonja blinked and sighed, then draped the back of her wrist over her eyes and closed them, wishing to stop the hammer swinging recklessly in her head. Beyond the canvas walls the bullwhackers unhitched their teams in the corral of the wagons, speaking to the cattle in quiet tones.

The tarp on the far side lifted, and Jackson peered in at her. "Still alive, huh?" He paused. "Guess that means we're back to bacon and beans."

Shock bubbled from Sonja's throat—though it sounded like a chuckle. "Bacon and beans . . . instead of me?"

Jackson nodded once. "Give these fellers a couple more weeks on the road, and they'll eat a mule and chase the rider."

Sonja laughed.

Jackson grinned back at her and began unloading crates from the wagon. "I'll get our own supper started soon as I dole out these here provisions to the other mess units."

She might have dozed, for it seemed only moments later that his spoon was indeed banging against cast iron, and the smell of wood smoke was strong enough to overpower that of the cattle. She blinked against the daze that was so hard to shake, like cobwebs—

"Tarnation, ain't you got supper cooked yet?" someone on the other side of the canvas asked. "All the other mess units is already eatin'."

Sonja held her breath to listen.

"Simmer down," Jackson growled. "I'm doin' the best I can. Can't cook but only so fast—"

"Ain't his fault," another voice chimed in. "It's that there girl been holdin' everythin' up."

Sonja breathed again and looked to the feeble tarp hanging between her and the half dozen or so bullwhackers in their mess unit.

"What's she doing out here all by herself?"

"Running from the law, I reckon."

"Or chasing a reluctant beau." This was followed by a round of laughter.

Just then Jackson lifted the far wall of canvas and reached inside for a small wooden box. He glanced up, his stare locking with Sonja's.

"I heard she was hurt bad," someone behind him said as the laughter died. "Heard she's right pretty, but she broke both legs. I heard the doc had to knock her out just to set her bones."

Jackson's eyebrows nearly met his cheeks, so deep was his scowl. With a grunt, he hauled the box into his arms and spun around, letting the flap fall behind him.

"Don't you know better than to harass the cook? Now get on with you, all of you, 'fore I toss some bullets in the fire. By gum, a body can't get no work done, what with stumblin' over the gawkin' and jawin'."

There was mumbling, but it grew distant—except it was a sure bet some stares tried to bore through Sonja's canvas sanctuary in their retreat. And they were wrong; it was none of those things. Not *from* the law, nor *to* romance did she run. It was for the love of Papa that she took herself away.

And would never go back.

Sometimes the jerk into reality was too much. Like waking from a dream to discover her eyes were open and she was standing up. Everything would suddenly snap into focus, as though the days preceding that moment hadn't quite happened. Not really. Not tangibly—except for the commitments she'd made in her absence. And this one capped the climax. She'd really walked away from Papa, and she was really part of this train headed for Santa Fe.

I want to go home.

But there was no home. And she had to go, for she couldn't stay.

So don't think about it.

What she needed to do was get to the bushes before she had an accident all over the store of food. She heaved a chuckle. Wouldn't the captain take her back to Diamond Spring himself if she did that?

She pushed aside the canvas and peeked over the side of the wagon. Had to be a five-foot drop to the ground.

The canvas on the other side of the wagon rustled again. Sonja whirled around.

Jackson worked his tongue in a vacant space in his bottom teeth and shifted uneasily. He jerked his mangled hat toward a spot behind him. "Don't take none of them too serious. They don't hold nothin' against you. I mean, they talk that way, but there ain't a one of 'em would leave you to fend for yourself." He shook his head once. "Bullwhackers is an odd lot, missy. They's mighty independent and ornery to boot, but you got to understand it's because they's alone so much. But ain't a one of them wouldn't fight for a child's safety . . . or a woman's honor."

Embarrassing tears wobbled Sonja's stare, and she swallowed hard, damming the deluge.

It was Jackson who saved her, clearing his throat and moving away.

"Wait!" she called.

He turned back.

"Could you help me?" she asked, cheeks already warming. "You see, I need . . . that is, I . . . I need to . . . tend to myself." Provided she didn't burst into flames of humiliation first.

Jackson's unruly brows lowered. "Thunderation, girl, why didn't you speak up? I'd have helped you down out of there."

Relief poured over her, then her gaze drifted past his shoulder. The men would be ringing the fire and talking about her.

Jackson's eyes narrowed into a squint. "Don't worry, little missy. You stay there. I got just the thing to fix you up."

Jackson's fix turned out to be the tin bucket he handed

her and the guard he stood a respectable distance from the wagon while she relieved herself into it. She emptied it into the grass over the side—saving herself that much humiliation—while he fetched her a plate of supper, grinning liked he cooked it just for her.

"This looks good," Sonja told him, although its aroma didn't tease her as it had before she'd crawled around the bucket. Her leg hurt like that hammer in her head was striking it as well.

"Just hot and lots of it," Jackson said, reminding her that she'd spoken. He nodded in the direction of the cook fire. "Them brutes wouldn't care if it was still alive, so long as they didn't have to wrestle it much."

A chuckle rose in Sonja's throat but died behind her teeth. She offered what she could manage—a warm gaze.

God had a sense of humor, providing such an unlikely friend, with his stooped shoulders inside a ratty shirt, cranky voice, and metal-gray hair poking out from under that tired hat. But he had a quick step and a thorough glance, and the creases in his sun-beaten face told how often he folded it in laughter. Besides, he was the only applicant.

It is no coincidence, Papa would say, his voice bouncing between the church walls. He'd wave a muscled arm, swirling the dust motes floating in the shaft of sunlight slicing the air in front of his pulpit. *Do not blame chance, and do not give luck the credit; it is the Lord who did it for you. Search your heart and see if it is not so.*

Papa would pause, his mighty baritone settling into the corners where the scarred planking didn't quite meet the plaster walls, his vivid blue eyes caressing the faces of his congregation. *Think on where you put yourself,* he'd say, *then thank Him for the mercy you do not deserve.*

"How's the leg?"

It was Jackson who asked the question . . . meaning she

was still with that freight train.

"Fine," she lied, not wanting to be the bother those bull-whackers were so sure she'd be, and not wanting to turn Thaddeus against her any more than he already was.

Should take another bite of food, to satisfy Jackson, except a spasm of pain made her clench her teeth instead.

"All right, men. Let me have your attention for a moment."

Even if the voice weren't distinctly the captain's, the tone would make it clear. Jackson exchanged a glance with Sonja before he turned away, letting the canvas fall behind him.

"As many of you have already heard, we have a guest," the captain said, obviously speaking to those around the cook fire. "In fact, Miss Thorseth is in your mess unit, and she'll be riding with us until other arrangements can be made. She's not feeling well right now, but the doc says she'll be up and around in a few days.

"Let me remind you that each of you signed a morality agreement before you hired on. I'll add that you're to give Miss Thorseth your utmost respect . . . and courteous distance. When we make stops, the north side of the train is hers; please use the south side to conduct your . . . business. Anything less than your unbroken honor will be judged as jeopardizing the safe and timely arrival of this outfit . . . its workers . . . and its contents . . . and will be interpreted as a challenge to my authority." He paused. "Any questions?"

Silence.

"Very well. Thank you."

Sonja stared at the canvas. It was Jackson who lifted it and gave her a guilty gaze.

"Reckon I better be makin' a fresh pot of coffee," he muttered as if to deny the grave interruption, while conversations behind him rose in a flurry of nonchalance. "I swear them boys swaller enough every day to float a barge.

You want some?"

Sonja rolled her head back and forth over the hickory rib she leaned against. "I'd take some water if you can spare it. And Jackson?"

He'd hefted a small barrel of coffee from the interior. Now he stopped.

"What will the captain do if anyone . . . bothers me?"

His eyebrows sprang into animation. "I reckon he'd do what any ship's captain would do when an order's disobeyed. He'd find hisself a hangin' tree."

He'd hang them?

Sonja closed her eyes and collapsed against that hickory rib.

Oh, Ander, I've really gotten myself into a mess this time.

She should be on the creek bank right now. Just like last summer, before death became more than a word in the dictionary. When chores were done, water gurgled over the rocks, and the only cool air in the world clung to the shade of the old tulip tree. With brush rustling under her head, twigs poking her back, little sparks of light darting between the canopy of leaves overhead . . . and Ander's voice dancing on, painting a story into the space she stared through. He'd roll his head to smile at her, cornflower-blue eyes laughing and his man-size teeth too big for his eleven-year-old mouth. It was still the smile of the Pest, except now he chose more distant victims for his pranks.

"Oh, Ander," she whispered aloud, the choking in her chest eclipsing the agony in her leg.

"Here's your water."

Sonja jumped. Thaddeus stood under the canvas he held in one hand; a tin cup was in the other.

Five

*T*hose eyes had held compassion in Independence—
enough to make Sonja follow them—but it must
have gotten heavy, for Thaddeus had obviously left it
behind. In fact, he'd worn a kinder expression earlier, when
she threw up in the bucket he held.

Sonja watched him over the rim of the cup while she
drank. His skin was clean of dust and the strands of his blond
hair were made light brown by the water gluing them
together. The hair curled on itself on either side of his
throat, and he smelled like soap. Gracious, if he wasn't handsome, his colors those of the earth.

"Don't drink it all," he warned. "Save some to wash
down the laudanum."

"No." She almost dropped the cup. "I don't want any
more of that awful stuff."

"Jackson said you were in pain, and for once the old
fool was right." He exchanged the water for the medicine
cup. "Come on, take it. Don't make me break my promise
to all mankind by letting you suffer needlessly."

She stared into the cloudy syrup. "What if I . . . get sick
. . . again?"

"I'll hold your bucket. Again. Now, drink it. You're anything but a coward, and martyrdom doesn't suit you."

Coward? Martyrdom? What was he talking about?

He gave her no time to wonder, only to drain the cup. She shuddered and wolfed down the rest of the water. "I can't believe you think you relieve suffering. Your remedy is worse than the pain, let me assure you."

"Tell me that in ten minutes when you can't remember your name, much less feel your leg. Do you want more supper?"

Sonja shook her head. "I wasn't very hungry."

Thaddeus took the plate and left. When he returned, he had a towel draped over his shoulder, a bucket in one hand, and a lighted lantern in the other.

"I thought you might want to wash up before bed," he said. He climbed up and settled cross-legged beside her, the canvas closed behind him.

"Thank you," Sonja mumbled, though the inside of the wagon pressed them together too tightly for his aloof tone.

"Don't thank me yet," he replied, his rumbling whisper adding to the intimacy. "I don't have your toothbrush. I put your knapsack in my box, but it's getting too dark to dig through. You can use this." He pulled a neatly folded red bandanna from inside his shirt cuff, adding, "It's clean," when she hesitated.

She paused only another second before plunging the bandanna into the water. Wrapping a section around her index finger, she used it to scrub her teeth.

"How old are you?" he asked.

The finger in her mouth stopped.

He gave her a casual lift of his brows. "Just curious."

Maybe it wouldn't hurt to tell him. "Eighteen."

His eyebrows twitched as if he were surprised.

"What about you?" she asked around her finger, though

Mama would have scolded at such a personal inquiry.

"Twenty-six." He traded the bandanna for a chunk of soap. "Where did you learn to read?"

"How do you know I can read?"

"My dosage cup. You read the monogram."

So she had, but everyone in her family could do that—in two languages.

Sonja scooped water over her face and held the groan of satisfaction. Such a simple thing, water, yet this was warm and wonderful. She worked up a weak lather with the crude soap—not as fine as Mama's—and set it to her face.

Thaddeus handed her a towel.

She wiped her face, then buried her nose in the cotton that smelled like him, all sunshine, soap, and male exertion.

He waited for an answer, except she couldn't give it—that it had been Papa's conviction that if "faith cometh by hearing, and hearing by the word of God," then everyone should have a Bible and know how to read it. Such a Norwegian pastor and weekday blacksmith would be too easy to find, so she peeked over the towel in silence.

Thaddeus' sunburn looked better this evening. His eyes were that unusual brown, and his lips looked soft, though she'd never thought a man's mouth could be so.

"Sonja?"

She jumped. She'd been daydreaming. She gave her face a final rub and handed back the towel. She dipped the bandanna in the water, wrung it out, and mopped her neck and arms.

"You were telling me how you came to know how to read," Thaddeus said.

"My father was a tailor," Sonja fibbed. "He had a shop, and I was reading patterns before I could walk."

"Really? Where?"

For heaven's sake, couldn't he just let it go? She'd done

all the lying she was going to do for one day.

She handed back the kerchief and began untying the strings binding her braids. "It doesn't matter."

"Why not?"

"Because he's dead."

He took the bucket from her lap and motioned with the damp cloth. "If you'd like to wash the dust from your legs, I can look the other way."

She shook her head. He'd already seen most of one leg, but she still couldn't wash with him so close—eyes averted or not.

Her hair was so stubborn tonight . . . and her fingers felt thick and clumsy. Oh yes, that medicine. It made her fuzzy and content like this.

Something tapped her hand. Thaddeus. Offering her a comb.

"Thank you." It took all her concentration to wrap her fingers around it. She pulled her hair over her left shoulder and worked on the only chore that was keeping her from lying down . . . just to lie down . . .

"How did he die?" Thaddeus asked.

"Who?"

"Your father. And what of the rest of your family?"

Not that again. Every time she said it, the words seemed to fuse the nightmare, to age it into something more solid, as if it weren't quite as true before. Say it enough times, and it would be irrevocable reality. Prophecy come to pass.

She said it anyway. "There was a fire. My house burned to the ground."

"I'm sorry," he said, except they all said that. Sometimes they were, and sometimes they were just speaking their lines. Saying what was expected, when what they really wanted was an admission of guilt—*None of this would have happened if she hadn't been where she wasn't supposed to be. If she hadn't disobeyed—*

"Sonja, why don't you let me help you?" Thaddeus said suddenly, taking the comb from her hand.

"I can't get this knot," she explained—except he made easy work of it.

He began to comb her hair, his brow furrowed in concentration, then relaxing as his eyes followed . . . up and down . . . the fluid rhythm of each stroke.

"That feels good," she told him.

His gaze swung to hers and lingered before shifting back. "It's very pretty. Like golden filament."

She closed her eyes. "Mmm, that even sounds nice."

"Lie down, Sonja," Thaddeus said suddenly though softly, hands cupping her shoulders. "You're about to fall asleep."

Her head floated away until her makeshift pillow captured it back again. She giggled. "Yes, Captain."

"Harley's the captain," he replied. "I'm just the doctor, and I'd like to check your knee."

"Go right ahead," she told him with a flick of her hand.

Thaddeus shifted, kneeling beside her on the sacks of food. He moved the lantern, setting it on the far side of him and out of her face. "Why did you leave? Why Santa Fe?" he asked as he pulled back her skirt, his fingers feeling soft and cool where they touched.

Sonja shrugged with boneless shoulders. "I don't know. No one knows me there, and it's where you're going."

"I thought you had an aunt in Santa Fe."

Caught!

She opened her eyes.

He stared back.

"Right. I do. An aunt," Sonja replied.

It was a stuttering moment before he returned to her leg. "Why not California? Or Oregon? Most people are—"

"No! Not Oregon!"

His glance locked with hers again, this time calmly curious. Reaching for the twist of red bandanna, he opened it and began washing her legs. Her eyes fell closed as if he commanded it. He'd forget his questions, and everything was all right again.

"You really took a beating this morning," he said from the other side of the softness. "I don't think you'll suffer any permanent damage, but it's going to take some time for this to heal."

"My head hurts. I think I bumped it."

"Really?" Thaddeus asked.

She opened her eyes.

He was already reaching for her head, probing carefully in her hair. "You didn't mention it this morning—though I should have asked. Where does it hurt?"

"All over."

The corners of his lips lifted as if he were amused. "Is there a specific place? A lump?"

"I don't know."

"Of course," he mumbled. "Are you nauseated?" he asked, bracing his weight on one hand and continuing his search, more systematically, with the other.

She nodded—but no, she only thought she'd nodded. So she nodded, while his fingers grazed her scalp for signs of injury, his touch feeling more like a caress than a search. Everything felt odd when varnished by that mysterious con-coction in his little white porcelain cup that had a gold mono-gram but no handles.

"How long will I need the lood . . . the loud . . . that awful medicine?" she asked.

He laughed. For the first time in thirteen days—since she first met him—he gave her what she hadn't realized she'd been waiting for. Oh, and it was a beautiful smile. Perfect and transforming, for what had been handsome before became brilliant and sweetly joyous.

"Not long. Another day or two at most," he said.

What? That didn't make any sense—but it was too much work to find her place in the conversation, so she whispered, "You smiled. You never have before, or I would have remembered. It makes you look so handsome."

The fingers in her hair fell still, and Thaddeus' gaze plunged into her face, stopping the next breath in her throat. Slowly, he devoured her, as if there were nothing but her chin and hair and the little places he found between.

"Sonja?" he said so softly, so urgently. "Who's Ander?"

"Ander?"

"Is he your beau?"

She laughed. "No, silly. Ander is my brother. My wonderful, sheep-headed eleven-year-old brother."

Thaddeus' eyebrows twitched. "Her brother," he whispered, then chuckled, so quietly that it sounded as if it were for him alone. "Should have guessed. Little slip of a thing like you wouldn't have a beau." His fingers sifted again. "Your hair is so soft. It's a shame to hide it in those braids."

Seconds stretched lazily as he stroked . . . shifted . . . braced his hands on each side of her head . . . and leaned over her . . . his face growing closer and closer. His burnt-amber gaze fell to her mouth. Lingered there. Climbed back to her eyes and . . . caressed her. And suddenly—but not alarmingly so—he was near enough to breathe the same air. She might have blinked. Might have slid into the fluff again. And she might have jumped in surprise, except his mouth was gentle as a whisper when it touched hers. Tender, his lips in their moving over hers, while she hung suspended in delicious flight . . . then lifted her chin, seeking more, her hands reaching into the thick sweeps of his summer hair.

Thaddeus had simply grinned down at her, acted her hero, that day in Independence. Though his eyes held a compelling promise, they showed no hint it would include the careful skill he provided her today . . . or the tenderness he gave her now.

Sonja sighed and whispered his name—the one that was far more fitting. . . .

Thaddeus lifted his head with a start.

Noble? Who is "Noble"?

Even while he stared at her, Sonja's hands slid out of his hair and folded heavily on her stomach. Her cheek sank into the blanket as the laudanum finally overtook her, while he sat back on his heels and huffed a breath. If that didn't beat all. She'd been kissing him and thinking about someone else, some guy named Noble. Her beau, no doubt. She had one, after all, the little liar—

And he'd had a snoot full of women's confusion. Marrying one man, but in love with another. And for what? So all three of them could be miserable.

Thaddeus chucked the bandanna into the bucket, preparing to leave, but only wrung it out again and set about completing the washing he'd started. Just as he'd expected, she'd lied about the aunt in Santa Fe. No telling how much truth there was to anything she said. They were all alike. Devils in angels' skin . . . And this little liar was indeed as soft as down and as lovely as they came. With all the pain and worry drained from her face, she looked quite innocent and sweet.

But she wasn't. She was a little sneak. She might have a brother named Ander and a father who was a tailor, but the house burning to the ground and killing her entire family? Everyone but her? Highly doubtful. And there was something that panicked her about Oregon. Maybe her family was sending her there, and she didn't want to go. Maybe she was running to meet someone in Santa Fe. Maybe that's where this Noble fellow lived.

Aw, he still had more questions than answers. It hadn't worked very well, giving her the laudanum, then lingering to pump her for information. And the kiss? Never should have happened. Old Professor Dawdy, the conscience and law of the University of Pennsylvania School of Medicine, would call him before his peers for taking advantage of a patient's weakened inhibitions and mild concussion. It only fueled the argument it was indecent for male practitioners to tend female patients. Besides, she'd been kissing someone else, not him.

Thaddeus dropped the bandanna back into the bucket and glanced a final time at Sonja's knee. The edema would go down in a few days. In the meantime he'd make her a crutch so she could get to the bushes by herself, else humiliation would make her swell like a sick fish.

She sure looked pretty, all that shimmering hair spilling around her and those soft lips parted slightly. Sleeping so peacefully, she looked too frail to get herself from Independence to here. A pistol she couldn't lift, a few clothes, a Bible, a bedroll, and some dried food—that's all she had with her. She was either profoundly foolish or stoutly brave.

Not like Amanda, who didn't even have the guts to face him after she kicked him in the stomach. No, she threw her punches from afar, the coward, using her attorney to tear his heart out—except the distance hadn't buffered the pain any.

Thaddeus pulled Sonja's skirt over her legs and tucked her into a wool blanket. The laudanum would depress her metabolism, including the functions that kept her warm; the May days promised summer, but the nights still remembered winter.

He jumped out of the wagon, closed the canvas behind him, hung the bucket on its hook, snuffed the lantern, and treaded through the brush to his own wagon in the circle. There he pulled off his boots, crouched under the conveyance—banged his shoulder on the grease bucket hanging from the rear axle—and crawled to his bedroll.

He stared up at all he had left of his former success—the desk, precious medical library, delicate instruments, and pounds and pounds of steel tools packed carefully into the freight wagon above him. Whether or not the shipping came at a discount was debatable, since he bought the privilege wielding the twenty-foot whip that kept forty-eight lazy hooves in motion.

Curse Amanda for that, too. He'd left his childhood home for the University of Pennsylvania a little lighter for believing he'd bullied his last stump of bovine flesh. Stupid animals—as evidenced by the fact that each one walked voluntarily to its respective teamster to be yoked at hitching time. But since the only thing certain anymore was uncertainty, he didn't dare part with the money to buy stage passage. He'd walk every mile to Santa Fe, for the twenty-five dollars a month it paid and because it could take weeks to get established once he got there. It was the peddlers of patent medicines who rode in and took over; doctors had to prove themselves first.

He groaned as he stretched and rearranged weary bone and sore muscle. Another day's work behind him, and his patient settled for the night. She was on her own once they reached Santa Fe, too, aunt or no aunt. Sonja could take care of herself, she'd proven that. Seemed to prefer it that way. And she could just fix those big blues on some other fool. He wasn't interested . . . even if her eyes caught the sun like a chunk of azure crystal. Even if her lips were soft as down. Even if he could still feel her fingers digging through his hair. . . .

Six

Thaddeus opened his eyes and blinked into the inky
night.

"It's the little missy," a voice said.

"What's the trouble?" he asked automatically, as he'd
done a thousand nights before, when other anxious fists
pounded on his door.

"She's tossin' and turnin' like she's in terrible bad shape,"
Jackson whispered loudly.

"All right," Thaddeus replied, already throwing back the
warmth of his bedroll. He palmed his face, wiping away the
last vestige of slumber, retrieved his spectacles from their lard-
can safe, curled the handles behind his ears, and shouldered
his dangling suspenders. Jackson followed him to the mess
wagon and watched while Thaddeus lifted the canvas tarp
and braced it on the stick. Warm air hit his face, and Sonja
whimpered. He found her arm, then walked his fingers to her
face. Her skin was damp, but no warmer than it ought to be.

"She's all right. It's only pain."

The news eased Jackson into a more relaxed stance.
"What can I do?"

"You could get me a lamp," Thaddeus replied, lifting

himself into the wagon while Jackson padded away.

Sonja was miserable, all right. Even as he felt his way to her side, she moaned.

"Sonja? It's me," Thaddeus whispered, stroking the damp hair from her forehead.

Which turned her cheek into his palm. "That you, Noble?"

Thaddeus' hand ceased its caressing. He snorted. Him again?

"I knew you'd come," she continued. "I knew you'd help me."

Without question. But she needed to know who he was, stop confusing him with this other fellow who'd been so callous—or stupid—that he thought she could make it to Santa Fe by herself.

On the other side of the canvas Jackson told Ennis, one of the night herders, that there weren't no trouble 'cept the little missy fussin', then the glow of a lantern grew closer and Thaddeus reached out a hand to receive it. He set the light on a barrel near Sonja's head and turned for his first look.

Her clothes were as wrinkled as though they'd dried in a sack, and the hair that wasn't stuck to her face was tangled about her shoulders. She winced and turned away from the light.

"Think you can fix her?" Jackson asked with a sympathetic grimace from where he stood on the hub of the wagon wheel.

Thaddeus grinned; Jackson spoke of his patient as if she were a broken clock. "I think so," he replied.

"Well then, tell me what you need, and I'll fetch it."

The list was long—laudanum, the medicine cup, a bucket of water, a drinking cup, and a clean cloth. Jackson strode away to fill it, while Thaddeus dug into his pocket for his watch: two thirty-five. Patients always suffered their sickest moments after midnight, and if they expired, they usually did so before dawn. Sonja would be resting comfortably by that time—which was still long after Harley and Lieutenant Mason had rapped on the iron tires with the command to "roll out" of those bedrolls that were the only thing warm.

Thaddeus untangled and lifted Sonja's skirt. Her knee had swollen more.

"I brung you the sleep-easy first," Jackson whispered loudly, waving the bottle of laudanum and dosage cup over the side of the wagon. "I figured you need it worst."

"Good thinking," Thaddeus said as he reached for the implements of his trade. When he looked up again, Jackson was gone.

Since it had been several hours since the last one, Thaddeus measured a full dose into the little cup.

"Sonja? Here's some more medicine," he said as he pushed his arm under her shoulders and lifted.

She opened her eyes and blinked heavily against the light. When he repeated his announcement, she shook her head drunkenly. "I don't want any more of your hideous revenge."

He held a chuckle. "No malice intended. This will relieve your pain."

"It does hurt something awful," she admitted groggily. Her eyes widened, deadly serious. "I think I might die."

Jackson—back in his position at the flap—chuckled.

"I hope not," Thaddeus replied, giving the cook a conspiratorial glance. "You'll make me look bad. Come on, that's a good girl. Drink it all."

Sonja shuddered but swallowed the laudanum, following it with an impressive measure of water before she collapsed against Thaddeus' chest.

"I'm so glad you came. I can stand it better when you're here," she said, snuggling into his neck.

Jackson grinned.

And Thaddeus explained. "It's the opium and a bit of a

concussion. She thinks I'm someone named 'Noble.' "

Jackson grinned. "Don't look to me like she's confused."

Thaddeus scowled at him.

Now Jackson laughed. "It ain't me you got to convince, Doc." Then he faded from the spray of lantern light.

"When will it stop?" Sonja asked.

"Soon," Thaddeus promised, laying his cheek against her hair before he caught himself. It wouldn't be right to be familiar with her. But then, what was the harm? She needed comforting, and he was the likely provider. He replaced his cheek and wrapped his arms around her, willing his strength into her.

She tensed suddenly and whimpered, taken by another spasm of pain.

"Very soon, Sonja," he told her. "You think you'll be sick again?"

She shook her head.

Good. She seemed hardly strong enough to lift her head, much less hold it over the bucket.

"Try to relax and let the medicine work. Can you do that?"

She nodded weakly.

He hugged her more deeply against himself and stroked her arm . . . such a little arm. Fragile. And her hair smelled as warm as it was soft. Enticing enough to make him rub his cheek into it.

What he needed to do was get that swelling down. One-handed, he reached for one of the cloths Jackson had brought, dunked it into the bucket, and squeezed out the excess water. He pulled up her skirt with a hooked finger, shook the rag open, and draped it over her knee. A soft breeze chose that moment to curl around the tarp.

"That feels good," she mumbled.

"Yes," he agreed, then wasn't sure if she referred to the

cloth or the fresh air. "Are you hot?"

Her clothes were damp with perspiration, despite the near chill of May.

She nodded. "I forgot to braid my hair for bed."

"Do you want me to do it for you?" he asked, smoothing the silk of it down her back and combing it away from her face with his fingers. She shook her head; fine with him. It looked pretty, loose.

He dipped another cloth, pulled back, and shifted, settling her against his biceps. He wiped her face while the lantern cast deep shadows, the occasional oxen bawled sleepily, and the air smelled of cattle and the dew that would settle in a few hours.

"That's nice," she mumbled, her speech losing its clarity as the laudanum weighted her efforts. Then she added, "Do you think he suffered?"

"Who?" Thaddeus half smiled. Stubborn girl wouldn't give up. Should be asleep by now.

"Ander."

His hand paused, stilling the cloth on her cheek.

"You're a doctor. Do you think he felt the flames?"

Thaddeus watched the lips that had spoken. Stared at the eyes still closed. His heart stopped.

"Ander was never afraid of anything, you know. Not like me," she said. "He was silly sometimes, but he could stare down a badger if he needed to." She licked her lips. "The fire was so bright. It melted the snow and started Mama's porch-tree on fire . . . the one she raised up for the shade. And someone was screaming . . . maybe it was me." She paused, sounding vague. Then, more certainly, "He was only eleven . . . just a little boy, really."

Something stabbed Thaddeus' heart, spanking it to life once again. He squeezed his eyes shut and pressed her face into his shoulder, willing her to sleep. To forget such horror.

"He carved me a comb for my hair . . . for my birthday," she mumbled against his shirt. "It wasn't very good . . . but it was my favorite thing . . . my favorite in the whole world. It burned up."

He began to rock her, feebly stroking her arm while he fought the lump in his throat.

"Will you tell him for me, Noble? Will you tell Ander I'm sorry I lost his comb?"

It all stewed together to concoct her doom—the miserable night, the decrepit road—walking would be preferable, even in her condition—the dusty oven of the wagon, and the remains of Thaddeus' vicious medicine boiling like poison in her stomach. Sonja barely grabbed the bucket in time.

"You sick, little missy?" Jackson called from where he steered the team of mules.

"Yes. But I think my stomach is finally empty—" She proved it by retching absolutely nothing into the pail.

Jackson whistled between his teeth. "Dry pukes. I hate that."

Poetically, Sonja heaved again, though Jackson had the mercy to keep his attention on the road.

"You want me to stop?" he asked.

And risk the wrath of the camp doctor?

"No. I'll be all right."

"Ain't she somethin'," Jackson said, obviously to the mules at the end of his tethers. "Pukin' up her toenails but don't do no swoonin' about it. You hang on, little missy," he called over his shoulder. "I'll slow her down for a spell, till you get your up and down untangled."

The jarring in the back of the wagon lessened somewhat, though Sonja still clung to the bucket, the cruel spasms working up a sweat until the urge—and her energy—were finally spent. Then she flopped onto her back and slid into a pool of heavy-lidded exhaustion.

"How is she doing this morning?" Thaddeus asked a little later.

The reply was muffled, but it was Jackson's voice.

"Again?" Thaddeus exclaimed, then he sounded very near when he said, "Sonja?"

She dragged her eyes open and rolled her head to see him where he stood beside the wagon. She blinked, struggling to clear the fuzz from her head, though she'd be better with it between them. Following him had been foolish. She was too impulsive. Everyone said so.

"*. . . You did not think this through, Sonja,*" *Papa said as they turned toward home,* "*or you would not join in such mischief as this—and it is not always impolite to say no, my girl.*" *He flipped up his collar and hunched his shoulders against the cold. His voice got quieter, as it did when he got to the important part of his sermons.* "*You must stand strong when your friends invite you into temptation.*"

That was the point. It hadn't looked like temptation. It looked like helping Margaret—whose parents wouldn't let her see Jonathan by the light of day. Margaret couldn't very well see him at night alone, and Sonja didn't think. . . . Didn't think Papa would get out of bed after he just got in it. Didn't think he would notice her coat missing from its hook. And didn't think he would come to get her.

He sighed. "*Such a place, America.*"

Sonja had groaned silently—not this again.

"*You have Norwegian blood, but you are as American as your birth,*" *he said. He shook his head.* "*Such a bold and outgoing people.*"

He'd come with the first Norwegian immigrants, as enthusiastic as any thirteen year old would be, though his new neighbors overwhelmed him a bit back then. His children, who were just like them, still did.

They walked from the trees behind the schoolhouse, father and daughter, along sleepy streets where dogs barked and house windows cast no light. The wind picked up, and the cold sped their steps as they hurried home. . . .

But they didn't hurry fast enough, for flames were already leaping victoriously into the early November sky when they reached the structure that collapsed over their beds . . . and Mama and Ander.

Then it was a blur—Karl, Papa's new apprentice, arriving from Norway, and Papa wanting to move the smithy to a new home in the Oregon Territory.

"Sonja?"

She jumped.

Thaddeus was pulling his hands out of his leather gloves. "Jackson says you've been sick. How's your stomach feel now?"

She looked away. "I'll live."

"You weren't so sure last night. How's the knee?"

She shrugged. Stared at the canvas overhead. She'd cost him a night's sleep, and any apology offered now would be feeble compared to the huge liability she was to him. Oh, to be back . . . back . . . *where?*

Nowhere.

"This will probably be a bad day, so let me know if you need some more medicine for the pain," Thaddeus said.

She nodded at the ceiling.

"I made you a crutch so you can get to the bushes by yourself. It's here beside the wagon. But if you get dizzy, call for help."

She thanked him, though she'd crutch her way over a cliff if one were nearby—except that stupid scout would just catch her again. Probably ruin her other leg.

"Jackson is cooking breakfast. Do you want some?"

Sonja shook her head.

No sound gave away his leaving, but when she looked, Thaddeus was gone. She leaned over the side of the wagon to eye the crutch. He'd stripped the bark from a long, stout stick and had wrapped a bandanna around its forked end—

"Running away again?"

Sonja's attention snapped to the knee-high boots planted in the grass a few feet away, climbed the sturdy legs in buckskin leggings, and crawled over a brown vest, green flannel shirt, and broad chest.

Seven

*T*he captain picked up the crutch and eyed it carefully. "Thad does good work. Have you tried it for length?"

Sonja fell back into her bed—which made her head spin—and gave him a lift of her chin. He didn't scare her. "With or without the crutch, it will be days before I'm well. Your scout chased me like I was a thief. Doesn't he have better things to do than attack innocent women?"

"I'm sorry you were injured," the captain replied casually, "but Lieutenant Mason was just doing his job. He says you fought him like a wildcat." He paused. "Perhaps you'll tell me where your family is so I can see you're safely united."

"Please don't concern yourself, Captain . . ."

"MacGregor," he replied.

"Thank you. Please don't concern yourself, Captain MacGregor. I'll be fine once I reach Santa Fe."

For the longest time, the captain studied her. "Very well. Russell, Majors, and Waddell will give you passage to Santa Fe, but I'm assigning you to help Jackson—as you become physically able, of course. In this outfit, those who don't work, don't eat, Miss Thorseth."

Sonja opened her mouth to reply, but Thaddeus stepped around the end of the wagon, brown hat riding far back on his head as if he'd pushed it away to scratch his forehead. The men stood eye-to-eye, but that's where the similarity ended. If the wagon master was built like a Clydesdale, the physician more resembled a Thoroughbred—strong and broad in the shoulder, but in a more refined and fine-stepping way.

"Ruff is looking for you," Thaddeus told Captain MacGregor. "One of the drivers has a lame animal you need to see."

"Which one?" the captain asked.

"I don't know. The brown one. I've done my best to forget how to tell them apart."

The captain chuckled. "Not the steer. Which driver?"

Thaddeus glanced at Sonja, his cheeks coloring as he broke into an embarrassed smile. Then a laugh burst free and he shook his head at his own foolishness. "I can't tell *them* apart, either," he confessed, resetting that hat. "The skinny fellow. The one with the pointy nose and lots of mustache."

"Black hair?" Captain MacGregor asked.

"Yes."

"Jochum. Nigel Jochum. Calls himself Butch."

Thaddeus' brown eyes widened behind his silver spectacles. "That's the one. Butch!"

And Sonja's heart faltered in its rhythm. He looked so handsome. So gentle and safe, his smile lighting his face—though he apparently gave that only to his friends.

The men's laughter rolled to a stop, and Captain MacGregor nodded toward Sonja. "Take care of our little stowaway, Thad. She tells me she's anxious to help Jackson with the grub. And Miss Thorseth? You really should smile more often. It becomes you." With that, he dipped the brim of his gray hat and left.

Good heavens, what brought that on? Sonja looked to

Thaddeus, in case he knew, but he just stared back. All the warmth and humor were gone from his eyes.

In Independence, Magnus surveyed the oxen and wagon he'd purchased with a heart full of hope. Every day they waited, Sonja would be further away—or more hungry; she didn't take enough money to feed herself. His own outfit was at its prime worth right now, while there was still enough summer left to get someone else across this sprawling land to the new life waiting on the other side.

"We will sell the wagon and team," he told Karl. "Today we will start back for Indiana. Sonja is there."

Thaddeus' boots squished as he waded through the grass. If water weighed eight pounds per gallon, then there had to be twelve pounds' worth in each one. He eyed his wool trousers, wet and splattered to his thighs. Had to be another six pounds in them—not counting the liquefied soil. But it was done. The Little Arkansas was crossed, thanks to the spades that dug out a gentler bank and the planks that made a temporary bridge over the hoof—and boot—sucking bottom. He sighed. The current was only five or six yards wide—not enough to have to cross at an oblique angle—but they'd still had to double-team and keep moving, or sink. Now the wagons were corralled and the oxen unhitched and grazing; if the creek rose during the night, it only made the water supply easier to reach.

Thaddeus passed one of the four other mess units and approached his own where Jackson already had a pot of drinking water on the fire to boil—clean water was hard to come by—and a good start on supper. That was his talent; Sonja's contribution ringed the fire in the tidy stacks of buffalo chips beside it and provision crates around it. Just how she coerced Jackson into repeatedly unloading and loading those boxes, to serve as makeshift chairs, two meals each day, Thaddeus would never know. The old fool grumbled about it, but he did it anyway.

Jackson whacked his spoon on the rim of the Dutch oven and straightened. "Hi, Doc."

"Jackson," Thaddeus returned and stepped up to the pot for a glance; beans again. "Where's Sonja?"

Jackson hooked a thumb to the north. "Needed some privacy." He shook his head and scowled. "You better quit givin' her that there laudanum, Doc. Makes her powerful sick. She'll be wastin' away to bones if she don't start keepin' somethin' down long enough to suck nourishment from it."

"Laud—She hasn't had any of that in days." Wouldn't take any more after that second day, three days ago.

"Then somethin' else is ailin' her."

Thaddeus looked to the little figure dotting the next dip in the terrain and followed it. The most common scourge of the trail was diarrhea, not nausea.

By the time he reached her, she was lying in the grass, the crutch beside her, a wrist thrown over her eyes. The air smelled of sickness.

"Oh, it's you," she said and sat up.

"Jackson said you've been ill," he said. "Why didn't you tell me?"

Her shoulders sagged. "He told you that? I didn't want him to know. He'll think it's his cooking."

"No, he thought I was still giving you laudanum," Thaddeus replied. He knelt on one knee to press his palm to her forehead. Her temperature was normal, and her eyes looked clear, though her color was a shadow of itself. "Do you hurt anywhere—other than your knee?" Appendix, maybe. But the railroad tracks in Youngstown made a better surgery than this short-grass prairie.

"No. I feel fine except for this . . . sickness. Sometimes all I have to do is smell food, and it rolls over me."

Thaddeus froze, his examination stopping at her eyes as all the little pieces tumbled into place. "When was the last time you had your monthly?"

She gasped. "That's none of your affair."

"I'm a physician, Sonja," he said firmly, "and I need answers in order to treat you."

She shook her head a little frantically before fixing her attention on the grass being crushed under her skirt. "I don't know. I guess it's been a long time. I forget."

"Do you get dizzy, or feel tired?" he asked. "Are your breasts tender?"

Her eyes widened, and she got her color back—in excess. She nodded.

"Which?"

"The last one. The one about . . . the tenderness."

Nope, no doubt in his mind. Or hers, the little sneak.

"What is it?" she asked, as if he'd believe she didn't know. As if her running—all her plans—didn't pivot around her little secret.

"Stop the innocent act, Sonja," Thaddeus said tiredly. "We both know why you're sick, and it has nothing to do with Jackson's cooking. Maybe you think it's none of my business, but I am responsible for you—as your guardian and doctor. You could have at least told me you were expecting a child. What if you'd hemorrhaged when you fell?"

Sonja's expression collapsed with theatrical drama, just before her eyes nearly dropped from their sockets. She was *good*.

"Me? With child? That can't be."

"Can't it?" It was a question of her purity. He watched, waiting for the answer.

Eyes wide with a believable confusion, she stared at the front of his shirt. "It never occurred to me."

Well, it occurred to him—kissing him and calling him by another man's name. Blast her deceptive woman's-heart, and blast her for believing him too stupid to discover the true and ultimate reason for her flight.

"What else could it be?" he asked.

She turned her face away. "Yes. What else indeed?"

Lazy, the licking . . . the fluid lapping of flames at the edge of the coffeepot . . . almost gentle . . . like the tongues that had curled over the eaves and twined around the porch posts of a house become funeral pyre. Pausing moments, those . . . moving slowly but relentlessly and heavy enough to press themselves into a memory. . . . And these moments, whose steep banks threatened to fall away, from calm into chaos. Jackson's lips moving beneath his tarnished mustache . . . *Sit* . . . The hard top of the crate rising to meet Sonja's bottom . . . and *Don't get mad at the doc for tellin' me* . . . That she'd hurt herself lifting them heavy things. Except it wasn't her *self* the doc was worried about.

Was that yesterday? No. The day before. Or another day when there was no catastrophe . . . except the men still spun yarns and laughed so casually, the breeze still teased the smoke into an enchanting dance over the bean pot, and the sun still rode its steady path in the sky . . . because the world was normal and faithful and safe after all. She still tied her braids. Still brushed her teeth. The men still ate. And they laughed. See? There was still laughter.

They knew, the bullwhackers in her mess unit. Oh, they

were polite enough, dipping their hats—*Evening*—as they ambled to the coffeepot for a refill, but they knew. They sprawled on the grass, legs stretched out before them and cups hooked in callused fingers. Threads of smoke trailed from cigarettes and puffed from sun-dried lips . . . and their furtive stares burned as they took turns pinning them on Sonja.

She sucked in her stomach, but her skirt still cut into her. She'd stopped fastening the top button and began loosening her corset at . . . some vague time ago. After the house burned down, maybe. But before she left Papa—

There it was again. The shock. A baby inside her.

There was actually a baby inside her.

Where was God? He'd gone. She was fatherless. And Fatherless.

It was none of his business, Sonja's crying, so Thaddeus buried his ear deeper into the rolled-up coat that served as his pillow. When it didn't muffle her much, he shifted to his other side. All right, it might be his business—as her doctor—but there wasn't anything he could do about it. Nothing he would do to take away her problem; his surgical intervention stopped at the entrance of an occupied womb.

He rolled back again. Adjusted that sorry pillow again. And tossed off his blankets. He'd figure out something to say before she woke the whole camp—or dehydrated herself.

"'Bout time," Jackson grumbled loudly from beside the cook fire, several feet away.

Thaddeus didn't reply. Just looped the handles of his spectacles around his ears, pushed his feet into the boots that had barely cooled, and stalked through the grass to the mess wagon. Sonja's sobs grew louder as he approached.

"Sonja? It's me, Thaddeus."

The sobs stopped. "Yes?" she asked, her voice as calm and clear as if she were about to break into song.

"May I lift the canvas?"

"I'm trying to sleep."

He shook his head. She'd been with the train only a week, but it was long enough to expect that defense. And she'd had three days to adjust to her predicament, but apparently it wasn't long enough. He pulled the tarp's grommet out of the eye holding it taut and, when she didn't object, peered into the cave of her makeshift sleeping chamber. The feeble moonlight reached no further than her elbow, and she didn't even sniffle, but the tension in her body fractured the air.

Thaddeus relaxed against the wheel. "You're keeping that baby awake."

Silence, then, "I don't care."

"Want to talk about it?"

"What would that accomplish?"

He shrugged, though she probably couldn't see it. "You might feel better. And who knows? You may hear an answer while sorting out the options."

"It can't be true," she implored him. "You must be mistaken."

He crossed his arms and drew a thoughtful breath. "Why don't you go back home, Sonja?"

Wood creaked as she flopped around on her bed. "No home to go back to. I told you, it burned down."

"No relatives?"

"None I'd care to shame."

She had a point. "All right, how about Noble—the baby's father?"

She hesitated. "He . . . He wouldn't want it."

Thaddeus' heart lurched. Who was the greater fool? Sonja, for having so little faith in the man, or the baby's father, for letting Sonja go so easily?

"There aren't any easy options, Sonja, but this isn't impossible," he finally said. "I suspect you're not one who gives up."

And it wasn't so unusual, her condition. Easily, one in six of his female patients came to him in similar circumstance. Those who analyzed society's advance and decline over their pompous cigars in their pompous parlors should seek their statistics from one who knew them; little had changed. If there were fewer births outside of marriage in recent years, it wasn't because lovers had suddenly risen above such passions. They were simply more skilled at not getting caught—or disposing of the evidence when they did.

"I'm not as strong as you think I am," Sonja replied. "I'm not up to this."

"You may surprise yourself."

She didn't agree or disagree, but at least she wasn't crying anymore.

"I should have prayed about going to Santa Fe," she said suddenly, almost in a whisper.

"You're a Christian?" he asked. She had a Bible—but so did Amanda.

"Yes. Are you?" she asked, sounding equally surprised.

Now there was a question. Too bad he didn't have a good answer. "I used to be—I guess."

"What do you mean, 'used to be?' Either you are or you aren't. Have you given your life to Jesus?"

Oh, to live where everything was so simple. Only in the mind of a child.

"Once upon a time," he said, "but He wrung it out and threw it back. Let's just say I haven't seen the hand of God in my life much lately."

And now she would start in with some simplistic drivel about how God loved him and had just been testing him. Not his idea of love, and he'd passed all the tests he needed to at the university.

"I'll pray for you," she said, surprising him again.

Better to pray for herself. As for him, he knew exactly where he was going and what he would do when he got there.

"How does your knee feel?" he asked, returning to a safer topic.

"Better."

"And the nausea?"

"Gone," she replied flatly. "Until Jackson starts cooking again. How long will it last?"

"Not long." He paused, letting the silence settle around them.

The night herder sang in the distance, calming cattle who didn't need much excuse to stampede. If Sonja remained silent, he'd steer the conversation toward saying goodnight.

"Noble isn't the baby's father," she said suddenly.

So much for goodnight.

"No?" Thaddeus asked simply. Maybe she'd give him some real information—but exactly how many beaus did she have?

"He's you," she told him.

"Me? I don't understand."

"You wouldn't tell me what the 'N' of your first name stood for, so I made something up. I guess I was feeling a little silly because of the medicine—"

"Let me get this straight," Thaddeus said. "There is no man named Noble? You made that name up? Then pinned it on me?"

"Yes."

Thaddeus could only chuckle. "That's not me, Sonja. In

fact, you couldn't have stepped further from the truth."

"Well, at this point I can't think of you by any other name. And it must be better than your real one."

"Anything's better than that," he had to agree.

"You aren't going to tell me what it is, are you?"

"Nope. Not even if you torture me." And he could stand a lot; jerking that whip back and forth in the air all day was adequate proof of that.

And this meant it was his name, after a fashion, Sonja had whispered when he'd kissed her. Not some other man. She knew it was him. Might have even—

"I think I'm ready to go to sleep now," Sonja said, yanking Thaddeus back into the conversation.

He stared into the blackness of the wagon. It wasn't fair that she could see him so well, while he couldn't see her at all.

"Thank you. For everything," she added.

"You're welcome." He reached for the tarp to let it down.

"Noble?"

He stopped, a grin springing to his lips. Silly name, but he answered to it. "Yes?"

"The Lord knows where you are," she said quietly. "He'll walk every mile to Santa Fe with you, if you'll ask."

"Sure, Sonja," he said, except it wasn't that simple. "Sleep well," he told her and closed the canvas.

Eight

*T*he sun struggled to drag itself over the horizon, and Thaddeus struggled to drag himself from the warmth of his bedroll. The boots he pushed his feet into were cold, but he huffed a chuckle. The silly girl had invented her own name for the N on his dosage cup. Where she'd come up with "Noble"—well, she wasn't lacking in imagination, he'd say that for her.

He set his hat and worked his fingers into his left glove, eyeing the golds that washed the eastern sky over the edge of the earth. Could walk the rest of his life and never get far enough. Some things followed you, like pine pitch that won't wash off. So the best you could hope for was to try to start again. A new history. A new place. New faces—

He stopped, right glove only as far as his palm. His stare slid to an obscure spot just in front of his boots. It was a silly name, "Noble." Not like him at all, except she believed it, this girl with the sunrise in her hair, who'd followed him simply because he'd shooed some bullies away. And this new name she gave him . . . it was such a proud name.

"Miss Thorseth."

Sonja jumped.

"I'm sorry. Didn't mean to startle you," Captain MacGregor said, though he grinned. "You shouldn't travel so far without a horse."

Heat climbed Sonja's neck. She stared at the fire. "I was thinking."

"Would you care for a walk?"

She looked up. He was serious. She looked to Jackson—

"You have a few minutes," the captain said firmly, as though he knew the thread of her thoughts.

He wanted something, except what it was wasn't plain on his face. She scanned the immediate area for Noble, but he wasn't anywhere around. Hadn't talked to him since he stood beside her wagon last night.

"Come on. We won't go far," the captain said with finality.

Her gaze climbed his frame again and settled on his face. She had no choice, really, and he knew it. He was the captain, which was probably why the flow of conversation around them caught momentarily when he fell in step beside her. He made her conspicuous, as the house fire had done last November. And the gossips acted the same, now and then, their words and laughter stopping, then galloping forward to catch up before they blended into an incoherent rumble behind her.

Sonja folded her arms over her stomach and watched each step swirl her skirt over her boots and stir insects into panic. *So simple, their tiny lives. Just leap out of the way.*

It was evening already, though the afternoon was a blur. What day of the week was it? Thursday? Friday, maybe?

Gracious, such an empty, wild land. Except for Pawnee Rock, the landmark they'd been approaching all day and hoping wouldn't blow away before they reached it. They'd tied kerchiefs over their noses and mouths against the relentless dust. Now there was hardly a breeze. No, it was nothing like home . . . where there were woods and the ring of Papa's hammer and Mama's soap on the fire and Ander—

"I'm sorry I haven't stopped by to pay my respects sooner," Captain MacGregor said, "but Thad kept me informed of your progress. I'm glad to see you're nearly healed."

Sonja nodded. The doctor had tried to stay more informed about her condition than he was, but she'd avoided his inquiries by heading for the range north of the trail whenever he wasn't greasing the axles on his wagon or maintaining tack, and clinging to Jackson's side at all other times. Nothing to say to him. No questions she cared to answer. Already enough humiliation—

"Have you ever been to Santa Fe?"

Sonja glanced at the captain and shook her head.

Papa said Oregon Territory was a lot like home, except there were mountains and an ocean—

"It will surprise you then. Not like anything you're used to, I'm sure."

What would surprise her? What had they been talking about? Just couldn't concentrate anymore. And forgot the simplest things—

"Easterners either love it or they hate it. The town has about four thousand people, maybe five. And the country is dry, but it's pretty in its own way."

Oh, yes. Santa Fe.

"Most of the houses are adobe—"

Whatever that is.

"And the people are amazingly gentle and polite." He chuckled. "It surprises visitors. It surprised me."

Sonja stopped, waiting to hear why the captain would find being polite and gentle so astonishing.

"Santa Feins love to celebrate. Anything. A fiesta can go

on for days. And the women tend to be . . . uh, relaxed in their manner. What you might regard as flirtatious. And their dress is rather . . . casual by eastern standards." He grinned. "By your standards as well, I see."

Sonja fell into step once again. "I would never presume to judge anyone." Not she, of all people. Not now, of all times.

"That's good. It's just their way. Their culture."

And no matter how relaxed, it had no room for one of her circumstance. No community was that forgiving.

She glanced behind her. This was far enough, with camp just out of conversation range.

The captain shifted, settling into a more relaxed posture, though he looked ready to wrestle the oxen himself, if necessary. If that didn't work, there was always the massive sidearm protruding from his left hip, its wooden handle arcing forward, pitted and worn.

Maybe she could threaten him somehow, force him to shoot her. Just to get it over with. But his eyes held her in place. It didn't miss a thing, that gaze. He probably stared the cattle into obedience.

"Thad told me about your family . . . about the fire," he said suddenly. "I'm sorry."

"Thank you," she replied.

"But no one seems to know why you're going to Santa Fe."

She looked to the horizon. "I can't say."

"Can't? Or won't?"

Her stare darted back to his face. So that was it. So insidious, this—the shield becoming a threat in its own right. Protecting her with his authority, then probing so calmly and patiently.

Sonja spun toward the cook fire. "You wasted your time, taking me on this little walk, Captain—"

"I'd prefer you call me Harley."

She stopped—though it surprised her that she did. She

waited for him to grab her arm, to use his power, but his sharp gaze contrasted more sharply with the softness of his tone when he said, "I'm not trying to get information, Miss Thorseth. I'm asking for myself. Personally."

Two days later—three weeks out of Independence— another stagecoach caught up to the wagon train, giving Harley the perfect opportunity to free Russell, Majors, and Waddell of its only female. He exchanged road information with the driver . . . then simply waved him by. When the train pulled into Santa Fe, she would still be with it.

"Have you lost your mind?"

Harley stopped grooming his mule long enough to cast Thaddeus a glance. "I don't think so. Why do you ask?"

"Don't be obtuse. You know what I mean."

"You mean Sonja?"

"Yes, Sonja."

Another glance. Then a tensing in Harley's jaw and heavier strokes over a ratty coat. "Don't sentence the entire female population for the sins of one. She isn't Amanda."

Thaddeus sorted through all the things he couldn't say— such as the truth—for something he could. "You know nothing about this girl."

A gust of wind angled the brush around them, prompting Harley to scan the sky. "Looks like rain."

If it was, they'd all be sleeping in it. "Don't change the subject," Thaddeus said.

"All right. Why are you so suspicious?" Harley asked.

"Because she didn't just wander onto this road. She's running to—or from—something."

Someone, actually. And he knew why.

"She says she followed you." Harley paused. "You interested in her?"

"You mean romantically? No."

Not with another man's baby growing under her heart. Not with another man's memory hovering in the shadows, pulling her eyes into a stare that didn't see, when she escaped to times gone by. Times with the one she loved.

Harley waited, eyebrows lifted skeptically.

"I told you, I'm not looking for company," Thaddeus continued, picking up the thread of conversation. He gave Harley a speculative stare. *Are you?*

The other man returned to grooming his mule. "She's sure pretty."

That was no answer.

"She's sure foolish," Thaddeus replied.

Harley chuckled. "Maybe she's a little fearless."

Making excuses for her, the man was. And he had more stubborn than any three men ought to have. "Suit yourself, Harley."

By one drop, then another, it began to drizzle.

"Just be careful," Thaddeus continued. "Sometimes you get pulled in so fast, you don't realize all the loose ends and little stories don't make sense until it's too late."

Until you've already given all you have.

"Remind me to never make you angry."

Sonja looked up.

Harley motioned to her lap. "You're cranking on that thing like you wish somebody's fingers were inside."

She followed his stare to the coffee grinder in hand.

Truth was, she'd forgotten it was there.

"Would you care to walk it off?" Harley continued without waiting for a reply.

"I may not be good company."

"I'll take my chances."

The men didn't even notice anymore, when the camp's only female set off on a stroll with its captain—and that was almost more irritating than their stares.

"So answer my question," Harley said as they walked the camp's perimeter, he on the outside. "Who you mad at?"

Sonja glanced at him and thought about saying it was him, just for the fight. She wanted to yell. Wanted to rip the sky from its hangings and pull it down on top of her. And wanted to throw something at those stupid bullwhackers to stop their infernal singing.

She needed to wake up. Certainly this wasn't her real life. Certainly God had some other form of justice to mete out.

"Is it me?" Harley asked.

"No," Sonja replied.

"Good. You want me to beat him up for you, then, whoever it is?"

Couldn't help it; she laughed.

He smiled. "That's better." Then he motioned to the distance. "I'll bet you've never seen a sunset like that before."

Long layers of clouds hovered over the horizon, bank upon bank whose undersides glowed the pink of fiery embers. Little over halfway to Santa Fe now. Jackson said they'd turn to the southwest tomorrow to take the cutoff across the Cimarron Desert, rather than travel the Mountain Branch that followed the Arkansas River. Jackson said Harley knew it was early enough in the year to make it across this dryer—but shorter—stretch.

"No," she told him of the sunset. "There were always too many trees in the way, back home."

"And where would that be?"

May as well tell him. "Home was Indiana."

And there was nothing for her there, now. There was nothing for her in Santa Fe. Nothing for her anywhere.

Harley gave her another penetrating look, as if he were trying to read words written in her ear.

Sonja stopped, arms folded snugly over her stomach. "How long have you been a wagon master?" she asked to distract him. Should have never come on this walk. It only encouraged his attention.

"Three years." He chuckled suddenly. "Can't believe it's been that long. I used to love nothing better than beating this road every summer. I think I'm finally getting tired of it."

"What would you do instead?"

He studied her face as if to find the answer there. "I don't know. Strike out on my own in something, I suppose."

"You really aren't much for working for someone else, are you?"

"What makes you say that? I draw pay."

Sonja shook her head and resumed her course around the camp. He fell in beside her. "Not the same," she said. "Russell, Majors, and Waddell may give you a salary, but out here you're the boss. It may as well be your business."

A grin played at the corners of Harley's mouth. "Very perceptive. Have you always been so analytical?"

She shrugged. "Anyone could see it."

His reply was a silence, then, "I usually make four hauls a year—two each way—which puts me back in Independence in the fall. This year I think I'll cut that by a leg so I can winter in Santa Fe." He paused. "If I did that, would you see me if I called on you?"

Nine

S onja's heart sank. Here it came again, another reminder. Sometimes she almost forgot about the problem—until she lost something else she might have
had. Not that she was looking for a man, but she wouldn't
even get the chance to turn this one down. Their acquaintance would end when he learned of her disgrace. He
wouldn't even speak to her again, except out of pity or oblig-
ation.

He'd asked earlier who she was mad at. The One who'd
forgotten her, that's Who. And the magnitude of aiming her
wrath at such an authority as He didn't even frighten her anymore. The insult was bigger. He'd left her the night the house
burned down, and He wasn't back yet, while Satan worked in
the empty silence, wringing her out and throwing her—

... *Wrung my life out and threw it back, Noble had said. Let's
just say I haven't exactly seen the hand of God in my life much
lately* . . .

"Sonja?"

Was it that simple?

I am with you always, even unto the end of the world. . . . *The
Lord is my shepherd: I shall not want.* . . . *Yea, though I walk*

through the valley of the shadow of death, I will fear no evil: for Thou art with me. . . . Surely goodness and mercy shall follow me all the days of my life.

She looked up. Apparently she'd stopped, and now Harley was staring at her, his brow furrowed with concern. She whirled away, giving him her back.

Are You there? she asked silently.

I will never leave thee, nor forsake thee.

But I haven't heard You, she added, still silent.

The Lord is nigh unto them that are of a broken heart; and saveth such as be of a contrite spirit.

Tears leapt into her throat.

Come unto me, all ye that labor and are heavy laden, and I will give you rest.

Her mind's eye saw Him, the shepherd, carrying His little lambs, the ones who just couldn't go another step on their own.

For my yoke is easy, and my burden is light.

Yoke. The oxen, their organization as well planned as that of the church. . . . One pair of leaders at the front, to set the pace and initiate turns. Three pairs of swingers, the young and unruly steers to carry out the turns—when placed carefully amidst the more experienced. And two pairs of wheelers, the heaviest and strongest, to pull the bulk of the weight. This toil . . . easy? and light?

Yes. An easy yoke because He partners gently. A light burden because He's the one who pulls it. In Him there is rest, for He plans as carefully as a wagon master.

The Lord knows where you are, she'd told Noble. *He'll walk every mile to Santa Fe with you, if you'll ask.*

And He'd walk every mile with her. He'd gather her into His arms, if necessary.

Tears made her breath stumble as peace—warm, welcome, and real—poured into her. Warming from the inside, dissolving the panic into assurance, clean and clear. She had choices; she could be bitter and disobedient, which would return anger and solitude, or she could accept her plight and seek God's face to deal with it.

The dishonor wouldn't be banished, but it would make no accusations. The sorrow wouldn't be healed, but it wouldn't pull her under. The problem wouldn't be solved, but it wouldn't defeat her. And tomorrow might be uncertain, but she wasn't going there alone.

She didn't cry. Was too exhausted for that. Rather, she gazed with longing at the grass that would make a gentle napping place as tensions melted from muscles that had been prepared to spring for months.

Harley shifted suddenly, reminding her he was still there and waiting for an answer. "I'm sorry. I must have assumed something that wasn't there," he said.

This wasn't going to be easy. Might lose Harley's friendship, not to mention his respect. For sure she'd lose his interest. No man wanted a used woman—or another man's baby. But no man was going to condemn her for a sin she'd never owned, or for those God had forgiven.

"It's not you, Harley. It's me. I lied to you," Sonja began, though it was that glorious artwork on the horizon she told it to.

"All right," Harley said slowly, uncertainty in his voice.

"My whole family didn't die in the fire. Just my mother and brother. I left my father. I ran away." She paused. "It was a sin to lie to you the way I did. I shouldn't have done it."

And it was real, this repentance. Not merely a matter of being sorry for the mess she was in; it was God's mess now. Oh, and it felt so good to give it to Him. She was clean . . . and this was right.

"I'm sorry. Please forgive me," she added.

"Okay. I forgive you," Harley said in measured words

from behind her. The next ones were spoken with more authority. "Why did you run away, Sonja?"

"You'll have to trust I had good reasons," she said to the new calluses on her palm. She half turned, looking over her shoulder. "What's important is that I can't go back. I would shame my papa. You see, I'm . . . I'm with child."

Magnus stepped up to the tulip tree Sonja and Ander used to play under, his heart sinking. If she were anywhere in the vicinity, she'd be here. He slammed his fist against the bark. If she were coming home, she'd have been here by now. He shook his head and stared at his worn boots, blackened by the hearth.

I wish I had Your eyes, Lord. You know exactly where she is. You can see if she is safe or if she is hungry or hurt or being mistreated.

His throat choked closed, and tears made his shoes ripple.

I cannot see her, but You can. . . . Please help it be enough. Keep her safe. Keep her well. But please tell me where to look for my little girl.

Thaddeus scooped up another spoonful of stew and glared at it. The menu hadn't varied much—bacon and beans, or beans and bacon, every evening for the past thirty-two days. Supposed he should rejoice to have reached Lower Spring alive, to have survived the sinkholes and quicksand of the Cimarron River that acted as prologue to the days across the Cimarron Desert. No water—unless one counted the hailstones yesterday.

Thaddeus pushed the food past his lips. Once again, it didn't matter; he'd eat shavings from the wagon if that's what Jackson cared to dish out.

"Aren't you hungry?" he asked Harley, glancing at the untouched plate between them.

"Not especially," Harley replied.

"I'll never understand why not," Thaddeus told him. "I'm sick of the monotony, but I could eat the south end of a northbound mule. I don't care what it pays, this isn't worth it, Harley."

The captain only hummed a reply from where he crouched on one knee, twirling a stalk of grass between his lips. He stared across the way, toward the fire. Thaddeus followed his gaze.

Sonja.

She was bent over the Dutch oven, obviously trying to coerce the portly Ruff into eating the last serving. Ruff shook his head, wrinkling his chin in reluctance, which she answered with a skeptical and somewhat smug stare. Then she said something, which broke Ruff into a laugh before the big brute conceded his plate to her.

Harley laughed softly. "She's something else."

Thaddeus scooped his spoon across his tin plate, getting more out of the noise than the promise of culinary satisfaction. "You've been on the road too long."

"I'll not argue that. In fact, I'm thinking of giving it up. A man can't eat dust all his life."

"Meaning?"

"Meaning, I'm thinking it's about time I stayed in one place instead of gallivanting all over the country. If nothing else, I worry my poor mother sick."

The robust Martha McGregor—back home in Youngstown, and mother of four sons and three daughters—had nothing to do with this. Thaddeus watched Sonja, selecting his words carefully. "Things may not be as they appear."

Over his shoulder, Harley stared at him. "Forget it, Thad. I know about the baby."

"You—she told you?"

"Of course."

As if she should.

"And you don't care?" Thaddeus asked.

"Of course I care," Harley said, facing forward again. "It's not ideal, but it's—let's just say it doesn't matter. Not as much as I thought it would."

"After what I went through with Amanda? You were there. You saw—"

"This is different."

"She was expecting another man's baby. And still in love with him."

"That was—"

"She went back to him," Thaddeus spat in a hushed tone. "She divorced me to go back to him. No one in my family— no one I even know—*divorced*," he groaned. "Doesn't that mean anything to you?"

Harley just knelt there, studying that stalk of grass as if it were important. "She isn't Amanda, Thad. It's tough in the West. You'll see. Far from family, neighbors, supplies—even the simplest things our mothers took for granted. It's hard to find a woman who'll even consent to making the trip, much less one who came up with the idea."

Thaddeus tossed his plate onto the grass in front of him. "There's a beau somewhere, Harley. Someone she favored enough to give herself to. What if he comes for her?"

Harley set the grass in his mouth and stared across the camp at Sonja, who was now washing dishes at the tub. The hem of her skirt dusted the backs of her boots in its swishing back and forth.

"I don't know, Thad," Harley replied softly, tiredly. He sighed. "Ask me something else."

It wasn't much of a day of rest—except for the oxen. No day was, in a working freight train, despite Russell, Majors, and Waddell's decree to observe the Sabbath. Sundays were a day to catch up—greasing axles, repairing tack, doing laundry.

Sonja swiped the back of her wrist across the perspiration building on her forehead, waved at one of those pesky gnats that could be heard but not seen, and plunged her fists back into the water, scraping another grimy shirt over the ribs of the tin washboard. She glanced over her shoulder at the few who'd already finished their chores and were now catching up on their sleep, hats shading their faces. Let them sleep, so long as they paid her for the clean clothes she'd hand back at the end of the day, if the wind didn't kick up a storm of dirt—

"Mornin', Miss Sonja."

Sonja jumped. Her stare darted to the young man who suddenly stood beside her.

Ennis tipped his hat and ducked his head nervously—though it was Sonja's stomach that turned somersaults. It wasn't his laundry that brought him to her side; that was already in the pile to her left.

So far the men in the other mess units were either too busy or too far away to pay her much mind, and the bullwhackers around her own cook fire were older—more like uncles than prospective beaus, the one they called Ruff being her favorite. Ennis was too young to be an uncle—

And he was too close.

Make him go away, Lord. Make him leave me alone.

"Need any help, Miss Sonja?" Ennis asked.

"No, thank you. I can manage."

"No trouble, ma'am. I can fetch you fresh water or wring out them—"

"Don't you have some place you have to be, Ennis?" a familiar voice asked.

The tension that had been building in Sonja's shoulders fell away in a wave of relief as the younger man jumped erect and actually backed up a step.

"Yessir, Captain," he said. "Thank you, Miss Sonja. Afternoon to you, now."

Sonja watched Ennis retreat. She turned further, her stare climbing Harley's chest. Oh, to be a man. To have that kind of power. That kind of security.

"He bother you much?" Harley asked.

Sonja returned to scrubbing, giving herself a moment to phrase an answer. Didn't want to get Ennis in trouble, but didn't want his attention either.

Obviously Harley was wise to her dilemma. "Ennis is young, but he's not stupid. He'll keep a wider perimeter."

In Lafayette, Magnus tugged on his boots and stepped to the open door of the loft. The sun rose before him; Karl snored behind him.

It was kind of Miles Tyler to loan them his barn. They'd slept in the back rooms of the church after the fire, but Magnus hadn't asked for a renewing of the favor. Sonja's stepping into the night to meet Jonathan Collier last November—even if Margaret Shanahan was there too—had already put doubt in the parishioners' minds about him.

He couldn't even control his own daughter.

Riding into town, looking for her, set the tongues in a new frenzy.

She's run away, don't you know?

The indiscriminate speculations stirred a battle in his soul. Could lash out in self-defense, except God's Word commanded he turn the other check. That was the way of the high road, to let them wallow in their babble. What did they know anyway? The Lord knew His heart—and that of his daughter, whom he didn't teach disobedience. She managed that well enough on her own.

Lord, save her from herself. Put Your angels around her and protect her from her own impulsive ways.

In the meantime, he wasn't leaving town until Sonja showed up or he knew she wasn't coming, whichever came first.

Ten

*I*t sounded like a shot. For that matter, the poppers on the ends of the whips cracked like gunshot up and down the line, but this was louder. More solid. Even the oxen started, trotting in stumbling sideways steps and rolling their eyes in wary glances over their shoulders. One at a time in the outfit's two parallel lines, wagons stopped and the obvious question was repeated—*What was that?*

Thaddeus' heart sank. The injuries associated with accidents were seldom trivial, and he was the obvious choice to tend it. Wasn't even sure he could handle anything as delicate as a suture and needle anymore; it took both hands—and all of a man's strength—to wield that whip with the precision required to make a maximum of noise and still not even touch the precious animals who pulled the cargo to paying hands.

He took off his hat and mopped his face and neck with his bandanna, then stepped to the side of the wagon to pull a swallow of water from the canteen hanging there. Sonja, at the mess wagon several teams behind, braced both hands at the small of her back, then leaned heavily against a wheel. At the other end, Harley joined the men clumped beside one of the lead wagons. The discussion appeared calm, which nearly guaranteed it was something mechanical, rather than physical. Harley nearly confirmed it when he crouched down and fingered something on one of the wheels.

"Looks like a broke wheel." James, the bullwhacker behind Thaddeus, added his commentary.

Wouldn't be surprised. The terrain changed 150 miles ago, monotonous prairie giving way to ravines, gullies, and knobby crags. Sure enough, within seconds, Lieutenant Mason mounted his mule and steered it down the line, distributing the news as he plodded along. "It's all right, Doc. Just a broken wheel," he said as he finally approached, adding, "Go ahead and corral up for the night."

"Thanks, Lieutenant," Thaddeus told him.

"What happened?" James wanted to know. "I thought the Indians had us for sure."

The second-in-command, the personification of patience—so unlike the first-in-command—merely chuckled. "Naw. They're peaceable. It was just a spoke that snapped. The wood dries out, and they sound like that when they're loaded down so heavy." Then he began the whole announcement again for the benefit of the last wagons in the line.

Thaddeus pocketed his bandanna as the wagon ahead lumbered into motion. A broken spoke. His luck, Harley would expect him to splint it.

"Doc!"

The cry froze conversation mid-word and poised supper spoons over plates, while a half dozen stares snapped expectantly toward the man who skidded to a stop in front of Thaddeus.

"I'm trying not to swear, Doc, but tarnation, you got to come quick!" he cried.

Thaddeus nearly flipped his supper into the grass between his boots. "What—"

"It's Zeke," the man panted. "We was changing that wheel, and the jack slipped. The handle hit him right in the face, Doc, and I swear I ain't never seen nothing like it. Knocked him ten feet, if it throwed him one."

Zeke was in bad shape, all right; blood nearly obliterated the right side of his face. It was hard to tell exactly what parts of him were damaged, but it looked as though the handle had hit him in the cheek. The weapon lay five feet away, and the left rear corner of the wagon slumped drunkenly where the jack had crumpled under it.

Thaddeus fell to his knees, whisked off his hat, and laid his ear to the man's chest . . . where the lung function was . . . regular and his heartbeat strong. Thaddeus nodded in satisfaction. The men around him seemed to sigh in unison.

He looked up into the ring of faces, their expressions identical in the deep furrows of their collective brows. "Let's get him over to the fire. Do it gently."

By the time Thaddeus had fetched his surgical and suturing wallets, Zeke was already stretched out on a blanket beside the fire, and it looked as if the entire camp was assembled on three sides around him. No doubt the curious would have crowded on the fourth side if they could afford to lose their britches to the fire. Even Sonja watched from where she washed dishes.

Voices told and retold the story, then announced Thaddeus' arrival as the group parted to make a path for him. He crouched beside Zeke and exchanged a look with Harley, who was already kneeling at the top of his head. Thaddeus wrapped his hands around Zeke's neck, staring at an obscure spot on the ground while his fingers walked the trail of delicate bones. If the bullwhacker's neck was broken, it wasn't obvious. He parted Zeke's eyelids, first one then the other.

Both pupils were responsive and equal in size.

"What do you think?" Harley asked.

Thaddeus shook his head. "Too soon to tell. He's still unconscious. I don't like that, but I'll know more after I clean this wound."

"What do you need?"

"A smaller audience would be a good start."

Harley was already rising. "All right, men. Let's give the doc some room. He has a job to do, and we have a wheel to change."

Where Harley left off, Jackson stepped in, herding the men to drop their dirty plates in the wreck pan and fan out to their evening chores—greasing axles, cleaning tack, and checking shaken loads. Thaddeus tossed the wash water always set out at meal time and refilled the basin from the pot on the fire. Hanging his hat on an eye bolt at the side of the wagon, he rolled back his sleeves and watched Zeke. The man hadn't even twitched. If his brain was hemorrhaging, he'd never see the sunrise. Would never regain consciousness. And if there was broken bone under all that blood—

"Noble?"

He spun around.

Sonja gave him a tremulous smile. "I've never done anything like this before, but I'd like to help."

She'd been washing dishes; the front of her man's shirt was dark where it was wet, and the floppy sleeves were rolled back to bells rocking around her elbows.

He glanced at her stomach. "Are you sure you're up to this? It can get messy."

That little chin elevated itself a degree or two. "I'll be fine."

Thaddeus looked to Jackson, who seemed the more sturdy candidate.

"I don't need her. All that's left is the heavy work—loading all them crates she fusses 'bout me puttin' out." He waved a gnarled hand toward Zeke. "And you don't want me near nothin' looks like that. I'm liable to dress him out and hang him in the smokehouse."

Thaddeus bit back a chuckle and nodded Sonja toward the washbasin. "All right. Wash your hands."

When she finished, he carried the water to Zeke's side and sat at the man's ear. She settled herself awkwardly at Zeke's forehead.

"What do you want me to do?" she whispered, staring at Zeke's wound as if something hungry might leap at her from the middle of it.

"You don't have to whisper," Thaddeus told her. "He's unconscious. He doesn't even know we're here."

"Oh," she replied, eyes and lips equally round.

He moved the surgical wallet between them and motioned inside. "Help me clean this wound with these bandages."

Her touch was gentle—actually a little timid—as she worked in pair with Thaddeus, steadily uncovering the man under the life that had leaked from him.

"It's very red, isn't it?" she said suddenly.

Thaddeus glanced up, then followed her stare to the wound, her words sending him to those initial days of medical school. The first time he saw blood flow so freely, he was certain he'd never be able to handle a real emergency, that all his patients would die of his incompetence. Now his skill was about the only thing he had confidence in.

"Yes," he said, "but you get used to it."

"I don't think I ever could. How much do people have in them, anyway?"

"A few quarts."

The next daub would uncover the center of the trouble. He rinsed the cloth and applied it directly to the wound, balancing a careful touch with his own curiosity. Clean, so far. No bone—

Sonja groaned. "That looks awful."

"Actually, it looks pretty good," Thaddeus said as he rinsed and sponged once more. The cheekbone looked intact, or at least it had neither collapsed nor had shards of bone protruding from it. Additionally, the edges of the wound were straight enough that a few stitches would pull them together nicely—if the opening didn't go all the way through.

Thaddeus pressed Zeke's teeth together, so he wouldn't get bitten, pushed his index finger past the man's lips, and probed the inside of Zeke's cheek, searching for broken teeth, broken bone, or a ragged opening. He found none.

"Is he going to die?" Sonja asked, as if the answer had been etched on the inside of Zeke's mouth.

Thaddeus uncorked a small bottle of whiskey and poured it into Zeke's wound. "If the blow didn't scramble his brain, I think I can fix him."

Jackson chuckled, calling Thaddeus to exchange a glance with him. Fix—it was Jackson's word.

Thaddeus smiled himself as he unrolled the suturing wallet to reveal needles, needle holders, and silk sutures. He set a needle in the needle holder and threaded it. "As this bleeds, and head wounds always do, daub at it so I can see." He set the needle to the farthest edge of the wound. "You'll have to be fast. All right?"

No reply—because she was staring at the needle as if it were some primitive form of torture he was about to turn on her. She was as white as—

"Sonja, don't you dare faint. Not now. The easy part's over."

With obvious effort, she pulled her gaze from the needle. "I think I'm going to be sick."

"Fine. Get sick," Thaddeus replied, drawing on Professor Dawdy's distracting strategy, "but please refrain from doing so in my patient's face. Now, please get that cloth up here where it will do me some good. I can't stitch what I can't see."

With that, while Sonja was still snapping into action, he drove the needle into the far outside edge of the wound. She grimaced as if she felt the tug of the suture herself. Skin didn't pierce as easily as cotton; that always surprised people.

Conversation would see her through this. "It's been five weeks since your injury. Any residual effects?"

"What? Oh. No. I'm fine. All healed."

He drew the needle toward himself, catching the near edge of the wound, stitching from the inside to the outside. "And your mess duties? They don't over-tire you?"

"Oh, no. I'm fine," she said again with a shaky voice, eyes still fixed on Zeke's wound.

Thaddeus nodded toward the blood that flooded the wound he was disturbing. "Sonja, the cloth, please."

"Oh. Sorry," she replied, rushing to soak up the runnel. Then, the pump primed, she ran on, chatting haltingly but amiably about how much she liked Jackson and how different the horizon-to-horizon sky, rolling hills of sagebrush, and wooded river banks were from the dense woods of Indiana— her home. "I miss it," she added.

Thaddeus tied off the second stitch and started a third. "Will you go home to your family and friends, then?"

The smile in her eyes sagged. "No. The Lord will see me through this."

God; her friend, not his.

"What sort of man is he, the baby's father?"

She didn't answer; he looked up and raised his brows, expecting an answer. Wouldn't go on until he got one.

"He was vain, very prideful about his strength," she said.

"Was?"

"Was."

She talked about the man as if he were dead. But then, what woman didn't?

Every time one of your patients died, I wished it were you, instead, Amanda had spat out, making him wish it, too.

No doubt Sonja's beau was a stocky man. Maybe even muscular and proud because he had that to boast about. He'd be built like a bullwhacker. Or a wagon master. Not like a doctor.

Thaddeus focused on the fourth and last stitch. "Will he come for you?"

"No."

And whose fault would that be? The flat line of Sonja's lips and the emptiness in her eyes said well enough.

Thaddeus took Sonja's cloth and wiped the area he'd just mended. Zeke would have a nasty scar, but he'd heal—if infection, the bane of his practice, didn't find the man. He began cleaning the needle and scissors.

"Shall I wash the rest of his face?" Sonja asked.

"That would be fine."

She fetched clean water for the job, while Thaddeus rolled up his suturing and surgical wallets. He reclaimed his hat from the side of the wagon, poured himself some coffee, and leaned against the wagon wheel while he blew across the cup. Zeke should be waking—

Thaddeus nearly smiled outright; Sonja concentrated so acutely on washing the dried blood out of Zeke's ear, the tip of her tongue poked at her upper lip. When her efforts got more diligent, her eyebrows got more animated, pinching and floating above her eyes.

He smiled anyway from behind his cup. She continued her cleaning, her touch gentling as she wiped the mess on all its perimeters—until she inadvertently touched the waistband of the man's trousers with her elbow. Then she jumped as if she'd touched a snake. She looked to see if Thaddeus had seen.

"Mr. Zeke never noticed," he assured her. "He's still out."

She blushed—then jumped again when Zeke stirred.

"Bessie," Zeke said as clearly as if he'd stitched his own cheek.

Sonja peered into his face. "No, Mr. Zeke. It's Miss Sonja."

Zeke groaned. "Takes so long . . . get home."

The hand Sonja set on Zeke's uninjured cheek lay soft and sweet against the stubble that needed plowed. "I know," she crooned, "but you rest now. You'll see. Everything's going to be fine."

Zeke turned his bristly face into her palm, nudging it as if it were warm. "Buy you . . . stove . . . promise."

A smile touched Sonja's lips, making her look far more a woman than the blond braids dangling at Zeke's shoulder should allow. "I know. You just get well. That's what Bessie really wants."

As if her soothing were a magic elixir, Zeke relaxed once again into painless sleep. She began to hum, some lovely little tune that lilted in fragile contrast to the heavy man—and animal—sounds civilizing the sagebrush.

Thaddeus finally sipped from the cup resting against his lips. Amanda hadn't shown as much compassion for Zachary, her own son, when the poor little thing was sick and too young to understand why. Sorry excuse for a mother—

". . . that steer," Harley said as he rounded the wagon, Lieutenant Mason walking a brisk pace beside him. "He looks lame. If you don't think he can keep up, butcher him."

Fresh meat—for an outfit in too big of a hurry to hunt.

The lieutenant smiled. "Tired of bacon, Captain?"

"Who isn't? But don't tell Jackson. The old guy gets touchy." Harley turned to Thaddeus—"How's Zeke?"— except it was Sonja he gave more than a glance. It was his hand that helped her to her feet.

"I closed the hole in his cheek," Thaddeus replied,

"and he's come around a little, but I'm certain he has a concussion."

"Then we'll put him in the back of the mess wagon, the way we did Sonja," Harley said, turning as if to discuss the arrangements with her.

"That's not a good idea," Thaddeus said, interrupting him. "Sonja bruised her knee; a little time, and it healed. Zeke rattled his brain. There may be hemorrhaging."

Harley had swiveled back. Now his brow lowered. "Cut the fat, Thad."

"His brain could be bleeding," Thaddeus replied tersely. "He may die or, at the least, never be right again."

Harley's shoulders lifted with a sigh nearly as deep as his scowl. He turned to Lieutenant Mason. "All right, we'll stay here tomorrow. That will give Zeke Saturday and Sunday to heal up. Have Jackson build another fire ring for his mess unit down the line a ways so Zeke has some quiet, and tell him to cook that beef we were talking about—but put a few extra nails in the tarp over the wagon with the whiskey in it. I'd hate to lose that freight less than two weeks from Santa Fe."

"We're only five miles from the fork to Fort Union. Shall I split off the wagons with the Army freight and take it over there tomorrow?" the lieutenant asked.

"May as well. You can meet us back on the trail Monday."

"Save us some of that meat," the scout added, then, "Anything else, Captain?"

Harley wrinkled his chin as if considering. He shook his head. "Naw. I think I can get my own coffee."

The lieutenant chuckled as he left, while Thaddeus shifted, ready for Harley to join him. But the wagon master wasn't interested in that cup he'd promised himself. He wasn't interested in anything Thaddeus had to say. He wasn't interested in anything but Sonja.

Eleven

*T*haddeus turned. "Pardon me?"

"I asked if you ciphered any answers." Jackson pointed to the fire. "You was starin' in there like you was readin' it."

"Just thinking," Thaddeus replied, turning back to where he'd been sitting since Sonja and Harley strolled into the evening.

"Dangerous pastime," Jackson said over the racket of taking utensils and foodstuffs from the cook wagon.

Thaddeus stared into the fire. Jackson would know. He spent more time with her than anyone else, except maybe Harley.

"Jackson?" Thaddeus asked.

"Yeah?" came the muffled reply.

"What do you suppose Sonja is up to?"

The rattling stopped, and Jackson's head peeked around the end of the wagon. "What you mean?"

Thaddeus glanced into the dregs of his coffee then at Jackson. "Do you think she's trying to get Harley to fall in love with her?"

Jackson gave him a long stare, but his reply was short

and definitive. "Nope."

Thaddeus hoped for more exposition than that, but said only, "That's good, because he knows every woman in every town between here and the coast."

"Which coast?" Jackson asked, adding the coffeepot to the pile.

Reluctantly, Thaddeus chuckled. "Both."

It was Jackson's turn to laugh, then change the subject. "Whole outfit's gettin' cantankerous. Time to bring out peaches for a pie and that jar of pickles."

That sounded good, though the near-forgotten foods didn't hold Thaddeus' attention long. "So what's Sonja up to? She's a different person every day."

"Yeah, she rattles around a little," Jackson replied. "Truth is, I don't reckon she knows herself what she's about, but she's been through a powerful lot, losin' her family and all. I figure she's just grabbin' at friends wherever she can catch 'em." He picked up the last item, the coffeepot, and straightened. "Don't scrape your nose, Doc."

"What do you mean?"

"Well, seems you're inspectin' so close, you can't see what you really got." He hiked the load higher in his arms and shuffled away, the swinging of the coffeepot handle squeaking in time with his steps.

Thaddeus turned back to the fire.

It was full dark by the time Harley and Sonja walked from Jackson's cook fire—and the laughter that had been rolling around it for hours—to the one Thaddeus stared into. During his own moving about he'd seen them earlier, walking the perimeter of the camp from mess unit to mess unit, she strolling so demurely beside the wagon master that her skirt didn't even brush his boots. She was at least careful in that much—or at least Thaddeus never saw them touch or step beyond where thirty-three sets of eyes couldn't chaperone.

Would that she'd been so cautious last January.

"How's Zeke?" Harley wanted to know.

Thaddeus tossed the remains of his coffee into the grass. "Not good. He still hasn't awakened fully."

"I don't even have to ask what you're doing tonight," Harley said. "You want me to take the first shift?"

"No, I can manage."

"I can help," Sonja offered from her spot beside Harley.

"You need your rest, Sonja," Harley told her before Thaddeus had the chance.

Yes, she was probably exhausted from her walk, but Thaddeus said only, "You should get off your feet. You were on them too much tonight."

The statement was still enough to swing Harley's attention to Thaddeus—and make his eyebrows twitch ominously before he turned back.

"He's right," Harley said. "You need your rest. Are you sleeping here, or down the line with Jackson?"

Poetically, a round of laughter rose from the direction of the other fire.

"I think I'll stay here with Noble," she replied. "The men are having fun. I'd only intrude."

Harley seemed perplexed by her statement—or something—for his brow furrowed deeply. "What did you call him?" he asked.

Sonja didn't make the familiarity any more casual when her expression collapsed. "Noble," she said in a small voice.

Thaddeus felt the flush clear to his boots—like he'd been caught flirting with another man's wife. And like he was about to lose something private and special.

"He wouldn't tell me what the N of his first name stood

for," Sonja explained lamely, "so I made something up."

"So you named him Noble?" Harley glanced in Thaddeus' direction. "Very clever," he told her, except his voice held no mirth.

Thaddeus could only stare. Jealous. Harley was actually jealous—as if Thaddeus wanted a woman whose entire situation reeked of one he'd been in before. As if once weren't enough.

"Thank you for the walk," Sonja said, effectively diverting the conversation.

Harley accepted the change like a gentleman. "Get some sleep. I'll see you in the morning."

Sonja gave him a smile void of guile, but the look Harley gave Thaddeus spoke of possession, before he raised his chin in a silent good-bye and faded from the light.

"I can help you with Mr. Zeke," Sonja said when Harley was gone.

Obviously Thaddeus had given her the impression he was suicidal; Harley would knock his teeth in for letting her stay up all night.

Thaddeus snapped his bedroll in place—though it was already perfect. "That won't be necessary."

"Oh, I don't mind," Sonja said brightly, then disappeared into the darkness around the back of the cook wagon. She returned a moment later with her own bedroll and knapsack.

"Aren't you sleeping in the wagon?" he asked.

"Jackson keeps taking beans from my mattress for supper. There isn't much left of it."

"Oh. Well, can I help you with that?"

Her movements were getting stiff and strained. She'd really blown up in the last weeks, testing the capacity of her man's shirt to hide her growing bulk. At five months along now, it was abundantly clear she was carrying a child; she was beginning to get that waddly look.

She gave him a grateful smile. "That would be nice. I might not get back up again once I get down there."

He cleared her a space across the fire from his own, carefully sweeping away the pebbles and sticks that would gouge into her sleep, then laid out the oilskin ground cover and the bedding it kept dry.

"Can I escort you to a bush for some privacy before you go to sleep?" he asked when he'd finished.

"No, thank you. Harley already took care of that."

Of course. Harley.

Thaddeus returned to his bedroll and wished he hadn't tossed the rest of his coffee. Sonja had a hairbrush in hand, but she only watched her thumbnail run through its bristles. Men laughed in the distance, and Ennis, the night herder, warbled a lonely tune on his mouth organ.

"I don't know why you're so mad at me," Sonja said suddenly and softly to her hairbrush. "I guess because I followed you. I'm sorry for that. I wasn't myself. But I'm earning my passage to Santa Fe, and you aren't responsible for me anymore." She looked across the fire, and her eyes snapped. "And I have no designs on your friend. In fact, I'm not looking for anyone to rescue me, so you can quit watching me so suspiciously."

Thaddeus' heart skipped a beat. She read him well. Better than he cared to be known.

He rose and went to Zeke's side, pressing fingers to the man's throat . . . where the pulse was strong and steady. His respiration was equally normal. His wound had swollen and was weeping, but Thaddeus had sewn in the minimum of stitches to allow it; infection grew least where it was exposed to air and light.

Thaddeus looked to Sonja, where she knelt on her bedroll, still staring at that hairbrush. She was wrong. He wasn't angry with her. He was just—

Never mind. It was of small consequence now and would be less so in another two weeks.

He snugged the blanket under Zeke's chin and was turning away when the man stirred. "Bessie?"

"Dear Mr. Zeke," Sonja called immediately. "It's Miss Sonja, Mr. Zeke. Please try to rest so you can get well."

The admonition worked, for Zeke mumbled and sighed into sleep again, and Thaddeus breathed a little easier. At least Zeke had the faculties to know his wife's name. And maybe it was merely exhaustion that kept him so still. Didn't take a medical degree to understand that.

Thaddeus returned to his bedroll. Sonja untied her braids. Then in a slow and steady rhythm she brushed the golden ripples.

Dear Mr. Zeke, she'd said, the tenderness falling so easily from her lips—to a near stranger. Amanda had never called him anything but Thaddeus. But then, he'd never been anything more than just Thaddeus to her.

He put another buffalo chip on the fire. She tugged at her left boot, trying to take it off.

"Are your feet swollen?" he asked.

"I beg your pardon."

"Your feet. Are they swollen?" he asked again.

Of course they were. Why else would she be struggling with that boot?

Sonja watched with wide eyes as he stepped around the fire and dropped to his knees before her. "No! I can't let— What are you doing?" she asked, sinking back on her elbows.

"Practicing my profession." He loosened the laces further and tugged the boot from her foot. In an instant he had her heel in the palm of one hand and her empty stocking in the other. He pressed a thumb into the top of her foot and watched for the tissue to spring back.

"Women in your condition tend to retain water," he said.

And she was; the impression of his thumb remained.

This wasn't good. If she was puffed up like this now, how would she be by the time she delivered in September?

"Are you visiting the privy when you need to?" he asked. "You aren't waiting so Jackson won't have to stop, are you?"

"That isn't it. There isn't any privacy out here. Where can I go that there aren't a million eyes watching?"

She was right—and he had absolutely no remedy for it, other than to stand guard for her, maybe even hold up a blanket to screen her, but that wouldn't—

Sonja tried to pull her foot from his hand. Thaddeus held harder and began to rub it, stroking the instep and massaging his thumbs into the sole. It worked; she let him have her foot, her eyes blinked slowly, and the handle of the brush tilted as her grip relaxed.

"This trip is taking more of a toll on you than I thought it would. Take it easy, Sonja. You're on your feet too much."

She just stared at him, her expression clearly void of commitment.

"You want to get sick? Maybe lose this baby?" he asked as he relieved her of her other boot.

Her eyes widened. "No."

So she really did want the child, despite the mean circumstances of its birth. Amanda had—

Never mind that.

"Then listen to me," he said. "Lie down for a rest when we break for breakfast. And after supper." When she opened her mouth to protest, he sent her a quelling stare. "You lose this baby out here, and you could die. Do you understand that?"

Sonja finally lay down all the way. She nodded.

Thaddeus shook his head. "I swear you're the second-worst patient I've ever had."

"Who's worse?"

"My mother—but not by much."

"I have work to do, you know."

"I'll talk to Jackson. He won't argue with me."

She seemed to accept that and let him knead her feet, one then the other and back again. They were cute, human anatomy in miniature. And no wonder they hurt. They were too small to support her properly. Put another ten pounds or so of child on her, and she'd need this ritual nightly just to survive.

"That feels nice," she said, the softness of her voice in stark contrast to the visions of Harley's fist crashing into his jaw.

And he wasn't as selfless as she thought. Her little foot was definitely the softest thing he'd touched in weeks, and her golden hair spilled around her—

"Do you have any sisters or brothers?" she asked suddenly.

He had a suspicion where this was going, so he was a little hesitant as he told her, "Two brothers. Two sisters."

She tried not to smile, but the urge was obviously strong. "What are their names?"

He almost laughed himself, for she was so ridiculously transparent. But he told her anyway. "My sisters are Antigone and Ophelia. My brothers are Dante and Agamemnon."

"Oh." Her eyebrows raised in steps but, to her credit, she didn't laugh. "Aren't those people in history?"

"Historical literature," Thaddeus corrected, changing feet. "Sophocles, Shakespeare, Dante, and Homer; my mother liked to read when she was in the family way."

Sonja bit the lower half of the smile that fought to break free. "So what was she reading . . . with you?"

"I'm not saying."

That loosed a chuckle. Then she only watched him knead her foot . . . until finally—to her foot—she said, "I owe you an apology."

"For what?"

"For lying. For making a nuisance of myself." She finally looked up. "I don't know what I was thinking when I followed you."

Sorry? A female? Impossible.

"Do you want to hear why I did it?" she asked.

"If you want to tell me," he replied quietly, as if it didn't matter whether she told him or not.

"I ran away." When he didn't react—an act of pure will—she continued, "From my father."

"So he is alive."

"Yes. And he's not a tailor. He's a blacksmith. But the other—the part about my mother and brother . . . there really was a fire."

Yes, the porch-tree and the comb Ander had carved for her. She spoke of it calmly, now—grief, finally accepted. Or perhaps dwarfed by bigger problems.

"I know," he said, adding, "I'm sorry."

Her gaze lingered before she finally said, "Thank you."

The quiet made itself comfortable while the fire danced, Zeke began snoring softly, and oxen bawled. Laughter burst from the direction of the other fire. Someone whistled. Another round of laughter followed.

"I didn't lie about the baby," Sonja continued. "I really didn't know about it when I ran away."

The rhythm of Thaddeus' hands faltered before catching again. If she hadn't known, the baby's father hadn't known. Still didn't know. But probably would want to.

"Why did you run away?"

It was a long moment before Sonja replied. "I won't lie to you, so I guess I can't say. You'll just have to believe I had good reasons."

Thaddeus waited for her to continue. She didn't. "What about the baby's father?"

She shrugged. "He wouldn't care. I want to forget him."

The man hurt her. Whoever he was, this beefy beau, he broke her heart.

Thaddeus stared at the little foot in his hands and held the urge to sigh. If he understood anything, he understood rejection, and that's all it was—tossed out like yesterday's newspaper when you no longer served a purpose. His gaze lifted. She stared back—no anger, no sadness, just fact.

"Thanks for the apology. I forgive you." He gave her foot a final squeeze. "You'd better get some sleep. I wouldn't be much of a doctor if I kept you up all night."

"I'll take the first shift," she said.

"No, I'll take the first one and wake you in a few hours."

"No you won't. You won't wake me at all," she replied, far too astute. Then she shrugged. "You may as well sleep. I'm staying up anyway."

Which didn't surprise him a bit. He fished in his pocket for his watch. "All right. Wake me at 1:00—or as soon as you get tired."

She sat up and cupped her hands to receive the time-piece, then held it as if it were butterfly wings.

"You've never seen one before?" he asked.

She looked up, eyes wide. "Papa always wanted a watch, but we could never afford it. Mama thought she might buy him one for a present someday."

Thaddeus reached into her hands and released the latch that held the cover in place. It popped open, revealing the white enamel face and black Arabic numerals.

Sonja's eyebrows lifted slightly over a soft smile. "It's so small. Like a little clock."

And it was only brass. Gold and silver were beyond his means.

"Wake me at 1:00," he said again.

"2:00," she said, the magic of the watch forgotten.

"1:00."

She lifted her eyebrows smartly. "3:00."

"All right. Get me up when you can't stay awake any longer. You won't wake me till then anyway." She was closing the watch with reverence as he stepped to his bedroll and took off his boots. "Mr. Zeke should sleep through the night, but wake me if anything out of the ordinary happens."

"What's not ordinary?" she asked, glancing at Zeke as she rearranged her boots and knapsack.

"Pain, tossing and turning, agitation, vomiting. You'll know."

She nodded.

He set his hat a few feet away and pulled off his spectacles, dropping them in the lard can. The final lying down pulled a groan of satisfaction from his throat. It felt so good to get horizontal every night. That bed in Santa Fe—once he secured one—was going to feel heavenly.

Thaddeus opened his eyes and rolled his head toward the fire. Sure enough, Sonja was watching him . . . brushing her hair again . . . slowly drawing the bristles through the shining shimmering length of it. It looked pretty, even seen through near-sighted eyes. No matter what she did with it, no matter how many times she brushed it, she couldn't drive the last of the curl away. Each little gathering of filaments waved in their own direction, like the chaotic ripples in a pond, making her hair fluffy.

She lifted her eyebrows in question, but he shook his head. Nothing she needed to know. He closed his eyes.

Twelve

*T*haddeus woke. Blinked his eyes into focus. Sonja was leaning over him, the firelight flickering on her cheeks; he'd set his attention on worse sights the first thing in the morning. Except this wasn't morning.

"What time is it?" he asked.

"Just after 1:30," Sonja said, sitting back on her heels. Her hand left a cold place on his shoulder when she took it away. "You fall asleep and wake up faster than anyone I've ever seen, you know that?"

Thaddeus cleared his throat, sweeping the sleep from it. "Oh? And how many men have you seen sleeping?"

She looked to the hands in her lap. "Just Ander."

Not her beau, the baby's father? It hadn't been much of a romance.

He combed his fingers through his hair. "How's Mr. Zeke?"

"He woke up once, but—"

Thaddeus' hands stopped in his hair. "He did?" He looked to his patient, who was rolled up on his side, his back to the fire. "What was wrong? Is he all right?"

"He's fine. I would have awakened you if he hadn't been.

Besides, you hadn't been asleep very long."

"What woke him?"

"I don't know. He just opened his eyes. Mostly he wanted to know what happened to him."

"He spoke to you? Did he know who you were, where he was, that sort of thing?"

"He didn't think I was Bessie, if that's what you mean." Sonja shrugged. "He felt the bandage on his face, drank some water, and went back to sleep."

"That's all?"

She speculated a moment, puckering her lips in thought. "No. Come to think of it, he said he was dizzy as a drunk skunk and that his head hurt like . . . well, like something I can't repeat."

The laughter rumbled from Thaddeus' throat. So pretty, she, all warm and feminine, her laughter sweet and her blue eyes dancing—even if she'd tortured that beautiful hair into braids again. Their laughter rolled to a stop. They stared at each other. The fire snapped. The night held its breath.

Visibly flustered, she looked away. Then she remembered the watch and held it over his chest as if to set it down. But that seemed too personal, judging by the way she caught herself, so she just held it there until he finally relieved her of it. Their skin brushed. The brass was warm.

She rose a little awkwardly and stepped to her bed. "I'm sorry I can't stay awake any longer, but I made you a fresh pot of coffee."

"Thank you, and that's all right. I'm used to this," he told her, pocketing his watch and rubbing his face with both hands. He set his spectacles on his nose, pulled on his boots, and went to Zeke. No change except, while Thaddeus knelt beside him, he rolled on his back and began to snore.

"That's why you wake up so fast, isn't it?" Sonja said.

"You've spent lots of nights like this with your patients, haven't you?"

He poured himself a cup of coffee and sat, legs bent and forearms resting on his knees. He set his hat on his head and stared over the rim of the cup at her, where she lay on her side, her arm bent beneath her cheek. He blew across his coffee and nodded.

He could sleep anywhere. On the floor. In a chair. He'd had plenty of practice, waiting for a fever to wear out, a baby to push into the world . . . or some poor soul to give up.

"I thought so." She yawned. "Have you ever . . . been there when a baby came?"

Thaddeus grinned behind his cup. "Dozens and dozens of times."

"What's it like? I mean . . ." Her voice trailed away, and she started picking at the edge of her blanket.

"I know what you mean." Thaddeus sipped gingerly and wrapped his hands around the cup's warmth. "It's never routine, and it's always a wonder." He chuckled. "I do so little of the real work, but I'm the one who gets paid for it."

She smiled.

"Am I being interviewed for the job?" he asked.

"What job?"

"Delivering your baby."

Her expression collapsed. "Oh. No—I couldn't let you do that."

"Why not?"

"Well, because," she replied indignantly. "I just couldn't."

"Who's going to deliver you?"

"I don't know. Not a man. Not anyone. I'll do it myself."

"It's not that easy, Sonja. You can't manage by yourself." He whispered, "I won't look. I'll close my eyes."

Truth was, propriety already dictated he work by feel in subdued light with his patient completely covered. He carried it one step further and insisted her husband be present for intimate examinations.

Sonja bit her lip and picked at that blanket as if it needed all her concentration. Were the light true, she'd be blushing.

He sipped again. First-time mothers always had the hardest labors. Unprepared and idealistic, they took the hours of drenching toil and agonizing pain as a slap in the face, as if it were the cruelest injustice that something so selfless, so virtuous in its intent, could be so miserable. They often begged for death—any relief from the torment. Many of his colleagues fanatically embraced the Bible verse, "in sorrow shalt thou bring forth children," but the oath he swore to included something about relieving sorrow. So he always carried a full bottle of laudanum to deliveries. Especially the "firsts."

Sonja couldn't go to anyone else. Not some butcher who knew nothing of cleanliness and not some midwife who knew nothing of real medicine. Not when the University of Pennsylvania School of Medicine boasted the first independent department of obstetrics in the country. Not when what he knew was built on the experience and research of some of the greatest minds in the world. Why, he was even a member of the American Medical Association.

"I'll take good care of you, Sonja," he said. "It will be fine. You'll see."

She closed her eyes to sleep. "No, Noble."

He blew across his cup. "Yes, Sonja."

"No, Noble."

"Yes, Sonja."

She lay still. He glanced at Zeke, who continued to snore quietly. Thaddeus sipped; not only was the coffee fresh, it was good.

"No," Sonja mumbled.

"Yes," Thaddeus whispered. He watched the fire. Then he watched Sonja . . . and maybe thought about how much the same, and how different, she was from another woman he'd known.

Amanda. Cascades of black hair and bottomless brown eyes. Skin the color of milk and the texture of cream. Thaddeus was helpless to her, that first time he saw her, dressed as she was in red—as if God had made the color just for her. She was the most beautiful woman he'd ever seen— till then or since. And he'd loved her to distraction.

Thaddeus shook his head. He'd had no stamina against her, not after working himself to exhaustion just to save the money for tuition to the finest university in the country, then more arduous months of study and apprenticing to earn the right to be called a physician. The only females he'd seen in an eternity had been feeble, in labor, or still wetting their britches. It was no wonder Amanda knocked him windless with her sparkling attention.

Thaddeus heaved a harsh breath, humiliated all over again. She wasn't in love with him. She wasn't a Christian. She wasn't even a virgin. He was all three and so determined to put his name on her, lest Frank Feiden realize his mistake and try to win her back. So he married her, took her home to Ohio, and believed the child that came a few weeks early was his.

The coffee in his mouth turned nasty.

They had no happiness, only tolerance—which she flung on the floor under her petticoat and Frank Feiden's trousers. Amanda was in love, all right. But not with him.

He flicked the last drops of coffee into the fire and stared at Sonja. She would say he was bitter. He raised an eyebrow. Okay, so he was bitter. Bring down lightning from heaven and sear his soles to the ground. He'd paid his hometown practice and reputation for the right to some resentment.

He braced his forearms on his bent knees and stared at the fire, at the buffalo chips that burned like charcoal. A pair of boots rustled just inside the firelight's reach as one of the teamsters served his two-hour, every-other-night watch circling the perimeter of camp. The man's silhouette created a moving column of emptiness in the uninhibited show of stars around it.

And Sonja slept peacefully. She'd shifted to her back but had turned her face toward the fire. One braid disappeared under her cheek then reappeared at her arm. The other lay in the black behind her head. Everything about her was soft—the delicate brush of her brows, the button of her chin, the down of her cheeks, her tissue-paper eyelids, and the pillow of her lips. She breathed so gently, she didn't even move the blanket over her.

Thaddeus refilled his cup, but only set it aside to go to his wagon. A moment later he reclaimed his spot, spread his sketchbook on his knee, and set a crayon of pastel to its surface, alternating between sipping coffee and staring across the fire as he sketched . . . the anatomy of arms and backs . . . his old office in Youngstown . . . and finally, Sonja.

For most of the night, Thaddeus watched Sonja sleep. When the air turned brisk, scattering its burden of moisture onto the brush, she curled into a little ball; he stoked the fire and tucked the blanket around her. The sun teased the horizon into soft blues and golds, and still he watched her, sometimes seeing Amanda, sometimes seeing a panicked girl, and sometimes seeing a pretty young woman with qualities he hadn't expected—courage, compassion, and maybe, a little integrity.

Much of the camp roused to full-life around them, those who weren't rolling on to Fort Union helping those who were. Jackson cooked breakfast, and Sonja washed her hair. Then she stood beside the cook wagon, combing it dry in the morning sunlight. Thaddeus watched her again.

She was bent at the waist, though her stomach kept her from bending far. Her hair was nearly dry now and brushed past her knees as she gathered it into a long rope, raised up, twisted it, then tucked it into a coil at the crown of her head. One hand held it in place while the other searched her pocket for the six-inch stick she drove through it. Tentatively she let go, but the hair started to fall. She cupped the knot again, withdrew the stake, and drove it home once more. This time it held.

Thaddeus' coffee cup stopped halfway to his mouth. Her profile was devastating, for the girl he knew in braids and men's trousers became a woman in full skirt and baggy shirt. Her golden hair was pillowed on her head, highlighting the delicate bones of her face and the slender line of her throat—which begged to be kissed. Her condition showed this morning in the way it pushed at her shirt, but it made her a more feminine picture. In fact, the shirt added a note of intimacy, its cut implying she borrowed it from her husband—perhaps because her own still lay in a heap on the parlor floor. He didn't need to ask; she would say she looked awful. He would say she didn't know what she was talking about.

As if she sensed his watching, she scanned the camp for the eyes that held her so steadily. He set down his cup and pretended great interest in the time of day.

Santa Fe.

It crept up in stages; prairie grass that had yielded to sagebrush now gave space to piñon forests. Lieutenant Mason had led half the wagons on a loop to the north to deliver contracted supplies to Fort Union; the empty wagons joined the rest of the train on Monday. Mr. Zeke swung along in a litter suspended between two mules, and Harley swore he'd never hire a doctor to crack whip again, claiming Noble's presence encouraged more misery and mishap than it remedied.

The train moved on to Las Vegas, a minuscule settlement on a well-watered meadow where the men rested before striking the final leg through the Sangre de Cristo Mountains. It was the first taste of this other relaxed yet polite culture Harley had told Sonja about. And it was her first taste of eggs, cheese, and milk in weeks, bought from the Mexican settlers who peddled them, and shared by Harley's generous hand.

They crossed the last river, another fork of the Pecos, at San Miguel, a pathetic little settlement of baked mud dwellings where naked children ran hither and thither along worn passages that could never aspire to be called streets.

The road had swung south at the crossing of the Canadian River to arc around the jut of the Sangre de Cristo Mountains. It was Glorietta Pass that cut through them, a narrow gateway between the southern spurs of the mountains and the red rock walls of Glorietta Mesa. It took all day to make the ascent, crawling past steep ravines and boulders, and around the turns almost too short for the double teams it took to pull each wagon's six thousand pounds to the top.

The last camp was six miles from Santa Fe at Arroyo Hondo, where the men "rubbed up," primping and putting new poppers on their whips for a splendid arrival the next morning. In clean shirts and tidy frock coats—their Sunday best—they climbed a final steady rise to the tablelands that gave their first view of cornfields and adobe buildings . . . descended a serpentine road banked by tall junipers . . . and finally thundered into the plaza of Santa Fe.

Sonja sat on the seat of the mess wagon, exactly where Jackson had told her to stay so she'd be out of the way. He'd jumped from his perch long ago. Now he was bellowing orders from somewhere behind the wagon, his gruff words carrying over everything in the vicinity. The teamsters worked with new exuberance and shone as bright as their smiles, clean as they were from their fussing that morning under the razor and over the washbasin.

Sonja grinned at a little boy swinging back and forth at the ends of his arms around a support over the dirt walkway. Every living thing on legs crowded around the train, as if the stores being handed down—pots and pans, cotton, muslin, silk, shoes, oil lamps, pocket knives, ink pens, silverware, reams of paper, bolts, screws, tools, hinges, mirrors, ammunition, clocks, watches, toothbrushes, spices, furniture, tobacco, champagne, and whiskey had been specifically ordered by them.

"Miss Sonja?"

She turned. Poor Mr. Zeke. His had been no grand entry into Santa Fe, lying in the litter. Noble had removed the man's stitches, but his wound was still a scabby gash, and he couldn't stand up straight. Even now he leaned against Noble.

"I wanted to thank you for your kindness," Mr. Zeke said. "You took care of me almost as good as the doc and were a powerful sight prettier."

"I didn't do anything special," she told him. "Just finish getting well."

"No doubt about that now that I'm home," he said. "But if you ever need anything, you let me know. I won't see your cupboard dusty, Miss Sonja." Then he tipped his hat—no bullwhacker was ever sick enough to leave off wearing his hat—and limped into the throng as if he were a little drunk.

One block front to back and a longer block from side to side, the plaza seemed to accommodate all of Santa Fe, as well as its visitors, teamsters, and oxen alike. Most of the natives were Mexicans—short and swarthy men in white pants, unbleached muslin shirts, conical hats or ones with wide flat brims, and brightly colored blankets folded over their shoulders. The women wore full but short skirts and blouses that displayed plenty of pillowy flesh, though they wrapped shawls over some of it. Military uniforms peppered the crowd, and nearly everyone smoked tobacco, even some of the barefoot children who jumped about, chattering in rapid Spanish and giggling in a language anyone understood. Papa would think this a prime mission field.

A trio of chickens pecked at the dirt just beyond the mules, whose harnesses jangled as they twitched at flies. High heaps of sticks trotted about with burros tied beneath them, oxen bawled a miserable tune, and dogs barked underfoot, churning up billows of orange powder that hovered near the ground but managed to float high enough to color the air.

Sonja looked to the doorway of the mercantile where Harley stood in the shade beside Mr. Gonzales, whose name graced the sign overhead. Harley said most of Santa Fe's merchants were foreign-born, but this was a New Mexican who poked a knobby finger at the ledger cradled in his palm. Harley replied in Spanish that came as easily as if it were a supper-table language and pointed to a crate floating through the mob on the shoulders of one of the bullwhackers—Ruff, judging by the bulk of him. Mr. Gonzales smiled, teeth gleaming ivory against his golden skin, then he nodded and motioned Ruff through the door of his store, pointing to a spot inside.

Harley looked to Sonja and smiled, then turned back to Mr. Gonzales. She groaned. Just how long did he expect her to sit here?

"Come on, Sonja. Let's get you out of the sun."

It was Noble who'd spoken, and Noble who was reaching up to lift her down.

Thirteen

oments later Noble pulled Sonja's hand through the crook of his arm and tugged her into motion from where she'd stopped. "I can't take you to a hotel, Sonja," he said. "Your reputation would be in tatters."

Sonja shot him a glance. He needn't worry about her reputation. She didn't. She knew the truth. Besides, no amount of chastisement—from herself or others—would change anything.

"I can take care of Mr. Zeke," she suggested.

"Mrs. Zeke will take care of Mr. Zeke. She was already in the plaza when we pulled in."

News traveled fast where there wasn't much to know.

"Are you going to just leave me there? When will I see you again?"

He didn't even give her a glance. "Have Harley bring you by my storefront as soon as I secure one."

Shouldn't have even asked. His attitude had curled up and flopped over again like a slice of bacon. Where he'd at least conversed with her the night Mr. Zeke got hurt, he now gave no more than the impartial expression of a casual acquaintance.

She watched the powdery soil disappear under her skirt. There was nothing more to do and nothing more to be expected from him. Between working her passage to Santa Fe and earning money doing the teamsters' laundry, she'd relieved him of the nuisance of her. And she'd apologized for entangling him in her troubles. Her following him was only her means of landing in Santa Fe now.

She swallowed the tears that wanted to rise and looked for distraction. They passed a row of sorry little shops and stepped onto a narrow street, the crowd evaporating behind them as if an imaginary line held them back. They stopped to let a man and his stick-laden burro pass before them; the smell was distinctive—sweat, beast, and fresh cedar.

Santa Fe was nothing like Lafayette, Indiana. Junipers, not deciduous trees, dappled the hills flanking town, and everything was shaded in those dry tones of orange, pink, and brown—not green. Some of the houses looked more prosperous than those in San Miguel, but many were just as sad. There was neither brick nor wood—except the poles sticking straight out of the walls in a line just below the flat roofs—and almost nothing distinguished one little dwelling from another.

. . . For I have learned, in whatsoever state I am, therewith to be content.

That seemed a stretch, but Sonja tried anyway. "I'm going to like it here."

Noble gave her a steady gaze. "Why?"

"Why not?" she asked. Papa would say it was a matter of decision. It worked for St. Paul; it could work for her as well.

"I guess I'm not so certain," Noble said. "I may starve."

"You won't starve."

"If I can't get my medical practice established, I will."

"Then why did you come?"

He thought for a moment. "You're nothing, if not optimistic."

No, just certain of his abilities. Certain the people of Santa Fe would recognize brilliance when they saw it. Would appreciate someone whose hands could heal.

"Why *did* you come?" she asked.

Noble only motioned with his head, saying, "This must be it."

Sonja followed his stare to where a rectangular wooden sign swung from the dirt-floored porch of a squat but tidy little house. The sign's skinny blue letters declared something in Spanish; smaller ones beneath them told the story in English—*Mrs. Trujillo's Boarding House, $1 a day*. Cloth in stripes of sunset colors hung in the window, falling over the sill to the outside as if a careless breeze had tossed them so. Five pots of red geraniums marched between the vertical supports.

"I can't stay here," Sonja announced.

Which made Noble's expression collapse. "You haven't even seen it yet, Sonja. Give it a chance—"

"That's not it," she replied, lowering her voice and glancing about. Little boys played, a young girl swept, two women bent over washtubs, and a man led a donkey and squeaky cart past, but none gave them any attention. "I don't have enough money for this."

"I don't think that's a problem," he replied flatly.

"I can't take Harley's charity," Sonja hissed. "Who knows when I'll be able to pay him back?"

Noble just turned and set one boot in front of the other. "You'll have to settle that with him. For now you need to get a room before they're all gone, and I have work to do."

He wouldn't even discuss alternatives. Within a blink, a young Mexican woman answered his knock and his request, leading Sonja over a floor that seemed nearly as noisy as it was hard and under a ceiling that seemed far too low. The cubicle she displayed so proudly—her last vacancy—was as clean as it was small, the powdery gold of the walls pulling light from a single window. The floor appeared to be clay, though it was smooth and solid, and it gave rise to a corner fireplace molded out of the walls on either side. A bundle of wood inside it lay ready for a spark, while the vivid colors in the curtains, quilt, and the rectangular rug relieved the smooth textures and solitary gold of everything else.

Sonja turned back to the doorway. It was empty, save for her knapsack lying in a heap on the floor. She found Mrs. Trujillo in the kitchen slapping a thin pancake of dough between her brown hands.

"Where is Dr. Staley?" Sonja asked.

Mrs. Trujillo nodded toward the door. "The man, he left," she said, her accent strong. "But don't worry. He pay for the room."

"Did he say he was coming back?"

Mrs. Trujillo shook her head. "He say you rest. You go. I have dinner quick."

Sonja returned to her room and stared through her window to the little courtyard the house seemed to be built around. They were finally in Santa Fe, she was finally on her own, and Noble hadn't even said good-bye. She folded her arms over her stomach and swallowed hard. Maybe it was for the best. He would need to gain the confidence of the community in order to establish his part in it, so he'd have to take care whom he associated with.

That evening Sonja stepped to the window overlooking the street. The fiery gold of the Santa Fe sun was dying, yet the city lived, lively music and laughter springing from the plaza and rising over the tops of the houses across the street. As if there were no work, no need for sleep, no tomorrow.

She hadn't planned very well. What did she think she'd find when she got here? Open arms and a family's welcome? She hadn't brought enough money, but she also hadn't been the one sweating over the forge to earn it. No, the only thing she thought about was following Noble, which never seemed more stupid than now, after he dropped her off without a glance back.

"*El doctor,* he is your husband?" Mrs. Trujillo asked behind her.

Sonja whirled around. "Dr. Staley? Gracious, no." She paused. "I have no husband."

She waited for Mrs. Trujillo's gaze to fall to her bulging stomach, but the woman merely nodded and looked away, though not before sympathy darkened her stare.

"Is there a Protestant church in Santa Fe?" Sonja asked.

"Protestant? *Sí*—how you say—John the Baptist?"

"A Baptist church?"

"*Sí*, Baptist."

Papa would prefer she attend a Lutheran church, but such were the choices. Her heart lifted with anticipation anyway; to hear them again, the hymns and prayer and God's Word. Even the thought felt warm and familiar and a little like home.

A raucous cheer rose in the near distance. Sonja turned back to the window.

"The *fandango*," Mrs. Trujillo said. "Everyone is happy when the bullwhackers come. It is good you took the *siesta*. All night long, they will make *loco*."

All night long? Someone whistled, sharp and shrill. Bits of an energetic tune followed it, while Sonja stared outside as if the noise made as much visible color in the air.

In Indiana, Magnus propped his forearms on his bent knees and stared into the fire.

"We will find her, Magnus," Karl said suddenly.

Magnus' focus passed through the flames to his apprentice on the other side of the fire. "My faith is losing its strength," he replied, fear for her paralyzing him then, just as quick, boiling into anger. "Almost eight weeks we have looked for her."

Karl shrugged. "Now we know she isn't coming home to Lafayette. We can go back to Independence. That was the last place we saw her."

Magnus' sigh hefted his stare to the night-blackened sky. "You are right. But the days are so short . . . and the nights are so long."

"Why shouldn't I be angry with you?" Sonja demanded of Harley the next morning. "You installed me here as if I were your horse and this were a livery. You didn't even give me so much as a farewell, while you and Thaddeus and your partners in sin were making racket all night long."

Harley's head snapped back in surprise. "I had no part in that. Not last night."

She cocked an eyebrow at him. If he'd been carousing until dawn, he didn't show it. His face was tanned but freshly shaved, his green cotton shirt crisp, and his hazel eyes clear.

He laughed and held up both hands, palms out. "I promise, Sonja. We were good boys. I doled out pay, then got friendly with the ledgers, and the most excellent Dr. Staley was unloading his medical practice all night."

"He found a storefront?"

"No, but he did manage to buy a little adobe a few blocks from the plaza. He says it's perfect. You know, easy to find but in a quiet spot." He pulled her hand through his arm. "Come on, I'll take you to breakfast."

"No." She stopped, staring past him to the street that would only grow more crowded as they approached the plaza. She couldn't go out there. It was no place for a round-bellied woman in a man's shirt and a sun-weary skirt. "Perhaps we could go for a walk," she said, scrambling for another option.

"You feel up to that?"

Given the alternative? "Yes. We'll go slow."

She panned the landscape that looked sparse compared to the lush woods of home, though it was beautiful in its own silent and waiting way.

"You like Santa Fe, don't you?" Harley asked as they strolled from Mrs. Trujillo's.

"Yes. Better than I thought I would," Sonja admitted to herself as well as him—even if all she'd seen of it was from a window.

"I'll have to teach you some Spanish if you're going to make your home here." He pressed her hand between his fingers and forearm. "You don't want to go into town because of the baby, is that it, Sonja?"

Heat flushed her face. Couldn't fool him any better than she could find any of that courage she'd been so full of a week ago. Reluctantly, she nodded.

He pressed her hand as if it were a reply and said, "I asked Tucker—he heads the office for Russell, Majors, and Waddell here in Santa Fe—for an extension. That means I'll captain the train leaving in a week, instead of in a few days . . . which would give us some time together but still put me back just before the baby comes—if you don't rush it," he added with a smile.

A suspicion crept into Sonja's stomach, raising little flutters.

"Thad will look out for you while I'm gone," he continued. "I'm a pretty independent man, you know. I've lived alone a long time. Too long, I'm beginning to think. But if anyone can polish my rough edges, you can. I'll take good care of you, I'll treat you well, and I'll love that baby as much as any we have together." He stopped and turned. Stared into her face. Into her heart. Right through her. "If you'll do me the honor, Sonja."

Ander would have grown into a man like Harley MacGregor. Backed as it was by steely strength, Ander's devil-may-care abandon would have become like Harley's bravado, his rebellious streak would have become such command, and his sense of mischief would have become this charm. Harley, like Ander, had heart, competence, and handsome—though aggressive—ways. She could do worse. Far worse.

"Marry me, Sonja," he said. "Marry me today."

Fourteen

*T*haddeus carefully unwrapped the spirometer, stuffed the newspaper wrappings into the crate with the others, and began to carefully wipe it clean of ink smudges and dust. They had made the trip well, his medical supplies, from the most delicate—the binocular microscope with the glass specimen slides—to the array of smaller tools—needle holders, bullet probes, bullet extractors, scissors, scalpels, vaccination lancets, and ivory tongue depressors. Good thing. They were probably the only ones of their kind within a week's ride. He scanned the room. Everything had traveled unscathed, thanks to RMW's premium hardwood wagons and Harley's expertise in packing the mix of shapes and textures, which included an oak desk and chair, an array of kerosene stage lights, adopted because of their light-amplifying reflectors, a tall examination table, boxes of medical texts, a cabinet of chemicals and medicines, these crates of precious instruments, and even the shelf clock Mama and Dad gave him when he opened his first—and last—office. From its post on the desk, its familiar ticking whispered into the quiet of the house.

Too quiet. Thaddeus looked to the door. As soon as the

sign painter got his sign hung, patients would begin knocking on that door.

As if raised by Thaddeus' will, a hard rap sounded on the wood, but there was no pause before it swung open. Harley drove the knob, and "unhappy" was etched into every plane of his frame.

"What's the matter?" Thaddeus asked.

Harley closed the door behind him, but rather than answering or even clearing a place to sit down on the room's only chair, he stepped to the small front window and just stared out, fingers jammed into the pockets of his trousers.

Thaddeus turned back to his tools. Only one thing on earth accounted for that kind of misery; this one's name was Sonja. He set the spirometer on the table and began unwrapping another bundle.

"I asked Sonja to marry me," Harley finally said.

The newspaper stopped mid-crackle. "You did," Thaddeus said, a question sounding like a statement. A spark of possession flickered to life—he'd found her first— but he snuffed it.

"She turned me down," Harley continued.

"She did." Another statement.

Harley finally swiveled. He shrugged, his expression stunned, as if he'd just taken a blow in the dark. "I took her for a walk. I made my bid. And she said no, plain and simple."

"I don't understand. Why—"

"She wouldn't give a reason. Just said she wouldn't make me happy."

Thaddeus could only stare. Imagine that. And who would have figured Sonja for this kind of judgment? And reserve? Or myopia? Harley was a good man. He wasn't ugly, and he sure wasn't poor; made five times a month what a bullwhacker made. And it wasn't like she had a bounty of better offers.

Thaddeus set the instrument beside the tub of wash water and reached for another package. "You all right about it?"

"Oh, sure," Harley replied. "Guess I'm more shocked than anything. It never occurred to me she'd say no."

That was an understatement.

"What's that?" Harley asked suddenly.

Thaddeus glanced then followed Harley's deeply puzzled stare to the vaginal speculum on the table.

"Female instruments," Thaddeus replied.

Harley nodded, then quirked his eyebrow at the obstetrical forceps Thaddeus was unwrapping.

Thaddeus held up the forceps before adding them to the table. "For dislodging impacted infants during delivery."

Harley's eyebrow lifted. "Every job has its hardware." He sighed and stepped back on course. "I'm rolling out day after tomorrow. The sooner I go, the sooner I'll get back." He drew a little pouch from his pocket and dropped it on the desk, the coins inside chinking softly. "I'll be busy loading up tomorrow, so I'll give this to you now. It's for Sonja. I paid her room and board for the next three months, but she'll need some clothes and female-things. She'll fight you, but make her take it. She can pay me back or something later." He paused. Finally met his friend's gaze. "Look after her, Thad. She's . . . pretty special."

"He say his name is Ruff," Mrs. Trujillo said, leaning into the room later that day.

"Ruff? The bullwhacker?" Sonja asked.

Why would Ruff be visiting her?

Sonja sat up and swung her legs over the side of the bed. "Thank you, Mrs. Trujillo. I'll be right there."

It was indeed the bullwhacker who waited so patiently

in profile on the porch, though he looked like a domesticated bear casually searching for food. His clothes and hair were no less dusty than they were on the trail, and his beard—so popular these days—was still nothing more dashing than a bush of wire poking from his jaw. His paws rolled and unrolled the brim of his sorry hat.

"Ruff. It is you," Sonja said, stepping out on the porch.

The rotund man turned, giving her the warmth in his green eyes. "I thought you were here. These are the nicest rooms in town."

"They are?" she asked, already certain. Harley had done that. Her heart split, one half given to gratitude and the other lost to regret.

"You getting along all right?" Ruff asked.

"Yes," Sonja replied—except there was no logic to what she was doing.

Ruff nodded and motioned toward the Santa Fe yard of Russell, Majors, and Waddell, just a few blocks away. "I guess you know we're pulling out day after tomorrow."

"Tomorrow? You're leaving tomorrow?"

"No, day after tomorrow."

"Oh." The word took all Sonja's breath with it.

"We usually spend some time in the yard, getting the wagons and animals ready for the return trip, but . . ." Ruff's monologue faded.

"Harley is captaining the train?" Sonja asked.

Ruff's gaze grew less careless. "I thought you'd know that, if anyone did."

She shook her head. Didn't even know what she was doing, much less what Harley was about.

Ruff's features scrunched up. "I don't mean to pry, but the rest of the crew and I thought you and the captain were something serious."

"No."

Her stomach roiled in misery. She'd hurt Harley. He tried not to show it, but it had to be the most profound rejection to be turned down by a woman in her desperate circumstances. Rather like, *Marry me or be stoned as a sinner,* and she preferred the stoning. It wasn't that Harley made an unattractive prospect, but she could have talked all morning and not convinced him of that. Besides, she deserved the stoning.

"Well then, I guess you'll be needing this even more than we thought." Ruff leaned back to push a meaty fist into his trouser pocket, screwing up his face as he dug deep. He pulled out a little package wrapped in newspaper and tied with wire. "Here."

"What is it?"

"Money, of course," he replied, as if it were obvious. He held it out until she finally lifted her hand to take it. "The boys passed the hat for you, considering you have no family here. Mind you, some of it isn't local coin, but the merchants will take it just the same."

She stared from her palm to his face. "I can't accept this."

"Oh, take it, Missy. It isn't an heirloom," he scolded, using a shortened version of Jackson's pet name for her. "You never complained, and you worked as hard as the rest of us. Then you were so good to Zeke, feeding him by hand and all. He'd be angry if we didn't see after you."

"How is he?" she asked, seizing the easier topic.

"Tucked in his own bed." He shifted and casually scanned the houses across the street. "You want us to spread it around you had a husband that died on the trail, we'll do that."

Sonja set her attention on the wire tie. She closed her fingers around the package and leveled her chin. "That's all right. I wouldn't want you to lie."

"It might be for the best, you know. I mean, I'm afraid ..." Ruff shifted. "Miss Sonja, are you sure you know what you're about? The Anglos aren't going to be any more forgiving of you here than they were where you came from."

"I—"

"Some folks have a bent sense of justice," he continued, each word riding on more energy than the one before it. "The Mexicans aren't so spiteful. About the only thing they won't stand for is adultery, but some of those other folks neglected to leave their Eastern ways back east. They can act pretty nasty with women in your situation. Outcast. Spit on. You'll be lucky if all they do is ask for a public confession. At worst, they'll kill the baby and—"

The ground tipped suddenly. "They'd kill my baby?"

She might have collapsed if Ruff hadn't grabbed her by the arms and held fast. He groaned. "I knew I shouldn't have said anything. Now you'll get all worked up—"

"Would they really do that?" she asked, her voice a feeble thing.

"Probably not," he said, but it was too late. And he was a poor liar. Wincing as if he'd just killed her dog, he stroked her arms clumsily, then shifted as if searching for a way to help her. Finally his features simply collapsed, and his arms dropped to his sides. "Most of us are going with the captain, even though it's a few days early," he said quietly, "so if you need anything, just ask for Mr. Zeke at the boot maker's. That's his father. He'll find him for you."

"I'll do that," Sonja said weakly. "Thank you, Ruff. For everything."

The sunlight was too young to push through the curtains, but the noise wasn't so feeble, carrying well the jangle of gear, the roll of wheels, and the bawl of oxen. Sonja almost rushed to the parlor window to look, but she wouldn't be able to see for all the houses in the way, anyway.

So she lay where she was, cozy under the quilts and appreciating them more for how temporary they were.

The baby shifted inside her. It would be born in three and a half months. Then it would cry, and feel cold or warm or wet. Or pain. Had to think. Had to devise some way to keep it safe once it was thrust where others could take it from her. Or hurt it.

Lord, they wouldn't really do that. Would they?

The tumult outside stilled suddenly, amplified by the quiet that followed. Then came the long and distant call of Harley's command—*Roll on*—recognizable by the familiarity of its pitch, tone, and rhythm.

Sonja threw back the covers and went to her knapsack, falling awkwardly to her knees to dig through it. The noise started again, the pistol-shot crack of a whip, a creaking of wheels. More whips. More wheels. Once she uncovered the book, she flipped through its pages—Judges, II Kings, Psalms . . . Isaiah.

He shall feed his flock like a shepherd: he shall gather the lambs with his arm, and carry them in his bosom, and shall gently lead those that are with young.

Sonja clutched the Bible in her arms, holding it between herself and her last visible hope. She bit her lip, mind whirling with disjointed prayers and stomach sore with panic.

Noble came to visit, but Sonja was taking a nap he obviously refused to disturb. So he left a note and a little pouch that was heavy with the sound and weight of coins. *Dear Sonja,* it said, *please accept this money on Harley's behalf. He wanted you to have it to buy clothes and some of the other things you'll need until he returns. He says you can pay him back later. Mrs. Trujillo assures me you're feeling well. Please let me know if*

you need anything or if your condition changes. Noble.

Sonja stared at the note and its tidy script. It was a lovely hand, but all its owner cared about was doctoring her, and she owed Harley enough, as it was. She folded the note neatly and slid it into her skirt pocket. The pouch she gave to Mrs. Trujillo.

Sonja slept one more night in the soft bed Harley had paid for, then she looped her knapsack over her shoulder and tucked her bedroll under her arm.

"The captain, he pay for your room until he come to Santa Fe," Mrs. Trujillo told her.

"I know," Sonja explained, "but I've made other arrangements. You just keep his money safe until then, and I'm sure he'll appreciate it."

She gave Mrs. Trujillo a smile of thanks and walked away.

Someone finally knocked on Thaddeus' door, but it was only Jackson.

"How's business?" the old man asked as he stepped inside and looked about.

"Still slow." Thaddeus reclaimed his chair and folded his forearms on the desk. "Truth is, I haven't had one patient. Not a single one, Jackson."

Even though that new sign—*N. Thaddeus Staley, Medical Doctor*—swung from its new post out front. Apparently no one bothered to read it.

"Well, you only been here a few days. It'll pick up," Jackson said. He stepped up to the certificate hanging over the twin bookcases and leaned forward from the neck to peer at it. He snorted. "Want me to shoot somebody so you got somethin' to doctor? Looks like some important folks think you can handle it."

Thaddeus couldn't help but chuckle. "That's all right. I'll wait until they come in on their own."

"Suit yourself," Jackson said. He dropped into the chair on the other side of the desk. "I been studyin' on it, and I reckon it's the womenfolk givin' you trouble, seeing as how they's the ones what tends to the healin'."

Thaddeus gave his full attention.

Jackson shrugged. "Well, they's nervous about comin' to a doctor that ain't got no wife."

Thaddeus puffed a sharp breath. "That's ludicrous."

"In English," Jackson spit.

"That's ridiculous," Thaddeus said more deliberately.

"Maybe, but you know how they are. And how they goin' to explain takin' off their clothes for a bachelor? Say, you got somethin' to drink? I'm parched."

"Coffee?"

"Ain't you got nothin' stronger?"

"Not unless you're sick," Thaddeus replied with a lift of his brow.

Jackson scowled but gave him a gnarly nod, so Thaddeus pushed himself from his chair.

"My female patients don't need to disrobe," Thaddeus said, picking up the conversation as he knelt to pour at the fireplace in the back corner. "I know about women's delicacy. I take every precaution to be discreet, uncovering only what I have to see to treat. Sometimes less. Sometimes it's a guessing game. Sometimes I'm working strictly by feel and a very vague memory."

Couple that with a list of symptoms just as sparse—modesty again—and it was enough to make a man want to go back to herding cattle.

Almost.

Thaddeus sat down and Jackson sipped his coffee.

"It's a weaker refreshment than I wanted, but you make a fine cup, Doc." Jackson growled a sigh and shifted, getting comfortable. "Maybe they don't know that."

"Perhaps I should take out an advertisement in the next issue of the *Santa Fe New Mexican*," Thaddeus suggested sarcastically.

"Maybe," Jackson said, "but it might be easier to just get a wife."

Thaddeus's back slammed into the chair. "A wife?"

Jackson looked perfectly sane and serious—which could only mean he was going somewhere with this.

Thaddeus crossed his legs, ankle on knee. "You talk to Harley before he left, by any chance?"

"Yep. I saw him," Jackson replied. "He wanted me to go with him, but I'm—"

"He tell you about his conversation with Sonja?"

"Yeah, he told me, but—"

Seeing Jackson had a particular wife in mind, Thaddeus shook his head. "Oh, no. You're confusing me with the stupefied wagon master. I'm the satisfied doctor, the one with some sense."

"Don't look too satisfied to me. You look bored. And that youngun needs a father."

"That youngun has a father, and the mother knows exactly where to find him," Thaddeus replied, lifting his cup to his mouth. "Besides, Harley already offered." He took a long swallow.

"She don't want Harley."

Thaddeus nearly choked. "What makes you think she wants me?"

"I got eyes."

Thaddeus chuckled again. This was ridiculous. "Well,

you're wrong. I've played this part, and I haven't anything left for an encore." He motioned around the room. "All I have is all you see, my friend, and I barely escaped with this."

Jackson's gaze narrowed. "Spit in your eye, did she?"

Thaddeus gave him a long stare—meddling old man. "You could say that." He paused. Lowered his voice and admitted, "She convinced me I got her with child, then laughed at me for a fool. All along she was wishing I were someone else. The court would have given me the child . . . but I guess I wasn't as cruel as she. I couldn't stay there . . . Everyone knew, and she . . ." He paused. "It took half of what I had left to clear my debts and get me started in Santa Fe."

"Pretty spiteful woman," Jackson said.

"I'll say."

"Don't reckon I ever knowed a woman so mean."

"She's a rare one, all right."

"Yep, pretty rare," Jackson said. "Good thing lightnin' don't strike twice."

Thaddeus stared through the top of his spectacles. The man hadn't heard a word he said. "I don't need a wife, Jackson."

The cook wasn't even fazed. "What you need's respectability—same thing the little missy needs." He shook his head once. "Peculiar thing, ain't it? You could give to each other what neither one of you got on your own. Think on that." He lifted his cup and sipped. "What this needs is a little whiskey."

"It's crazy, and there's whiskey in the plaza."

"I like the company here, thanks. Seems to me you're up to your britches in stubborn. Fact, you got more pride than paying customers."

"I don't need a wife, Jackson," he said again.

Jackson sighed. "Naw, I reckon not. It was just somethin' I studied on, that's all. You know, like a business arrangement.

People do all sorts of things in business they might not do otherwise. Leastwise, there ain't much at risk 'ceptin' time and money." He motioned casually with his cup and grinned. "And you know about time and money. Ain't neither one worth much till you spend 'em."

Fifteen

*T*haddeus filled his mug with the dregs of the day's coffee and stepped to the doorway of his house, leaning his right shoulder on the jamb and taking a sip. The day had been hot, but the evening was cool, and the night would be cooler. The Santa Fe climate suited him just fine so far. Too bad he couldn't make a living.

Jackson was wrong about the womenfolk hesitating to seek a male medical practitioner. And Sonja was wrong for him.

Ludicrous.

It would be a poor business decision and a terrible match.

Forget it.

He took another sip of coffee.

Nasty.

He chucked it into the dirt.

Once Sonja filled her pockets with dried apples and jerky, she stepped from Mr. Gonzales' store to the soft dirt of the plaza, passed its sundial, and turned left, following its perimeter and nibbling slowly on her breakfast crackers to make them last. Seemingly no one realized the excitement was over, that Harley's train had unloaded days ago and was already on its way east. Either the bunches of people she shouldered through expected another to arrive, or they loved to visit. No wonder so little grew underfoot.

She approached another gathering of Mexican men and women, who fell silent and stared as she walked by. She hiked her blanket higher over her protruding secret and set her attention on the doorways as she passed them, strolling by this entry, that one, and the one after that. Most—except those that were clearly and crazily still residences—erupted with laughter, the tunes from mandolins and those guitars with twelve strings, and the smell of tobacco and liquor.

She paused in the next one, where a man leaned over a pair of boots, hammer in hand and a row of tiny spikes pinched between his lips. Her heart stopped. Had to be Mr. Zeke's father. He glanced up, but the words choked in her throat, and she rushed on. She wasn't hungry, but she sure wasn't prosperous either. She'd stop by and say hello when she was.

She ambled down a side street, pressing past clusters of people and the occasional forlorn burro. A row of white canvas canopies shaded the sandal-footed Mexican women on their straw mats, and if the landscape was single-minded in its color, the wares they sold—sweet cakes and rolls, coffee, ribbons, brown earthen mugs, little mirrors, firewood, alfalfa, and garden foods—made up for it.

The first woman smiled from behind pyramids of onions and garlic. "Good morning. All I have is yours."

Sonja's steps faltered. She wasn't certain she'd heard correctly until the next woman—pounding corn in a stone mortar—added, "I am at your command."

Sonja nearly laughed out loud. Harley said the Mexicans

were polite. He should have been more specific; they were nothing short of courtly, so in contrast to their free and easy smiles—which partnered more comfortably with the fact that the woman behind the baskets of freckled beans was rolling tobacco into a corn-shuck cigarette.

The woman beside her said something to the others in Spanish; they looked to Sonja and agreed, smiling and nodding their heads as they added their own commentary.

Sonja's confusion must have shown, for the woman who'd spoken waved a pale green ribbon at her and said something.

"I beg your pardon?"

The woman fingered her black and silver tresses. *"Su cabello."*

Sonja's hand flew to the braid falling over her breast and beyond. "My hair?" She panned the women down the line.

"Sí. Hair," one of the others said.

The rest nodded, obviously remembering the English word.

The woman fingered her hair again but motioned toward Sonja's. *"De oro,"* she said. "Gold."

The understanding came as a warm and welcome relief. Sonja smiled. "Blond."

The door closed behind her with a solid thud that echoed softly in the cool and quiet dimness. For a moment Sonja stood just inside, letting her eyes adjust to the dark, letting her pores pull in the peace . . . and letting the interior find form. It was as different from Papa's church as it could be. Nearly as narrow as it was tall, and shapeless, the packed-earth floor stretching unbroken from one adobe wall to the other. Sonja smiled to herself. Let old Mr. Emmett try to sleep during one of these services—with no benches, no pews, and no chairs. The windows would offer no distraction either, for they were tiny, few, and set just beneath the soaring ceiling, casting their first light on its smooth logs and the carved braces supporting them.

Leaving the entry, Sonja stepped softly to the front of the church, where the figures shelved on the wall weren't really big enough to call statues. More like large dolls and not even particularly pretty, though the mural around them, clear to the ceiling, was. And no pulpit stood ready to receive an open Bible, but the musty air held the memory of whispered prayers. It was calm here. Tempting to stay— except she needed to find a necessary, and there was probably one out back.

Sonja trod once again to the entry but was startled by the sunbeam that caught her eye. She stopped and looked up. The ray leaked around a rope hanging from a hole in the ceiling, drilling a tiny circle of light on the floor; the rope was tied off around a cleat on the wall far above her. She moved her head until the shaft of light caught her square in the eye. Had to be the bell rope. She scanned to her right, then to her left and spied the little door—whose handle was cold in her hand. The door needed coaxing to open . . . until the dim wedge of light from behind her fell on a narrow stone staircase. She followed it around . . . full circle . . . to a trap door, a line of light leaking around its edge and tracing its square shape. Hands flat, she heaved the weight of it.

It opened onto the belfry.

The next day and three blocks away from her destination, Sonja's heart ran ahead of her. It would be so good to be in church again. To sing the hymns and hear the Word of God.

Two blocks away, Sonja's steps slowed a little. The best

she had to wear was a man's shirt and a dirty skirt, while the Mexican women draped themselves in those beautiful lace scarves—*rebozos*—and the Anglo women wore layer upon layer of flounces over voluminous hoops.

Within sight of the plain little building, knots tightened in Sonja's stomach. No ring graced her finger; there was no husband to put one there. Her shame was there, protruding from her shirt and arriving before she did.

Sonja stopped and stared—then jumped aside when a woman in black taffeta skirts brushed past her, the woman's long lace scarf blowing gently behind her. The heels of her satin slippers stepped smoothly. The scent of lavender powder drifted in her wake. Such were the prosperous Mexican women, dressing as if the day were new and money lay about for the gathering. This was church attire for one of the Catholic churches. Weekdays it was still those beautiful shawls, jewels for their hair combs and ears, and taffeta, but in vivid colors.

A family of Anglos overtook her. The girl on the end was about her age and gave her a glance as they passed—she, in her clean dress and shiny hair curled so carefully. She who stepped through the door as if she belonged there. As if her walking inside would inspire smiles rather than curiosity. As if there were no sermons written for her circumstance.

For a long moment Sonja watched the door . . . before she tiptoed beneath the side window and listened in secret.

Thaddeus strolled the perimeter of the plaza, shirt and waistcoat crisp. He slowed as he approached a woman with a black-headed youngster against each pocket of her skirt. She was working on another one, except she probably thought her shawl and hiked-up waistband concealed it. But he was no casual observer, and someone would have to deliver the child.

He watched her face, waiting for the chance to tip his hat and strike up a conversation, maybe mention his new practice. His opportunity came when she looked up from speaking to one of the children. She smiled—and he looked away. He groaned inside. He looked again. She was already passing by.

Every day he walked to town, intending to shake some hands, get to know his neighbors, spread the word about his practice, but such outgoing demonstrations didn't come naturally, and they hadn't been taught at the University of Pennsylvania School of Medicine. Such social fluency was better left to vivacious people, people like Sonja, who could get away with it.

He stopped now, at the end of the walk. Should go visit her, see how she was getting along . . . and enjoy her sweet smile. Maybe Jackson was right. Maybe if he were married, looked a little more solid, a little more safe . . .

No, he'd build his practice in Santa Fe the way he'd built his practice in Youngstown—a little at a time. Even now there could be someone knocking on his door. Or maybe he'd place that ad.

There was much to know about this new home; Sonja was introduced to most of it from the lofty height of the belfry of the Chapel of San Miguel. Such as the coolness that surely clung to the elm trees tracing the ditch irrigating the corn and wheat fields to the south. Locals called it Acequia Madre, "mother ditch"; the Santa Fe River cut through the dirt to the north. That the little burros and their firewood—packed as carefully as if the skill were a science—came down Canyon

Road from the mountains to the east. That most everyone farmed, and that only a few owned horses or hogs; everyone else owned sheep, goats, and mules. That the majority of the little mud houses were only one story, though there were some that were three, and others of wood structure with pitched roofs, and that their simple exteriors were misleading, giving no hint of the central courtyards flourishing with decoration, foliage, and activity. That Burro Alley, far west of the plaza, was to be avoided, for all the gambling parlors there. That Fort Marcy, on a hill northeast of town, was quite an installation, with its thirteen cannons on its high walls. That there were about a half dozen Catholic churches and no schoolhouse. That any reason was reason enough for a festival, including a parade about the city. And that the Chapel of San Miguel held a worship service every day; Sonja's ears continued ringing for hours after the bell overhead had stopped—but only the first time. She made a point to be somewhere else every time after that.

Ander would have delighted in the view. And had she found her eyeing place sooner, she could have watched Harley's outfit, right below her, as it ambled away with its cargo of blankets, *serapes,* beaver furs, and wool, and its herd of Mexican mules so valuable to the U. S. Army in Missouri. As it was, she stayed long hours in the belfry, far from curious eyes that might notice too much. Occasionally she caught a glimpse of a familiar brown hat and smooth stride passing on the other side of the river. She watched closely at these times. So closely her eyes watered with the strain.

In Independence, Magnus eyed the crowded street. Wagon and harness makers, sellers of livestock, and blacksmiths had no trouble making a living where there was always another party to supply for a westward sojourn.

"We will stay busy. There is no doubt," Karl said.

Magnus nodded, except it wasn't feeding his belly that held his attention. Rather, before he even looked for a place to fire his forge, he would stop at the print shop to order handbills, *Reward for information . . .*

"Oh? Has she walked to town or something?" Thaddeus asked from where he stood under the overhang of the porch the next day.

"No, *Señor,*" Mrs. Trujillo replied, her brow wrinkled as if she were perplexed. "*Señorita* Thorseth, she no live here no more."

The words, broken as they were, hit Thaddeus in the stomach. "What do you mean, she doesn't live here anymore?" Surely the woman didn't understand.

"She move away. She—"

The stomach again. "Moved away? When?"

"*El sábado.* Saturday."

"Saturday? That was five days ago." More gently Thaddeus asked, "Did she say where she was going?"

Mrs. Trujillo shook her head. "She just say she make the other arrangements."

"Did she take anything with her?"

"*Sí.* She have the bag and the blanket."

"And the money I left for her," he added—or rather, the money Harley left for her.

"No. She no want the money."

The woman's words fell more easily than Thaddeus' steps as they crossed the plaza to the other side of Santa Fe. And Jackson wasn't nearly fast enough in answering his knock.

"Why didn't you tell me you'd taken Sonja in?"

Thaddeus asked as he rushed inside Jackson's house.

Jackson's head snapped back in surprise. "Sonja? What you talkin' about?"

For the third time, the punch in the stomach. Thaddeus scanned the room. It was empty of anything feminine, including Sonja. "She's not with you?"

"No. Ain't she at the boardin' house?"

No more punches to the gut; this time it fell to the floor. "She left. Mrs. Trujillo says she moved out five days ago."

"Five days!" Jackson closed the door and dashed his fingers through his hair, which flopped back over his ears anyway. "Thunderation, I knew I should of gone to visit, but I been busier than a diarrhea-ed cat at the yard." He met Thaddeus' stare, his own determined. "Where you figure she went?"

"I don't know. All she took with her was her knapsack and bedroll."

Jackson was already crossing the room. He grabbed his hat and threw his arms into his vest. "Come on. We're wastin' daylight."

Sixteen

*T*haddeus sighed heavily, braced his forearm on the window frame, and stared outside. All day they'd looked, even splitting up to cover twice the ground, but two grown men couldn't find one foolish little wisp of a woman. People had seen her—the Anglo with the gold hair—but no one knew where she lived. At least that's what they said.

Still, he and Jackson stayed at it until long after the sun gave up. Until long after the vendors in the market went home and the smells of supper billowed from chimneys. Until long after it got ridiculous. But it was no use. Sonja didn't want to be found.

Frustration welled up in Thaddeus for the twelve-hundredth time that day. She had her clothes, a blanket, and the money she'd earned doing laundry. Nothing more. Blast it, where was she?

Sonja peeked over the edge of the belfry and scanned the western sky. Looked like rain. Smelled like rain. And if it fell at any angle at all, it would drive right over the belfry's low wall.

She might get a little wet.

Lightning snaked the sky. A roll of thunder chased it, followed by a spattering of rain against the windowpane.

And Thaddeus got a lot determined.

Enough was enough. Sonja was clever, but he was smart enough to piece this together, and he was going to find her if it took him till dawn. Then he was going to blister her reckless little bottom.

Whirling from the window, he stepped to the fireplace, banked the fire, and pulled his coat from the peg augured into the wall. He wouldn't bother with the plaza. The only people there this time of night were the smokers, drinkers, and monte players.

He shoved his arms into the sleeves of his coat, set his hat, and grabbed the lantern from the table. She would seek shelter, and it would meet two criteria—it had to be familiar, and it had to be a place she could get into undetected. Perhaps a smithy, since her father was a smith. It could be perfect—stables she could sneak into during the day, straw she could hide under at closing time, shelter at night.

Cold dollops of rain had soaked the shoulders of his coat by the time Thaddeus stopped at the first smithy on the north side of town . . . where the footprints he eyed around its perimeter were too large for Sonja's tiny feet.

Standing in the lee of the livery, he dug in his pocket for his watch and held it in the lantern's light. A runnel of rain poured from the brim of his hat, and it was just before eleven. He scanned the street; no people, no stick-laden burros trotting about tonight. Should have worn his sidearm.

Naw. Wouldn't shoot anyway. Not a person. Not even a dog. Had taken an oath to relieve suffering, not cause it.

He hunched his shoulders and stepped back into the onslaught. On the north edge of humanity now, he'd zigzag his way to the south side, checking every livery between here and the river. . . .

Which took an hour and a half, and brought no obvious profit except to tell where Sonja wasn't. Every barn and out-building empty behind him, he stood at the Santa Fe River. The only place left was the *Barrio de Analco*—the "Ward beyond the River"—a less prosperous section of town.

His steps sounded hard and hollow on the wooden bridge. He stopped in the middle to stomp off the clods of mud stuck to the boots that had walked eight-hundred miles—and then some—in the last two months. A little weather wasn't going to scar them at this point, but they sure wouldn't make it through the winter. Have to cash in that promise Zeke made for a discounted pair.

With a sigh, Thaddeus resumed his pace, the lantern swinging beside him—until he stopped again, gaze fixed on the silhouette ahead. A church. Yes. Should have thought of that sooner. It would never be locked, and Sonja loved all things related to the Lord.

The heavy door opened on agonized hinges and closed with a hollow thud behind him. For a moment he stood, getting his bearings. The room was stark and empty, judging by the reverberation. He stepped out of the entry onto the clay floor and lifted the lantern, though its feeble light found no corners. His gaze rose to the abyss overhead. Tall. That's where the echo came from.

Slowly he walked across the center of the room toward the altar—or whatever was up there—holding the lantern high and scanning left and right in the vacancy. But no shape bent the shadows—

Something moved at the back of the church. He spun around and raised the lantern, but whatever had moved was beyond the power of the light. Had to be Sonja. Now, what did the noise sound like? Not steps. More like a door. To the outside? No, not that heavy. And she wouldn't go out there anyway. Not unless she had less intelligence than he gave her credit for.

Thaddeus didn't even bother to check the shadows as he passed them on his way to the front half of the church. He stopped in the entry and moved the arc of the lantern's light past every corner. Nothing. Just a bell rope rising from its cleat to a hole in the ceiling. Probably to the—

Belfry? No, she wouldn't. Or maybe she would.

He stepped to the left . . . let the lantern's light find the door, and clenched his jaw even as he opened it and ascended the narrow circle of stone steps. Sonja was up here, and she was going to wish she'd opted to stay in Independence to face her father by the time he got through with her.

He had to set the lantern down and push with both hands against the trap door that had swollen in the rain. She must have stomped it closed behind her. It came free, and rain pelted his face as soon as his hat and shoulders cleared the opening. He retrieved the lantern and peered around the other side of the door. . . .

And there she was, huddled against the short wall of the belfry, her eyes as large and luminous as those of a trapped animal.

"Sonja, what in the blazes do you think you're doing?"

She allowed him to march her back through the streets to his place. There, inside, she turned a slow circle in the center of the room then stared at him from beneath the brim of his hat, which he had placed firmly on her head. Finally she spoke.

"I didn't mean to hide. I didn't know it was you." Her first words since he'd found her; the first words he could hear over the downpour.

Even now his coat hung heavy over her narrow shoulders, dripping into the few inches of skirt below it, which then dripped on the rug. She looked like a pudgy little sister playing dress-up in her brother's clothes.

Except Thaddeus didn't smile.

He'd frightened her? The woman was more in danger of herself than of anyone prowling an empty church at one A.M.

He pulled her sodden blanket—which made a feeble coat—from his shoulders and hung it on one of the hooks behind the front door, then strode to her side to sweep the hat from her head and help her out of his coat.

He motioned behind him. "This front room is an examination room. You can take your hair down and get out of those wet clothes while I build up the fire."

She reached for her knapsack on the table.

"There are nightshirts in that room," he told her from where he was adding the coat and hat to the hooks.

"Are they yours?"

As if there were an impropriety regarding whose body had touched the cloth before hers. "You weren't too concerned about donning men's clothes two months ago," he said.

"They were Papa's."

Which explained why they were large enough to accommodate her condition.

At the table, Thaddeus lit the lamp and handed it to her. "The nightshirts are for my patients. There are towels and blankets in there too."

Sonja didn't argue for once. Just thanked him and moved silently past him, closing the door as quietly behind her.

With icy limbs, Thaddeus hurried to fill the hearth with flames and ring its edge with cobble rocks. By an act of will he stepped from its heat to his own chilly room, where he struggled with wet clothes that refused to slide over goose flesh. Dry once again, he set a pot of cornmeal to cook on the fire.

A few minutes later the door opened and Sonja finally emerged, a blanket wrapped around her, a towel draped over her head, and a bundle of clothes in her arms.

"Here, let me have those," Thaddeus said.

"I can do it." She scanned the room for a place.

He eyed the bundle more closely. Had to be the petticoat and pantalets that were surely in there—and so demurely hidden from sight—that made her clutch it as if it concealed stolen jewels. As if he weren't a physician and hadn't had sisters. And as if her enveloping herself from neck to toe and clutching the edges of that blanket together in the center of her chest lent any more propriety to their middle-of-the-night solitude.

He motioned toward the table. "Lay them over the far end."

"The wood will warp."

"I don't think you can hurt it, Sonja," he said of the secondhand table, and turned back to her supper.

Heaven only knew what she'd been eating. Dried fruit? Crackers? Hardtack? Whatever was cheap and ready to eat—which wasn't much. Not enough.

"Don't you have a rack for your wash?" she asked after she spread her clothes to dry and sat on a bench, close to the fire.

"I take my clothes to a laundry." He filled a bowl from the cupboard with cornmeal mush and set a spoon, napkin, and tin of molasses in front of her. "I'm sorry. I don't have any milk." Hadn't been to the mercantile in a few days, else she'd be spooning eggs and bacon.

Her eyes grew wide with surprise. "Aren't you eating?"

"I've already eaten today." Earlier, when the coffee hadn't been simmered to an elixir.

He claimed the bench opposite her, while she leaned over the bowl and inhaled deeply of its steam, eyes closed in ecstasy as she reveled in either the smell or the warmth. Maybe both. Then she paused; that was prayer.

Thaddeus pretended not to notice what was so profound, and opened Sonja's knapsack. She had her Bible, of course, her other skirt, a pale green ribbon . . . and nothing of what he looked for.

"What did you eat today?"

She stopped chewing and looked up in alarm. "Am I eating too fast?"

"Are you trying not to?" he asked. When she simply stared back, he pointed to the knapsack. "You don't have any food, Sonja. What have you been eating?"

"Food."

"What food? Which foods?"

"I had a *tortilla* today," she said as if it were a boast.

"And what else?"

"Some dried fruit." Sonja paused. "I won't lie, so don't ask any questions you don't want me to answer." She spooned some mush, giving it her full attention. "I haven't been eating very well, just what I could buy from Mr. Gonzales, but I haven't been very hungry either."

She ate like she was plenty hungry now.

He folded his arms on the table. "Why did you leave Mrs. Trujillo's?"

"I don't expect this to make any sense to you, but I have to hide. As I understand it, people may try to harm the baby.

Maybe even . . . kill it . . . because it has no father." She paused. "Is that true?"

As long as he could, he held out, but finally he had to nod. "Rural settlements are generally more tolerant of women in your circumstance, but it's not just a moral issue, Sonja. A child with no mechanism for support becomes a burden to the community."

"I've never asked for anything from anyone," she said vehemently. "I even worked my passage to Santa Fe."

"So why did you turn down Harley's proposal? You love him, don't you?"

"I care for him as a friend."

He searched her face. She looked truthful enough. "Good marriages have started on less."

"I had other reasons."

"Such as?" Thaddeus all but held his breath, waiting to hear what was inside that head haloed so sweetly by the fire that crackled in the roaring silence.

"He's not a Christian," Sonja replied finally. "We'd be unequally yoked."

Good thing the bench under him was a sturdy one, else Thaddeus might have tumbled from it. It wasn't that Sonja didn't love Harley. It wasn't that Harley was too poor. It wasn't even that the man's work took him away from home too much. The only strike against the respected wagon master was his faith—or lack of it.

"Even if we could have gotten past the obvious differences," she said, "I just kept thinking about how disappointed Papa would be."

Thaddeus raised his brows in question.

A grin tickled Sonja's lips. She smoothed the napkin in her lap. "He's only a blacksmith part of the time. Mostly he's a pastor."

The bench held once more. "Your father's a pastor?"

The belfry. She'd been in the right place, and his reasoning had been faultless. Then his heart fell. She was the pastor's daughter and carrying an illegitimate baby. No wonder she'd donned men's clothes and run away from her father.

"Where is your father?" Thaddeus asked.

She shrugged. Poked at her mush. "He was on his way to the Oregon Territory when I left him."

"You were headed for the Oregon Territory and just walked away from the train?"

She nodded.

She'd doubled back to where the roads to Oregon and New Mexico forked. She'd walked for days. She'd wanted to leave pretty badly.

Thaddeus went to the hearth to add fuel and to retrieve the last of the cornmeal mush. Sonja simply thanked him for scraping it into her bowl, added more molasses, and daintily spooned it in.

He reclaimed his seat and motioned with his head. "What's the stew pot for?"

"My mother made the most wonderful soap," she said between bites. "If I use her recipe, I can sell it in the plaza to support myself and the baby."

"Where are you going to make it? You'll need a fire. Ingredients."

"No one would notice a little fire in the brush beyond the Barrio, and I have enough money for the ingredients. I was going to buy them today, but . . . well, I'll start tomorrow."

Because she'd been too tired today. He'd tended enough women in her condition to know that. And it would be a poverty existence—though as prosperous as selling soap could be. The women would buy her cakes for the quality. The men would buy them to win her smile. Face it, he'd buy her soap. Of course, winter snows would fight her for her manufacturing site, but she hadn't thought that far. Such was Sonja's habit.

The inquisitive lift of her brows made him jump. He was staring. "Finished?" he asked to cover himself.

She nodded. "Thank you. You're a good cook."

Anybody could make mush, but he only took her bowl to the kitchen on the back wall. When he turned around, she was all but lying on the table, her chin braced on her arm. She stifled a yawn.

He motioned toward the spare room. "Come on. Time for bed."

Sonja adjusted the blanket carefully before she stepped around the bench and away from the table. Then she followed as he returned her to the examination room. No patients had needed it for the past two weeks; have to believe they'd be as habitual tonight.

He set the light on the overturned crate beside the bed, and his heart fell. The roof was leaking—

Sonja yelped. Thaddeus jumped. Eyes wide and hand clapped over her mouth, she stared at the far side of the room.

Seventeen

*T*haddeus followed Sonja's stare. His shoulders collapsed in relief.

"What is that?" she asked, her voice little more than a squeak. "Is he—was he one of your patients?"

"One of—" Thaddeus chuckled. "No. I mean, he was probably someone's patient at some time, but not mine."

Sonja gave him an uncertain glance before staring again at the skeleton hanging on the stand in the corner. "Was he in here before? I didn't notice."

Thaddeus nodded. "One of my colleagues from the university shipped him to me as a joke, but it ricocheted when I refused to send him back. A skeleton is nearly impossible to come by, especially one that's intact. You know, no broken bones or anything, although this old boy—and he was a man—did once break the phalanges of his right hand. Probably when he was young. You can see where—" He stopped. Sonja wasn't getting anything out of his oration. "Sorry, I'll put Siege in my room." He strode to the far corner for the stand of bones.

She gave him plenty of space as he passed, but her eyes held a scolding when he returned, and it had nothing to do with his leaky roof.

"Siege?" she asked.

He shrugged as he aimed the bucket under the stream of brown water dripping from the ceiling. "It seemed to fit. He looked like he'd been through one."

Mentally, he shook his head. Walls two and a half feet thick, but the roof leaked . . . and water seeped in where the wall met the floor. Too bad he didn't know that before he bought the place, even if it did have its own well and real glass—rather than mica—windows, and shutters to close over them.

"You scared me half to death, you know," Sonja said.

Thaddeus gave her his attention and snorted. "You've never been afraid of anything in your life, Sonja."

The humor in her features dissolved. For a long moment she simply stared. "I get afraid," she said finally, softly. "I try not to let it catch up to me."

So she ran. In the opposite direction of her only family. Down a road to no one she knew. To a home in the belfry of a church—and still managed to look pretty enough to beg a sketching, though pastel lines could never do her skin justice. It was flawless. Translucent. Baby-new, with the hint of a freckle or two across her nose. Her smile had relaxed. Even the blanket had slipped from her left shoulder. The loose neck of the oversized nightshirt threatened to follow.

Her eyes widened suddenly but gently. Her hand flew to her stomach. "He always seems to know when I'm about to go to bed. He thinks that's playtime."

But she grinned like it didn't matter. Like it was amusing. Like a woman who knew how to love.

She motioned to the bucket beginning to make music on the other side of the examination table. "I always wondered about that. They're only dirt, you know—the roofs."

"Are they?"

She nodded. "I could see from the belfry."

So she could.

"But I don't know about the floors," she added. "What are they, to be so shiny?"

"Clay," he replied; he'd asked the same thing of Harley. "They mix animal blood with it and let it dry." He paused. "Pretty ingenious, working with what's at hand."

Again she nodded. Blinked. Such pretty eyes . . .

He shifted. "I'll get your warmer."

In the parlor Thaddeus set his attention on filling another tin bucket with the cobble rocks he'd strung around the fire. In the examination room he set it in the space between the examination table and the bed where Sonja would sleep.

"These will stay warm for a while," he said. "Sleep late. You need it. There's a chamber pot under the bed, and you can keep the lantern; I have others."

"Thank you," she told him, wrapped up cozily in her blanket with her tiny white toes barely peeking out. She never did comb her hair, so it lay tousled and—

"Will you open my door when you go to sleep?" she asked. "It will be warmer, and I'd feel . . . safer."

"Uh . . . sure," he said, the epitome of intelligence, adding, "I won't be long."

Every movement he made felt watched as he set the house right for the night, as if she could see through the door between them. As if the finer details of his life were being explained to her.

When he finally went to Sonja's door, Thaddeus waited for a moment and listened. No sound came from the other side.

"Sonja?" he whispered.

No reply.

Slowly, he opened the door, firelight sneaking around him to spill where she was curled on her side facing away, toward half of the house's windows. He stepped into the room and peeked around the foot of the bed.

The blanket she'd wrapped around herself was now folded on her feet, but her hair was still loose, a strand of it dangling over the edge. It wasn't like her to forget her braids, but then neither had she brushed her teeth. Too tired, no doubt, though she'd never been that tired before.

He listened. Her breathing was too faint to disturb the air, but the rain still pattered into it. If he hadn't found her, she'd be under it. If he hadn't found her, she'd be wet and hungry. If he hadn't found her, he'd be introducing himself to every door in Santa Fe.

Eighteen

Noble was sitting at his desk when Sonja opened the door, the parlor silent, warm, and smelling of coffee around him.

"'Morning," she said.

"'Morning."

She snugged the blanket around her and searched for appropriate conversation.

"How about some coffee?" he asked, saving her.

She nodded. He rounded his desk and crossed from the front half of the parlor to the back, fully dressed in brown trousers, a yellow shirt with billowy sleeves, a brown figured waistcoat, his boots—minus the mud—and brown suspenders. He plucked a cup from a peg on the back wall and crouched at the fireplace to fill it, while the morning sun poured soft light through the room's only window. From its spot beside the front door, it honeyed the woods, walls, and his sparse furnishings.

He returned to his desk and set her coffee before the guest chair on the other side of it. He motioned toward the vacancy. "Why don't you sit down?"

"I should dress," Sonja said, bunching the blanket even

more tightly over her chest.

"I'd prefer you wait, if you don't mind," he told her. "I have something to discuss with you."

His words stirred eddies in her stomach, but she shuffled across the floor, dragging a bit of the blanket behind her. Always the gentleman, Noble waited until she sat before reclaiming his own seat. The rug was warm under her toes—all that would reach the floor—and the chair was more comfortable than the benches on either side of his eating table. His desk faced the room, a massive shiny thing cut of oak in simple line and design. An oil lamp and small shelf-clock graced the left corner, an ink bottle and pen, the right. He'd been reading a magazine, the *New York Journal of Medicine*. The window sat in the wall behind him, and to his credit, his coffee tasted as good as his cornmeal mush.

"What did you want to talk to me about?" Sonja asked.

He set his forearms on the desk and began fingering a clean chicken leg bone sitting at the center edge. "Some of my questions may seem a little personal, Sonja, but it can't be helped. Just try to be patient with me." He paused. "What were the terms of your relationship with Harley when he left?"

"Terms?"

He peered through the top of his spectacles. "You know, did you agree to write each other? Or to resume your courtship when he returned?"

They'd already talked about this last night, but she answered him. "There's no courtship. We didn't decide anything, except to be friends."

"Is there any possibility your father will find you?"

"Why?"

He shook his head. "Just answer the question."

It pressed her into the chair. "I don't know. I suppose he's looked, but he didn't know where I was going."

"Where do you think he would go? Would he look here?"

"What are you—"

"Just answer the question."

Sonja shrugged. "He probably went back home, but I don't know where he would look after that. He won't come here. I picked Santa Fe by chance . . . because that's where you were going."

Noble chewed on her answer for a moment, furrowing his brow as he rotated the bone between his fingers. "Why didn't you go home to Indiana?"

"Because it was the first place he'd look, and I didn't want him to find me."

"Why not? You said you didn't know you were with child."

"I didn't, but I knew I had . . . shamed him. I didn't want him to find out about that. He's hurt enough."

"And the baby's father won't look for you?"

"No." Silly man, there was no father. No one worth remembering.

The clock ticked softly. He stared. She looked away. Whatever he was digging for, he wanted it more than she. She adjusted the blanket, pulling it closed where it wanted to fall open over her knees, and reached for her coffee. She sipped and glanced at him over the rim. He simply watched, sympathy in his eyes.

And he could keep it.

Her cup landed hard on the desk. "I'm getting dressed." She pinched the blanket, preparing to rise.

"No. Stay," he said, his gentle tone belying the urgency of the words.

"I don't want your pity, Dr. Staley."

"The point is, you're out of options, Sonja, and that's what I needed to know."

Fine, but he didn't have to remind her of that. Tears

balled in her throat. He'd ruined it, the pleasant night spent eating mush and talking. The cozy bed. Then this morning, with its coffee and the rug and the fire—almost like home. She was better off in the rain. Better, before he showed her everything she didn't have anymore. Might never have again.

She swallowed hard. "Can I go now? I have things to do."

"Just a few more minutes. Do you want more coffee?"

"No, I don't want more coffee," she snapped.

Apparently he did, for he stepped around the desk and out of view. A moment later he returned with the pot.

"Well, maybe a little," she told him.

He grinned.

"What are you smiling at?"

"Nothing." But neither did his expression change as he poured the coffee and returned the pot to the fire. Not until he was back at his desk, then the line of his brow grew serious again. "You can't continue living in a belfry, Sonja. I understand you feel compelled to hide, but your circumstances will eventually catch up with you."

This sounded like the introduction to a court sentence. Her heart beat faster.

"I may be able to offer a solution," he continued, his gaze watchful and maybe even a little grave. "Your baby needs a name, a father. And you need a protector. I can provide both."

Nineteen

*O*hmygoodness.

The blood left Sonja's head—only to swirl in her stomach. "I have a protector," she replied on what little breath she could push through her throat. "The Lord."

"I'm thinking of something a little more earthly," Noble replied patiently. "I suggest we marry."

Just like that. As if he'd only been waiting for the opportunity to ask her. As if she had social standing or wealth to offer. As if she could give him anything he didn't have or couldn't get.

"Why?" Sonja asked, though the word was hardly out before her heart plummeted to her toes and her stare shot to the open door of his bedroom—

"No. Not that," he growled.

Sonja jumped.

"That has nothing to do with anything," he continued. "For heaven's sake, Sonja." He paused. Actually blushed before he started over. "I came here to start a new practice, but it seems the one thing I neglected to pack was a wife and family. I'm told the women in town don't feel they can trust themselves to a bachelor or their children to a man who has none of his own. You can give me a more trustworthy image."

Gracious, gracious, gracious, it was too much. She couldn't receive it all. She got to her feet.

"Sonja?"

"Just a minute," she said, walking away. "Let me think."

Noble. The man from Independence. The man whose burnt–amber eyes held deep thoughts and keen perception. Her husband?

Sonja scanned the room he'd filled with pieces of himself. It was the framed certificate hanging over the bookcases between his desk and the fireplace that caught her attention first. Impressively scripted by the University of Pennsylvania School of Medicine, it told the world that N. Thaddeus Staley had earned the title and privileges due a doctor of medicine. She knew nothing about him. Less than nothing. His desk, the clock, the chicken bone—they all had a history. Moments in his life, and she shared none of them. Didn't even known they were there to wonder about until a few moments ago.

She scanned the spines of the texts neatly columned on the shelves. *Medical Inquiries and Observations; Domestic Medicine, or, a Treatise on the Prevention and Cure of Diseases by Regimen and Simple Medicines;* and *Lectures on Midwifery and the Forms of Disease Peculiar to Women and Children*. Dozens and dozens of them, and he'd read them all. Understood the complex words and concepts presented inside, while her education was limited to the fifteen books at the schoolhouse— and the Bible, of course.

"I'm not a man of Harley's means," Noble said into the quiet. "People more often pay me in sacks of flour, feed for my horse, or a laying-chicken, than coin."

Money? He thought that was why she hesitated?

Sonja swiveled her head to watch his answer as she asked, "Are you a Christian?"

He'd stood when she rose from her chair. Now his left

eyebrow arched. "I'm not where you are, but I'll support you in it."

She didn't need a supporter any more than she needed a protector; she had the Holy Spirit for such fortifications. Her husband—if she had one of those—needed to be a leader who knew how—and Whom—to follow, a partner to shoulder his half of the yoke.

"There have been some . . . circumstances I've had to deal with," he added.

The breath stopped in her throat—in suspense for the bark of laughter or wail of tears that would follow, as soon as she decided which to give him. Circumstances? Who didn't?

"All right," he said, as if he heard her thoughts. "I'm stumbling right now. You can pray for me."

He looked so disgusted with himself. Not a pleasant place to be, where he was.

"I never stopped," she said softly.

That brought his stare crashing into hers.

Bolstered by his candor, she asked, "Where did the bone come from?"

Fleeting and quick, the pain—sparking in his eyes before he buried it again. "I . . . knew a little boy once. He . . . cut his teeth on it."

When Noble said no more, only stared at the bone on his desk, Sonja turned back to the bookshelves. Two of them, side by side, each fingertip-to-fingertip wide, chin high, and as finely crafted as his desk. The rest of his furniture—a table, two benches, and a kitchen cupboard—looked as if they might serve more rightly in a bonfire. The table sat diagonally in the center of the room, where he and his guests would get equal pay from the corner fireplace, while the cupboard sat on the back wall. The sum total of his coffee mugs was four, judging by the number of pegs on the wall, and he didn't have a stove. She'd do all her cooking in the fireplace.

"I didn't bring any domestic things with me," he said. "It was ridiculous to ship them when my priority was to bring my office and as many medical supplies as possible. I didn't know what I'd find when I arrived." He paused. "I . . . I bought what I could afford. . . ."

Sonja turned and nodded, absolving him of having what he thought was too little money. What he had was so much more than she. And so much more than a pastor who fed his own by smithing.

The bedroom doors stood side-by-side, the one with the examination table in the front half of the house, his room in the back half. She peeked inside . . . at the bed neatly made—

"That would be your room," he said suddenly. "I'm sorry it isn't the room with the window, but my examination room has to be the one with the best light. My patients seldom stay the night, but they do come and go at all hours, so I'll move into the examination room to give you your privacy."

Granted a measure of permission, she looked again, at the blue wool blanket pulled smooth on the bed and the shipping crates stacked three high and four wide, open side out, against the wall. They stored his clothes, which were folded neatly, though they didn't even fill half. The top displayed a brush, a wash bowl and shaving cup, and other items too flat to have a discernible shape. A mirror hung from the wall. The floor had no rug, but it was clean, and a brown coat and another shirt and pair of trousers hung from a row of wall pegs. *Siege* smiled from the corner, no doubt humored by the ridiculous ideas he overheard.

"What about children?"

That question Noble had been expecting, judging by the speed of his reply. "I'll be father to your baby, in name and all ways. You give me your word your old beau won't be a problem, I'll give mine that the child will have no other father as far as I'm concerned."

"He won't. I meant . . . other children. More children?" Noble's children.

The floor undulated beneath Sonja's feet, and the clock ticked louder than it had all morning. She turned around to see Noble's eyes, to see if what he said and what he thought agreed. Whether the child she gave him—not his own— would be enough.

"That's entirely up to you," he replied quietly. "If you . . . don't care to . . . Well . . ." His face colored, and he rushed forward, telling his desk, "I'd already prepared myself for . . . a solitary life."

He stared at the cup held negligently in his hand, the flatness in his features saying he was certain he'd already lost the battle. "I can provide for you," he told the cup, "but I have to admit I'm a little stretched right now. Stocking the house cost more than I planned. I didn't even have sheets, much less beds. And I'm not exactly turning patients away." A muscle in his jaw tensed. "But the only other doctor in town is old and more enamored with his tools than healing; I know I'm better."

Such conviction, not to mention confidence. Would that she could reach for the world with such certainty.

Sonja turned to the door jamb and lunged for the courage to ask him what she didn't want to ask but had to know. "Do you ever have couples who want children? I mean, could you find a home for the baby if . . ."

"Probably," he said after a second of silence.

What he didn't say was that he had already found a home—his own. That made her heart smile.

He must have sensed it, for he said, "You're considering it, aren't you?"

She turned. Obviously he wasn't as certain about his ability to husband as he was his ability to doctor.

"How do you know I can cook?" she asked.

His whole body relaxed by degrees. "I can cook, and you're teachable."

"When would you want to do this?"

Just slightly, he stood a little straighter. "Today. This morning. You see, your reputation is compromised further for having slept here last night. I'm afraid we'd never convince the gossips there was a wall between us."

Her attention darted to the door—though it was a silly reaction, as if an angry mob were about to beat it down and take her to the plaza. Should have thought of that last night.

"There's one thing you should know," he added.

She swiveled again, but he made her wait.

"I'm divorced," he said finally.

Divorced! Goodness! Didn't even know anyone who was . . . that.

Sonja concentrated on keeping her features level, on not letting the tumult in her stomach show on her face, for Noble watched her as if he expected it—and volunteered nothing more.

"Well, aren't you going to tell me about it?" she asked.

"The details are immaterial to our situation," he replied.

"That depends. Are you going to divorce me?"

That muscle tensed in his jaw again. "That depends. Are you going to commit adultery and leave me for your lover?"

It was a tidy life he'd made for himself, packing up his possessions as if his work was all he had, all he was. He hadn't packed the hurt—had probably left every reminder of his wife behind—but it had followed him anyway. It was there, in the set of his shoulders that was just a little too proud. He glanced at her, defiance hovering behind his eyes. He gave himself to his coffee again.

"What was her name?" Sonja asked.

"Amanda."

"Was she pretty?"

The defense melted. "She was the most beautiful woman I've ever seen," he admitted as if it were his misfortune.

It was Sonja's heart that fell in dismay. She tucked the blanket around her bloated belly.

His features hardened. "She was also the coldest."

"Is there any way to reconcile your relationship with her?" Sonja asked.

"No. She married the father of her child."

"She . . . got with child with another man?" Had trouble even thinking it, much less saying it.

"She was expecting a child when we married. I thought it was mine," he replied quietly.

It took a moment for the thoughts to connect—which provided a trail for the shock to bolt through. Oh, goodness. *Before* they were married. It was scandalous. It was sin. Sonja nearly gasped, except Noble stared at the top of his desk as if he might never look up—never face her—again.

What a picture he made standing there in his tidy clothes, jaw firm against the censure he was so sure was coming. As if she'd give him more of what he already provided well enough himself. His eyes were fixed on the desk, but if he looked up now they would startle her again with their depth. This was Noble. Not some paper image of himself, but a person with a history, a heart, and moments when his confidence crumbled. He'd sinned. But he'd paid. And though it might look as if he'd walked away from the Lord, the beliefs and values were still there. That was plain in his shame. He hadn't turned his back, he'd turned his face. Not because he was disappointed *by* God, but because he was disappointing *to* God. He was so certain he deserved abandoning, that when God didn't give it to him, he gave it to himself.

Not by works of righteousness which we have done, but according to his mercy he saved us, by the washing of regeneration, and renewing of the Holy Ghost.

Except Noble didn't hear that.

"The little boy, Amanda's child," Sonja said, "Was he the one who cut his teeth on the chicken bone?"

"Yes."

"Do you still love his mother?" she asked softly.

"No." Only Noble's eyes moved as his attention swung to her, their expression challenging her to disagree.

Silly man. As if he could hide the hurt from her. As if she couldn't see he expected her to reject him too. Obviously he didn't know her very well.

A final objection raised itself. "I'm not so sure I'm the one to lend you respectability."

"Give it a couple months, and everyone will think we've been married for years," he said, then waited with silent expectation that roiled knots in her stomach.

No more questions. No more answers. Time for a decision.

Wherewithal shall a young man cleanse his way? by taking heed thereto according to thy word. Thy word have I hid in mine heart, that I might not sin against thee.

No, wrong verse. Frantically, Sonja searched her memory.

Be ye not unequally yoked together with unbelievers: for what fellowship hath righteousness with unrighteousness? and what communion hath light with darkness?

Right verse, but how many Sunday services did Noble have to miss before he was an unbeliever? How far did he have to turn before he was given up for lost? He couldn't be too lost; the distance wasn't so great that shame couldn't reach him. And, approached from the other side, there seemed to be no reason not to marry N. Thaddeus Staley.

Sonja stared hard across the clay floor to the man who had draped cool cloths on her knee and wrapped her against the rain with his own coat and hat. So calmly, he volunteered to father her baby. So calmly, he proposed they lock their lives together.

Tell me now, Lord. Tell me this is the man you want me to commit myself to. Or tell me no. But say it clear, for this is the man from Independence. The man with the burnt-amber eyes.

As if the building were on fire, the territorial official positioned Noble and Sonja before his cluttered desk and sped through a ceremony that held as much sentiment as an agreement to trade cattle and feed at the end of the season. Jackson stood to the side, as if he could make credible what was already absurd. Sonja cast a furtive glance at N. Thaddeus Staley, the man beside her who suddenly seemed very much a stranger.

O the depth of the riches both of the wisdom and knowledge of God! how unsearchable are his judgments, and his ways past finding out!

She stared at the gold band he pushed onto her finger, seeing the dollars it cost, but Noble wouldn't be talked out of it, this announcement that the woman with the gold hair and bulging stomach had a proper husband. Like the larger band that told Santa Fe its new doctor was solid and safe.

For as the heavens are higher than the earth, so are my ways higher than your ways, and my thoughts than your thoughts.

"I do," Sonja said, her voice sounding small in the smaller room crowded with papers and men—one of whom was now her next of kin.

"You can kiss your bride," the territorial official said on a leering grin.

Sonja's gaze jumped from the man's crooked teeth to Noble's face, her breath lodging in her throat. Kiss. She'd forgotten all about that.

For my thoughts are not your thoughts, neither are your ways my ways, saith the Lord.

For a long moment, Noble peered over the round of his shoulder at her before he shifted all at once, as if to make up for the lag. She couldn't even move, couldn't even think, as he cupped her face in his hands, closed his eyes, and lowered his head. Maybe she couldn't even breathe, though they were surprisingly gentle lips he set on her mouth—and barely known, the tender pressure and movement, before he took himself away.

The official shook Noble's hand and Jackson pounded his back, but Sonja only stared from man to man and wished for a chair. Only a few months ago she'd been sweeping crumbs from a supper table in Indiana.

Twenty

S onja could say it had been a beautiful marriage ceremony, except it was only thoughtless recitation. She
could say the weather was nice, except last night's
rain had made a muddy mire of the streets. She could even
say it was good to see Jackson again, except he disappeared
as soon as they cleared the door. He thought he was giving
the sweethearts time to be alone together. But they sure
weren't sweethearts, and they had the rest of their lives to
enjoy such silence as they practiced now.

So it was a great relief when Noble broke it, saying,
"Let's stop at the mercantile."

"That would be nice," Sonja replied—with a little too
much exuberance when contrasted with the silence that
followed.

He could go days in contented quiet, depending on her
to tell him when it was about time he said something. She had
no such suggestions today. What did a wife say to her husband
in the first twenty minutes of their marriage? This one said
nothing until Mr. Gonzales greeted her from behind his
counter.

"Buenos diás," Sonja replied. *"Como está?"*

Noble gave her a startled stare. He needn't. It was only a little Spanish she'd picked up here and there.

"Very well, thank you," Mr. Gonzales said in his flawless English. He turned to Noble, brown eyes twinkling. "I see you found her."

"Yes."

It was Sonja's turn to be surprised. "You came in here looking for me?"

"I went everywhere looking for you," Noble said softly.

Mr. Gonzales heard anyway and chuckled. "I have dried apricots today. Five cents a pound."

"No dried fruit this time—unless my husband likes it," she replied, announcing the news at the same time she tried the title for fit. Her stomach rolled over. Such a marriage. Hadn't even known it was coming until a little over two hours ago.

Mr. Gonzales' smile widened—if that were possible. *"Muy bien.* And no more living in the church."

Now both the Staleys stared at Mr. Gonzales in disbelief. "You knew?" Sonja asked.

"There are no secrets in the Barrio—except to strangers," Mr. Gonzales added, giving Noble a pointed stare.

"I didn't want you to lie for me," Sonja said.

"He didn't lie," Noble said, eyeing the merchant. "He just avoided the questions—rather smartly, I might add."

Mr. Gonzales' smile warmed. "And so we're not strangers anymore, I am Jaime Gonzales."

"Thaddeus Staley," he said, shaking the hand offered him.

Mr. Gonzales bowed slightly and waved an arm, indicating his store. "Welcome to Santa Fe. Everything I have is yours."

Noble grasped Sonja's elbow and led her toward the long tables against the opposite wall, while Mr. Gonzales greeted the two Anglo women who breezed inside.

Sonja had landed near the door, where women could

glance in the window and see the goods now spread like a feast before her; lacy fingerless mitts, brooches, lacquered jewel boxes with roses painted on the lids, ivory fans, dainty shoes with shapely heels—

Noble asked her something.

"I beg your pardon?" she asked.

"Can you sew?" he asked again from where he stood behind her.

"Yes."

"Then please pick out some material for a dress."

She followed his stare to the cloth folded thickly on shelves at the back of the table. He never had cared for Papa's shirts and trousers, but they couldn't eat new dresses. "Are you sure?"

"Let me worry about the money," he said gently.

A new dress would be nice. Wasn't as if she enjoyed looking a frump. She eyed the red calico . . . then a yellow gingham. Maybe—

"Do you like this? It would compliment your coloring." Noble's long arm reached past her to a peach cloth with tiny orange blossoms.

Sonja stared. Men weren't supposed to have an opinion about women's clothes. At least, Papa never did—except whether it was ladylike or not.

She looked up.

He smiled at her. "Don't you trust me?"

"I don't know."

He laughed. "Try. I have a fair eye—and a better view of you than you do."

He waited until she nodded her assent before he lifted the cloth over her head, then waited again while the two women passed to a deeper part of the store. He led her back to the counter, where he selected more items—flour, corn-meal, lard, eggs, soap, scissors, thread, and sewing needles.

"Don't spend money on scissors for me," Sonja told him. "I can use yours."

That got her a stern expression. "I appreciate your flexibility, but I'm a little particular about my instruments, Sonja. They're not made for cutting cloth."

So well, she remembered. "My husband is a doctor," she explained to Mr. Gonzales.

The man continued measuring the fabric against notches in the edge of the counter. "Are you a good doctor, or a good salesman?"

Noble's head jerked slightly, as if the question were a physical affront.

Sonja jumped in. "Oh, he's a good doctor. He was educated at an impressive medical university in Philadelphia, Pennsylvania, you know."

"Yes? Then tell me what you can do for my hands," Mr. Gonzales said.

Anything that might have gone on before was forgotten as Noble's attention slid to Mr. Gonzales' knobby hands. "What's the matter with them?"

"They hurt." Mr. Gonzales dropped the cloth and held his hands out, fingers spread.

Noble was just as quick in initiating his examination, gently probing the length of each finger. "Did you injure them?"

Mr. Gonzales shook his head—then winced when Noble touched a tender place.

Noble nodded. "Arthritis. Salicylic acid won't cure it, but it will relieve the pain."

"Acid?"

"Yes, but it doesn't burn you."

"I rub it on my fingers?"

"No, you drink it, and it will give you a vicious stomachache." Noble shrugged. "You'll have to decide if it's worth it."

"You have some of this acid?"

"Yes."

The merchant resumed measuring cloth as if there were nothing else to say. "I don't mind a bellyache."

It was the stall in Sonja's activity that made Thaddeus pause in his, stopping him in the center of the parlor, razor and strop in hand. "Pardon me?" he asked.

She didn't have much but he'd given her more room for it, moving his clothes to the examination room where she slept last night. The shaving equipment was the last of it. From this moment, his old room was her new one.

She stared at the peach colored cloth in her hands. A smile tickled her lips. "I've tried but I just can't remember which book of the Old Testament it comes from."

It took less than a second to know what she was talking about, and it started with an N.

"Don't say it, Sonja," he warned, striding into his room and arranging his things on the crates that held his clothes.

"Daniel, maybe?" she continued.

He returned to the parlor.

Her delicate brow knit prettily. "Yes, I think it was—"

"I mean it, Sonja. If we're to live amiably, you'll refrain from saying that . . . word."

"It's your name."

He strode to his desk. "It's a curse."

She rolled her lips inward except her eyes smiled well enough for her whole face. "You're named for royalty, you know . . . Your Majesty."

He glared at her.

She laughed. "Nebuchadnezzar Thaddeus Staley. No wonder you won't tell anyone what the N stands for."

"And you won't either." But neither would she forget it.

She proved it, saying, "Your name is a whole spelling lesson in itself. I'll bet—"

"Sonja—"

Someone knocked on the door.

Thaddeus nearly jumped. Hadn't heard the sound of it but only twice before. Since Harley was far from Santa Fe, and Jackson couldn't leave fast enough after the ceremony, it had to be someone else. Thaddeus pulled himself from dumbfoundedness and stepped to the door.

The fist that had knocked on it rotated the rim of a work hat, and its owner asked, "Are you the new doc?"

"Yes."

The man broke into a grin. "My Molly was in town today. Said she heard you was here, but I couldn't believe it. Now I'm sure glad."

Thaddeus swung the door wide. "Why don't you come in?"

"Thanks." The man stepped inside and nodded a greeting at Sonja. "It's my boy," he continued. "He fell off the fence and busted his leg. My wife tied it to the other one to keep it still, but somebody needs to set it. Think you could come?"

"Sure. I'll get my things," Thaddeus said. He motioned toward Sonja, who was smoothing the new cloth on the table. "This is my wife, Mrs. Staley."

"Pleased to make your acquaintance, ma'am. I'm Benjamin Carney."

Sonja smiled with a warmth that could disarm a general and smoothed the tail of her man's shirt over her tired skirt. "Forgive my attire, Mr. Carney. I'm dressed for working. Won't you sit down?"

"No thanks, ma'am."

Thaddeus smiled with satisfaction as he went to the examination room for the special saddlebags containing his medical wallets. Amanda was never so gracious when her tranquillity was invaded. He'd chosen well today.

"How old is your son?" Sonja asked, proving it again.

"Eleven," came the reply, while Thaddeus rooted through his bag to be sure everything he needed was inside.

"I'm so sorry about his fall," Sonja said. "He must be in terrible pain."

"Yes, ma'am, but he's taking it pretty good. He's strong."

Thaddeus plucked his hat and sidearm from their pegs, as Sonja added, "I'm sure he's a lot of help to you."

"Yes, ma'am. Jacob's my only boy, so I lean on him pretty heavy."

"Jacob?" Sonja said. "That's a name from the Bible. Are you a believer, Mr. Carney?"

Thaddeus had been buckling his gun belt; it slipped through his fingers and slapped the floor. Couldn't get anymore direct than that. He glanced into the parlor to see if Mr. Carney had survived the inquisition.

The man smiled—though a little sheepishly—while he worked the brim of his hat. "No, ma'am. Can't say that I am."

Sonja wasn't even fazed. "Oh, this is something to look into, Mr. Carney. The Lord has been so good to me, especially when I've been the most foolish."

"Yes, ma'am."

Amen. And too bad Thaddeus didn't need to shave more splints or mix some medicine. Sonja would put the delay to good use. She'd have Mr. Carney reciting the Sinner's Prayer before he could shift his weight to his other leg.

"Would you mind if I pray for your son?" she asked.

"I'd consider that a kindness, ma'am. Thank you."

Thaddeus put on his vest and strode into the parlor, arms full of saddle, tack, and medical saddlebags. "How far out do you live?" he asked Mr. Carney.

"About a half hour."

Thaddeus glanced at the clock on his desk. It was

already six-thirty. He turned to Sonja. "I'll be back about nine or nine-thirty."

The smile she'd held for Mr. Carney disappeared. "Oh."

This was a long walk down a tired old road. As if he'd promised her a special evening. Or storekeeper's hours. As if he wasn't already sick to death of women who couldn't—or wouldn't—be pleased. What he had promised her was his provision—which he earned by tending the sick.

"Lock the door. I have a key," Thaddeus said while Mr. Carney opened the door for him. Then Thaddeus told his wife goodnight and stepped through it.

Sonja stared at the door Noble had passed through. She huffed. He'd just called her Amanda. *Good night, Amanda.* Just like that.

I'm married now, Mama, and he doesn't even know who I am.

Sonja heaved another breath. She probably should cry about that, but she couldn't. Too shocked.

Noble's and Mr. Carney's voices rumbled from the front to the back of the house, then faded into a silence troubled only by the snap of the fire. Sonja crossed the room to the door and locked it.

He was angry. Maybe because she talked to Mr. Carney about the Lord. Or because she didn't help him get ready to go. Or because it looked as though his medical practice had been on the verge of picking up on its own—without marrying her.

She was the most beautiful woman I've ever seen; that was Amanda.

Sonja stroked her stomach. Her very large and misshapen stomach. Noble better have someone check his spectacles, to have mistaken one for the other.

Sonja opened her eyes. Blinked . . . at the world tilted sideways. She sat up—but shouldn't have done it so fast. Her head spun a little. She blinked again. Apparently she'd fallen asleep at the table. The peach-colored cloth was mashed where her head used to be, and the needle and thread were looped around her fingers. She looked to the clock, except it was a moment before her eyes could focus. Ten-fifteen, and Noble wasn't home yet.

Sonja braced her hands low on her spine and bent backward. The movement was agony. Lest she be so careless again, her back reminded her that tables were for eating.

She glanced at the clock, then stared at the door. He could ride into the yard at any moment, or be another hour. He was already later than he said he'd be. Surely it wouldn't take two and a half hours to set Jacob's leg, and no other patients knew to fetch him from the Carneys'. So it was probably a piece of fresh pie or a warm cobbler that kept Noble someplace other than home . . . someplace with preferable company.

Sonja folded her sewing, pulled her bulk from the bench, and shuffled to bed.

Thaddeus fitted his key in the lock and stepped into the room quietly. Sonja was asleep. He already knew that. There was no light in the window, no light in the room.

He shook his head at his own foolishness. Why had he even hoped she would wait up until . . . nearly ten-thirty for him? Amanda never had.

$\mathcal{M}$r. Gonzales laughed the instant he entered the examination room the next day. "I think you like skinny women, *mi amigo*. Does your wife know about this?"

Sonja looked up from the parlor table. All she could see was Mr. Gonzales' back, but she didn't have to see more to know what—or whom—he was talking about.

"Yes, she and Siege have met," Noble said—and actually laughed. In fact, good humor rolled from his throat as if it had been there all morning. As if he'd had more than the barest *good morning* for her.

"Now, let me show you where the problem is," Noble began. Siege's bones rattled in apparent illustration. "Knobby spurs form on these bones. See? Imagine the pain when you flex this joint."

"What causes this?" Mr. Gonzales asked, voicing Sonja's own curiosity, while she turned back to an endless space waiting for an endless line of stitches.

"We don't know, but this powder, salicylic acid, has been a miracle discovery." One of the drawers of his supply cupboard opened and closed softly. "People used to chew white willow bark to get it, but we're more advanced than that now."

So advanced, in fact, that civil manners were a thing of antiquity.

Sonja pushed the needle into the peach-colored cloth she hadn't wanted in the first place. The red calico was much livelier.

Noble strode into the parlor and to his desk where he wrote something on a carefully folded paper packet that he handed to Mr. Gonzales. "This will relieve your pain, but drink it on a full stomach to make the bellyache bearable."

Mr. Gonzales nodded and reached for his pocket.

Noble interrupted him. "You can keep that on account at the store if you prefer."

Mr. Gonzales broke into a fresh smile. *"Sí. Muy bien, el doctor,* and if this works, we will do a lot of business, you and I." He turned to Sonja and bowed. *"Buenos días, Señora Staley."*

Sonja smiled and waved, but it was a pity to see Noble's good mood whistling his way out the door—which hardly closed before someone knocked on it again.

"Morning, Doc," a masculine voice said from the threshold. "I thought we should meet before the need came up. I'm Leland Coghill, the undertaker."

Sonja's needle stopped. She leaned to catch a peek of the man who tended the more gruesome tasks in town, except she couldn't see around Noble. Mr. Fetter, the man's counterpart in Lafayette, had been a skinny, bent little fellow who, it was whispered, had a system of pulleys hanging over his supper table to move the bodies about. Margaret Shanahan said he just folded their arms over their chests and cranked them up and out of the way when he ate. Sonja had almost asked Papa if it was true, but asked Ander instead. He said he'd seen it for himself.

"Pleased to meet you, Leland. I was about to look you up," Noble said, extending his hand.

People only nodded when they met Mr. Fetter. Except for Papa. He said Mr. Fetter was a nice man with an unpleasant job. Noble seemed of like mind.

"This is my missus," Mr. Coghill continued, making Sonja lean further.

It wasn't necessary, for Noble was stepping aside. "Why don't you come in. I have fresh coffee."

They stepped into the parlor, the undertaker and his wife, and they didn't have long and cadaverous faces. They didn't even wear black. Mr. Coghill wore blue, and he was a sturdy man of average height with brown hair, a dense mustache, and a jaw so solid and square, the rest of his head appeared to be set atop it. He wouldn't need any pulleys, though if an extra hand were ever needed, Mrs. Coghill looked up to the task. Her dimensions were stumpy, but her face fought back with a pert gaze from huge blue eyes and full lips sweetly bowed.

"This is my wife," Noble said, motioning toward Sonja.

Mr. and Mrs. Coghill smiled at Sonja, who smiled back and then jumped into action, bundling her sewing and casting about for a place to set it—not on Noble's desk, not on Noble's bookcases, and not on the kitchen cupboard. She finally decided in favor of her bed.

Be not forgetful to entertain strangers: for thereby some have entertained angels unawares—that's what Mama always said. As for Papa, he said there were usually three people folks sent for when bad things happened to them—the doctor, the pastor, and the undertaker; two of them were at her table.

"We've been here about two years," Mr. Coghill said. "We lived in South Carolina for a while, but the politics was getting bad. Then we heard business was good in the Territory. As it turned out, there was no undertaker, so we're not sorry we come." He paused. "And how about you folks? You like Santa Fe?"

Sonja's hand stilled in taking down their remaining cups.

"So far," Noble said. "I'll like it better as soon as my medical practice occupies a full day's activity."

Sonja released the breath she'd been holding and retrieved the coffeepot from the fireplace. Should have known Noble would glide right through that explanation, as if the two of them were the premeditated couple they appeared to be. Didn't need to look up from pouring to know the room was barren of pictures, decorations, and memories—except that chicken bone that had belonged to another wife's child. It was a concocted marriage—and no less evident, its blandness, than beyond the parlor, where the husband's clothes hung in one bedroom and the wife's in the other.

"That Cash Conklin is the height of greed," Mr. Coghill was saying. "He'll ask top price when it's your money, but you're in for a bidding war when it's his turn to pay."

"He thinks the only effort worth anything is his own," Mrs. Coghill added.

"You want a good buy on a buggy, talk to Percy Jones over on the west end," Mr. Coghill continued. "Folks respect him."

"I didn't know you were planning to buy a buggy," Sonja said, replacing the pot at the fire and sliding onto the bench beside Noble.

Who scooted over to make room—where it wasn't necessary—and gave her a patient glance. "I ride miles sometimes, at all hours and in all weather."

She should already know that. The heat of humiliation poured over her, and even Mrs. Coghill's grin slipped before it caught again.

Noble turned to Mr. Coghill, and Sonja explained, speaking softly enough to pull Mrs. Coghill into a separate conversation. "We haven't been married very long."

The other woman nodded.

"We just got married yesterday," Sonja added lamely. If anyone was going to gossip about the Staleys, at least they'd have the facts. "The baby's father . . . doesn't want me."

Except Mrs. Coghill's expression softened. "You're so new to town, most folks will never know. In any case, they'll never hear anything so personal from me."

Which washed Sonja in a relief that was rivaled only by her gratitude. But of course Mrs. Coghill would rush forward with such compassion; who would know the sting of community rebuff more sharply than the undertaker and his wife? She herself had considered sweeping them from her porch.

"Did you know we were so newly married?" Sonja asked to see how broad her own rejection might extend.

"Didn't know you were married at all. Mr. Gonzales told us he'd heard someone had hung a doctor sign in their yard, but he hadn't met anyone claiming to be the man, and he surely knew nothing about a wife."

Meaning the doctor's bachelorhood hadn't kept any patients away. They hadn't called because he simply hadn't made himself known. Sometimes a person could be too shy.

"I'm sewing myself a new dress," Sonja said, shifting topics.

Mrs. Coghill brightened. "Is that what you're making of that pretty orange fabric?"

"Yes. My husband picked it out."

"He has a fine eye. You'll look beautiful."

Sonja folded her arms over her stomach. "With all due respect, 'beautiful' might be a little more than a piece of cloth can manage."

Mrs. Coghill laughed, a warm, light sound that gave Sonja the sudden impulse to devour her. So long—months, actually—since she'd talked with another woman.

"Call me Berta," the woman replied, then whispered,

"Is this your first?"

"Call me Sonja. And yes."

"When?"

"Just over three months."

Berta nodded knowingly from behind the cup she held to her mouth. "I declare, the last few months are the worst. Seems like it takes forever."

"You have children?"

"Three girls—Gladys, Molly, and Daisy." She waggled her fingers. "Don't worry, each one gets easier."

Perhaps, though this would be both Sonja's hardest and easiest time; there wouldn't be another.

"I'm no dentist," Noble said into the sudden lull.

And Berta obviously knew what prompted the declaration, for she made one of her own. "You're the closest thing to it within a week's ride."

Sonja looked from Berta to Mr. Coghill. "You have a bad tooth?"

"Been tempted to cut off my head for the relief," Mr. Coghill replied.

Sonja stifled a laugh. It wasn't funny—even though it was.

And the Coghills watched Noble with such hopeful anticipation.

Noble set down his coffee. "I can take a look, but I won't promise anything." He turned to Sonja. "I'll need someone to hold the lamp."

Mrs. Coghill looked as if she wanted to volunteer, but Sonja shook her head. "That's all right, Mrs. Coghill. I'm used to this"—if one time assisting could make a person accustomed to the things Noble did to a body in order to advance its healing.

Mrs. Coghill relaxed onto her bench and Noble rose from his, rounding the table the long way around—away from Sonja—and striding to his examination room. Leland followed.

"Why don't you lie down, Leland," Noble directed, pointing to the examination table as he strode to the supply cabinet to light one of the three theater lamps on top.

He drew a hand mirror from one of the drawers, gathered the footlight, and stepped to Mr. Coghill's side. He handed the lamp to Sonja.

"Stand at his head so you don't block the light from the window," he told her, then lapped his hands over hers to position the lamp just so over his patient.

Then to the man under it, "Okay, Leland, let's have a look."

Mr. Coghill opened his mouth and pointed to a tooth on the bottom and in the back. "Righ' 'ere," he mumbled around his finger.

Noble used the hand mirror to reflect lamplight into a place that didn't gather it easily. Carefully . . . intently he peered . . . before he stepped back again, decision obviously reached. Sonja let the lamp settle to the corner of the table.

"The tooth looks pretty bad," Noble said. "How miserable are you?"

Mr. Coghill was wiping his wet finger on his shirt. "Miserable enough."

Noble nodded, then turned to Sonja. "Go ahead and put the lamp on the cabinet. This will take a minute."

Then he strode there himself. By the time Sonja joined him he had that familiar bottle of laudanum and monogrammed dosage cup in hand. Sonja rolled her lips inward to keep from laughing at the ridiculous secret—that ridiculous name—she now knew. Noble must have sensed it, for he cast her a sidelong stare that was as stern as it was playful. He sent another, just for measure, as he poured a dose of the painkiller. Then he swiveled and gave the cup to Mr. Coghill.

"That tastes hideous," Sonja warned him as he sat up to drink.

"I don't mind," Mr. Coghill replied. "Something tells me this is going to hurt pretty good." He drained the cup, shuddered, and lay back down.

Noble disappeared into the parlor . . . to wash his hands, apparently, for he returned, sleeves rolled to his elbows.

"Mrs. Coghill is working on your dress," he said so softly that only Sonja could hear as he opened one of the cabinet drawers.

"She is?"

"Let her, if you don't mind," he said. "She's worried, and it will help."

Sonja looked to the doorway and the sliver of view into the parlor. Berta's head was bent over something at the table, and that was probably all right. With all those daughters, surely the woman knew how to sew.

Noble drew two white squares of cloth and a tool that looked like a pair of pliers from the cabinet. He wrapped the tool inside one of the cloths and set it on the cabinet. Then he turned around, folded his arms, leaned against the cabinet, and actually asked Mr. Coghill about where he'd learned to be an undertaker.

Sonja stared in disbelief. This was no time for idle conversation. Not with—

Then it dawned on her. It was all on purpose, what he was doing; engaging Mr. Coghill in easy diversion would allow enough time for the laudanum to fuzzy the man's mind. And it was working. Mr. Coghill droned on, his monologue growing slower and slower until he stopped mid-sentence, as if he needed all his concentration to blink. Which he did. When he spoke again, he started at a different place from where he'd left off.

Noble unfolded his arms and returned to the table, taking both cloths with him, though the full one was set on the space of table beside Mr. Coghill's leg. The other was draped over the man's chest and tucked under his chin. Sonja grabbed the lamp and returned to the head of the table where Noble helped her position the fall of light once more, his hands warm and soft over hers.

"Open your mouth, Leland. Open wide," he had to tell his sleepy patient.

Then he unwrapped the tool, but he did so out of Mr. Coghill's line of sight. *So smart, Noble.* So quick with the laudanum and careful to keep those pliers where the man— who had to be scared out of his wits, despite his outward calm—couldn't see them. *So sensitive to a person's unspoken needs, Noble.* So sensitive to even Berta's fears.

The lamplight honeyed the top of his head, sending a spray of gleaming into his blond hair. All shades of beige and yellow and gold, it was. Sonja's whole life, she'd been surrounded by fair hair, except none of it captured this many colors or surrounded brown eyes. And even these were unusual among browns; light enough to be rare, dark enough to be warm.

There were always messages in his eyes, telling of the books he'd read, the sorrows he'd eased, and his relentless search for the suffering he would always find. Oh, to be the sort of woman those skilled and gentle hands would reach for. To win the privilege of tracing the line of veins along the back. Or to lay her head there, in the hollow of his shoulder, and listen to the rhythm of his heartbeat. To be good enough to be wanted for . . . herself.

The blond head bent before her nodded as if its owner had come to a decision. Then Noble lifted the instrument he'd had hidden at his side, and reached into Mr. Coghill's gaping mouth.

His fingers gripped the tool that gripped the tooth. Gripped again. Firmly. Worked back and forth with a strength and concentration that furrowed the brow over his spectacles and flexed the muscles in his forearms.

Mr. Coghill groaned.

"Just another moment, Leland," Noble said quietly, the tone so soothing. The rocking gained speed. His arm jerked, and the tool emerged with a bloody tooth pinched in its teeth, a string of red spittle spanning the space between—

The floor sank. The walls tilted. Sonja spun away and clutched for a hold on the corner of the table. She stumbled a step. And threw up.

Twenty-two

A little later Sonja watched the door, listening as Noble said good-bye to the Coghills, assured them she'd be all right, and closed the door behind them. Then there was only silence and his footsteps moving to the examination room and lingering long enough for him to make order once again. He returned to the parlor . . . approached the door . . . slowly pushed it open, and looked inside.

"I hoped you'd be asleep," he said.

His expression was unreadable. He could be silently seething or disgusted beyond speech.

"I'm sorry I got sick," Sonja said. Was really sorry Berta insisted on cleaning it up.

Noble stepped into the room—as if he might check her forehead for fever—but he only sat on the edge of the bed.

"I didn't mean to embarrass you," she continued.

Then all fear of how she'd disappointed him fled when his eyes smiled.

He shook his head. "Sonja, Sonja. A simple tooth extraction? You've held up under worse. What was it? Your own cooking, maybe?"

"It had nothing to do with my cooking," she replied indignantly. "I couldn't help it. It just made me sick."

"I can hardly charge full price when the patient's wife has to clean the examination room herself—even if you did give her something to fuss over that she could actually fix." He shook his head again and chuckled.

His gaze climbed to the top of her head and lingered for a moment. "I'm sorry I didn't come to you when you were sick. I didn't dare leave Leland for fear he'd roll off the table. He turned as white as Siege."

"The poor man. Was his tooth very bad?"

Noble looked to the top of her head again. This time whatever snagged his attention drew his hand as well. He pulled at the stick holding her hair in a twist at the crown. "His tooth was rotten to the tip. The pain must have been maddening." He eyed the twig, picked from a Texas tree and stripped smooth. "Buy some hair pins from Mr. Gonzales tomorrow."

"You can't—"

He slid the stick under her pillow. "I can afford pins for your hair, Sonja." He lifted his hand and began smoothing her hair over the pillow in gentle strokes.

Sonja's heart beat a little faster.

"Once Leland's better, he's going to work off my fee by helping Benjamin Carney build me a chicken coop."

"Do you have chickens?" Hadn't heard any. Didn't have any eggs. And she could hardly make her mouth work with his fingers working her hair so gently. She was tired, after all, and he wasn't helping.

"No, but I will. And I think they'll do a fair job. Benjamin has a tidy place, and Leland is a practiced carpenter." He paused. "Thank you for what you did yesterday. Benjamin Carney knocked on the door last evening because he knew I was here and heard favorable things about me. You instigated that by introducing me to"—he grinned—"practically anyone who'd listen."

"I was just being sociable."

"You accomplished more in one day than I did in ten."

Sonja quoted Jeremiah on the subject, saying, *"For I know the thoughts that I think toward you, saith the Lord, thoughts of peace, and not of evil, to give you an expected end.* God promises that—and I prayed about it."

Noble's brow furrowed. "You prayed about my medical practice?"

"Of course. *Be careful for nothing; but in every thing by prayer and supplication with thanksgiving let your requests be made known unto God."* A memory raised a smile in her heart. "Papa always said to pray specifically, that you should never ask for good weather when what you really want is a calm day. If you're a seaman, good weather means a sailing breeze."

He nodded—*I see*—though the expression in his eyes said he didn't, and didn't believe all that nonsense anymore.

Sonja's smile felt suddenly ridiculous and out of place. It froze, then fell. She, of all people, was quoting scripture to a man who didn't care to hear it. She—too godly for Noble, not godly enough for anyone else.

She'd wanted a Christian man, meaning he'd married her under false pretenses, for he couldn't believe even as well as Harley did. And if Harley had no faith, he at least had money.

Thaddeus pulled his hand from the silk of Sonja's hair and curled his presumptuous fingers upon themselves. He rose from the place he didn't belong and gave his wife the due of a business partner, saying, "If you think you'll be all right, I'll ride out to the Carney place to check on Jacob."

She nodded. "Will you be home for supper?"

"Yes."

After that, he'd spend the evening reading and she'd sew. He was practiced at solitude, she'd settled for second-best, and the parlor was big enough for two.

Sonja looked up from her sewing to the other side of the parlor. Lamplight glowed in the gold on Noble's bent head, his left arm lay along the top of his desk, and his right was draped over the bent knee of his crossed leg. It lifted long enough to turn the page of the medical book he was reading. He sat up straight to peer into the twin tubes of the contraption—a microscope, he called it—to the right of the book, then nodded as if to say what he found agreed with the text. If devotion to study made a good physician, he had to be the best on the continent.

The baby kicked her in the left ribs. She pushed back with the heel of her hand, fending off the second and third hits, for they never came in singles. It worked; the baby rolled over, striking elsewhere. She palmed the knob where the tiny foot poked. Just six more weeks, and they'd both be more comfortable.

Without moving his head, Noble suddenly looked up through the top of his spectacles, his stare seeming to shoot right through her. It was always like that, a quiver to her heart and a flutter to her stomach. As if she'd been waiting whole minutes for him to finally look at her. He raised his eyebrows—*Everything all right?* When she nodded, he returned to his book. She returned to her sewing. And the fire crackled softly in the corner.

Nearly two months they'd been married, and it wasn't so special. It wasn't tender and comfortable, as Mama had promised. It was . . . polite, the silence spaced with controlled and cautious phrases. "More coffee?" "Sure is hot today." "Good night."

Sonja glanced across the room. Stared at the little bone in its paramount spot on Noble's desk. Then watched the blond hair, the spectacles that looked so scholarly, and the straight line of his nose. He shaved so carefully every morning—not that she watched, but she heard, and had seen how that hand could move so steadily and precisely. She peeked again before taking another stitch. His cheek looked soft . . . in a masculine way. Would it be? Would it be—

Never mind. No sense in starting a pursuit she'd never finish.

Sonja braced a hand at the small of her back and stretched. Couldn't even see her feet anymore—though their aching proved they were still there. Her wedding ring pinched, her breasts were tender, her stomach itched, the Santa Fe heat baked her energy away, her body had forgotten how to roll over without sitting up to do it, and the chamber pot was never more handy—or more awkward. *Easier the next time? Not for anything in the world, Berta.*

Someone rapped on the door.

Sonja froze mid-stretch and watched as Noble crossed to the door. The man behind it was short and wiry, his shirtsleeve was torn at the shoulder, and his trousers were striped with dirt. He swept his hat from his head. A bead of blood hung from the corner of his left eye.

Sonja held her gasp, though Noble was already motioning toward the examination room.

"No, not me," the man said and glanced at Sonja uneasily. "We had a . . . fight at the Blue—at the . . . cantina in the plaza. I'd be obliged if you'd come, Doc. Looks like Mel's got some busted ribs."

"I'll get my bags," Noble said and repeated the routine

he performed nearly every night, except this time he left his saddle and tack in his room. The plaza was within walking distance.

The intruder nodded a contrite apology and farewell.

"I'll be late," was all Noble had to say.

Mel's ribs were added to the list of ailments Noble visited routinely—along with Grandma Ortiz's consumption and the Smiths' sick baby. When he returned from the Ortiz home, he smelled of fried *tortillas* and *chile* sauce. When he returned from the Smiths', he smelled of fresh bread. When he came home from Mel's, he smelled of tobacco and perfume.

Noble stopped in the doorway, hands on the collar he'd been straightening over his vest. "Pardon me?"

Sonja set the knife to the cutting board, slicing beef into thin strips for drying, and put a more casual tone in her voice. "Would you mind filling the lamps? The kerosene . . . I don't care for the smell."

Noble set his hat on his head. "Is it the baby?"

She shrugged and kept right on slicing. "No. It just . . . bothers me."

He opened the door. "Sure. Anything you need from town?"

She shook her head. "Just fill the lamps."

Noble paused in the doorway—as though he wanted to know more—but he said only, "I'll take care of it this afternoon."

Sonja nodded and gave him a grateful smile. She waited

until the door closed behind him before she sighed with relief.

But the relief was brief.

When Noble returned, he opened the door briskly, closed it sharply, and marched to his bedroom without a glance.

Sonja rubbed the bar soap over the collar of his white shirt and resumed scraping it over the washboard in the tub of water on the table. Noble was angry about something. Had to be over one of his patients. He never got emotional about anything else.

He strode into the parlor and tossed some medical journals on his desk. The mail must have arrived.

"Coffee's old," she told him, "but I can make a fresh—"

He'd been striding to her side. Now he stopped uncomfortably close. Her stare climbed to his face, then dropped to the envelope in his hand.

His eyes narrowed. His voice was cold. "This came for you. It's from Harley."

"Har—" Sonja's hand flew to the base of her throat. What would Harley be sending her? Surely, not good news. At least, Noble didn't look too pleased about it.

She accepted the envelope and opened it, turning slightly to settle onto the bench as she read, *Dear Sonja, Sit down before you read this. I found your father and Karl.*

She gasped. One hand dropped to the ball of her stomach.

They were working in Independence and had handbills about you nailed to every post in town. Your father is a remarkable man, Sonja, and he talks of nothing or no one but you. He and Karl have hired on with the train. We'll be in Santa Fe about the end of September.

Her stomach somersaulted. One month. About the same time the baby was supposed to come.

I haven't told him about the baby. That's for you to manage, but

I believe he'll understand. Be well. Regards to Thad and Jackson. Fond wishes, Harley

Sonja looked all the way up to Noble, who still stood a breath away, eyebrows low over the narrow slits of his eyes.

"Well?" he asked.

Nothing had worked. She'd run away, earned her passage stooping over a bean pot and stacking buffalo chips into her arms, moved to a town she'd hardly even heard of, lived in a belfry, and married a man who had no room in his life for her—all of that so Papa could find her, anyway?

"Harley found my father," she said. "He's coming with the next train."

Noble's expression collapsed into shock.

"They hired on with the train. They'll arrive in four weeks," she said.

"They, who?"

"My father and his apprentice, Karl."

"Did Harley tell your father about the baby?"

"No."

"He won't know we're married, either. How's he going to take it all?"

Sonja opened her mouth to reply, but someone knocked on the door. She groaned. Couldn't they have a moment of privacy? Just once? Couldn't he stay home long enough to help her deal with this . . . this panic?

Whoever it was, Noble knew them, for even now he was stepping back for them to enter the parlor. It was a woman, and though the planes of her face were set as if the morning had not treated her well, she was dressed for placement in a store window. Her pink blouse swooped low across a bosom whose beauty lay not in its size but in the flawless expanse of soft skin the color . . . of warmth. A full taffeta skirt of a pink, blue, purple, and even red pattern cinched her narrow waist, and didn't even try to conceal the ankles so dainty in satin slippers. Her hair, so black its highlights shone blue, was pulled up into combs and adornments; an orchid *rebozo* fell from her hair to drape around the lace ruffles at her sleeves, and a fan dangled from lovely fingers. She was the picture of Santa Fe—rich and festive and earthy.

She bowed her head to Sonja, then to Noble.

"I am wholly at your disposal," she said. It might have been memorized as a phrase, for her next words were halting and reshaped by her accent. "I walk to you, this time."

This time? There'd been others, but Noble hadn't mentioned them. Hadn't said anything about any female patients beyond Grandma Ortiz and the Smith baby.

"*Muchas gracias. Como está?*" he inquired in the Spanish he was learning as he motioned the woman into the examination room and pushed the door all but closed behind him.

Sonja stared after them in disgust. He hadn't even introduced her.

The woman's reply was muffled—but there wasn't much mistaking Noble's request. "Remove your blouse, please."

It sent Sonja's eyebrows to her hairline. Good heavens, he intended to examine the woman intimately.

Sonja looked about for a distraction and found a worthy candidate in the letter still in hand. Papa and Karl, coming here. Her stomach rolled over. Nothing was ever simple.

"Does it hurt here?" Noble asked in the other room.

The woman's answer was too soft to understand.

Warmth crept into Sonja's cheeks. Here, where?

"How about here?" he asked again. Then he announced, "These ribs look much better. In fact, all of your injuries are healing nicely. *Muy bien.*"

"It is your very well hand that makes good," the woman replied. "I can working liké I never hurt." There was laughter in her voice. "I can no speak your *Inglés.*"

Noble seemed just as jovial when he replied. "You're

doing fine. Don't work too hard. Go slow, Mel. Please, *no dificil.*"

Nothing difficult.

Sonja eyed the tub of wash water getting cold and the clothes mountained in it. The doctor obviously wasn't talking to her. She drew herself upright and ambled to the bedroom to put the letter away. If Papa was—

Wait a minute. What did Noble say? What did he call that woman?

Go slow, Mel. Mel?

Sonja's heart seized. It hadn't been Mel who'd broken *his* ribs. It was Mel who'd broken *her* ribs. Mel, a pretty woman Nobel had visited nearly every day for two weeks—and been conspicuously silent about.

"Don't jump. I'll help you," Noble said, obviously speaking of the examination table's height.

Their feet shuffled toward the parlor. Sonja closed the bedroom door behind her and leaned against it.

"You think I have no money?" Mel asked on the other side of the door.

"No—I just—I mean, I know you haven't been able to . . . work for a while," Noble replied.

"Here. You take."

And it was apparently too much, for Noble told her, "I'll have to get change from the mercantile."

Stupid little town didn't even have a bank.

"No. Take all," that woman said.

"It's too much—"

"No. *El doctor es mi amigo.*"

That struck Noble into silence, then, so quietly, "You could do something else for a living, Mel. Next time, you might not—"

"No talk we this once more," she replied. The woman sighed melodiously, as if she were tossing aside all previous conversations. "If I can work for you, you come to see me."

"I've told you—"

"Very much thanks. I see you." Mel's footsteps sounded lightly, then the door opened and closed.

Noble appreciated pleasing things. Tidy rows of stitches. Crisp shirts. Gleaming wood. And pretty women. *She was the most beautiful woman I've ever seen,* he'd said of Amanda.

Sonja stared at the floor in front of her feet—far in front of her feet, considering the stomach obstructing the view. She was all belly. All swollen, ungraceful, and . . . repulsive. No wonder he set himself at a distance—which started about the time Mel broke her slender little ribs. Because his wife wasn't a proper wife. Not a whole wife.

Indignation rose in her. That was no excuse for sin. And she hadn't asked for this marriage. He had, and he'd promised to be faithful, to forsake all others. If he didn't intend to keep that, she at least deserved to know.

Twenty-three

S onja set her jaw and swung the door open. Noble was sitting at his desk, leafing through papers.

"Is that the Mel whose ribs were broken the night there was a fight at the cantina?" she asked, the sound in the silence nearly as shocking as the question threatened to be.

Noble didn't even look up. "Yes." He found what he was looking for and set the other papers aside.

Sonja straightened her shoulders, determined to put a little more strength into her voice. "I thought she was a man."

Noble glanced up, brow furrowed—either with puzzlement or irritation. "No." He reached for the pen standing in its holder. "Though I see why you misunderstood. Her full name is Melina."

As if that mattered.

"Noble, have you . . . known that woman?"

He dipped the pen in the ink bottle and tapped it lightly on the rim. "Did I know her before?"

"No. I mean, have you known her? You know, *known* her?" Humiliation—that she would even have to ask—found a home in every pore, except in the hollow where her stomach used to be.

Now Noble gave her his full attention. He looked profoundly puzzled. Then the understanding dawned, creeping into his features. His brow furrowed deeply. "You mean . . . in the biblical sense?"

"Yes."

"No." He poked the pen in its hole with vicious force. "What would make you ask such a question?"

"You've spent a lot of time with her lately—*looking* at her ribs."

"I wasn't *looking* at her ribs—not the way you imply. The bones were broken. And she had other injuries." He picked up his pen again. "The idea is ludicrous, Sonja. She's a . . . a prostitute."

The warmth in her cheeks drained to her feet. "You went to her—to her—to one of those places? You just walked right in?"

"That's where my patient was. What would you suggest I do? Have her meet me on the street?" He dipped the pen again and finally began writing with an angry flourish. "Our relationship is purely professional."

"Which? Yours or hers?"

Noble homed his pen and rose so quickly, his chair teetered on two legs before settling noisily. "If you're accusing me, perhaps it's because your conscience is weighted with guilt. What else is in that letter from Harley, Sonja? Why didn't your father write you, or did Harley have news of his own to share?"

"I don't—"

"I want to know why my wife is receiving mail from another man," he yelled, full voice.

"Harley only intended to warn me of Papa's arrival. It's nothing like what you've been doing, approving what that woman does by tending her."

Noble's voice fell to an ominous calm. "That's odd. I

thought I was caring for someone in pain. Of course, I could have refused to treat her, based on principle, of course. That would have made a big impact on turning her life around. I'll be sure to consult you next time, so you can help me get my theology correct. I wouldn't want to offend God by showing mercy to someone who doesn't deserve it."

She had asked for that, grabbing at sticks to throw; this one had been handy. And wrong.

"I just take care of sick people, Sonja," he added tiredly. "I try to leave the judging to those more qualified."

He hadn't judged her. That he didn't mention that now spoke louder than any reminder.

When she didn't say anything, he continued, "So what can I expect from my wife and best friend when Harley returns?" His tone was quiet, but his stare was intense. A muscle flexed in his jaw. "Never mind. Surprise me—if you can." He strode to his bedroom, emerged with his hat, and left.

Thaddeus steered for the river, away from the plaza. Didn't care to see anyone he knew. Not tonight. Nothing civil to say.

Carrying on with a harlot! Two months on the same train and more than two months married, and this is what Sonja comes up with? It was insulting.

She really had no idea, no idea at all how long he'd loved her. But neither could he let her, not while she was still so far gone for Harley—or the beau who'd fathered her child.

Sonja stood in the space between Noble's desk chair and the window, staring at the sun that hung so stubbornly on the horizon. If it would only give up, she'd at least get some relief from the heat. She scanned one end of the street then the other. Nearly night, and still no Noble. Fine. Let him stay away.

She braced her hands at the small of her back and stretched gingerly. Such was marriage—dirty floors, dirty shirts, and dirty mattresses. And days of silence punctuated by moments of warfare, though Mama and Papa never fought like that.

Sonja sighed and turned from the window. If she couldn't make sense of it, how would she ever explain it to Papa? He'd be crushed with disappointment. She wasn't proud of the person she'd become. So distant, that silly girl who'd chattered and laughed as if no bad could ever reach her. She didn't want to feel . . . joyless, now, except there just never seemed to be any other options—

In an instant tears built and a sob shook her shoulders. She stumbled to the bedroom and collapsed on the bed, curling on her side in the dark. Noble should be here, helping her figure out what to do. She had no words to give Papa, no way to tell him why she was married to a Santa Fe doctor she hadn't known long enough to make the baby she was carrying.

She sobbed again.

Harley should have told Papa about the baby, so Papa wouldn't have to learn it all in the space of fifteen seconds— and in the middle of the plaza.

Papa, this is my husband . . . and this is my baby—

He'd be furious. Or so ashamed, he wouldn't accept the infant. His own grandchild—

Don't let that happen, Lord. Give him love for the baby.

The next sob couldn't even break free. It just trembled in her stomach.

Help me, Lord. Help me not be afraid. Help me figure out what to say. And make Noble come home. Make him see he's wrong about Harley and me. Help him trust me.

In the moon-washed middle of the street, Thaddeus stared up at the belfry. He would have searched until dawn, if that's what it would have taken to find her. He heaved a breath. That was probably his most recent lucid moment. Until now. Things were all too clear—all too real—now. She'd have no reason to stay once Harley and Magnus hit town. She'd married him for the security, and either of them could provide her that. So he had four weeks to make her see he could give her more. Four weeks to help her remember why she'd refused Harley's offer and accepted his own. Four weeks to guarantee she wouldn't regret either one.

Sonja blinked. Blinked again. It was night. She'd been asleep.

She looked to the door, let her eyes adjust to the only source of light—the fireplace—and let her ears adjust to the silence. Her door was open and she was still in her dress, but Noble must have come home and draped this blanket over her.

She threw back the cover and swung her booted feet to the floor. Bracing her back with both hands, she stepped into the parlor and peeked into Noble's room . . . where there was a sizable lump in his bed, though the deep darkness made it difficult to tell. As usual, he made no noise when he slept. Papa rattled the window in the loft with his snoring, his night noises something the whole family—

Pain. Sudden. In her stomach. Couldn't breathe.

Rooted to the spot, Sonja forced herself to inhale—but gasped as the misery wrapped all the way around her. Hugging the source of it, she hobbled from Noble's doorway to his desk chair and eased into it. She bit her lower lip. Couldn't be the baby. Noble said it would be another month.

The pain finally began to subside, though she relaxed gingerly lest it return. It was the baby. Couldn't be anything else. She looked to the blackness of Noble's room. He hadn't even wiggled. Good. She needed time to think. She stared into the parlor, whose shapes she knew more by rehearsal than sight, and searched her memory. She was only seven when Ander was born, so the only birthing she knew anything about was Margaret's mother's. And Margaret didn't know much herself except to say the midwife was already there when she woke up, it took all morning for the baby to come, and Mrs. Shanahan did plenty of screaming about it. She, Sonja, didn't have a midwife, she had a doctor—who treated her with indifference. He hadn't even come home for supper.

If ever I needed you, it's now, Mama. I can't go through one more thing without you.

Berta. Yes, Berta would know what to do. Except how would she get to her house? Sonja glanced at Noble's doorway. Maybe she could sneak his saddle and tack from his room. No, that wouldn't work. Someone might need him in the middle of the night. She slumped back in the chair. She'd just have to walk.

Sonja stepped carefully to her room and fetched her shawl, then turned back again to grab up a diaper and gown for the baby—but made it only as far as the front door before another pain crept around the hard ball of her stomach. This one wasn't as bad as the one before it—maybe because it wasn't such a surprise—though she still supported her stomach with one hand and gripped the door jamb with the other. Her breathing eased once again as the pain subsided.

A fist pounded on the other side of the door.

Sonja jumped hard and cried out. Her stare darted to Noble's room. Whoever it was, they knocked again, and Noble was already moving. She spun around.

"Just a minute," Noble said in a loud whisper, seemingly right behind her as she slipped into her room and pushed the door closed.

Noble opened the parlor door.

"Evening, Doc," a male voice said, too loudly.

Sonja set her forehead against her door and closed her eyes.

Please, Lord, make it something quick. Better yet, something that takes Noble away from the house.

Noble shushed the man. "My wife is sleeping."

"Sorry," the man replied, his voice nearer but not much quieter.

The door closed, and boots shuffled.

"This here's George," the man said—and, oh glory, he was drunk.

The chimney of the lantern rattled, then light seeped around the edge of the bedroom door.

"His mule done bucked him off tonight," the man continued, "Fool ornery thing. I told him when he bought him. I said, 'George, don't never buy no mule what's got an evil eye.' And Doc, this mule has got the evilest—"

"I'm sure," Noble stepped in. "And your name is?"

"Bartholomew Terence Sullivan, but you can call me Bart."

"Fine, Bart," Noble said easily, then obviously to George, "Did you hurt yourself tonight?"

"That, he did," Bart answered for him, "And where it's at, I ain't gonna bandage. No, sir. I said, 'George—'"

"George, why don't you step in here, and I'll take a look at that?"

The suggestion was followed by additional uneven and broken shuffling of boots, the door banging against the wall, someone swearing about it, then more jostling. There was conversation, but it was lost to the onset of another pain. Sonja hugged her stomach and felt her way to the bed—

The door opened, and Noble's silhouette filled the slice of light.

"Sonja—" he whispered, then, "You're already up. I'm sorry. Did the noise wake you?"

She shook her head.

"Are you all right?"

She managed to nod, though the pain was at its worst. "I'm fine," she whispered with unintentional softness.

He motioned toward the parlor. "If you're up to it, I could use some help. There are two of them, and they're intoxicated."

Poetically, Bart chose that moment to yell, "Doc? Ho, Doc? Is George supposed to be on this here table?"

"I've got to get in there," Noble said. "Will you help?"

Sonja nodded.

"Thanks." He started to turn, then stopped. "Are you sure you're all right?"

The pain eased enough for a reply. "I'm fine."

Just as Thaddeus suspected, Sonja's simple entrance was enough to calm Bart and George; if a woman's presence called for a measure of self-control, one in her condition called for some outright manners. Obligingly, Bart tipped his hat and gave her a loose grin, though George tried to get off the table, mumbling something about having his britches down in front of a woman he weren't inclined to be romantic with.

"I'm just an assistant. I won't even look," Sonja told him, stepping up to the table. To Bart, who hovered near George's dusty boots, she said, "There's a chair at the desk in the parlor, if you'd care to sit, Mr. Sullivan." Then to George, "What was it you said you did for a living, Mr. . . ?"

"Higham, ma'am," George replied, launching into the prologue of his biography, while Bart dragged a bench—not the chair—into the room and sloshed himself dangerously close to the end of it. He watched Sonja with schoolboy fascination. Better keep an eye on that one.

The tear in George's left buttock mimicked the shape of the one in his trousers—about two inches long and as jagged as if Bart had cut it for him.

"Did you fall on a bottle, or a rock, Mr. Higham?" Thaddeus asked.

"It was a rock, Doc," Bart answered for him.

"How do you know?" George wanted to know. "I'm the one what fell."

"Yeah, but I saw where you landed—'less you got eyes where no one's ever had a pair before."

Sonja's grin was reluctant but true.

Thaddeus grinned himself and dunked a clean cloth in the basin of water he'd brought from the parlor. With no glass to dig out, he could have this gash stitched up and Sonja back in bed in a few minutes. He cautioned a glance at her. She chatted amiably with George, but it was a sure bet her parlor back in Indiana had never entertained guests such as these. As if to prove the delicacy of her sensibilities, she caught a glance at George's wound—and the dimpled flesh surrounding it—and blushed prettily.

George tensed his gluteus muscles and gasped; the water wasn't warm.

"Are you going to give him anything for the pain?" Sonja asked softly.

Without the precious nitrous oxide that had been too bulky to make the trip west, his choices were limited to laudanum, chloroform, and ether. The first, mixed with the alcohol already in George's system—enough to light every lantern in the house—would kill him. The second and third would put the man to sleep until mid-morning, making him not only a patient, but a house guest.

"I think he's consumed enough analgesic on his own," Thaddeus replied.

"I can handle it," George assured her with a gallant flourish of his hand, except he yelped when Thaddeus began washing the wound. He looked over his shoulder at Sonja and blushed.

She patted that shoulder and said, "You just hold still, Mr. Higham. Dr. Staley has some very careful work to do, and you wouldn't want him to make any mistakes, would you?"

All women had it, that voice of a switch-wielding mother, and it had been snapping little boys of all ages to attention for centuries.

George wasn't immune. "No, ma'am," he replied, then obediently folded his arms under his chin.

Sonja rewarded him with another pat before she stepped to the parlor to wash her hands, brushing past an enamored Bart who gave her more than enough room and a silly puppy grin. As if she'd read Thaddeus' mind, she brought him more clean cloths from the cabinet.

Thaddeus watched her unfold one of them and begin gently cleaning George's ravaged but most private flesh, blushing furiously the whole time. She poured a trickle of whiskey into the wound but didn't bother to chase the spill-overs where they ran downhill.

She'd never be unfaithful to him. It was ludicrous to even ponder the question, with such simple and certain honesty in her eyes. If her thoughts lingered anywhere near Harley's train, they were with her father—and how she was going to explain herself.

Thaddeus set a needle in the teeth of the holder and threaded it. Harley would be no problem. He'd understand. In fact, if their roles had been reversed, Harley would have insisted Sonja marry him for the same good reasons Thaddeus had.

"All right, here we go," he told George, who tensed but nodded.

"So what did you do after you moved to Santa Fe?" Sonja asked, picking up a diversion.

Thaddeus set the needle where he wanted the first stitch and pierced the skin. George jumped and hissed through his teeth before rushing into his recitation with more energy. When he grunted with the first half of the next stitch, Bart laughed and told him it served him right.

Two more stitches would do it.

"Hey, it's all right, ma'am," George said suddenly, right over the top of what Sonja had been telling him about an obstinate horse her father once shod. "It don't hurt that bad."

Thaddeus looked up. Sonja's brow was furrowed, and her left hand gripped the edge of table so tightly, her knuckles protruded. "Are you all right?" he asked.

She nodded.

"Is it your back?"

"It does hurt."

Bart slapped his thigh. "You want to sit down, ma'am? You come on over here. I can help the doc."

"That's all right, Bart," Thaddeus told him. "I'm just about finished."

Sonja eased her grip on the examination table and

sighed. Three pains now since Noble summoned her assistance, and she'd managed to keep them all a secret. Now he was at his desk, settling accounts and giving final instructions to Mr. Higham. Some coins jangled. Hallelujah, real money this time.

"'Night, Mrs. Dr. Staley," Mr. Sullivan called from the front door, loudly enough for the noise to spill into Noble's room and crash into the opposite wall.

"Good night, Mr. Sullivan," Sonja called back, then rolled her eyes when Mr. Higham began grumbling about how his rear end was already paining him and it was going to be a long walk home—'cause he sure weren't getting back on that fool ornery mule.

The din faded out to the yard, Noble muffled it further with the door, and Sonja stuffed the last bloody cloth in the basin with the others to be washed tomorrow. She glanced around the room. Noble would make fast work of cleaning his tools and equipment before he returned to his bed. Good thing, since the pains were getting stronger.

Make him fall asleep fast, Lord, so I can get to Berta's.

Except Noble didn't look especially tired when he filled the doorway, the strands of his blond hair well placed and his shirt tidy, as if he'd taken more than the minimal time to dress for a pair of intoxicated men. His height didn't weary, the breadth of his shoulders didn't slump, and his hands didn't hurry as they collected his tools. Rather, he looked as if he had enough expertise and compassion in reserve to tend a dozen hind ends—

He looked up suddenly, his gaze stopping her heart and nailing her in place, as those burnt-amber eyes always did. All qualities worth seeking could be found there. Papa would meet him in four weeks. But he would like him. What was there to dislike about Noble?

"I can clean this," he said of the examination area. "Why

don't you go back to bed?" He paused. Glanced away shyly, though his jaw tensed. "I can rub your back . . . in a minute . . . if you want. It's the least I can do."

All summer Noble had been there, waiting faithfully in the background, then stepping forward when she needed something he could give. He didn't always agree with her, but he never thought less of her because of it. Never punished her for it.

Obviously tired of waiting for an answer—or certain her silence was one—he stepped from the doorway to the end of the table where he began to clean up.

An impulse too appealing to question threw Sonja against him, pushing an "uumph" from him as she wrapped her arms around his waist and held fast. He was warm and solid . . . and gave back no reaction. He just stood there while humiliation coiled around her. She started to pull away.

Twenty-four

"No. Stay," Noble said.

Sonja froze.

"What is it?" he asked softly, his voice rumbling beneath her ear. "Is this about our fight?"

Sonja shook her head.

"What then?" He actually set his hand on her hair and began stroking.

Sonja closed her eyes and rested against him. Noble wasn't angry. He didn't hate her. He could—would—spare a portion of that compassion in his eyes for her, even though she'd shamed Papa. Shamed herself. Even though the baby in her womb was another man's. Should be his . . . whose fingers tickled tenderly and whose cheek rested against her hair. If ever there was a man she could—

Oh no. Another one.

She opened her eyes as the familiar tension started, easing into her stomach. She stared at the examination table beside them. It would be so simple to tell him about the baby's coming, except for the not knowing what he would do to her. Would probably put her on that very table. Might even use some of those vicious blades or hooked instruments on her, since they were so convenient in the drawers just behind him. And he wouldn't ask permission. He'd simply assume the authority over her vulnerability—with no regard for her modesty.

"Sonja?"

She squeezed her eyes shut. The pain was taking possession now—

"Sonja, if it's—"

"The baby is coming."

Oh, why did she say that? She'd really done it now.

Predictably, his fingers stopped in her hair. "Right now?" he asked, infernally calm.

Sonja nodded frantically, her face rubbing his shirt buttons. She tried not to tense, but the pain . . .

Thaddeus set the palm of his hand on the side of Sonja's stomach . . . where the tension was unmistakable.

"Let me help you through it, Sonja," he said. "Let's say it's going to last another twenty seconds, all right? Let's count. Come on, Sonja, count with me."

She joined him in a voice that was already a whisper, under the peaking of the contraction—which he shared in a way he never had, with her stomach pressed hard against him. It was a solid one. This labor wasn't going to fade into the night, even if it was a month early. She'd be a mother by the end of the day.

Sonja relaxed as the pain eased, slumping into his embrace. Thaddeus squeezed her shoulders and laid his cheek against her hair for the sake of a moment that came too seldom and wouldn't last nearly long enough. Whatever it took, he'd make her want more of these—once the business at hand was settled.

"When did the contractions—the pains—start?" he asked.

"I don't know. They woke me up just before those men came," she replied.

"You were having contractions while you helped me tonight?"

She nodded.

He leaned back, cupping her cheek and turning her face up where he could see it. "When were you planning to tell me?"

"I don't know."

She never did. Mrs. Staley wasn't a woman to be bothered with planning. Should have known something was up, though. His mattress was freshly beaten, and she wasn't her usual slow-to-wake self when he knocked on her door— except she'd undoubtedly argue that point.

"Come on, we have a lot to do," he told her, tucking her under his arm, leaning to blow out the stage lamp on the cabinet, and grabbing the one from the parlor table.

"Where are we going?" she asked.

"Back to bed. You should sleep while—"

"You aren't going to put me on your examination table?"

Thaddeus looked down at her, and the serious concern lining her features. "No. Whatever gave you that idea?"

Sonja just stammered and blushed furiously.

"I think this will take longer than that," he told her.

"How long?"

He set the lantern on the crate beside her bed and pulled his pocket watch from his trousers; a quarter 'til two. She seized the opportunity to extricate herself from his embrace and stood aside, clasping and unclasping her fingers.

He gave her a smile meant to calm. "The baby should be born by sometime in the afternoon, I would expect."

"Afternoon?"

"You have somewhere else you have to be?"

She laughed sheepishly. "No."

"Good. This is always easier if you're nearby."

She smiled with shaky lips and motioned aimlessly about the room. "Should I sit down or something?"

"Not unless you want to," he told her and began stripping the bed. "Some say the baby comes more quickly if you walk through the contractions. Could be, since you make gravity work for you, and you will be lying down most of the day. You might want to put it off while you can." He glanced over his shoulder. "Tell me when you have the next one."

She nodded and watched him carry the bundle of bedding into the parlor and drop it on the table. "What are you doing?"

"Getting your bed ready."

"Oh . . . well, let me help."

She manned the other side of the bed as they spread an oilskin over the mattress, then the under-sheet, then absorbent toweling on top. She had another contraction, seven minutes after the one before it and strong enough to have her gripping the foot rail as she counted down the seconds of pain.

"How are you doing?" he asked when it was over.

She let go of the bed by degrees. "All right. Maybe not as scared as I was. It helps to be doing something."

The woman who said that was calmer—and not nearly as surly—than the girl who'd tried to outrun a mule and rider this side of Independence. It was early yet in this day's ordeal, but the smile in her eyes said her core attitude would remain, even when she grew weary of the pain, as she surely would.

Thaddeus pointed to the nightshirt hanging with her other clothes. "Why don't you change while I get some of the things I'll need?"

Sonja nodded nearly as vigorously as she blushed—as if

she expected to cover her modesty with it. Such reserve would be a forgotten luxury by afternoon.

In the parlor, Thaddeus set pots of water at the edge of the fire and stepped outside to fill the bucket and pitcher from the pump. In his room he pulled his obstetrical wallet from its drawer, then fetched his desk chair and returned to her room. She was tucked up to her chin in bedding and staring over the edge through big eyes—as if he were a man stepping into a woman's bedroom and not a doctor striding into a patient's. He held back a smile; she wouldn't believe herself even that safe if she realized how cute she looked.

"Would you like to walk about, or lie down?" he asked.

"Which would be best?"

"I think you should sleep if you can." This would be one of the longest days of her life.

"Are you going to give me some of that?" she asked, attention fixed on the laudanum.

Thaddeus set the chair near her head, uncorked the bottle, and poured a healthy dose. "It will help."

Sonja shuddered and even groaned, but she swallowed the laudanum without argument, then contemplated the dosage cup's monogram with blue-eyed mischief. "You know, if the baby is a boy, we could name him after his father. How about Nezzar, or Neb for short?"

He glared at her. It was only a matter of time. Never tell a woman anything you didn't want to hear again—and again, and again, and again.

"He was a prideful king, you know," she added.

"My mother hadn't read the whole story when she picked it, which is all the more reason to forget it."

She started to dish out a reply but lost the retort to a wince. She closed her eyes and began counting. He checked his watch; fourteen minutes since the contraction when they were making the bed, and she'd had one while she was dressing. If anything, she was consistent.

"You're doing fine, Sonja," he said, stroking the hair at her forehead. "It's just about over."

"How do you know?" she asked, eyes closed.

"They last about a minute."

Sure enough, she eased into the pillow at the mark of fifty-two seconds.

"Do you want to get up and walk around until you feel sleepy?" he asked.

"That might be better," she said and gave him a grateful glance when he handed her a spare blanket to wrap around her so-very-modest self.

"If I cooked you something, would you eat it?" he asked.

"I'm not hungry."

They never were, but he had to ask. She hadn't eaten any supper.

Blanket wrapped about her shoulders, she walked the house, stopping to cling to pieces of furniture or doorjambs when the contractions came. She tried to distract herself with sewing baby clothes or reading her Bible, but she had no patience and even less concentration. Even when her eyelids grew thick and her feet shuffled, she refused to surrender to her bed, as if she might miss the excitement. As if she had any choice.

The sun had coaxed the sky from navy to shades of pink and light blue when her next contraction came two minutes early and markedly stronger than the one before it. So ended the "easy" part and began the hours of toil that gave labor its name. Thaddeus doled out more laudanum. Sonja finally went to bed.

She drifted in and out of hazy misery, wanting to sleep

in that billowy place where Noble's fingers feathered into her hair, but too weak to crawl away from the pain that kept pulling her back.

My grace is sufficient for thee: for my strength is made perfect in weakness. . . .

When the new day cast its light into the parlor, her heart fell in broken disappointment. It had already been an eternity. How much longer? Noble gave an answer, but it was vague.

I am with you always, even unto the end of the world. . . .

Mr. Sullivan and Mr. Higham came back, still loud and still hurt. The latter had split his stitches open, so Noble sewed him up again. A woman brought a baby. The baby wailed, and the woman rattled hysterical explanations in Spanish, which Noble patiently picked through until he understood the baby had been feverish for three days. Tonsillitis, he determined, then quieted the mother, quieted the baby, and sent them both home with a mixture of morphine and quinine, and the hope that the child would heal without surgery. Then Mr. Gonzales stopped by for more of that acid medicine for his hands. He left as soon as Noble told him about the baby, but not before he congratulated Noble on the birth everyone in town would know about before it even happened.

I will bless the Lord at all times: his praise shall continually be in my mouth. . . .

Berta came at mid-morning, so it was she who mopped Sonja's face with a cool cloth when Noble was called away to stitch and soothe others in the next room. She was still there when he returned and gave Sonja more of his nasty medicine. She was there when he lifted the sheet to touch her.

He wouldn't hurt her, they both said. It would be worth it, they both said. Not true. They didn't know—the indignity. The shame. Shouldn't have let him touch her—do that vile thing—that man. Would never let anyone again.

I will fear no evil: for thou art with me. . . .

Berta was there when Noble tucked the upper sheet back in place. But she was gone when Sonja curled onto her side and cried . . . for the front porch and tulip trees and Papa's voice, certain in prayer, and the ping of his hammer and the smell of Mama's bread and the rhythm of her fine and steady stitches and Ander's blue eyes and infectious laughter. . . .

Oh, the laughter. Someone took the laughter.

Weeping may endure for a night, but joy cometh in the morning. . . .

It was Noble who set his face near hers and stroked her cheek. . . . Don't cry sweetheart you're over halfway there you've been so brave be brave a little longer the baby will be born soon you'll see.

Now unto him that is able to do exceeding abundantly above all that we ask or think. . . .

No. Soon was too long. Couldn't do it. The pain was relentless. Never left her alone. Would be embarrassed tomorrow for whimpering and moaning and begging this way . . . but couldn't help it. When, oh when, would it be over?

On Christ, the solid Rock, I stand. All other ground is sinking sand. . . .

Thaddeus braided Sonja's hair into two ropes, but even they annoyed her. Repeatedly, she tossed them to the edge of the bed—as if she wished someone would drag them away. Back labor plagued her. He offered to push on her back, to apply a pressure counter to the one inside. She declined. But not nearly so vigorously as she refused to let him examine her. Wouldn't even come out from under the sheet, regardless of the temperature or how much she rolled about to find a comfortable position—until he forced more laudanum on her.

The drug weakened her modesty—and fight—though she whimpered pitifully through the whole ordeal.

But he got some answers. Her cervix was dilated two-and-a-half inches—nearly there—the baby was in a head-down position, and her pelvis would accommodate it. Sonja was well assembled for birthing babies, though she'd die in a spasm of embarrassment if he told her so.

Thaddeus cast her a sidelong glance. Usually the intimacy it took to get with child dampened such schoolgirl modesty, and labor killed what was left. Odd situation, this; Sonja, his wife, was more timid with him, her husband and doctor, than just about any woman he recalled delivering.

Just before noon, she passed into unabashed agony and the final phase of her labor, winning that last inch of dilation. The expression in her eyes grew crazy with pain and her eyelids thick with fatigue, while the scriptures she recited—and she knew dozens of them—grew more simple and common. She finally fell to mumbling phrases from hymns.

Her hands grew clammy and perspiration beaded her face and neck. Yet her limbs trembled and she complained of cold feet, when she wasn't calling to him in plaintive moans and clawing at his hand as if he could pull her from drowning waters. She begged for relief, for him to do something. If ever he wished he could, it was now.

Sonja groaned. "First you want me to push, then you don't want me to push."

"Don't push," Noble said again. "You'll tear. Just let the next contraction push the baby out gently."

He no more said it than another pain sliced through her. Sonja tried so hard not to yell, but nothing could hurt this bad. Give her more of that nasty medicine. Get her out of here. Let her die. Anything. Just make it stop.

"Good, Sonja," Noble was saying—and said more, but not loud enough.

The child was a boy, just like the time before. The son became Thaddeus', just like the time before. And the mother never voiced regret, never cursed her predicament, and never spoke the name of the man who put the child in her, just like the time before.

Scrawny, wet, and angry, he didn't look like any baby Sonja had ever seen. And he didn't wail like one either. She didn't blame the little fellow. She'd had enough, herself, and Noble only aggravated her exhaustion with more of his intrusions, kneading her stomach and insisting she push again, even though the baby was clearly born.

She bore down one more time, to give him what he wanted, then collapsed. There was sand in her head and surely she'd been poured into the mattress. Certainly she'd never again move as efficiently as Noble, who was cleaning the baby at the foot of the bed. She watched what she could see and waited, then held her breath when he finally set a lumpy blanket in her arms.

He bent, dropped a kiss on her forehead, and hovered there. "Mrs. Staley, meet your son. Son, this is your mother."

The shadows stopped their creeping across the floor as Sonja pulled back the blanket with a careful finger. He was tiny. So tiny. And pink and puckery. And looked like Papa.

"Pretty special, huh?" Noble said, eyes smiling. "Now you see why I'd rather deliver babies than just about anything." He paused. "You did a fine piece of work today. I'm proud of you."

She ducked her chin and gave her attention to the baby. "I made a fool of myself." Didn't remember much, but that much was unforgettable.

He drew himself upright and stepped to the end of the bed again. "I believe you held together quite well, and I'm somewhat of an expert. You certainly schooled me in Scripture. I feel like I've been to church."

Water spattered as he wrung out a cloth, which he applied to her. Sonja tried to concentrate on the fact that the water was warm, rather than where he was touching.

She stroked the baby's cheek and palmed his round little head. "Do they just sleep like this?"

"Pretty much," Noble replied. "He'll let you know when he wants you to fuss over him. The desire seems to be strongest just after midnight."

He finished his cleaning and bandaged her the way she bound herself that one week a month. The man knew entirely too much about women. Then he lay the baby in a crate he'd fashioned into a cozy bed sometime during the day, and brought her a clean nightshirt.

"Let's get you settled so you can rest," he said, sliding a solid arm under her shoulders and lifting her to a sitting position.

Too fast. Her head whirled. In fact, her neck threatened to let it roll away, except Noble's grasp was firm. He pulled back the sheet and swung her legs to the floor, then held her close to his side as he walked her to the chair.

"Are you all right?" he asked once she'd sat down.

"I think so."

"Good. Stay there, and I'll change your bed."

He needn't concern himself with it. She wasn't going anywhere. She watched her son, who lay sweetly in the blanket and crate bed that so easily overwhelmed him.

She jumped when Noble set the nightshirt in her lap and dropped to one knee in front of her. He already had her bed made. "I'll turn my back, but I'm going to stand right here while you change, Sonja," he said.

Not this again. "I'll be all right," she told him.

"You'll be better if I'm here to catch you," he replied then backed the conviction in his eyes by standing up and turning around, right in front of her. In fact, if he bent his knees, he'd land in her lap. But he behaved himself, staring straight ahead while she slipped out of her dirty nightshirt and pulled the clean one over her head. She knew; she watched him the whole time.

"Okay," she told him once the gown was smoothed over her knees.

His body followed his head around, and he grazed her from hairline to lap, saying, "That's better. Do you want to wash your face or comb your hair?"

She shook her head, which seemed to swing a few more times on its own. "I just want to lie down."

His reply was to all but lift her by her elbow to the bed. She groaned. It had been a day of mosts—the most pain, the most exhaustion, the most hours.

She watched him gather up her dirty nightshirt and soiled linens and take them to the next room.

The most humiliation.

Then he lifted her son from his bed and laid him in her arms. The baby was perfect and miraculous, and it was just like God to begin a forever-relationship by building on the one half's dependence on the other. Love welled in her heart and choked in her throat; she wasn't sure which half she was.

The most joys.

Twenty-five

S onja must have fallen asleep, because in the next moment Noble stood in the wedge between the door and its frame; the baby was still nestled at her side.

"If you're up to visitors, Berta is back."

"Berta? Yes."

Noble pushed the door open further, giving Berta space to breeze past him.

Sonja was already scooting to sit up. "Thank you for coming."

"Don't get up for me," Berta told her, dropping her bonnet on the foot of the bed as she came and smile beaming when she reached for the infant. "Oh, he's beautiful. Early, to be sure, but he looks none the worse for it." She pulled back the blanket and poked his chin. "Hello, little fellow. Do you have a name yet?"

"No," Sonja replied. "I—we haven't had time. I've been asleep."

"Isn't it dreadful? I might have told you to expect the worst, but I didn't want to frighten the wits out of you. It's bad enough as it is. But you did fine, and it will be easier the next time. You'll see."

"There won't be a next time," Sonja told her—just as Noble returned with two cups of coffee, though he acted as if he either hadn't heard or was content to deliver everyone else's babies.

He set Berta's coffee on the crate and motioned toward the baby. "You might want to feed him."

Feed him? at her . . . breast? in front of him?

Noble grinned as if he heard every thought. "Berta can show you how. I'll be in the next room." The door closed quietly behind him.

It wasn't as embarrassing as it sounded. Berta suggested she lie on her side with the baby snuggled up to her—and he seemed to know what he wanted, once Sonja guided his little mouth. He latched onto her breast with delicate greed and a tiny gnawing—though Sonja still cast a hesitant glance at Berta.

"You're doing fine," the woman told her. "Relax and enjoy him. Before you know it, he'll be rushing out the door with hardly a promise to come home for supper."

Sonja slumped into the mattress and peered at the little face whose cheeks were pressed tightly against her. It was amazing he could breathe. She palmed his fuzzy blond head. If holding him had been wonderful, nursing him held a joy one hundred times deeper. She stroked the row of bumps that were his fingers; he sighed and hummed a delicate little noise as his breath scraped over his vocal chords.

"I love it when they sing like that," Berta said softly.

Sonja looked to her. Their gazes held for a moment. "Thank you for coming . . . earlier. How did you know?"

"I didn't. Dr. Thaddeus sent for me. He let the little boy down the street take a peek at that skeleton of his in trade for bringing the message."

"Why would he do that?"

"I think he knew you'd appreciate the company of someone who could empathize." Berta glanced at the doorway. "That's quite a man you have there. Does anything ever rattle him?"

Sonja gave her stare back to the baby as heat started in her cheeks and bled into every pore. "I might have preferred a midwife," she said softly, disregarding the question.

"A midwife! Land's sake, any woman would love to have such a skilled and gentle man to see her through her birthing. Why, he's taken care of every detail. If he weren't such a fine doctor, he could make a handsome living running a laundry."

Sonja glanced at the washed bedclothes that now hung in the corner to dry.

"And to have your husband, rather than a stranger . . ." Berta added.

Embarrassing indelicacies of the day paraded through Sonja's mind. Berta would never understand; her husband *was* a stranger.

Berta shifted in her chair. "You're just tired. You'll feel better soon, and you'll forget all the bad parts. You'll see." She patted Sonja's arm, then rose. "I'd better get home, and you need your rest. I'll be back tomorrow to bring you some more supper and more clothes for the baby."

"You don't have—"

"I know, but I want to." Berta reached for her bonnet and set it on her head. "Can't have that baby lying about the house naked. It isn't decent. Now, you get some rest— and give that child a name. Can't keep calling him Baby."

On her way out, she handed back her untouched coffee and assured Noble she'd take care of supper tomorrow.

Sonja stared at the ceiling and sighed. There were baby clothes to sew, they were out of butter, Papa would be here in a month, and she was useless.

"Sonja?"

She jumped and hastened to cover herself as Noble strolled into the room and pressed a warm palm to her forehead to check her temperature. He gave a meaningful glance at the baby. "Switch sides after a few minutes, or you'll get sore."

Sonja nodded, though Noble would find that fever he'd been looking for if he felt her face again.

He seemed not to notice its probable color. "I guess you know Berta brought supper. I'll bring you a dish."

He returned to the parlor, the baby hummed, and Sonja smiled. He held to her breast like he'd paid two months' rent in advance.

He wasn't the only one who was hungry. No food had ever looked or smelled as good as the *tamales* in corn husk wrappers and spiced *frijoles* Noble held out to Sonja. Obviously Berta had mastered some of the wonderful dishes of the Mexican women, who were decidedly the superior cooks.

As discretely as possible, with Noble standing over her, Sonja broke the baby's connection and covered herself. And as if they had a memory of their own, his lips continued sucking. She looked up. Noble politely looked away, but his eyes twinkled.

"Still feeling all right?" he asked, once he claimed his seat and crossed ankle over knee.

Sonja nodded, except it would be nice if they talked about wagons or horses or the price of rope—anything except all these intimate things they could talk about.

He forked some beans, holding the plate at his chest in a way reminiscent of suppertime on the trail. "Did the baby eat much?" he asked, obviously just getting his momentum up.

"I fell asleep."

Noble nodded. They each chewed. The baby slept. And they'd hear the squeak of Noble's beard growing if it weren't for the occasional scrape of fork tines against plate.

Sonja stole a glance at him. He had shaved but must have swiped with one hand while he washed bedding with the other, and his even features and intriguing coloring gave no hint that he was as tired as he should be. Couldn't have slept much more than two or three hours before a gashed rump called him to stitching. He'd been doctoring ever since.

"Thank you for everything," she told him. "You even did the laundry."

"Don't thank me. I'm adding that to my bill."

She would have laughed if she had the energy. She smiled instead and asked, "What do you think we should name him?"

"After your father, maybe?"

Sonja looked to her son to see whether the name "Magnus" suited him. "He does look like Papa."

"Then you look like your father, because your son looks like you," Noble said. He carried more *tamale* to his mouth.

"Do you think so?"

"Boys usually resemble their mothers, and daughters, their fathers."

"I suppose so," she said, though Papa might not appreciate the baby—*this* baby—being titled after him, even with the resemblance. "I thought we were going to name him Nebuchadnezzar, after you, since you worked so hard to get him here."

Noble's eyebrow arched sardonically. "Then name him Sonja. You did the real work—and he'd probably like it as well as I like that word my mother hung on me."

She laughed. When the effort called for more than she had, she closed her eyes and let her head collapse into the pillows.

"Are your afterpains very bad?" Noble asked.

She opened her eyes and rolled her head to watch him drink his coffee. He knew everything about having babies—

and women, for that matter. As if he'd been privy to every giggle and whispered conversation behind every schoolhouse.

"I'm fine," she said, except her head was still full of medicine. It might be next week before she felt anything clearly again. "Why don't you name the baby?"

He might have more love for a child he'd at least named, though it seemed hardly possible for him to love the son when he didn't love the mother.

"All right."

He sipped his coffee, considering for a long moment. "How about Lars?"

"Lars? What made you think of that?"

"It's a good Norwegian name. Your father will like it, and his opinion matters very much to you."

He read her well. Like he could pick out all her pieces, assemble them, and see every moment of her life.

He tilted his head. "No?"

She glanced at the baby. "Yes. I like it."

"Fine. Lars . . . How about Donovan? . . . Staley."

"Donovan?"

He shrugged. "It fits. Rather like bridging the Norwegian and the British with something Irish."

"You're of English descent?" He seldom shared such information. He almost never volunteered it.

"Practically the first landing. We just keep working our way west. My great-grandsons will bring us full-circle, breaking trail over the Thames once again." He looked to the baby. "Won't they, Lars?"

Sonja was in good shape, but a difficult patient because she hated being waited on. She insisted on walking to the privy—rather than use the chamber pot—though she arrived more slowly than she departed. She showed no signs of puerperal—childbed—fever; no elevated temperature, excessive bleeding, swelling in her reproductive tissues, or abnormal pain in the lower abdomen—but then her physician had taken the greatest care with cleanliness. She wasn't much for carrying babies to term, but she'd be complaining about nothing to wear in a few days.

The member of the Staley family Thaddeus worried about was Lars. He'd avoided looking too closely, but now there was no denying what he couldn't miss. The infant's respiration was too fast, too labored, his nostrils flaring with the effort of each breath.

Thaddeus lay Lars on the examination table, unwrapped his blanket, and stared at what shouldn't have surprised him, what sent his heart rattling against sharp edges in its descent. He glanced at his stethoscope. No. Wasn't necessary. The working of the little chest . . . the tiny grunts of struggle . . . these told the story well enough.

Twenty-six

*T*haddeus stared at the baby's chest for a long while, willing Lars' immature lungs to draw a full breath.
Blast it.

He stroked the velvety skin over the belly and down the skinny legs. He caressed the little feet that were so perfect but would never take a step. Then he wrapped Lars snug, scooped him into his arms, and pressed the tiny cheek to his own, palming the baby's head and giving himself a moment with another son he'd almost had.

Blast it all.

And there'd be no consoling Sonja. She'd already lost so much.

Blast, blast, blast.

Hands buried deep in his trouser pockets, Thaddeus paced past his bedroom window. He turned at the wall and retraced his steps, stopping to stare at the slices of the horizon visible between the houses across the street. The day was not the only thing dying.

He'd give Sonja a few more minutes to fall into deep sleep, then he'd take Lars—if she'd release him. He'd been trying to get him away from her for the past two hours, to spare her the shock of the baby's passing in her arms, but she always stirred awake. He pulled his timepiece from his trouser pocket; almost nine-thirty. Maybe now—

A scream from the other room; too late.

"Noble! Nooo. Oh, no!"

He spun, legs swallowing the distance between his room and hers. He found her standing beside the bed, ghastly pale and holding Lars tightly to her breast. Her eyes were wild with panic and already wet with tears.

"There's something wrong with him," she cried, thrusting the baby at him. "He's gasping. He can't breathe. Do something."

As if it were that easy. Save my baby. With a stethoscope, some sutures, and a dosage cup, stand against the foe. Fight, hearty and hale—and win.

He knew so much. Everything in his stock of books and some things he'd observed for himself, but it was flimsy fare against all there was to know, and it wasn't enough to pull this baby from the cold clutches reaching to take him.

Still, he took Lars in one arm and Sonja in the other.

She pulled away. "Aren't you going to do something?"

Only to appease the pleading in her eyes, he looked at the baby. Lars' breathing was labored and shallow, and he grunted loudly with the effort to stay alive. Thaddeus pulled his arm back, moving Lars from Sonja's view, and gathered her to him again.

Sonja's delicate brows furrowed deeply. "What . . . ?"

Thaddeus searched for words—any words—and parted his lips to speak.

"You knew," she cried. "You knew all along he was dying, but you didn't tell me. You just let me hold him and talk to him—" She jerked out of his hold and wrapped her arms around herself, cradling her stomach as if it were the source of her pain. "You let me suckle him, knowing he was going to die. How could you?" She snapped upright again, as if bobbing on an ocean whose whim changed with each wave. "Let me have him. Is he dead yet? Is he?"

"No. He'll—"

"Let me have him. I don't care. He needs me." She shrieked, the picture of panic, then was painfully gentle in setting the baby against her shoulder and cupping his head in her hand. "Ssshhh," she crooned, eyes closed as she hugged him between her hand and cheek. "It's all right, little boy. It's all right. Jesus will carry you. He'll come."

Just like that and so obviously without a teacher—else she would have known what to expect of her own labor and delivery—motherhood rose up in her . . . while the tears slipped from her lashes and rolled freely down her face. A sweet and melancholy melody floated from her throat, and she began to swivel, back and forth, on her feet.

"It's all right"—ever so softly—"Mama's here."

Thaddeus looked away. Curse him, for an inept physician. Curse him, for a bungling man. And curse her for making him care when he'd promised he'd never do it again.

Thaddeus' gaze walked the circle of faces the next day. They'd all come—Jackson, Leland and Berta, Mrs. Trujillo from the boarding house, Mr. and Mrs. Gonzales, Zeke and Bessie Fairchild, Ruff, a handful of other bullwhackers, and Jorge and Evangelina Ruiz, the couple who lived next door. They stared back, mute and waiting, as if he had an answer.

Thaddeus' attention lingered on Leland and Berta. He'd find some way to repay their kindness for providing the tiny box at no cost, though they claimed they never charged for babies under six months. Then they'd circulated the news that brought the mourners to the yard behind the house and set a pot of stew to simmer on the fire. And it was Berta's patient hand that had Sonja looking so tidy this afternoon. She wouldn't let him near her.

She hadn't slept much. She'd finally retired to her bed, Lars cradled deeply against her as she curled up on her side. And that's where he died. She held him, just held him, for a long time after that. Then she'd asked for no help in preparing his body, accepted no laudanum for her pain, and wanted no comfort for her sorrow. Just cried into her pillow . . . into the night.

Now she sat in his desk chair, at his left hip, while the early afternoon shadows fell across the box Lars rested in. He started to set his hand on her shoulder but caught himself. Balled his fist and shoved it in his pocket instead—but not soon enough, not before she could stiffen and lean away, under the guise of shifting in her seat.

Thaddeus looked down at his Bible, taken from the far corner of the bottom bookshelf and now lying open in his palm. He was no preacher. Speaking to more than three people at a time was a thing to be avoided, so he couldn't possibly do well at this. And no one had asked, but neither was there anyone else. It seemed his place.

He cleared his throat. "Mrs. Staley and I appreciate your coming today. It means a lot to us." He paused. Cleared his throat again. "I suppose the first thing that comes to mind in times like this is, 'Why?' "

He scanned the circle, trying to guess which of these eyes had looked into the face of Jesus and which knew Him only as a character in a holiday story. *Why?*—God knew, he'd had plenty of time tending sorrowful bedsides to ponder the question.

"I don't know why things like this happen," Thaddeus admitted, heartbroken and disappointed to the point of disgust. "I don't know why little babies die before they have a chance to live. I don't know why mothers die and leave newborns behind, or why there are little children who can't walk, or fathers who can't work. I don't know why any of those things happen to good people through no fault of their own." He paused. Stared at the little box. "But I know God knows about it."

Sonja lowered her head. Her shoulders shook on a silent sob.

"And I know God weeps," he continued softly. "He doesn't like this any more than we do. Some things we bring on ourselves, and some are just the logical result of natural laws that were perfect in their design but corrupted by sin."

Mrs. Trujillo daubed the corners of her eyes. Zeke clenched his jaw and hugged Bessie to his side. Jackson swiped his cheek with his thumb.

Thaddeus shrugged. Shrugged again as he tried to crystallize a concept. "Maybe we aren't supposed to ask why." He shifted his weight and rephrased himself, saying, "Perhaps it's a little presumptuous of us to think we can use a finite mind to comprehend the concepts born of infinite thought."

They stared back. Ruff looked a little blank. Zeke looked perplexed. Jackson scowled.

So he tried again. "It just seems arrogant to question what we could never understand, when maybe what the Lord wants us to do is trust Him. We have a hard enough time understanding the simple things—like grace."

He turned to the verse he'd found in Psalms. "The Lord also will be a refuge for the oppressed, a refuge in times of trouble. And they that know thy name will put their trust in thee: for thou, Lord, hast not forsaken them that seek thee."

And the one that was his mother's favorite, "I will not forget thee. Behold, I have graven thee upon the palms of my hands."

He looked up. "Maybe we shouldn't ask why, but how—how to get through this. How to find His peace in it. Maybe even how to make it a victory. It isn't perfect, it isn't fair . . . but nothing catches Him by surprise, so . . ."

His gaze fell to the box. He heaved a breath. "I make it sound so easy. It isn't easy. It's . . . so hard. But God seems to specialize in the insurmountable—or at least that's what it says in here." He motioned with the Bible he used to read so faithfully. "All I know is, the first step is usually the hardest . . . and sometimes all you have is desperation and just enough faith . . . to ask for faith." He paused. "The Lord can do the rest."

And maybe he should take his own advice.

He sighed. "Lars is in the arms of Jesus, the same Jesus who sees us here . . . and wants to help us get through this grief . . . If we ask Him."

Then, because it seemed a more comfortable ending than the one he'd backed himself into, he began, "Our Father which art in heaven."

Two voices joined in, "Hallowed be thy name. Thy kingdom come."

Several more added their own, "Thy will be done on earth as it is in heaven. Give us this day our daily bread. Forgive us our debts, as we forgive our debtors. And lead us not into temptation, but deliver us from evil: For thine is the kingdom, and the power, and the glory, forever. Amen."

Sonja said nothing. Only stared at that box. Even after Thaddeus helped her stand. Even after he set the chair near the fireplace and Berta brought her a bowl of stew she never ate, she stared at that place in space . . . as if that wretched box were still there. As if it followed her.

Thaddeus tapped on the bedroom door that evening and wished he didn't have to move the air that felt so fragile around him. Wished he didn't feel as if any measure of his presence were an imposition.

"Sonja?"

No answer. He called again and finally just opened it.

She was propped against her pillow, Lars' blanket and one of his rabbit-skin diapers in her lap. She watched her fingers swirl through the fur, her gaze the blank stare of a distant time and place.

"Do you want something to eat?" he asked. "There's stew left."

Without looking up, she shook her head.

"I could read to you . . ."

Another head shake.

"Perhaps you'd like some company. I could get my chair and—"

"I'm fine, thank you," she replied tersely, about the longest string of words she'd given him all afternoon. She hadn't been so stingy with even the Ruizes, whom she hardly knew.

Thaddeus sighed. "There was nothing I could do, Sonja. If there was anything, I—"

She looked up then, and her eyes would have murdered him on the spot if they'd had the power. "You lied to me," she hissed. "You knew he was going to die, and yet you encouraged me to name him, just as if he'd be going off to school one day. How could you do that?"

"I wasn't sure. He might have—"

"Why didn't you warn me? Prepare me, somehow?"

Prepare? *Prepare?* How? By mangling her heart with the news when it was about to be mangled, anyway? It had been years since he'd chalked sums, but that looked like an additive effect—one and one makes two. Twice the pain.

"And if I had, Sonja?" he asked quietly. "If I had, what would you have done? Could you have saved him any more than I? And how about the time you spent? Would it have been any happier? More precious? Would it have made a better memory if you'd known?"

She simply stared.

"I did what I thought was best . . . for both of you," he said.

Sorrow woke Sonja in the morning and tucked her in at night. It had a name—Lars. Lars, who had disappeared into a mist hovering behind her. Like the nowhereness that had swallowed Mama and Ander. The same haze that threatened to suck her in—except she fought it, managed to hold her own at its edge.

The afterpains of the first few days were an insult, a womb aching unfairly, for the trade was one-sided. The child she'd earned with such pains couldn't be reached.

Then sometimes Lars was only napping and would be waking soon. Sometimes he needed changing. Sometimes he would enjoy a walk. But most of the time, he wasn't even in the next room. He was . . . at that vague somewhere . . . with Mother and Ander, wherever that was.

It was incomprehensible, this place where God resided and took His own with Him. It had a name—heaven—but no address. Where were they? And how could she get there?

The reply kept her company at those times when the haziness receded. So cruel, when the reality caught her. When it told the answer—never. Never would she hold him. Never would he be a little boy. Never would she be a mother.

Thaddeus set a cup of coffee on the table before Jackson and straddled the opposite bench. "Sonja's well enough." It had been five weeks. He shrugged. "She sleeps a lot."

"You worried about it?" Jackson asked.

"I'm starting to be." Thaddeus sipped. Didn't have to look over his shoulder to know Sonja's door was closed. The clock ticked softly, its hands descending from 3:00.

"What you reckon you'll do about it?" Jackson wanted to know.

"Give her time, I guess. I hoped she'd get excited about her father and his apprentice coming, but she doesn't seem to care."

"Day after tomorrow, ain't it?" Jackson asked of the train's arrival.

"That's what Harley told the stage driver who passed him a few days out." Thaddeus stared into his coffee. Truth was, he wouldn't look forward to the sound of the train's wheels rattling either. She had a lot to explain to her father. And to Harley.

So did he.

Thaddeus watched Jackson sip his coffee. The old cook always knew more than he let on. Eyes in the back of his head and the intuition of a mother of nine, that's what he had.

"Maybe Sonja's afraid to face Harley," Thaddeus finally ventured, then watched, surreptitiously, for any reaction.

"Why? 'Cause she married you instead of him?" Jackson asked.

The jealousy of it punched Thaddeus in the gut, but he replied, "Yes."

"Bah," Jackson growled. "She don't want him."

"They looked pretty friendly on the trail."

"That's all they was," Jackson replied adamantly, the flags of hair above his ears flapping with the shake of his head. "Friends. And he weren't so fixed on her as he was with the idea of gettin' paired up. The captain's just scoutin' around for a wife, and Sonja was handy. And pretty."

If only Jackson were as correct about the first part as he was the second. Even if he were, tomorrow's reunion was bound to be monumental in its awkwardness. Magnus would be meeting a son-in-law he'd never had the chance to anticipate, much less approve, and Harley would be greeting his best friend, who'd succeeded where he'd failed. Worse, Harley probably planned to propose to Sonja again. No, the situation didn't make the sense it had two months ago. In fact, the whole thing stunk.

"You jitterin' about meetin' your new in-law?" Jackson asked, frighteningly perceptive.

"I might prefer having a tooth pulled."

Jackson laughed. "Don't go twistin' your bowels over it. That papa ain't got no cause to disapprove you."

Didn't know why not. Sonja wasn't sleeping in a belfry anymore, but he hadn't exactly blessed her with smiles to spare. She had empty arms and no joy in her heart. In fact, the best she could find to do all day was lie on her bed and stare at the wall.

"I may fail in convincing the man I'm the best thing that ever happened to his daughter," Thaddeus said. "I'm not convinced myself."

Before Jackson could argue, Thaddeus vaulted to his feet and bent to reach the coffeepot where it sat at the edge of the fire. "I've never felt so helpless—or useless—in my life as I did when Sonja handed me that baby and begged me to save him." He straightened, pot in hand, and stared at the ceiling, his back to the room. "'Do something,' she said. As if I had the power but refused to use it. She'd already lost nearly everyone who was ever important to her."

He sighed and turned to freshen Jackson's coffee, avoiding the man's eyes. Jackson would laugh at his foolishness, now.

"This ain't workin'," Jackson said instead. "You got to chuck this contract notion."

"Chuck it? It was your idea!"

Jackson shook his head. "It was a bad one. Ain't no way to run a marriage, like a business. People ain't signatures on a page."

"Even if I wanted to redefine the relationship, there's no guarantee she'd go along with it. I'd be changing the rules on her."

"So what? She gets riled up easy, but she simmers down quick."

"Well, nothing I can do in the next day and a half is going to make her father happy with me—or do a thing for Harley's disposition."

"Harley don't matter. As for that papa, he ain't got women figured out any better than you do. Treat his little girl good, and he'll be happy. Don't worry, Doc. He's gonna like you just fine."

That evening and from across the room, Thaddeus watched his wife read her Bible, a caravan of images parading through his mind. A real marriage. Companionship. Laughter. Intimacy . . . and the children it would create.

So foolish, believing he could share three rooms with this woman in . . . detachment. He loved her, as surely as his gaze searched for her eyes, his ears listened for her voice, and his heart needed her proximity. Foolish, because the feelings had started long before he spoke any vows. Their former agreement was off. He wanted it all, now. All her attention. All of her. Anything less was unacceptable. And unbearable.

She looked up suddenly, met his gaze, then looked away. He'd been staring. He turned back to *Principles and Practice of Obstetrics,* though he didn't read the words. Mentally kicked himself instead. Should have said something to her. Anything. Or at least smiled. But he'd never been good at this sort of thing. He looked up to recoup the opportunity, but she was already rising and stepping to the kitchen, giving him her back. He dropped his gaze to the page. Had to maneuver, come up with ways to change the structure of their . . . arrangement. And make her care for him.

Sonja's fingers stopped over one of Lars' little gowns she was sewing. She looked to the door. Was it? She listened. Yes. Thunder—not from the sky but from the ground. She looked to Noble. He stared back from where he sat at his desk. He'd heard it, too.

"Let's give them some time, Sonja," he said quietly. "They'll be busy for a while."

Yes. He was right. She dragged her attention back to the sewing.

It was just like Harley to be on time. Papa would appreciate that, for his heart didn't beat. It ticked. She scanned the parlor. Everything was in place and as clean as she could get it, what with Noble hovering behind her all the time and forever reminding her not to lift anything heavy, or overdo. And just exactly how did anything get done under those conditions? Easy for him to say. It wasn't his papa coming to inspect his homemaking.

She sneaked a glance at him. He didn't look the least bit nervous. Of course not; Papa would like him, and he had nothing to explain. She, on the other hand, would be talking until dark.

She tossed her sewing on the table. "I can't wait anymore."

"Sonja, he won't—"

"I can't just sit here. I have to get this over with."

Noble gave her a you'll-be-sorry look but slapped his palms on the desk and pushed to his feet.

Twenty-seven

*T*haddeus glanced down at the top of his wife's gleaming head. She'd never make it as a doctor. Not patient enough. Even now Sonja strode toward the plaza as if her skirt were on fire. She didn't even have the decency to look nervous, while his guts were about to double him over; he wasn't exactly pastor-pleasing material, and Harley was going to knock him onto his soft side.

Her steps slowed when they rounded the corner, bringing the train and the plaza it filled into full view. Her head moved in little jerks as she searched. He looked himself, scanning the crowd for blond hair, but most everyone wore a hat—

Sonja squealed suddenly. He tried to follow her eyes, but she was already grabbing her skirt in both fists and running awkwardly across the plaza. He followed . . . lost her in the crowd . . . then found her again in front of Mr. Gonzales' mercantile.

"Papa!"

Her call was barely audible above the din, but a man—tall, with the arms of a blacksmith—whirled around and swallowed her up. His hat tumbled from his head. His hair was blond.

His eyes closed in ecstasy, and it looked as though his squeeze might make a widower of her husband before he finally released her. Thaddeus stood by patiently—awkwardly, actually—though the man had no attention for anyone or anything but her. His greedy gaze checked her over in a quick but careful study, and he looked as though he would weep with relief. It put a lump in Thaddeus' throat. This little woman with the dawn in her hair and sky in her eyes was truly all the man had left.

Magnus cupped Sonja's face and said—

Wait a minute. The man wasn't speaking English. Sonja nodded her head and replied—in Norwegian. She spoke—

"Thad."

Thaddeus turned. His heart stopped. "Harley."

Harley threw out his hand to shake, teeth flashing in his sun-ripened face, and pulled Thaddeus into a back-slapping embrace. "Hey, it's good to see you. And thanks for bringing Sonja."

"Sure," Thaddeus said, though the captain's attention had already shifted back to her . . . and held with gentle intensity. In fact, the evidence was written in every cell of the man's eager stance; it was Sonja's face Harley had pinned on the horizon.

She pulled away from her father and gave him a smile. "Hello, Captain. It's good to see you've returned to us again."

The greeting was reserved—no doubt out of regard for her husband's proximity.

Harley's eyebrows twitched—puzzlement—but she was already turning to her father. "Papa, I'd like you to meet Dr. Thaddeus Staley."

Apparently the pastor-blacksmith spoke English as well, for his blue gaze slid to Thaddeus.

"He's my husband. I'm married now," Sonja added, as if it were as casual as an invitation to lunch.

Everything seemed to stop except the whir of Harley's head—toward Sonja—and the fall of Magnus' smile. The man had been lifting his hand for Thaddeus to shake. It froze, then dropped.

"Married?" Harley said, his stare swinging from Sonja to Thaddeus. "When?"

"A little over three months ago," Sonja replied.

Thaddeus searched for something to say. He'd seen that fury in those hazel eyes before. He tried to put words into his stare as he explained, "It's a long story, Harley. It was time, if you know what I mean."

Harley's brow leveled somewhat, but his glare said the discussion was only postponed. He dragged his attention to Sonja's waist and the dress that was too baggy. The frown slid away, replaced by more surprise. Thaddeus gave him another I'll-explain-later stare.

"You are the doctor Harley talks so much about," Magnus said.

Thaddeus turned to the blond height and blinding blue eyes. The man was broad in the chest and thick in the neck—like Harley—and the heavily accented voice carried well—like a preacher's.

"I suppose so, sir," Thaddeus replied, stretching out a hand that had been steadier with its first needle and suture than it was with this meaty paw.

"And you have married my *lille venn*?"

"We didn't know you were coming, Papa," Sonja said hastily. "We were married by a territorial official. There wasn't time for anything else."

Magnus' left brow lifted sternly. "You are Christian?"

"Yes, Papa," Sonja said, quicker than Thaddeus once more.

"Magnus?"

Magnus swiveled to the young man who'd spoken. He

smiled and gave introduction, saying, "This is my apprentice, Karl. Karl, this is Sonja's husband, Dr. Thaddeus Staley."

Karl's golden eyebrows shot up. "Husband?" He gave Thaddeus a quick scan and Sonja a familial glance, then offered his hand and a smile. "It is good to meet you. I wish you much happiness in your marriage."

The young man's accent was thicker—fresher—than Magnus', but Thaddeus managed to understand and thank him.

He might have said more, except Sonja interrupted, turning a pleading gaze on the wagon master. "Captain, I need to talk to my papa."

"No, *jenta mi,*" Magnus said. "I have work to do. I cannot ask these men to—"

"You didn't ask." It was Harley's voice that broke in with such authority.

No, Sonja had done the asking, except she didn't know Harley. He was notorious for his unwavering standards. Hadn't even taken a day to be sick since—

"Go on, Magnus," Harley said, jerking his chin. "You can help me later, at the yard."

Thaddeus could only stare. Then Sonja gave him a see-you-later glance, tucked herself under Magnus' arm, and ambled away. Karl dissolved into the activity around them. And Harley stared after Sonja, his arms folded over his chest.

"What happened?" Harley asked finally, quietly, still staring after her. "Where's the baby?"

"Buried behind the house," Thaddeus replied, which brought Harley's head around. "She delivered five weeks ago, at the beginning of the eighth month. It was too soon. He didn't make it ten hours."

Pain skipped over Harley's features. "It was a boy?"

Thaddeus nodded. "We—she named him Lars."

"How's she taking it?"

"You know Sonja."

Harley nodded. "Strong woman." He scanned the unloading activities going on around them, nodded to someone over Thaddeus' shoulder, and pointed them toward the mercantile. "So tell me why you married my girl, Thad."

"She was living in a belfry," he replied without preamble.

And had Harley's full attention once again. "But I paid—"

"She wouldn't stay at the boarding house because she couldn't pay you back. She won't accept charity."

"It wasn't charity."

"Convince her. I dare you."

Harley heaved a breath of disgust—and frustration—then digested the full impact of the information in silence, though the expression in his eyes showed a flurry of thought.

"It was more of an agreement than anything," Thaddeus continued after a moment. "She needed a protector, a name for the baby, and I needed a family to give my practice respectability. No one would trust a bachelor doctor." He paused. "She told me there was nothing between you but friendship. I would never have married her if I'd known she promised you anything."

"She didn't, but I hoped she'd warm to the idea while I was gone."

Thaddeus studied his friend's face for any signs of anger. He found none.

Harley suddenly broke into a grin. His head tilted and his eyes narrowed in speculation. "You love her, don't you?"

"Don't you?" Thaddeus asked.

"I could if I fed it."

That's what Jackson had said. The old coot was right again.

Harley raised his brows for Thaddeus' answer.

Love her? Thaddeus sighed. "I'm afraid so."

"She love you?"

"I'm afraid not."

Which made Harley chuckle. "Well, Thad, old buddy, looks like you've done it again."

Magnus' eyes reflected the joy of the sky itself as they greedily grazed Sonja's features. "It's so good to see you, my girl," he told her in Norwegian, calling her by one of her two pet names—*jenta mi.*

She cuddled into his side, heart beating in cadence with their lively pace, for the delight of seeing him and the dread of telling him what he must know. So she kept the conversation light—his trip, Santa Fe, and the weather—and took him to the house, for lack of anywhere else as private.

He swept his hat from his head and surveyed the parlor. "Your young man provides you a good house," he said, still speaking Norwegian, watching as she stepped into the bedroom to hang up her shawl.

He was still where she'd left him, standing and staring, when she returned. They were Ander's eyes beneath the wheat–colored eyebrows, full of laughter and the unexpected prank. Mama was there in the gold band he still wore on his left hand—as if she would return any day. And God's steadfast love and perfect judgment were behind his sun-beaten lips, spoken firmly over his open Bible. A dozen Christmases, summer picnics, and hundreds of ordinary days, they were all there. He was home, her history, and the careful instilling of what she should have become. . . .

He would be disappointed that she hadn't come to better than this—living where her own feet, not God's direction, had brought her, mother to a lifeless child born of sin, and married to a man who didn't love her.

Sonja wiped her hands on her skirt and motioned toward

the fireplace, asking in Norwegian, "Would you like some coffee?"

Magnus nodded, then strolled the room, perusing Noble's diploma and rows of books. She filled the pot with fresh water and coffee.

"He is an educated man, this husband of yours?" he asked.

Sonja bent to set the coffee on the fire. "Yes."

"And he has a merciful heart?"

"Yes. He is a very good doctor." She clasped her hands together when she realized she was wiping them on her skirt again. "There's . . . compassion in his eyes. That was what I noticed first. . . ." Further explanation abandoned her. She looked away under Magnus' steady scrutiny—though he should have been pleased to hear such an admission.

Except his gaze bore deep. And his voice was agonizingly quiet. "If this is true, why do your clothes not hang beside his, *lille venn?*"

"Little friend," he called her, but the question preceding the endearment felt like a shout, draining Sonja's blood to her feet—except for what remained to warm her cheeks.

"Cleave, Sonja," he continued softly. "And the twain shall be one flesh. We taught you this." When she didn't reply—couldn't say anything—he looked about the room in obvious frustration. "If only your mother were here to talk to you." Then back to her, he said, "He seems a gentle man. Surely he was . . . careful with you. It . . . gets better, Sonja. . . . But I can talk to him if you want."

Humiliation rolled over her. "Sit down, Papa. I'll explain everything."

Before he entangled them further.

Magnus folded his height onto one of the benches, while Sonja bought another few minutes, setting out the mugs. When she finally settled onto the opposite seat, he stared over the table at her, his patient waiting saying there was a good explanation for her running away, that she would never do anything to hurt him or shame her Lord, and that she was the same little girl he'd known in Lafayette, Indiana. So how was the little girl to begin? Each word she uttered would chip away at the trust that had always been there, in his eyes.

She dropped her gaze to the table. "I ran away because I was ashamed," she began. "I didn't want to bring my humiliation down on you." She swallowed and licked her lips. Closed her eyes and rushed headlong. "I had a baby, Papa."

There was only a moment of stunned silence. "A baby! This soon? How could that be?"

"He was born five weeks ago," she continued to tell the table, "but he was too early. He died."

"Oh, Sonja," Magnus moaned. He reached for her hands and encased them in his own.

She would have looked up, except her chin refused to rise. Then, unbidden and unwelcome, tears welled in her eyes and rolled down her cheeks. Off the tip of her nose, they splashed onto the table . . . soaking into the scratched and scarred wood.

Magnus gave her a kerchief from his pocket. She wiped and sniffed, heart breaking open . . . bursting in her chest . . . and choking her throat. Her shoulders shook—and the bench tipped to the floor as Magnus stepped around the table and dropped beside her. Gathering her in his arms, he held her while she cried.

"You gave me a grandson?" he asked softly after a moment.

"We named him Lars. Thaddeus picked it out."

"Lars—it's a good name," he said, pressing her head to his chest. "And your husband is exceptional, taking a wife who carries another man's child. He's forgiven you for this?"

She sniffed and nodded, then sat up and swiped her

cheeks with the kerchief—which she began folding. "Our marriage is an agreement, Papa. He married me to give the baby a name, and I married him because the ladies in town wouldn't trust an unmarried doctor."

"That's a sound agreement," Magnus replied—and couldn't surprise her more, with such an admission.

"He doesn't love me," Sonja said, in case he didn't understand.

"Every marriage is an agreement, Sonja, whether there's passion or not." He shrugged as he returned to his own bench, righting it first. "Even if there's this love you moon for, it's overwhelming one day and feeble the next. But the covenants don't disappear. You'd do well to learn this early." He nodded. "You'll have more children."

"No," she told her lap. "Before we married, he said it was my decision."

"And you decided not?" he asked as if she were absurd. He groaned. "You disappoint me, Sonja."

She looked up. "I had a baby outside of marriage and you get upset about this?"

His stare slid to an obscure spot on the floor. "I was afraid. . . . When you ran away, I knew it was something . . . that it could be . . . this." He looked up, eyes flashing with conviction. "You have asked God's forgiveness? You wouldn't sin again?"

"Yes. I mean, no. I wouldn't do such a thing."

"Then it's in the past. But this—this is wrong you commit right now. And don't plan to repent. This is hardness—disobedience—in your heart." He paused. His brows lowered, and his jaw tensed. "You would give a coward—a man who refused to marry you—what you won't give to a kind man who promised to keep you all your life? You hold your heart from him? My girl, he is not only your husband, he is a Christian. You can't treat him like that."

She jumped up and spun away awkwardly, caught as she

was where the table, bench, and kitchen came together. When the blood rushed from her head, she braced her hand on the wall, giving him her back. "I can't do what you ask, Papa. I can't explain it. I just . . . can't."

He groaned in frustration again. "If your mama were only here." He paused. "Try to understand, Sonja, there is more to . . . the . . . sharing part of marriage. It is intimacy—of the heart. Oneness. Emotionally. It's about trust, not . . . lust, Sonja."

She stared at the kitchen table Noble had purchased secondhand but so carefully. The joints met in seamless care, and the blue paint seemed to rise out of the wood like the velvet color on the petal of an iris.

"Who was Lars' father?" Magnus asked quietly.

"No one."

"You mean, you won't tell me?"

"I won't hurt you," she said, turning away from the kitchen and brushing past him to the fireplace, where the coffee was boiling. "Please, Papa, don't ask."

Footsteps suddenly sounded on the other side of the door. It swung open.

Twenty-eight

*T*haddeus halted just inside the door, knob still in hand. "I'm sorry. I didn't know you were here."

Sonja stood in profile near the fireplace, and she'd been crying. Hard. Even now, she gave her attention to a limp kerchief, folding it as she always did when she was upset.

"It's all right," she told the square of cloth. "We were finished."

Magnus sat at the table. The furrow in his brow said he wasn't finished. The very air between them hung heavy with heartbreak, misunderstanding, and issues yet unresolved.

Magnus said something to him—in Norwegian.

"In English, Papa."

Magnus shook his head. "I am sorry. I forget." He motioned Thaddeus into the room. "It is all right. Come in."

"Thank you, sir."

Thaddeus closed the door and stepped into his room to hang up his vest and hat. Then he simply stood for a moment, bracing himself for the inevitable inquisition—*Where is your family? What do your people do? What brought you to Santa Fe? How will you provide for my daughter? Will you bring sickness home to her and my grandchildren?* Fathers were worse than prospective employers.

The parlor was so silent, Thaddeus' boots tapped lightly on the clay floor as he stepped to the kitchen for a cup. He filled it from the pot on the fireplace and offered to refill Magnus'—except Magnus hadn't had any in the first place. Thaddeus pretended not to notice, poured both their cups, and sat beside Sonja. She scooted away just a little.

The crackle in the fireplace had nothing on that in the air. Cup in hand, Thaddeus set his elbows on the table and waited for someone to fire the first charge.

Characteristically, it was Sonja. "I told him everything," she announced to a spot on the table.

Thaddeus glanced at Magnus. The man's eyes looked hollow—as though someone had smacked him alongside the head with a hammer—but he didn't appear excessively angry. It was an admirable calm. If Sonja were his daughter, he'd be tearing up all of Indiana to find the devious cretin who'd whispered lies into her naive little ears.

"Okay," Thaddeus said slowly, his pitch inviting Sonja to continue.

"Except about Lars' father," she added. "He doesn't matter."

Magnus looked to Thaddeus, as if to ask his opinion.

Thaddeus took a leisurely sip of coffee and set the cup on the table, his finger hooked in the handle. "I told you, Sonja, I can live with your past—so long as it stays there." Heaven help him—the cretin—if he didn't.

"We have no interest in each other," she replied.

It was Magnus who jumped on her confession, saying something in Norwegian.

Sonja's reminder was markedly more patient. "English, Papa."

Magnus darted another glance at Thaddeus—"I am

sorry"—before he turned back to Sonja. "What manner of man is this that you gave yourself to him, and he cared so little for your virtue? It was a gift, Sonja. Was it Jonathan?"

Jonathan? This was a name never uttered before. And Magnus was human after all, giving a fatherly reaction and asking fatherly questions. Perhaps he'd get a daughterly answer.

But Sonja only gave Thaddeus a quick glance and her father a stern stare. "Papa," she warned.

Magnus shifted angrily on his bench and made a fist of the hand that lay on the table. "You ask too much of me, Sonja. What kind of father would I be if I did not defend you?"

"God will deal with him," she told the table.

Magnus heaved a frustrated sigh, but it was Thaddeus he spoke to. "You have a challenge before you, young man. My daughter has a warm, affectionate heart, but she is just as impetuous."

Every doubt, every misgiving about The Papa melted away with those words. In fact, Thaddeus fought not to laugh out loud. "I've noticed all those qualities, sir."

"She is a danger to herself," Magnus added, as if Thaddeus weren't convinced.

"I've noticed that as well, sir."

Magnus waved his hand in dismissal. "You are respectful, but I do not require it. You are family now. Call me Magnus."

Oh, yes. This was looking better all the time. "Thank you, sir—Magnus."

Sonja offered her only defense. "I didn't want to run away. I didn't know what else to do."

Magnus pardoned her with a kind expression. "Oh, *lille venn,* I am sorry. I should not make humor about you. It is not—"

The gentle words were her undoing. She buried her face in her hands, and her shoulders shook on a silent sob. Magnus was beside her in an instant, lifting her to stand in his embrace, where she poured her misery into the front of his shirt.

Thaddeus stared into his coffee. She'd been crying in little whimpers for weeks. Would do her good to let it go, full force. Except there were less embarrassing places to be than witnessing it. He glanced to the door. To remain was surely eavesdropping . . . but the movement it would take to leave seemed too intrusive. He watched the light reflect off his coffee, and thought about physics and the liquid's surface tension.

And Sonja cried, her voice muffled in Magnus' flannel shirt. "I'm sorry, Papa."

"I know," he crooned, amazingly in English. "And I forgive you. I have no anger in me. Only relief . . . And I blame myself that you did not come to me. Have I been so harsh with you—am I so cold—that you could not ask my help?"

"I didn't want to hurt you."

"It is the way of children, *jenta mi.* Nothing gives so much pain or so much joy. You will see when you and your Thaddeus have sons and daughters."

That lifted Thaddeus' brows—though only his coffee knew it.

"There, now, Sonja. The Lord has provided for us and brought us together once again. What is done is done. We will go forward from here."

Magnus patted her back. She sniffed. Then they shifted and Sonja landed gently beside Thaddeus. She scooted away again but more discreetly, and she waited until Magnus was distracted with taking his own seat before she did it.

Magnus wiped his eyes with his thumbs and hooked his finger in the handle of his cup. "Thank you for taking care of my daughter, Thaddeus. Your actions say much about you."

"Thank you, sir—Magnus."

The next silence limped a little in its passing. Sonja mopped her face with the kerchief and folded it again. Magnus sipped his coffee. The fire snapped around the coffeepot.

Predictably, Sonja was the one to speak. "Did you bring your tools, Papa?"

"Yes. Both of them, my Bible and my forge."

And he, Thaddeus, thought he brought a lot of heavy equipment with him. All the otoscopes, ophthalmoscopes, and bone saws in the world were nothing compared to an anvil.

"You'll establish your business here, then?" Thaddeus asked.

"My family is in Santa Fe."

True enough.

"Captain Harley will give me work at the freight yard with the other bullwhackers for a time, reconditioning wagons and tending animals. My needs are small; I can make a smithy anywhere, and I have preached from my parlor. I can do it again."

Have to be a bigger parlor than this one—

Thaddeus' coffee stopped halfway to his mouth. An opportunity, this, for Sonja might step a little closer if she had less pasture, and Magnus could help him pull in the fences. Besides, it was the neighborly thing to do.

"Have you made any arrangements for where you'll stay until you're established?" Thaddeus asked.

Magnus shook his head.

"Why don't you and Karl stay with us?"

That spun Sonja's head around—and threatened to make nails of her stare, which she turned on her father.

"With you?" Magnus repeated. He glanced at the bedroom doors as if to count them. "Yes. Thank you. And tonight we will have a proper wedding. Before God. You will need His help to keep your promises."

No doubt about it. Sonja was mad, and she was making sure Thaddeus knew it, slapping empty mugs in the wash-basin and scrubbing the table as if the top quarter-inch just had to come off. Thaddeus didn't need to ask what had her so hot. And he wasn't about to get her started anyway.

Never mind. She had enough momentum on her own.

She chucked the dishcloth in the washbasin and spun around, hands on hips. "Just what do you think you're doing, asking my father and his apprentice to stay here? There are hotels, you know." She swung her arm in an arc toward the plaza. "Mrs. Trujillo's is a perfectly fine board-ing house. They could have stayed there."

"Sonja," Thaddeus said calmly from where he sat at his desk, "we couldn't let your father stay in a hotel or board-ing house. Not when we have room here."

"We don't have room."

"We have room. I grew up in a house not much bigger than this, and there were five of us. Seven, counting my parents."

"Your parents were—" She stopped.

Really married? More than business partners? In the habit of sharing the same bed? If it were in his power, the Staleys of Santa Fe would be too, but Thaddeus kept that to himself and lifted his eyebrows, bidding Sonja to continue.

Her mouth worked angrily; if eyes could spark blazes, he'd be in flames. She whirled around to her wash water. "I hope you snore. Papa wouldn't blame me for making you sleep in the parlor, since I just had a baby."

For a long moment Thaddeus stared at Sonja's back. Watched the rigid set of her shoulders and the way her skirt quivered as she punished that poor coffeepot with the wash rag. She acted as if she were being asked to sleep with the chickens.

Forget it. Didn't need this. Had already had a lifetime's worth.

"I'll go to town and find them a room," he said.

Though the selection would be limited. Quiet and private—no fancy women sashaying provocatively through the halls—came at a price.

Sonja stopped scrubbing, and her shoulders sagged— only to be lifted again by her sigh. "Never mind. They can stay here. It won't be for that long."

Victory . . . that felt like defeat.

It didn't take many people to fill the parlor that evening; Harley, Jackson, Leland and Berta Coghill, and Karl were enough. They sat at the table and leaned against the kitchen, while Magnus stood with his back to the door, his tattered Bible lying in his hand as if there were grooves in his flesh for it to fall into. Sonja stood beside Thaddeus. He glanced at her, at the hair that was clean from her bath and pillowed now on her head. The length of it would be pillowed beside him in a few hours.

Sonja glanced up and gave him a little grin. Not a woman alive who could cling to her anger when she attended her own wedding—even if this was the second time. And wasn't she pretty, even with the distress of the past five weeks wearying her features. Give him a week or so to act on the future he had planned for them, and—

"Thaddeus, take Sonja's hand, please," Magnus said,

snapping Thaddeus' attention to front.

The animated conversations behind them ceased as Sonja lay her hand in his. It was soft and delicate. He squeezed. She actually squeezed back.

"This is my commandment," Magnus began, *"That ye love one another, as I have loved you."*

Thaddeus smiled to himself. His father-in-law—now there was some reality for you—was made to preach. His voice was quiet but commanding, his stance gentle but sure, and his bright blue eyes peered deep, as if he could search out the truth, lies, and scars where they hid.

"Our God Himself commands this," Magnus continued. "And He gives His blessing." He lifted his Bible closer to his eyes and read, *"Thou hast ravished my heart, my sister, my spouse; thou hast ravished my heart with one look of thine eyes, with one chain of thy neck. How fair is thy love, my sister, my spouse! how much better is thy love than wine! and the smell of thine ointments than all spices!"*

A passage from the Song of Solomon? Not the usual wedding speech. Thaddeus listened more intently. Magnus was going somewhere quite specific with this.

"Listen to the way Solomon loves his woman. It is with the eager love of courtship and newlyweds. Man to woman and woman to man. He sees nothing but her, and she stops his heart with her eyes." He set concentrated attention on his daughter. "It is fervent . . . as it should be."

The expression in Magnus' eyes softened, and he looked over their shoulders, far away and beyond. "Your mama, Sonja. How I loved her. How I love her still. And it was this way, as it is written here, with us. So . . . " He stopped. Closed his eyes as if he wanted to say more.

Thaddeus looked to his wife. She was blushing furiously. Behind them, throats cleared and feet shuffled.

Even Magnus cleared his throat. "This doesn't always

happen by itself. Some will marry for love. Many will marry because it is a good match. You must make certain it stays that way, that it is always a good thing for both of you. You do that by deciding it will be so."

His stare shifted between them as if addressing a pair of naughty schoolmates. As if Thaddeus needed the encouragement. As if Thaddeus didn't already spend long moments appreciating how well he'd chosen . . . Sonja's gentle touch on hurting flesh, her steady toil over a washtub of bandages she hadn't bloodied . . . and the delicate curve of her throat. How he ached to kiss and nuzzle and taste the tender skin—

As if he hadn't already decided his life had grown as dry as the dust he trod.

Magnus turned pages and read again, *"Set me as a seal upon thine heart, as a seal upon thine arm: for love is strong as death; jealousy is cruel as the grave; the coals thereof are coals of fire, which hath a most vehement flame."* He looked up. "I did not choose your mama, Sonja. My papa chose for me. But we decided very early to love one another. To respect one another, to pray for one another, to never stop trying to win each other's affection, to make no room for jealousy, and to make no room for selfishness."

He paused to scan faces, to test the effect. "Learn this early, and you will spare yourselves pain, for do we not often give kinder words to strangers than to our own family?" He paused again. "Love fervently . . . do not divide your attention . . . because you have made the promise as husband and wife, because you are family in the Lord, and because Christ will accept nothing else."

Magnus directed Thaddeus and Sonja to face each other and led them in exchanging vows. Holding Sonja's hands and beholding her face, Thaddeus spoke his promises slowly, letting the words settle into every corner of their parlor.

Willing them to speak back to her at unexpected moments, when she might receive them. And he listened intently, watching her eyes and the movement of her lips, as she returned her vows. But she gave no hint that she meant them any more now than she had the first time she promised to love, honor, and obey him.

Those lips took on new meaning when Magnus gave Thaddeus permission to kiss them. Might be his only chance to show her how pleasant courtship could be. Might be the brightest moment until he convinced her. Worse, might be the only kiss she granted him for days. So he took his time, cupping her face in his hands and pausing to stroke his thumbs over the down of her cheeks. Men walked into battle for such as this, so captivatingly sweet and creamy . . . though chapped a little, right here and here, where her tears ran a seemingly steady path of late.

An intensity stepped into her blue eyes, as if to ask what he was about. If he had an answer, he wouldn't share it. So he gently set his lips on hers . . . and fought a deep sigh. This was a place to stay. And revisit. Repeatedly.

"I'll be along shortly," Noble said that night.

To which Sonja replied, "Take your time," and rose from the table. They all stared—Noble, Papa, Harley, Jackson, and Karl—but she didn't even give them a glance. The kiss she set on Papa's cheek—the traitor—was barely a brush.

Silly, this. As if a Christian ceremony would make a love match of such an accidental arrangement as theirs. As if hanging their clothes in the same room would erase everything that had come before. As if it were planned for.

The men were too busy staring to resume their conversation as Sonja strode to the door of Noble's bedroom, lamp in hand. That's right, she was angry. Furious, maybe. So let them gawk and clear their throats in the awkward silence—as if Noble was in big trouble as soon as they left. Maybe he was.

Sonja closed the door quite solidly behind her.

Twenty-nine

*L*ater Thaddeus turned the knob and pushed the door open, letting a wedge of feeble light trace details in the room. Sonja was curled on her right side, facing the wall, and she'd definitely given him the larger half of the bed. Her dress hung on a peg beside his trousers, and it was bulky. No doubt her petticoat was hidden under it, as if he didn't know such frilly attire rocked back and forth beneath her skirt. As if a woman's clothes—a wife's clothes—had never hung in his room.

This marriage needed to be different. This one needed to last. This one would. This one had a Christian wife, a woman of morals, a woman who would no more step out into adultery than she'd step into the fireplace for a cozy respite.

He stripped to his small clothes, a compromise between a nightshirt—ridiculous twisting contraptions—and what he usually wore—or didn't—and slid into bed beside his wife. He rolled to his back and stared into the blackness, lying perfectly still to the point of even breathing carefully, though she was awake. He'd tended enough bedsides to know when someone was sleeping.

"What is it your father calls you?" he asked quietly.

Her answer was a long moment in coming, as if she were weighing whether to grant him the courtesy. *"Jenta mi?"* she finally asked, the phrasing clipped.

"That's it."

"My girl," she translated, then after another eternity, added, "Or *lille venn*—little friend."

Thaddeus smiled to himself. Such was a father's love for his daughter. For this daughter. He understood perfectly.

"Thank you for treating him . . . for your hospitality," she said begrudgingly. "I would hate for him to be sleeping somewhere else."

Thaddeus folded his hands behind his head. His motives hadn't been that virtuous. "This is your home too, Sonja, and he's my family now." And the sooner she made friends with their familial merger, the easier life would be.

"He likes you," she said.

"He does?" As if Thaddeus had given Magnus any reason to. Had given the man's daughter a countenance of joy.

"Yes," she replied, sounding as if he were silly to think otherwise.

Stillness and the night settled around them, and Thaddeus turned his head very carefully to catch a whiff of Sonja's hair. He scanned the lump she made in his bed. It was a short one, curled up between the levels of his shoulders and calves. And it was a slight one, hardly making a dent in the mattress.

"What was your mother's name?" he asked, mentally sketching a woman of blond hair wound up from her waist to a pretty twist on her head, the sky in her eyes, and baby skin over delicate bones.

"Oleena."

Mmm, it even sounded pretty. Graceful. Wise and serene; the clay from which Sonja was made, though it would take an earthquake to shake the rigidity from her posture now. She hadn't moved a molecule since he opened the door.

Since the surrounding geology appeared reasonably stable, Thaddeus tried an easier way to loosen the woman lying beside him. "My folks always prayed in bed. I heard them sometimes . . . after the light went out." And he could almost hear Sonja's surprise at his raising the topic.

Her reply was predictably hesitant but nearly immediate. "Mine did too."

He reveled for a moment in the delicate timbre of her voice, how it lifted into the night around him, seeming to dissolve there without even disturbing the air it passed through.

He made another brave move and unfolded his hands from behind his head. He nudged her back and held up his hand. "We always held hands at my house."

Jackson was beating a metal spoon on a metal pot, reminding Sonja it was time to get up. Reminding her there was supper to cook and dozens of hungry bullwhackers to feed. But her bedroll wasn't made for leaving. Not yet.

"Just a minute," she told him.

No answer. He banged the spoon again. She opened her eyes . . . Not Jackson . . . Rather, Noble.

Noble?

Sonja scanned the room. Oh yes, his room. Papa occupied hers.

And Noble was half naked in this one, chest and arms bare while his suspenders dangled around his legs.

He swished his razor in the bowl on the crates stacked next to his side of the bed and gave her a glance. The left side of his face was buried beneath a layer of soap, but the right was clean.

"'Morning," she said.

"'Morning," he said, then puckered his face to the right and took a long and steady stroke with the razor—which came back foamy and left a clean swipe behind.

She looked to the door, listening hard. "Is Papa up?"

"He's reading."

His Bible.

"Don't worry. I made a pot of coffee," he added.

No matter. She should still be cooking breakfast, yet she couldn't get dressed—or even out of bed—until he left the room.

"Exactly what is it about me that reminds you of Jackson?" he asked.

Her attention snapped back. His and Jackson's similarities? It was a short list; they were both men, and that was about it, for Jackson wasn't tall—not even in his boots, much less in bare feet—Jackson wasn't broad in the shoulder—though she tried not to look—and Jackson didn't have all that shimmering blond hair curling around his neck.

"Nothing," she said. "Why?"

Noble took another stroke in front of his ear. "You just called me Jackson in your sleep."

Sonja nearly laughed but said only, "Oh."

"And last night you called me Ander."

A mistake nearly as severe. Cheeks warming, she moved her stare to the half of the bed now vacant but still dented with another's shape.

The man whose shape it was rinsed his razor then tipped his head to give attention to the underside of his jaw. "Call me Berta," he said, "and I'll hang myself."

Sonja laughed, and her cheeks warmed. Such a subject to be discussing—bed things. She tugged the covers around herself and studied the weave of the oversheet.

Noble sipped his coffee and resumed shaving beneath his chin. "Do I snore?"

"No."

"Good. You do."

Sonja gasped and almost laughed again—until she saw Noble watching her. Then she saw what he was doing, and it wasn't going to work, all this praying and holding hands and teasing. She wasn't a child who could be so easily distracted.

"I'm sorry. Perhaps I'd better sleep in the parlor," she said.

All the way around, Noble swiveled. "That's all right, Mrs. Staley. I fall asleep as easily as I wake up."

Later that morning Thaddeus looked up from the sketch-book on his desk to the table where Sonja was taking in the seams of one of her dresses. For four weeks she'd worn each garment baggy, even though she hadn't eaten enough to require it. As if to deny Lars wasn't under all that cloth any-more. She should keep the garments intact for her next child—except she didn't think there was going to be one. Thaddeus knew different.

He also knew her well enough that he didn't need to refresh his memory to sketch her, but he looked anyway . . . just as she tilted her head and began to hum softly. Sonja never was much for raw silence.

Smiling where it didn't show, Thaddeus passed the pastel over the paper . . . in lines . . . that began . . . to assume the shape of . . . his wife.

He already had a sizable collection of sketches at the bottom of his left desk drawer, but there was always room for one more and one more that had to be drawn. This one would be Sonja in full length, almost in profile, and gazing at the sunrise. She'd be as she was on the road to Santa Fe, in the skirt that was weary from work and Magnus' shirt that was her badge of pluck. She'd be a little round with the baby who promised nothing more than upset, though her chin would be lifted—eager, brave, yet soft and humble, and always, always buoyed by a mixture of the optimism that came with morning and the hope she hadn't spent the day before.

"Drawing again?" she asked into the quiet between them.

"Yes."

"You should sell your sketches. They're better than any I've seen in your medical books."

She thought he was drawing bone and sinew. He didn't correct her. "You think so?"

"Yes. Don't you?"

"I've never thought about it."

This scribbling was nothing special, just a logical use for the nub of color that seemed to have been in his hand at birth. He'd started with pictures of Mama and Dad, progressed to pets and the animals about the farm, and advanced to exaggerated and ridiculous portraits of a few select schoolteachers—who weren't as entertained as his friends. He couldn't sit down for an hour after that discovery and its resulting trial, sentence, and punishment. When he cast about for a new topic, he discovered the intricate and exquisitely fashioned mechanics of the human body. He'd been drawing them in detail ever since.

"Well, you're talented," Sonja told him. "You shouldn't keep it to yourself."

Just like that. Think it, and it's done. It was always so simple for Sonja, who expected events to simply play out the way she rehearsed them in her imagination. In contrast, were he in Sonja's position last May, he'd still be on the way to Oregon, trying to decide the best day to run away.

She returned to laying little stitches, and Thaddeus began framing the sketch with smaller images—memories, really—

of Sonja in her various moods and roles; stirring a pot over Jackson's fire, plucking eggs from the beds in the chicken coop—with feathers in her hair—holding a cloth to a vicious wound as he stitched it . . . and suckling Lars. It was here that he lingered, recreating the delicate curve of her hand around the tiny head. . . .

The art tool paused over the paper. Would that he could so easily make her love him. He surely would—or die trying. And his demise would indeed mark his failure.

That afternoon Thaddeus forked another tangle of hay, carried it from the crib to the corral, and dropped it over the fence, where Hippocrates bent his head and flapped a fleshy lip to gather a mouthful. The horse crunched loudly while Thaddeus lifted the bridle from where it was draped over the fence. Good tack was worth some maintenance. So he stepped to the overhang that gave the impression of a front porch, straddled an overturned crate, and began working oil into the leather.

". . . good coffee, Sonja," Karl said from inside, his voice and its heavy accent tumbling from the little window between them.

Thaddeus smiled to himself. Karl loved to practice his English. And he was pretty good at it.

Thaddeus dipped his cloth-wrapped finger in oil and resumed rubbing in slow and careful strokes . . . and Sonja still hadn't given Karl a reply. Thaddeus rubbed more slowly, lest the din of cloth on leather mask her words.

"Magnus said you had a baby. He said the baby died," Karl said.

More silence, then, "Yes."

Such a feeble admission, though Sonja was making some

progress. She wasn't crying herself to sleep anymore. Except one of these days she'd have to admit the child lay in a grave, and wasn't temporarily misplaced in some obscure corner. She hadn't visited the little mound since the day Lars was buried.

"It was a boy?" Karl asked.

Thaddeus dipped his finger for another daub of oil, and Sonja replied, "We named him Lars."

We, not I. That was another inch of progress.

And it wasn't polite to eavesdrop. He didn't need to. This wife was virtuous. Thaddeus rose to return to the corral.

"That is a good Norwegian name," Karl told her. "Any father would be proud of such a name for his son."

"Yes," Sonja replied. "it was my husband who chose it."

That made Thaddeus smile to himself.

The next afternoon, Noble stepped into the parlor from outside. "Where's Sonja?"

"In her room," Karl replied.

Sonja stared at the door from where she sat on the bed, knowing Noble was doing the same from the other side. She paused over the dress seam, waiting—listening—for Noble to open it, but his boot steps merely crossed to the back of the parlor.

"Magnus found a house," Karl continued. "It is on the other side of the plaza, near the freight office."

"Russell, Majors, and Waddell's office?" Noble asked. Water splashed softly, as if he were washing his hands.

Sonja poked the needle into the cloth, taking another stitch.

"Yes. We should get business from the freight office because we are close by," Karl said.

"Is there an outbuilding already there?"

"No, but there is a corral and room for a barn. We will build as soon as we can hire someone to work the adobe."

And yesterday wasn't fast enough, in her opinion. Nevertheless, Papa would be whistling when he came home.

Someone knocked at the parlor door, and Noble crossed the room to answer it. "Ben Carney. Good to see you."

"You might change your opinion about that when you find out why I'm here," Mr. Carney said.

"Let me guess," Noble said. "Jacob?"

"Yep. He was cutting weeds and got himself in the leg with the sickle."

Sonja winced. Farm implements accounted for most of the stitches Noble sewed.

"How bad?" Noble asked.

"It's pretty long but not too deep. Mrs. Carney about had the bleeding stopped when I left, but she couldn't bear to sew it."

Sonja shuddered. She wouldn't even try.

She jumped when the door opened and Noble peeked inside.

"You're awake," he announced, then, "What are you doing in here? I thought you were sleeping."

It was a logical question. Too bad she didn't have a logical answer, so she asked instead, "Is Jacob all right?"

Noble stepped into the room and strode to his primary medical wallet, the one he kept at ready on top of the supply cabinet. "It doesn't sound too serious."

He paused in adding folded strips and squares of cloth to the supplies already in the case. "Would you like to go with me? It's a nice ride—if you're up to it." He looked over his shoulder, waiting for her answer.

Five weeks since the baby and she felt well enough physically. It was the ache in her heart and the emptiness of her arms that refused to heal. Berta said she would forever grieve the son she'd mothered less than a day.

"Sonja?" Noble asked again.

She'd have to ride behind the saddle. And the only thing to hang onto would be her husband's waist. A part of her wanted to back up from that . . . while curiosity made another part of her consider stepping forward. She glanced at the window, and Karl shuffled about in the parlor. He should go back and help Papa, and there weren't many warm days left.

"All right," Sonja said.

Noble grinned and closed his medical wallet. "Good. Let's go."

Across Thaddeus' line of sight—across the road—the rabbit darted, scurrying to get out of the way—

And smacked right into a tree.

Thaddeus might have asked, "Did you see that?" but Sonja gasped from her spot behind him on the horse, saying without a syllable that she had.

"Noble, he's hurt," she added, clarifying further.

Sure enough, the little fellow remained where he'd toppled over.

"I suppose you expect me to tend him."

"Well, you could at least take a look."

The real patient—Jacob—was already resting comfortably a mile behind them, so Thaddeus drew Hippocrates to a stop near the wounding tree, handed Sonja to the ground, then dismounted himself. Sonja held the reins while he waded through the scrubby brush and crouched on the balls of his feet. Would never tell her, but he'd doctored plenty of rabbits in medical school—which was always a little short on human volunteers—so they were somewhat expert fingers that dug through the fur to find a heartbeat. There was one, fast and strong.

Thaddeus pulled open an eyelid, then looked to Sonja, who was chewing nervously on the inside of her lip.

"He just knocked himself out."

"Are you sure?" she asked—

Her eyes widened. Pain shot into Thaddeus' hand.

"Ouch." He flinched so hard, he landed on his rear end, just as the rabbit scurried drunkenly away. As for his hand, it bore the unmistakable impressions of rabbit teeth.

And Sonja was the picture of sympathy—"Are you all right?"—until she got all of two steps. Then she broke into a laugh, though she was kind enough to clap her hand over the top of it.

"Go ahead and laugh. It was your stupid rabbit I was trying to save."

She laughed harder. Couldn't even walk, but just turned away with one hand over her mouth and the other on her stomach. She swiveled back and got more serious when he pulled his kerchief from his pocket and pressed it to the wounds, top and bottom of the heel of his hand.

Sonja hurried to the horse, managed to dig through his medical saddlebags, and came forward with a roll of clean bandage and the corked bottle of whiskey. "Here, let me help you."

"I can manage."

"Let me help, or I'll tell your patients you're nothing but a big baby yourself."

And she would. So he let her have his injured hand, hissing through his teeth when she poured the alcohol over it.

She gave the injury a critical examination. "Hmm, I don't think it needs stitches."

"Would you suture it if it did?"

She gave him the full effect of her blue eyes, wide with

grave solemnity. "Of course." Though the gravity was lost on her next giggle.

Sonja set the bottle aside and began wrapping his hand in the bandage. Her shoulder shook on a laugh. "You really should have seen yourself. It was as if the rabbit were playing possum"—another chuckle—"just waiting for you to be distracted"—and another—"so it could open its eyes and bite you. And the look on your face!"

Thaddeus chuckled himself, though he pretended deeper wounds. "Very funny. Next time, you can take care of your own damaged wildlife."

Anything to keep him from being distracted from the way the sun found a home in her hair and how sweetly her lips curved. How much richer, his life, since she'd pried her way into it. Hard to believe he'd been so diligent in keeping her out. That he'd actually been satisfied with the hollow bitterness he'd nurtured every day. If ever there was a man made to have a companion, it was he. And how well he'd chosen her. How very well indeed.

She looked up suddenly . . . stared long into his eyes . . . then just as suddenly rose from her crouch, leaving the strip of bandage to dangle from his hand.

"Don't. Don't do that. Don't look at me . . . that way. Don't try . . . to make me something I'm not. Can never be."

She whirled away and stepped around sagebrush with sharp steps. Sonja never did anything in an ambiguous way. So why would her rebuff be anything but quick and sure?

All the way home, Thaddeus felt every shift of her weight rocking from side to side behind him. Felt every accidental brush of her on his back. Felt a waist that ached to have her arms wrapped around it. Who knew what she held onto? Horse hair, maybe.

Perhaps she'd done Harley a favor, turning him down. Brides were fine, but they soon became wives, and wives were impossible to get along with. Love didn't even help, for that was nothing more than shock without the head injury. She was right. Their relationship was best served by remaining in its original state—business. He'd already prepared himself for solitude. A marriage that kept its distance wouldn't be much different. He had the advantage, in fact. He'd already lived through one.

Which made him want to climb off Hippocrates to kick himself for being so repeatedly, monotonously stupid. Whatever it took to make a woman happy, he didn't have it.

So it was no surprise that the one who bore his name verified that fact; she said nothing on the way home. She said little while she prepared supper. She said less while she ate it. And she hardly let the rest of the world know her destination was bed when she lit the lantern and strode away from the table.

She was facing the wall when Thaddeus slid into bed beside her.

He gathered a shred of fortitude and tried once more. "Is it my turn to lead the prayer?"

"I'm sorry. I've already prayed," she informed him.

Questionable. She might have already prayed, but she wasn't sorry about it. She'd never feel such a benevolent emotion where he was concerned. Her tone was cold, and he'd had just about enough of it.

"Sonja?"

Just then someone knocked on the parlor door.

Thirty

*I*t's Jack Schmidt," Noble whispered once he returned to the bedroom, the glow from the fireplace making a silhouette of him. He crossed to the peg that held his clothes, leaving the door open far enough to borrow some of the fire's light. He pulled his shirt over his head and stepped into his trousers, one leg at a time. "His daughter is ill. I shouldn't be gone long, but it depends on what's making her sick." He tucked the shirt and fastened his britches over it. "If anyone else comes while I'm gone, send them over there or get some particulars so I can take the call when I get home." Then he grabbed his boots and sat on the bed.

"Schmidt?" Sonja asked, writing the name in her memory.

"Right. Jack Schmidt." Noble strode to the stack of crates and combed his hair. "He says he lives just beyond the RMW freight office."

Sonja nodded and whispered, "Okay."

He grabbed his coat from its peg and his hat from Siege's head. He'd gone to his supply cabinet when he suddenly turned around and stepped to the bed. He stared down at her, then bent at the waist, braced his hands on either side of her pillow, and dropped a kiss on her forehead.

"I'll be home as soon as I can," he whispered.

Then he gathered up his saddle, tack, and medical wallet, and strode from the house.

Behind him, Sonja cried—for what she wanted but couldn't have. For having married a man of healing to a . . . *a* . . . *bad girl.* And for loving him with all her heart . . . with no capacity to love him without bounds.

The Schmidt house would have been silent except that Hannah breathed through a stuffy nose, her dog Gustav snored from under an abundance of jowls, and a fire crackled in the fireplace. The fire provided the only light, though it was ample, being one of the best fed fireplaces in town—and in Hannah's own room. Her parents slept down the hall for the first consecutive hours in two days, and a maid waited in the downstairs parlor, at ready to show Thaddeus out.

Hannah coughed. Thaddeus touched the backs of his fingers to her forehead. Her fever had broken and she was breathing easier, but percussion—tapping the middle finger of his left hand with the fingers of his right—on her back would still answer with a dull thunk rather than a healthy drumlike sound. Would have to watch this little one and her lung fever over the next several days, but the battle was won for tonight. In another half hour he could return to his own bed. And Sonja.

He would win her. Whatever it took. However long, for he had such patience as it might require, and he would succeed.

For now, pastel in hand, he returned to the sketchbook resting in the triangle of space between his crossed leg and the opposite thigh. He stared at it, drawing imaginary scenes on its virgin surface—Sonja soothing seemingly the entire Carney household today. Or wrapping a doctor's injured hand. Or nothing more dramatic than mixing a bowl of corn dodgers for a room full of hungry men.

He smiled to himself, for himself, for there was no one to see except Gustav, whose eyebrows rocked up and down, first one then the other, when Hannah whimpered and rolled over. Thaddeus shifted in the creaky chair to reset her blanket. She was a sweet little thing. They always were at four years old, with their features caught between baby and child. Still pudgy and dimpled but growing tall and thinning out. In another six months, there'd be little of the baby left to see.

His gaze fell to the paper, an idea forming. It might work. Should have thought of it sooner, except he never had such a high opinion of what he did—not *this*—that he made gifts of it. Except that time he gave a sketch of her horse to Gertrude Newstead. She seemed well enough impressed.

The drawing—this one thing he could give Sonja that was impossible any other way except through the connection between his memory and hand—might make her happy. If she didn't laugh at his foolishness. And if he remembered well enough and translated it clearly. One who was gone . . . for one left behind. Baby . . . for Mother. Lars . . . for Sonja.

Thaddeus began to sketch.

Sonja hadn't even reached the property before Noble, Magnus, Karl, and Santiago, the man who knew all about adobe, stopped their work to head her direction. Three sets of eyes fastened on the crate at the ends of her arms. One set fastened on her.

Its owner rushed to relieve her of the crate. "Sonja, I'm going to turn you over my knee," Noble scolded, just above a whisper. "That crate's too heavy for you to carry all the way across town."

"How else was I supposed to get it here?" Sonja asked.

He bent, setting his mouth at her ear. "You might have asked your husband. He would have come to get it for you."

"You're not my beast of burden, and I'm not made of glass."

Besides, he'd had enough interruptions. He'd hardly reached Papa's property at mid-morning before she had to fetch him back to the house. The youngest of the Gallegos daughters had toddled into the fireplace, three in the Escobar family were sick with the mumps, then Grandmother Gee suffered a blinding headache and fell on a right leg that was suddenly numb. Noble reached her just before she eased into death.

All this before afternoon had even gathered its momentum.

Now Noble was filthy with the mud and straw he'd been packing into wooden forms, shaping the adobe bricks that would become the new barn and Papa's smithy.

"You need more patients," she told him. "You worry too much about me."

He gave her a long gaze. "It wouldn't matter."

He was always doing that, saying things like that. And her mind always went blank when he did.

"What have you brought us, *jenta mi?*"

She turned to Magnus, who was as wet as any day he spent over the forge, despite the hint of winter in the October air. He pulled a kerchief from his pocket and mopped his face, just as she'd seen him do at least every work hour in every year for the past dozen. It brought familiar things to a dusty town far from them.

"I cooked you fried chicken and corn dodgers," she told him. "Is that all right?"

"It is more than all right," Magnus replied, already digging in the crate for the treasure buried under the towel. "I know who taught you how to cook, and she cooked the best chicken in the country." He came away with a leg in one hand and one of the chunks of fried corn bread in the other.

Noble was dousing his face and neck at the trough filled for making adobe. The water dribbled down his chin and back, clumping the hair over his collar and creating spots and streaks of darker color on the placket of his blue shirt.

He'd come home from his call to the Schmidt house sometime during the night and slipped under the sheet without her knowing it. She knew it well enough when she came awake with him snuggled up to her back, his arm draped possessively over her waist and face buried in the side of her pillow.

Even the memory made her nerves tingle in chaos.

When she threw back the covers to flee, he held tighter.

. . . Amazing, the strength in a man's arm. Like the one he was rinsing at this very minute . . . the bands of muscles cording as he rotated this way and that.

"Don't go," he'd said, his voice muffled.

"I'm getting up," Sonja had replied.

"I'm your doctor; you need your rest."

"I'm the cook, and I've had my rest. And stay on your own side of the bed." She lifted his arm by his hand, set it aside, and sat up.

He gave her a glance out the corner of his eye. "I forgot, Mrs. Staley."

"I haven't, business partner."

He just closed his eyes again.

And she couldn't look away. Simply stared at the hair tousled wildly about his ear, face, and the pillow. At the fresh beard shading his jaw and the hand that lay where she left it. The size of one and a half of her own, its fingers curled loosely over the sheet . . . the skin looked soft. It was soft, if memory served her, with clean nails and veins that stood in relief under the dusting of golden hair. And he could make a study of his own anatomy, so clear were the muscles that shaped his shoulder and spread into his naked back.

The room was empty until he filled it with his presence each night, pressing the mattress with his length and weight, then groaning and growling gently—but no less deeply—as he stretched and settled in. Long after sleep took him, she listened to the sound she'd never heard before, a man breathing in the night silence around her.

He opened his eye, the one that wasn't embedded in the pillow. "Something wrong, partner?"

Heat surged into her face. She spun away. "Did Mr. Downey find you? I sent him to the Schmidts'."

"Yes. His son has swollen parotid glands."

"I beg your pardon?"

His voice was muffled.

"The mumps," he replied. "There appears to be an epidemic. I'm going to sleep for another hour or so. Tell Magnus I'll be there as soon as I can."

Before she could grab her clothes from the peg, he faded into sleep—or at least he never rolled over to watch her dress, as he could have done.

She cooked breakfast for Papa and Karl so they could get to work at the property, then walked to Mr. Gonzales' mercantile. When she returned at mid-morning, Noble was dressed and gone, the bed made neatly behind him. His coffee cup stared back at her from the washtub, and his chair sat open toward the room, as if he'd just risen from it.

Now at mid-afternoon, she watched him wipe his face, neck, and those arms on a kerchief he folded and stuffed back into his pocket.

Nothing was stationary between them. Nothing was defined—not like it was on the trail. There he kept his distance. Here . . . well, it was like that time Ander cornered a raccoon in the back stall of the barn. She stepped forward to peek—and jumped back, caught between curiosity and caution. Being married to Noble was like that—the wanting to study every profound difference between him and herself, but held by the tingling in her stomach when she did.

From across the way, Noble's gaze snapped to hers. There was possession in it, telling any who cared to see, that she was his, that they were husband and wife. That it had been his arm cinching her middle and his nose nuzzled into her pillow. That they shared everything from the same name, to the same bar of soap. That he wanted more. Wanted a wife. Wanted her—

She looked away. Too bad. And how dare him. They'd agreed. He'd promised. Besides, he'd change his mind if he knew the truth.

She eyed the rows of adobe drying in the sun. "How long will it take the bricks to dry, Papa?"

"About a week to dry and cure once we get them all made, and there are very thousands, *lille venn,*" Magnus replied. "Then there are the vigas—the roof beams—that must come from the mountains."

Sonja's stomach fell to her feet. "But you don't have to wait until the smithy is built before you move in, do you?"

Magnus waved his chickenless bone toward the house. "No, but it is very dirty. It will take a few days to evict the animals and make it suitable. We will begin as soon as the bricks are formed and cured." When she waited for more, he shrugged. "A few days."

"Oh." That was better. "Well, I'd better go home," she said to no one in particular. "I need to bake bread and get something ready for supper."

She turned to pick up the crate, but Noble was already bending for it.

"Thanks for thinking of us."

For her alone, that quiet tone. She looked up—and wanted to die for the sorrow of seeing what she couldn't have. He wouldn't want her if he knew the truth.

His eyes . . . so like that day in Independence . . .

Flutters stirred in her stomach.

Quickly, to show him he mattered no more than he ever had, she looked away. "You're welcome. I'll see you at supper."

Then she left the crate—and perhaps a little of herself—behind. She hurried but didn't look back.

Sonja's skirt didn't sway—it twitched as she strode out of Thaddeus' view.

Women.

She wrapped his hand yesterday. Let him kiss her on the forehead last night. And scowled at him now as if she might invite him to kiss his horse instead.

Women.

He shook his head. When Amanda got tight like that, it was usually for some capital offense like taking the last cup of coffee or wanting a little marital attention. His stomach soured, although this situation was nothing like that one had been, and this woman shared no similarities with the one who had come—and gone—before her. Sonja was just tired and not sure about him, yet. Give her a little more time and him a little more opportunity. He'd convince her.

"I am going to the market for some fruit," Karl announced suddenly.

Magnus just waved him away. "Hurry back."

"I will," Karl replied, already resetting his hat and striding away along the same street Sonja had retreated on. When Karl returned an hour later, he didn't have any fruit with him, and he was ravenously hungry.

It was only the next evening when Thaddeus' heart was dashed again. She was actually going to decline, and he had no contingency.

Then Magnus stepped in. "Go on, Sonja. Go for a walk with your husband. It is a pretty evening."

"I have sewing, Papa," she said. "I have to take in my dress."

The one of the two that still had room for a child.

Magnus gave her a gentle gaze. "In truth, I would enjoy the quiet. I have a sermon to prepare." He motioned toward the Bible he'd just opened. He would hold church in this very room the day after tomorrow.

And these were the right words, for her mouth formed an O. "I'm sorry. I would have—"

Magnus waved a massive hand. "Do not apologize. You forget how it is with a pastor." He chuckled. "Now you keep the schedule of a doctor. So go while you can. It will be good for all of us."

It was Sonja who kissed Magnus' cheek, but it was Thaddeus who silently pledged his fealty to the man who seemed as determined to make a proper couple of the Staleys. Thaddeus would take all the help he could get. It was harder to woo a wife than a sweetheart.

He shortened his steps to accommodate hers as they strolled down the street toward no place in particular. He watched her surreptitiously, eyeing the arms locked in her shawl and the hands occupied with holding it closed. He could try for looping her arm through his, but it wouldn't be a casual move. Perhaps if he commented on the autumn evening that was cast in hues of blue and purple, and peppered with childish giggles, front yard conversations, and dozens of suppers' fried foods.

Sonja nodded to Mr. Ruiz and three of his brood as they passed their yard. A goat stared around the corner of a house at them. It bleated but stood its ground. Not so for the chickens in the next yard, who scattered in a wave as they approached. The Vegas' dog barked from the open front door, then the oldest Vega boy came to get it. He waved as he dragged the animal inside.

"Thank you for helping Papa with the barn," Sonja said suddenly, quietly, and with little warmth.

The way she always thanked him for every little thing was too neighborly for husband and wife. For even business partners.

But Thaddeus said only, "You're welcome. I enjoy that sort of thing, once in a while."

"It gets you away from your desk." She scanned the horizon nonchalantly. "It's a good thing you don't hold your books very close, or you'd rub off the ink."

Levity, almost. This was better.

"Is that a polite way of saying I study too much?" he asked. "You wouldn't think so if it were you I was operating on."

"I think if you don't know it by now, you never will."

He glanced at her—and cautioned a truth. "I think I wouldn't have to read the same paragraph three times if you weren't so distracting."

"I try to be quiet. Just tell me the next time I'm bothering you."

She really didn't know. Foolish girl.

"You're bothering me now," he said, then more quietly, "Could you try a little harder not to be so pretty?"

Her next step fell a second out of rhythm with the ones before it. The one after that stopped altogether.

The day was reduced to gentle shadows. She looked lovely in them . . . cheeks downy and all that hair pillowed on top of her head. It teased him, made him think of dragging the pins from their duty . . . slowly, gently, until the spun gold cascaded past her shoulders and danced about her waist, trickling through his fingers on its way.

She looked up at him . . . cautiously, carefully . . . as if she suspected the war he waged—how he fought not to haul her into his arms and tumble into the sky of her eyes. Such lips . . .

Need me, Sonja, the words formed in Thaddeus' mind. *You don't have to fight anymore. You can lean on me now.*

She looked away suddenly but didn't seem to have any place for her attention to light. "I should get back. I need to work on that dress."

The smallest nuance in her stance signaled she intended to do just that. It prompted him to touch her arm, which gave him the courage to grip her shoulders and turn her toward him. He rubbed her arms through her shawl, wishing he could pull the right words from the warmth of her.

There probably weren't any right words. Just honest ones. "Don't take in the seams on that dress, Sonja."

She shrugged. "I really don't mind. It's not difficult work, it's just tedious. And I have only one dress that really fits until I finish."

She smiled, though it was a shy replica of her usual enthusiasm. It put him in the ascendancy, made him the authority placed there to ease her distress.

"Go to the mercantile tomorrow and buy some material for a new dress," Thaddeus said.

"That's not necessary. I can—"

"No, keep it the way it is." Then more quietly, "Save the dress. Save it for the next baby, Sonja."

Thirty-one

The amiable expression dropped from Sonja's lips, and the sky in her eyes turned stormy with realization and accusation. "You promised."

"I know," Thaddeus said. "It was a foolish idea, this arrangement. We should have a real marriage, Sonja. A real marriage with—"

"You promised."

This wasn't going as planned. She wasn't supposed to be so upset. Thaddeus searched for gentler words, wooing words—

She turned and stalked away.

He grabbed at her arm. "Wait. Sonja—"

She wrenched free, picking up her skirt with her pace. "Don't make a spectacle of us," she warned when he caught up to her. "I mean it. You've done enough."

"Sonja, let's talk about this."

"There's nothing to talk about," she whispered fiercely. "You want to go back on our bargain—a bargain that was your idea." She groaned. Her steps faltered. "Of course. That was the plan all along. How could I be so naive that I didn't see it?"

He caught her arm and hauled her to a stop. "Now wait just a minute. I didn't trick you—"

"Dr. Staley?"

They both looked up as a man skidded to a halt in front of them, his chest heaving with exertion. "Are you Dr. Staley?"

"Yes."

"It's my wife," the man said on raspy gasps for breath. "She's . . . in the family way, but she's having trouble."

"She's in labor?"

The man glanced hesitantly at Sonja before he nodded.

"How long?" Thaddeus asked.

"Since last evening," the man said. "After supper."

"Twenty-four hours?"

The man nodded. "She's getting so tired. She can't last much longer." He impaled Thaddeus with eyes fraught with worry. "I live quite a piece out. Can you come?"

"Go ask Magnus, my father-in-law, to saddle my horse," Thaddeus said. "I'll be right there."

The man spun away, running at a full stretch toward the house, while Thaddeus slid his arm around Sonja's waist and drew her into a brisk walk. The timing stunk. The sketch of her and Lars was already framed and under her pillow, but he'd have no chance to make a gift of it—or to press his case for a real relationship between them. He glanced at her. Have to convince her later. Until then, he had to suspend her actions—and reactions. Hated to wield his authority over her, but he'd use anything he had.

"I probably won't be home until tomorrow, but we'll continue this discussion then," he told her. "In the meantime, go to the mercantile in the morning, buy five yards of cloth, and get started on another dress. One for now."

She shot him a glare full of anger and a heap of unsaid words.

He tried again, more gently. "Please, Sonja. Leave that

other dress as it is until we can talk about this."

The problem was, Mrs. Bewel's baby was breach, and she hadn't the width to pass it. Once Thaddeus turned it—a difficult and agonizing manipulation she was miserable enough to beg for—and employed some obstetrical forceps, she delivered her first daughter.

Then she began to hemorrhage.

Sonja hugged herself against the late October chill and stared at the marker Noble had painted for Lars' grave. She closed her eyes and let herself go back . . . to feathery hair and a tiny face. So much like her, Noble had said. And so much like her.

She lifted her chin and inhaled deeply. Fireplace smoke, a variety of foods, and moisture. Smelled like fall. Everyone said it would snow soon, which would relieve the sameness of the orange-brown landscape. And Noble would probably come home today, as he said.

It was going to be awkward when he finally rode into the yard. She hadn't composed a speech for him yet. Anything she told him would lead to more questions, until they finally reached the place where she couldn't—wouldn't—answer any further. Oh, why couldn't everything go back to the way it was?

"What did he look like?"

Sonja didn't even bother to glance over her shoulder; she knew that voice.

"Lars," Karl said—as if she hadn't heard. "Did he look like his father?"

Noble's sketch would show him. It was beautiful. She'd stared at it for long moments, convincing herself there'd been a child she'd held and kissed and loved. She'd been foggy . . . so tired . . . but Noble remembered. Sketched every detail. And added a kindness to the lines in drawing her.

"Thaddeus said he looked like his mother," she told him. "Did Papa come back with you?"

"No, he is still working. I came back to get a coat."

She scanned the horizon. It wasn't cold, just chilly. Papa would come home with perspiration rings on his clothes. She glanced over her shoulder. No coat.

"Where is this husband of yours?" Karl asked. "Does he often leave you alone so long?"

"That's none of your concern," she replied tiredly.

Karl didn't press further. A moment later his shadow rippled over the Santa Fe soil as he walked away.

As if he felt the race of Thaddeus' heart himself, Hippocrates sped his pace when they passed the freight yard of Russell, Majors, and Waddell. Sonja was only blocks away now, her hair gleaming and her eyes bright. She'd smile and laugh again, their disagreement forgotten, because that's the way she was put together. Sometimes she teetered and wobbled after she leaped into something—as if its reality was bigger than she'd expected. But with a little time—sometimes only minutes—she'd settle in and get as happy as if she'd planned things that way all along.

Thaddeus checked his time piece. Two-forty. He hadn't been home in nineteen hours. Certainly long enough for her to miss him. Maybe long enough to see he wasn't going back on their bargain. He was trying to strike a new one.

Wait a minute. Wasn't that . . .

"Karl?"

The young man stopped mid-stride. "Oh. You are home."

"Finally. How's the construction?"

Karl motioned in the direction of the property. "We are almost finished making bricks. Harley has been able to help us. Monday we will begin cleaning the house so we can move in while they cure."

Thaddeus nodded, then leaned on the saddle horn and glanced around, but there wasn't much else to say, and the person he really wanted to see was Sonja.

He shifted, making ready to depart. "Well, tell Magnus and Harley I'll be there as soon as I can."

"Yes. I will do that," Karl said.

Thaddeus nudged Hippocrates in motion. At the house, he tethered the horse to the stake buried for that purpose—he'd unsaddle him in a minute—grabbed his medical saddlebags and stepped inside.

Sonja was just coming out of the bedroom. Her features fell in surprise and her hand froze at the nape of her neck, where she'd been smoothing her hair. "Noble."

She looked wonderful—healthy and creamy and soft. Her golden sweeps of hair were coiled at the crown of her head, and she wore the dress she'd already taken in. He glanced into the room behind her. The one they'd fought over was hanging on a peg, not noticeably narrower than it had been, but it would be impossible to know without asking. He'd get to that in a minute—after he controlled the urge to haul her into his arms and press her against the door in a kiss that would make them both senseless.

"Hello," Sonja said, then resumed her progress into the parlor.

She walked right by him. Just like that. As if he'd simply returned from the market to fetch flour for bread.

Okay, he'd play the hand dealt him.

"Hello," Thaddeus said with a pretty admirable semblance of calm.

"Did everything go well?" she asked, heading for the kitchen.

"Eventually. It was an instrument delivery—risky. Then she hemorrhaged."

"Did Mr. Peña find you?"

"No."

"His mother is very old and sick. She's probably dying, but her daughter wants you to come. She gave me directions to their home."

"All right."

There was coffee on the fire. He set his saddlebags on the floor beside his desk, strode to the kitchen, and reached in front of Sonja to take a cup from the wall. She leaned away. Ever so slightly, but obviously she hadn't talked herself into anything—not anything he cared for, anyway. He poured himself a cup of coffee and sat at the table, while she asked no questions and made no comments. She didn't even turn around. He scanned the parlor walls for his sketch, but it wasn't hanging on any of them.

Thaddeus held a sigh. Time to gather clues. "Sonja, are you angry because I was gone so long?"

Heaven knows, he and Amanda had turned circles over this one.

She looked over her shoulder, eyebrows raised. "No. Should I be?"

Ouch. That was worse. Never again was too soon for another shot of cold indifference. Had enough of that from the *first* wife—thank you very much, Frank Feiden, you sneaking worm.

Thaddeus blew across his coffee. "I thought you might be upset because I left you alone for so long."

"I wasn't alone. Papa was here."

That was worse still.

"Are you upset about our fight last evening?" he asked.

"No, not upset," she said with caution. She'd been pouring ingredients into a mixing bowl. Now she paused. "I did as you asked, but we need to . . . discuss things."

"All right." Except her tone said he wouldn't like what she had to say.

The motion in Sonja's arms stopped, but she didn't turn around. "I want to take in the dress. I want things to stay as they are."

"I want to be married, Sonja. Really married."

No reply.

"Don't you care for me?" he asked—a monumental act of bravery.

"Of course."

He breathed again. It was a beginning. "Don't you want children?"

"Yes, but—" She must have spoken too quickly, for she stopped and said, more definitively, "No."

"I don't believe that."

She wouldn't either if she'd seen her face while she held Lars. Not if she'd seen her smile as the child nursed at her breast.

"Well, it's true," she said.

Thaddeus sipped from his cup and set it down, wrapping his hands around its warmth. "Sonja, I know you're grieving right now. You don't think you'll ever be able to love another baby the way you loved Lars, but it will get . . . Give it a chance. You'll change your mind."

She was already shaking her head. "That's not it."

"Are you sure?"

"Yes." She sighed, the effort lifting her shoulders. "Can't we be friends? Why do we have to complicate what is already good?"

That was simple. Because what they had wasn't good. It was less than nothing. And he wouldn't settle for it. Not anymore.

"Thank you for the picture," she said, as if her gratitude were a suitable consolation. "It's very good, especially of Lars. It looks just like—" She choked on her words before gathering herself in the lifting of her chin and the squaring of her shoulders. "You should be selling your work. Women would stand in line to have you draw them, so. You're . . . very complimentary."

No. He drew what he saw.

He got to his feet and went to her. He lifted his hands to touch her shoulders, but let them drop to his sides—the presumptuous appendages. Something had happened. She hadn't talked herself into embracing his suggestion as if it were what she planned all along. She hadn't even eased herself into making the best of a bad situation. She hated where she was. Wanted out. *Stay away from me, forever,* that's what she was really saying.

He stepped back to his coffee and stared at the diploma hanging over the bookcase. If he'd been one to give up at the first obstacle, he'd have never made it to the university, much less *through* it. The war wasn't over yet.

"I'm going to repack my saddlebags and head over to the Peñas'," he said, turning the empty mug around, one way then the other, on its bottom. He drained the dregs and reached past Sonja to set it in the washbasin. "I should be home for supper. If I finish sooner, I'll go help your father."

"He'll appreciate that," she told the mixing bowl.

He paused before turning away. She turned sideways, putting him on one side and the cupboard on the other. He studied the soft little hairs tickling just below the tender ear he could see so well.

"You look very pretty today."

"Thank you," she said, but her chin lifted and turned away even further, making it a terse piece of gratitude.

He headed for his desk and medical saddlebags. "Oh, I almost forgot. I saw Karl on my way home. Did he—"

"He came to get his coat."

Thaddeus nodded . . . and stared. Sonja answered before he even asked the question. And Karl might have intended to get a coat, but he hadn't left with one.

It was interesting to watch—and so obvious. Thaddeus didn't understand why he hadn't seen it before, the way Karl watched Sonja, while she pretended she didn't notice when the young man tested and flexed the muscles his age and hard labor were growing. Interesting, this, and disappointing. And all too familiar.

It took Magnus, Karl, and Thaddeus all of Monday and Tuesday to clean the new house and to fill it with the belongings stored at the Russell, Majors, and Waddell freight yard.

Each time Sonja checked their progress, counting down the minutes until she could have her own room back, it slapped Thaddeus in the face. And each time she left, Karl had reason to leave, following not ten minutes behind her. He never returned in fewer than forty-five.

It had been four days and four nights since Thaddeus returned from the Bewel place. Four days of Sonja avoiding him. Four nights of her hugging her side of the bed. Roughly one hundred hours of near silence—and worse than living with Amanda had been. At least she pretended to love him, even right up to the last vicious moment.

Sonja was standing at the kitchen stirring something in a mixing bowl when Thaddeus stepped into the parlor from outside. He glanced to her room—and huffed a silent breath. That was quick. Magnus and Karl had barely moved out; she was all moved in.

He watched her work. Watched her skirt swing back and forth, propelled by the rapid motion of her right arm. Just the two of them for dinner tonight—unless she'd invited Magnus and Karl to join them. He snorted again at the prospect of another opportunity to observe his wife trying to ignore a man who studied her every move.

"What's between you and Karl, Sonja?" Thaddeus asked, his voice assaulting the quiet as if the room were a tomb.

But it was nothing like the sound of the bowl thudding on the clay floor. Sonja stared down at it as if it had jumped from her hands. She looked to Thaddeus, then looked away, eyes darting in confusion.

Thirty-two

I beg your pardon?" Sonja asked, almost dazed.

A tension began to build in Thaddeus' stomach. He wanted to run, but pressed forward. "Karl. What's going on between you and him?"

"Nothing," she replied, dropping to a crouch to retrieve the bowl. She could have merely bent at the waist to pick it up. And her tone was anything but convincing.

She stood again and brushed at absolutely nothing on her skirt, then cast her attention into the bowl—except she didn't seem to know what she was looking for inside it. She turned to the cupboard, giving him her back. "He's Papa's apprentice. The son of an old friend in Norway. That's all."

Thaddeus strolled to the fireplace and topped off his coffee, then straddled the table bench . . . while he felt strangely split, watching himself be so calm when the world was about to drop out from under him.

"He follows you. Every day you brought something to eat to your father's smithy, Karl made some lame excuse to leave a few minutes after you. He never returned in fewer than forty-five minutes."

Sonja looked over her shoulder. "He followed me?"

"It looked that way."

She turned back to the kitchen, though she made no move to salvage—or abandon—the cornmeal she'd spilled. "He didn't come here."

"The day I came home from the Bewels', he'd been here."

"He came to get a coat."

"He left without it."

Silence.

"And you were coming out of the bedroom when I walked in, just a few minutes later," he said, so controlled, as if he were a hired barrister interviewing a witness.

"I would never do what you imply," she hissed.

The calm fled. "You'd never do such a thing with me, you mean."

She stiffened. "That's crude . . . and cruel."

Anger fired as if it had been only sleeping, finding every corner of himself that had been cool and methodical. "No, cruel is the way he looks at you—at my own table, Sonja. Cruel is the way you look at everyone but him. You try to pretend he isn't there. Something's going on, and you're my wife—despite what you prefer to think of the matter."

She lowered her head and told the cupboard, "You must have more faith in me than that. Forget him. He's only my father's apprentice . . . and a vain man."

For a moment it was only any statement she might make, then the words drilled a hole in him. Flushed him with cold—*He was vain. Very prideful about his strength.* That's what she'd said about the father of her child, the night she helped him tend to Zeke.

"Tell me the name of Lars' father, Sonja," Thaddeus said, then held his breath. Stared hard at her back, right hand choking the coffee cup and welcoming the burn while he watched to catch every nuance in her body.

Sonja shook her head. "He was no one."

In three steps, Thaddeus was at her side. "Tell me Karl wasn't Lars' father."

She already faced the cupboard. Now she turned her chin away. "It doesn't matter—"

"Look at me, Sonja. Look me right in the face and tell me Karl wasn't Lars' father."

Her shoulder collapsed, and a sob burst from her throat.

And the floor fell away.

No. No. Not again.

She buried her face in her hands and cried, while he could only stare. Karl. It was Karl, all along. It was still Karl. In his own house. In the rooms he thought his own. Behind his back. Furtive glances. Stolen moments. And laughing at him, the heartsick fool who was too stupid to see what was right in front of him.

Not again. Never, ever again.

He turned and strode to her bedroom. This time would be different. He swung the lantern and her hairbrush from the overturned crate beside her bed, set the lantern on the floor, plopped the crate on the mattress, and dropped the hairbrush inside. He spun, snatched her clothes from their pegs, and began to fill the crate, tossing in every evidence of her . . . her Bible . . . the old bedroll . . . the sketch of Lars that had been hanging under her clothes—

"What are you doing?"

Sonja stood in the doorway, her eyes rimmed in red but open wide.

"Taking you back to your father." Thaddeus surveyed the room, looking for pieces of her to cram in the crate.

"Why?"

Why? Surely she wasn't as naive as she looked, standing there with her delicate brow creased so deeply. He heaved a bitter laugh. The drama called for a look of shock, not innocence. She should work on that.

He turned back to the room. It looked like this was everything. If he found something else, he could always leave it on her doorstep.

He jerked her shawl from the last peg and shoved it at her. Then he braced the crate against his hip, grabbed her hand, and led her through the parlor and out the door.

She trotted to keep up with him, her shawl a bundle in her arms. He should slow down, but that was a caring person's thing to do.

"What are you doing? Where are we going?" she wanted to know.

"You don't get it, do you?" he asked quietly. They would already give the neighbors an eyeful. No sense in filling their ears, as well. "I won't tolerate an unfaithful wife, Sonja. Forgive me, but I'm just peculiar that way."

"I haven't been—"

She tried to pull free. When that didn't work she tried to stop. He didn't let her.

"And seeing as how the marriage was never consummated, this should be a pretty simple matter," he continued. They turned the corner, heading north toward Magnus' house. "I'll start the proceedings on an annulment—"

"No—"

"—as soon as the territorial offices open tomorrow. Then you'll be unencumbered, and Karl can sweep you off your dainty little feet." He gave her a glance. "But take some care, Sonja. Make him marry you. You weren't cautious the first time, and you might already be with child again." He turned back to the street. "You were about a week early for resuming marital activity, but I assume he caused you no damage. If you need someone to deliver you—or you'd like to know how to have your fun without getting caught—go to a midwife or get your information from Berta. I have all the patients I can handle right now, and I don't anticipate any openings in the future."

"Noble, you don't understand—"

"I understand just fine, Sonja, believe me. I simply won't shield you." He stopped. "Tell me, just how were you going to explain it when he got you with child again?" His blood turned cold. "Would that have driven you to accept my attentions? So I'd believe the child was mine—if you could bear to have me touch you?" He shook his head. Gripped her hand tighter. "I've been a fool once. I won't be again."

Sonja watched him march just a little ahead of her. Watched him pull her along—

He was really doing this. For whatever reason, he was really—

Don't do this. Please don't. Please.

She couldn't even speak. Couldn't seem to make her mind work. Because none of this was happening.

The air around Magnus' door held the dusty, musty smell of swept floors and wet mud, and no sound trickled from inside. But Thaddeus rapped his knuckles on the paint-chipped planks. Sonja sniffled beside him.

Let her cry. Let her go right ahead and pretend it hurt. In fact, the scene—for her later defense—wouldn't play quite the same without it.

When no one answered his second knock, he tried the knob. It turned freely. He pushed the door open and peered inside, then dropped her crate in the dim wedge of evening light that sneaked past him.

"Noble. Please. It's not what you think."

He turned to her. "No? What is it, then?"

Sonja swallowed hard but said nothing. Only stared back. He snorted. She had nothing to say—except excuses and lies and deceit.

He touched his fingers to the brim of his hat. "I'll let you know as soon as I have the paperwork for you to sign."

Sonja cast about frantically, so frantically, for a reason to give him. Anything.

Don't just . . . throw me away. Don't believe what you believe, for it isn't what you think.

But she couldn't tell him what it was.

Don't let him do this, Father. Please, Daddy, make him see. Make him understand. Tell him, because I can't. I just can't.

She swallowed hard but sobbed anyway . . . and found the courage to look into his eyes. "I've never even kissed another man."

"I'm the only man who's ever kissed you?"

Thaddeus asked it only because repeating it came automatically. The idea was so ludicrous, he couldn't even qualify it with a laugh.

Sonja nodded in reply to his question, and fresh tears rolled down her cheeks, toward her swollen lips.

Lips that had never—

He did laugh. "Sure, Sonja. Whatever you say." Then he walked away.

Later Thaddeus sat at the table, hands curled around the cup of coffee he'd left behind. It was cold. It didn't matter. The fire crackled to embers in the corner, the clock ticked softly on his desk, and Sonja's room loomed large and empty over his shoulder. The shadow of the mixing bowl crept along the cupboard and climbed the kitchen wall. The light turned pink and gold and dim around him. And no patients knocked at the door to offer rescue.

Don't do this don't do this don't do this to us, his mind chanted, as if Sonja could hear him.

Fool. There'd never been an *us.* Never a chance for an *us,* because she never stopped loving Karl, regardless of what she told Thaddeus every time he asked. How she must have laughed inside when he held her hand and prayed with her. What a silly simpering fool he was, giving her moon eyes and thinking her a marvelous gift from God. She was some gift, all right.

He sneered, peering up through his brows. "Pardon me if I don't appreciate Your generosity, won't You, God? And I can do without Your bent sense of humor, too."

He waited, but no lightning sliced through the ceiling to strike him dead. It never would—to his dismay. God had already taken His revenge, choosing more insidious ways to play.

Sonja would be cooking supper about now. Maybe already cleaning the dishes.

Ha! Would like to have been a mouse in the corner when she explained her presence to her father. Magnus would do some marching of his own—with Sonja in tow. Would pound on his door and demand an explanation. Probably tonight. But there was too much to tell and nothing to reconcile.

Sorry, old man, but your daughter is an adulteress and your apprentice, her accomplice.

Her partner. Her lover. Kissing her and touching her.

Putting his babies in her.

Thaddeus threw the cup at the wall. Coffee arced beautifully before the metal twanged against the adobe and fell to the floor, rolling awkwardly to a stop. He rubbed his face with the palms of his hands and groaned. Blast it all, not again. He'd tried so hard not to make the same mistake twice. Only this time was worse. He'd loved Sonja. Really loved her, for all the right reasons. He still loved her. Would almost take her back. If she came to the door and cried and promised she'd never do it again. He'd believe her, if she came. Would do anything to have her back.

No. Couldn't take her back.

Someone knocked on the door.

Oh yes, he could.

The bench tipped over in his rush, and its wind lifted his hair as he yanked the door open. He composed his features, but his heart fell anyway, and the breath left his lungs as he stared at the threshold.

"Oh."

"Oh?" Jackson bellowed. "Who was you expectin'? President Buchanan?"

"No, I thought you might be Sonja . . . or maybe Magnus."

Jackson's chin jerked into his throat. "Why would you think that? They got some particular way of knockin'?"

"No," Thaddeus replied tiredly and stepped out of the way. "Come in. You want some coffee or something?"

The man passed inside and set his hat on the desk. "Ain't no sense in askin' for nothin' stronger. Already know you ain't got it—unless I'm sick, and it ain't worth sufferin' your pokin' and proddin'."

Thaddeus heaved a breath. Too bad he wasn't a drinking man, else he'd be doing it now. Too bad he wasn't given to dipping in his own laudanum, as some physicians were.

Heaven knew he had the pain to warrant it.

"Where's the little missy?" Jackson scanned the room, his attention lingering on the spilled cornmeal, the tossed cup, and the overturned bench.

Thaddeus righted the latter. "She's gone."

"What you mean, she's gone? Dead, you mean?"

"Of course not. I took her back to her father. We're getting an annulment."

"An annulment? Thunderation, boy, what you been tryin' to do to yourself? Ruin everythin'?"

"If you must know, she's been committing adultery," Thaddeus said, plucking his coffee cup from the floor.

Jackson's head jerked as if Thaddeus had struck him. "Sonja?" He scowled and pointed to the bench. "Here, sit before you fall down. You look like you just stepped in a mine shaft. I'll make the coffee. My hair's as white as I care to have it."

Thaddeus collapsed on the seat, set his folded arms on the table, and stared at the scars in the wood.

Jackson gathered the pot from the fire, lifted the lid, and peered inside. "What makes you think Sonja's creasin' somebody's sheets? And you think you could fire up some light? I don't see as good as I used to."

Thaddeus started to get up.

Jackson waved him back. "Naw. Sit. I'll do it." Then he did, and set the lantern on the table.

Thaddeus sighed. "It's Karl, her father's apprentice. He watches her all the time. And he was always making some excuse to leave when we were working on the smithy."

"That don't mean he was comin' here. What does Sonja say?"

"That he wasn't coming here."

What did he expect her to say?

"Was she moonin' after him?" Jackson asked.

"She made a point to look everywhere else. That's how I knew. She acted so strange when Karl was around."

"Maybe—"

"Anyone could have seen it, Jackson . . . and she admitted Karl was Lars' father."

Jackson's gnarled old hand stopped over the pot, heaping spoon of coffee and all. "That so?"

"Yes. They're lovers. Right here in my own house."

"She tell you that? She won't lie, you know."

"She didn't need to. I have eyes."

Jackson dropped the coffee in the pot, smacked the lid in place, and set it at the edge of the fire, which he began to build up with corn cobs from the little pile beside the hearth. "Well, it don't figure by my cipherin.' Sonja don't like men."

Thaddeus chuckled. The old man had fallen on his head. "She likes you."

"I'm old."

"She likes Harley."

"Like a big brother."

"Well, she don't like me," Thaddeus said, slipping into Jackson's bad grammar.

"No, I reckon she don't sometimes, but that ain't no need for alarm. People are all the time lovin' folks they don't much like."

Thaddeus' head came up. "She doesn't love me." The idea was ludicrous.

Jackson shook his head as he stirred the fire. "You ever get a hankerin' to go cuttin' on me, remind me to do my consultin' with the barber. Your eyes ain't any better than mine, Doc. 'Course she loves you. Who you think she was followin' when she left her only kin and walked for days the other direction?" He grunted upright and chucked his stirring stick into the fire. "I'll give you some clues. It weren't me, and it weren't Harley, and it sure weren't some other fuzzy bullwhacker she ain't seen since."

"She didn't even know my name."

"Don't matter. She knew your face." Jackson waggled his fingers in the air. "Somethin' about you havin' tender eyes. Or maybe they was beau-tee-ful. I don't know, it was some such female nonsense."

Heat crept into Thaddeus' cheeks. If she thought that, she never shared it with him. Secrets. Always secrets.

Quiet settled between them. The clock ticked softly, the water on the sides of the coffeepot sizzled, and Jackson claimed a seat on the opposite bench.

Needing to think, Thaddeus pushed from his spot and stepped to the window behind his desk. The sun was hanging over the horizon, casting a long shadow behind the sign and hitching post in the yard.

"What do you mean, she doesn't like men?" he asked, pitiful question that it was. Surely he knew more about her than to even have to ask. She was his wife.

Had been his wife.

But he loved her anyway. Always would.

"Them bullwhackers was all the time sniffin' around, askin' her to go for walks and teasin' with her and such," Jackson said. "Even after Harley made it plain he considered her his property. But she wouldn't have no part of it. Not with the young ones. The old ones, she treated like uncles. The young ones? She said her polite no-thank-yous and found some work to do at the wagon."

Thaddeus had braced an outstretched arm on the window frame. Now he looked over it at Jackson.

"If Karl was the one what got her with child, he must have been powerful mean to her," Jackson continued. "The little missy acts like all young bucks is out to hurt her."

Thaddeus pressed his mouth into his arm and rested there, narrowing his eyes in thought. Come to think of it, the old man was right—but it was an odd smattering of pieces that just wouldn't quite take shape. All summer she insisted Karl didn't matter anymore. Whatever the man did to hurt her, he did it well enough to convince her he didn't care about her or Lars—and that she didn't love him anymore.

Until she saw him again. Then their romance fired again.

Thaddeus sighed into the sleeve of his shirt. There was nothing more to see than what he already knew. She'd lied. About everything.

"You ever know her to kiss Harley?" Thaddeus asked, just to confirm it.

Jackson swung his head wide. "No, sir. And I wouldn't have neither. Why, Harley was grumblin' hisself when he left for Independence, how Sonja wouldn't even give him a kiss good-bye. Said she'd never given him so much as a peck on the cheek." He laughed. "Should have seen his face when she tipped up those pretty little lips for you to kiss on your weddin' day—and her papa standin' there smilin' his encouragement."

Thaddeus turned back to the window. So she told the truth about that. It didn't mean she'd told the truth—

Wait a minute. Never been kissed by any other man? No one but him? Not even by Karl? What kind of romance was it when a man seduced a woman, made love to her, got her with child, without—

Thirty-three

No.
        Thaddeus closed his eyes in pain. The room wobbled as if it were on water.

No.

All the blood rushed to his feet. His stomach turned over and turned again. He stepped from the window frame then grabbed it again for balance.

No.

It was true—and it was all there. Sonja hadn't ever been kissed. A man could tell these things. Her lips were hesitant and unschooled. She blushed at even seeing him in his small clothes. She shrank away from any nearness to him in bed, as if she were timid and shy.

Sonja had never had a shy and timid moment in her life.

And Lars' delivery? She'd hated it. He'd assumed it was the pain, but it was more than that. She'd despised the . . . *indignity* of it. As if there were shame in her body.

Swiveling, he caught Jackson's attention. "Rape."

In an instant, Jackson's stare grew intense.

"Karl raped her," Thaddeus said again.

Jackson stared back with brown eyes turning old, right

there in front of him. The man winced. "You sure, Doc? That's a powerful accusation."

Thaddeus' heart collapsed on itself. "She told me, but she didn't realize it. She said I was the only man to ever kiss her. Jackson, she's so innocent, she just had a baby and doesn't know she was supposed to have been kissed."

Softly but quite succinctly, Jackson cursed.

Thaddeus shook his head, as if it would level what had been set to teetering. "I've got to go to her. I've got to apologize and bring her back."

"Thunderation," Jackson hissed.

"What?"

Jackson jumped to his feet. "You got to do more than that. I saw Magnus this afternoon. He was horsed up and headed to Taos on business. Said he'd be gone a few days."

"And Karl stayed behind," Thaddeus said, the cinch on his stomach already providing the answer.

"Yep."

Thaddeus dived for his room to grab his coat and hat, while Jackson pulled the coffeepot from the fireplace and prepared to leave the fire he'd just built up. Thaddeus was strapping his sidearm on his hips when he met Jackson at the door.

The man nodded at the weapon. "That for self-defense or justice?"

Thaddeus met his stare. "I haven't decided yet."

They just ran, silently deciding against saddling a horse. It would take too long, and Thaddeus only had one, anyway. They should have brought a lantern, though. Night was chasing them.

They'd hardly turned the first corner when a wagon met them coming from the other direction.

"Doc!"

It was his neighbor, Mr. Ruiz, who hauled a team of mules

to a halt beside them and motioned to the bed of the wagon. "Doc! It is your wife's family. The young man—he ran into the road, and I hit him."

Thaddeus' gaze darted from Mr. Ruiz to the wagon. "Karl? You hit Karl? With the wagon?"

"*Sí, sí.* It was an accident. He ran very fast."

"How bad is he?"

"I do not know. He is—what you say? Looks sleeping."

Thaddeus stepped to the back of the wagon where Karl was laid out, his feet hanging over the end. It was difficult to see in the fading light, but there didn't appear to be any dark stains of blood on his clothes. He pressed two fingers to Karl's throat; the pulse was fast but steady.

They were all watching him—Jackson, Mr. Ruiz, and the crowd of neighbors who'd come to feed their curiosity. Wouldn't they be surprised if he just walked away, saying he'd wanted the man dead anyway? That Mr. Ruiz's mules had saved him the trouble? Or he could be more cunning about it—take Karl home, bandage him, then provide him a generous dose of chloroform. No one would ever suspect that Karl hadn't died of his injuries.

No one . . . except himself and God. And he'd already disappointed both of them enough today.

"Doc?"

Thaddeus gave Jackson a glance and looked up to Mr. Ruiz. "Where is my wife? Did you see her?"

The man shook his head, obviously confused as to why he should have seen Sonja.

Thaddeus motioned the other direction. "Take him to my house. I'll be right there."

Mr. Ruiz cracked the reins over the mules' backs, lurching the wagon into motion.

Thaddeus turned to Jackson. "Sonja must still be at her father's."

"I'll go check," Jackson told him then paused. He nodded toward the departing wagon. "Not many men would be doin' what you're doin'."

"I don't have any choice."

"Sure you do. Just wanted to let you know I respect you for it." With that, he ambled away as quickly as his wearying body would take him.

His heart following Jackson, Thaddeus turned toward the house and broke into a fast walk.

There were plenty of watchers from the crowd who were willing to carry Karl's unconscious body into Thaddeus' bed. Then there were just as many who were eager to fetch and light lanterns, fill pots with water and set them on the fire to heat, and help strip Karl down to his bare chest and the hair on his legs. At that point, someone, probably Mrs. Ruiz, judging by the sound of her voice, shooed all the hatted heads out of the house. The resulting silence was deafening.

She was just closing the door when Thaddeus stepped into the parlor. She turned at the sound of his boots. "Pardon me, Doctor. I help?"

"No, thank you. I think I can manage from here. I appreciate everything you've already done."

She glanced toward the bedroom, brown eyes puddling with worry. "The man. He will be . . . not dead?"

Thaddeus nodded. "I'll do my best." Despite his desire to do otherwise.

"*Sí.*" She nodded sadly and scanned the room. "You want I bring food?"

True enough, there wasn't a morsel in sight—unless one counted the corn dodgers hardening in the bowl on the cupboard. She'd obviously cleaned up what was on the floor.

Thaddeus shook his head. Wouldn't be able to push it past his teeth.

Mrs. Ruiz wasn't satisfied with that, but she left on a warm smile and a dozen reminders to come and get her if he needed anything. He stepped into the examination room.

Karl wasn't as banged up as he probably should have been, considering. The left half of his face had long scrapes where he'd ridden the road on it, his left knee was scratched and swelling under a bruise, and his left wrist was broken. Those were the injuries Thaddeus saw with his eyes. He set the bell of his stethoscope on Karl's chest to gather information about the less visible . . . and revised his assessment immediately; Karl's left lung gurgled sickeningly with each breath. Thaddeus searched gently with his fingers. Sure enough, two, maybe three, of Karl's ribs were broken. One, or all, had punctured his lung.

Thaddeus fell back in his chair and pulled the earpieces from his ears. There was nothing he could do. Karl wouldn't make it through the night. As if to confirm it, the young man coughed, spattering blood on his lips.

Thaddeus pulled the blanket to Karl's chin. Then he sat back and stared at the man who was so proud of his budding blacksmith physique. So proud of the muscles that had overpowered that little woman.

He snorted. Which of them hurt Sonja more? Karl, by his invasion, or him, with false accusation and rejection? He shook his head. He'd never forget the things he said to her, the way he dragged her—cast her—from her home.

He leaned forward, setting his elbows on his knees. He rubbed his face with his palms, then set his chin on his balled hands.

If she never forgave him, he wouldn't blame her. But Sonja wasn't built that way. She'd forgive him, take him back, because that was the way she was made. She'd be standing at his shoulder right now if he'd had a measure of such grace.

Grace. Unmerited favor. Nothing deserved. Nothing earned.

He stared at the floor, gathering words. His throat closed. He swallowed. Swallowed again, but the tears rose anyway . . . puddled . . . and rolled from his eyes.

I don't deserve any of it. None of it. Not where I am. Not her. Not You. I don't even have anything to offer—no redeeming qualities—for even my skills at healing come from You.

He sniffed. He swallowed again, then just gave up, letting his shoulders shake with the sob that threatened to tear him into pieces from the inside.

God . . . forgive me. Forgive my disbelief and my arrogance . . . my bitterness—and the blame I placed on You. I've been angry all these years because of Amanda . . . and You didn't do it. I did. You told me not to marry that woman, that she'd be no good for me.

He sighed, a ragged sound.

She wasn't. So, left to myself, I can make a pretty tidy mess of things, you know that? Yes, You know that. I know it, now.

You gave me a Christian wife, and I didn't even ask.

He removed his spectacles, wiped his face with his hands, then combed them through his hair.

Give her back. Please bring her back. I'll appreciate her now. Just help me take care of her. Help me treat her like the gift she is. Help me be the Christian man she deserves. Help me live up to the faith she always had in me.

His eyes closed on a new wave of remorse, followed closely by the warmth of hope.

Help me accept Your forgiveness. Help me forgive myself. And keep me, Lord. Never let me walk away again.

For a long time, Thaddeus sat, sniffing and praying and silently crying. Sometimes leafing through the sins that needed absolution. Sometimes profoundly thankful that they were swept away so quickly, so cleanly, as if they'd never been. And he recalled a Scripture . . . something about God forgiving sin and taking it as far away as the east is from the west. . . .

Sonja would know. Would quote the verse from memory.

Had to get her back. And he would. Because the Lord would help.

Thaddeus sighed deeply, lighter than he had been, and straightened, taller than he had been. He wiped his spectacles, cleaner than he had been, then reset the lenses and rose from his chair to gather up his tools and bandages. He had all but his stethoscope in their proper places when he paused over Karl, who fought so desperately to live, chest heaving as he tried to fill his damaged lung. Very soon, he would stand before the Lord, Who would demand an accounting of his life.

Thaddeus' jaw clenched. Karl didn't deserve it—but then, who did? Certainly not himself. But he'd gotten another chance. Would get as many as he needed. And it would be the thing Sonja would do, regardless of what the man had done to her.

He reclaimed his chair and spoke, his voice not gruff but not gentle. "Karl . . . there's nothing I can do. You're dying. And you don't have much time."

Karl didn't even twitch. Not even an eyelash. But Thaddeus felt compelled to speak, just in case Karl could hear him.

"I know you've heard all this before, from Sonja if not from Magnus," Thaddeus continued, "but I'll remind you, in case you can't think straight. The Lord isn't going to be . . . pleased with what you've done. He's not pleased with any of us, because we're all bent on sin and making our own way. The only defense—the only good work you can take to the throne of God—is the shed blood of Jesus." He paused and recited the only Scripture he could lay his hands on at the moment and under those circumstances. "If we confess our sins, he is faithful and just to forgive us our sins, and to cleanse us from all unrighteousness."

He paused again. "They don't accept any other coin, there, Karl. So ask forgiveness. Just ask. It's so simple, most people miss it, but don't wait until it's too late. You're almost there now."

For a long moment Thaddeus watched for any recognition. Maybe Karl hadn't even heard him—

Karl's eyelids fluttered . . . and finally opened. His gaze cast about aimlessly, as if no one controlled it, before it found Thaddeus. Oh, and the expression in his eyes—so heavy with terror and regret.

Karl stared. Thaddeus stared. And Sonja hovered between them. Until something—Someone—greater spanned them.

Karl coughed, and tried not to for the pain of it. His gaze needed . . . reached . . . knew . . . relaxed . . . then peace settled into it—just before his eyes closed. Thaddeus pressed his fingers to Karl's throat. The rhythm was still there . . . perhaps beating from a forgiven heart, now.

Thaddeus sighed, stepped into the doorway, and leaned against the jamb. He alternated between glancing at the clock and staring at the fire. Jackson should be back by now. He must not have found Sonja, or he would have been.

He'll return soon, and Sonja is safe.

Thaddeus froze. Hadn't heard that voice—that assurance—for a long time. Was it his imagination? No. Yes. No, he'd definitely heard it.

Someone rapped on the door. He rushed to answer it.

"She ain't there, Doc," Jackson said before Thaddeus could even ask the question. He trudged into the parlor, shaking his head. "I checked Magnus' place, then just walked the streets, figurin' there ain't too many places she could be, but she ain't nowhere. It's like she don't want to be found." He jerked his head in the direction of Thaddeus' room, where the lantern still burned. "How's he?"

Thaddeus shook his head in reply.

"That bad, huh?"

"A punctured lung. And who knows what other internal injuries."

Jackson cocked back his hat and sighed. "S'pose it's a sad thing when somebody dies. Even when they was a varmint. How long, you reckon?"

"Soon."

Jackson stepped to the table and peered into their cups, trying to decide which was which, then bent to the fire and poured them both full of coffee. It would probably keep him awake, but Thaddeus accepted a cup. Wouldn't be sleeping anyway.

He sniffed and cleared his throat. If Jackson had noticed he'd been crying, he didn't make it plain. Stepping to the doorway of the examination room, he leaned against the jamb. Karl coughed again, a weak and feeble effort compared to the energy he spent reaching for breath. If God were merciful, the man would die quickly.

Thaddeus turned, putting the woodwork at the center of his back. "Did you go into Magnus' house?"

"Yep. No sign of her."

"Anything tossed about, like there might have been a fight or something?"

"Nope. Every place should look as good as that one."

Thaddeus nodded and stared into his coffee.

Tell me where she is. Help me make it right.

"All I can say is the little missy hides pretty good," Jackson added.

Hides? Of course.

Thank You.

Thaddeus pulled himself upright. "I know where she is."

Thirty-four

*J*ackson looked up sharply from the seat he'd taken at the table. "You do?"

Thaddeus nodded. "In the belfry."

"Thunderation," Jackson breathed. "I'll bet you're right."

Sonja had returned to familiar territory, but she could be in any emotional state imaginable—anything from fury to despondency to terror. It all depended on what had transpired between her and Karl—who chose that moment to sputter and struggle.

"He's going right now," Thaddeus said, setting his cup on the supply cabinet just inside the door and striding to the bed. He pressed his fingers to Karl's throat. The pulse was already thready. His body—the strength and power he'd been so proud of—tensed, fought, then the pulse faltered and stopped altogether.

Thaddeus looked to Jackson, who stood at the foot of the bed. They exchanged a long glance before Jackson jerked his head at the door. "Go on. I'll take care of this here mess."

"Have Leland come for the body?"

"Yep. Now go, before the little missy gets lung sick. It ain't summer no more."

In fact, the cold was enough to make Thaddeus hunch into his coat and step up his already brisk pace. The lantern swung and bobbed at his side. He gripped the handle more tightly, wrapping his thumb over his fingers. Should have thought to wear gloves—but since when had he been thinking, today? Maybe he'd done too much thinking and not enough listening.

He'd crossed the river and had the Chapel of San Miguel in sight when a man and youth approached from the other direction. He was about to pass when the walk of the shorter one caught his attention.

He held the lantern high. "Sonja?"

Her voice was small. "Yes." She ducked her chin, dipping her eyes in deep shadow. She was buttoned into someone else's coat—someone four times her size.

"Dr. Staley?" the man beside her said. "How fortunate that we encounter you on our way. No doubt you've come for your wife, but your search is over, and she is safe and well. I was escorting her back to your care."

"You're the priest?" Thaddeus asked, clued by the man's long robe and wide-brimmed hat.

The man introduced himself, but the words were only mumblings in the background. Sonja didn't look hurt by outward appearances, but there could be any number of injuries under all that coat.

"She seems to have been upset by something tonight," the priest was saying.

Thaddeus cleared his throat. "Yes. We had a bit of an upheaval."

She wouldn't let him see her eyes. Thaddeus clenched his jaw. Maybe Karl had hit her in the face.

The clergyman shifted. "Yes . . . well . . . these things happen. She tells me you've been married only a few months."

"Yes."

Silence stretched between them, becoming awkward.

The priest cleared his throat again. "Well, I suppose my mission is complete. Good evening, Mrs. Staley. Dr. Staley." He tapped his hat in greeting and retreated into the darkness.

Thaddeus still held the lantern up. Sonja still hid her face. His tongue still lay in a useless heap behind his teeth, seemingly unattached to his brain—which couldn't seem to put two thoughts together. She'd materialized before he'd had a chance to plan anything.

He lowered the light and started walking, pausing for her to step beside him. She didn't ask where they were going. She probably guessed when they turned down their street. But she didn't ask why Thaddeus had come looking for her. Fear gripped his heart. It wasn't like her to be so quiet.

"Are you hurt?" he asked.

Don't let her be hurt, Lord.

"No."

Thank You.

And that was the entire balance of their conversation.

At the house he opened the door for her and followed her inside, casting a quick glance into the examination room. Karl's body was gone, and Jackson had stripped the dirty bedclothes. Thaddeus closed the door then stepped into the rear bedroom—what had been Sonja's room—to hang his coat and hat.

Sonja was standing in the middle of the parlor, much the same way she had looked—oversized coat and all—the first time he brought her from the belfry. Except that night she'd been turning a slow circle, looking at his parlor. This night, the little figure stood still and mute, staring angrily at a spot somewhere near the leg of the table.

"Is that your father's coat?" he asked, walking past her to the fire—which Jackson had already built up.

"Yes."

"Why don't you take it off? It's warm enough."

Far too obediently, she did—but jerked away when he moved as if to help. His hands fell limp at his sides while she draped the coat over her folded arms. She turned her face away, chin high.

She didn't look injured—no visible cuts or bruises where Karl might have hit her—but she didn't look well. The coil of hair that was supposed to be at the crown of her head hung drunkenly at the side, looking as though it would fall free at the next turn, and entire strands had come loose and were tangled down her back. Her cheeks were red from the cold, her eyes sore from crying, and her lips swollen.

Where to begin? The way she held her shoulders tense like that, it was obvious she didn't want to be here. She glanced at the door as if she were thinking of bolting through it.

"Do you want something to eat or drink?" he asked, lame for anything else to say.

A little jerk served as a no. Perhaps if she sat down—

"Why am I here?" she asked.

Could have predicted her directness, but the question itself made a pitiful statement. The stare she turned on him was sharp, telling him she'd had enough. Sonja would fight.

Thaddeus didn't blame her—and couldn't be more proud, once he recovered from the surprise. Harley was right. A man wanted a soft woman beside him at night, but by day she'd better be strong enough to bully the animals, work under the weather, and improvise her way through the ceaseless doing-without. This one had that kind of courage—and more. This one sacrificed herself for the sake of those she loved. This one turned away from a rescue when it wasn't in the best interest of the wagon master who offered it. This one conceived a child in hate, but bore it in peace.

Thaddeus thanked God all over again for giving so wisely and well what he hadn't even known he needed.

"Well?" she asked.

"Why don't you sit down, Sonja?"

"I don't want to sit down."

Trying for a relaxed stance, Thaddeus folded his arms and leaned against the bookcase. "Prepare yourself. This will be a bit of a shock."

The only sign of her bracing was a tensing around her mouth.

"Karl is dead."

Her expression fell. Then her dumbfounded stare dropped from his face to his sidearm. "Did you shoot him?"

He nearly burst into startled laughter. "No—but I thought about it. He ran into the street and was struck by a wagon and team."

She whirled around to the closed door. "Is he in there?"

"He was. Leland took his body away. I imagine we'll have a funeral whenever your father returns, provided it's soon."

She nodded numbly as she stepped to the bench and sank slowly onto it. For a long moment, she stared at the floor in front of his boots.

"Did he hurt you tonight, Sonja?"

She gave him a dazed stare. "No. Why?"

Here it was, the time to cast her secret from the place it held between them, and he hadn't the slightest idea how to approach it. She'd do anything to conceal it, she'd already proven that. She'd left her only living relative, lived in a belfry, offered no defense when her husband falsely accused her, then let him take her back to her father as if she were merchandise bought under false pretenses. All this to keep from telling anyone how she'd been tortured by a sadistic "friend" of the family.

Thaddeus pulled away from the bookcase and sat beside

her on the bench. Warily she watched him.

"I know about Karl, Sonja."

"What about Karl?"

"About—" He stopped. She probably wouldn't even know what the word "rape" meant. It wasn't something mothers taught their daughters. It wasn't something they should need to. "I know that he forced himself on you."

The caution in her eyes fled on the heels of horror. She swiveled away on the bench, giving him her back. Then she jumped from the seat altogether, not stopping until she reached his desk, far from him and just a few steps from the door.

"How do you know that? Did he tell you?"

"No. I figured it out—"

"Does Papa know?"

"No. At least I don't think—"

"How did you figure it out? How did you know?" Panic was building in her voice. Her shoulders lifted and fell rapidly, as if she struggled for breath.

"By some things you said."

"What things?"

"Just things. I'll explain later." This was beginning to embarrass him.

"Tell me now. What things?"

More than the words, her tone said she wouldn't let the topic rest. He stared at her back and bent head, congealing all the things he could say into one or two best attempts.

"You said I was the only man to kiss you," Thaddeus began slowly. He paused, letting that much settle. "Couples . . . when they're . . . intimate, Sonja, they kiss."

Slowly she turned her head to look over her shoulder at him, naked curiosity in her eyes. "They kiss?"

She asked it as if he just discovered a lamp that lit itself. And his heart wrenched, for the expression in her eyes begged for it to be true. Silently she cried for his assurance that knowing a man in a way that made babies could be something better than what she knew of it. Something more than terror and agony and humiliation. It was worse than cruel.

. . . That poor girl back in Philadelphia. Her mother had summoned him to come quick, for her daughter had been raped—except it looked as though her attacker tried to slaughter her. Her mother attempted to clean her up before he arrived, but there'd still been blood—clear to her ankles and still weeping from her torn and tortured flesh. If that hadn't been enough, one of her lovely eyes—green eyes, they were—was nearly swollen shut, and her lips looked as though they belonged on a larger face. But she didn't cry. Just stared at the ceiling—until he came near. Then she fought like a trapped animal. He had to put her to sleep with chloroform just to patch her together.

Sonja stared, waiting.

"Yes, they kiss," Thaddeus told her. "And it's not what you think. Not what you . . . know it to be. It's . . . tender and . . . exciting." He said that last word with as much decorum as he could muster, then buffered it by adding, "It brings couples closer together."

Sonja whirled toward the desk, shaking her head. "Stupid," she spat. "And naive. I've had a baby and know less about it than . . . than . . . than anyone. An adolescent boy knows more than I do."

He rose and approached carefully. "You're not stupid. You're innocent. There's a difference, and it has nothing to do with intelligence."

He stared at the delicate neck holding her head, at the narrow shoulders on either side, and fumed with rage. How could something so small and delicate incite such blatant disregard and violence? What was the point? Certainly not for the contest; there was no challenge in making a woman two-thirds your weight bend to your whim. Even if she matched Karl pound-for-pound, his superior muscle structure gave him—

"I should have fought," she said suddenly. She shook her head. "Never mind. It was my fault."

"What was your fault? I don't understand."

"Never mind. I'll go back to Papa's."

Wait a minute. He had this all figured out. Now she was mixing it up again.

She began searching the interior of the coat for the sleeve hole.

"What are you talking about?" Thaddeus said. "Karl forced you."

"No, I shouldn't have gone out there," she replied, still searching for that opening. "Mama told me to never be alone with a boy, and Papa didn't like me in the smithy when Karl was working by himself, but I didn't think it would matter. I just didn't—"

"Sonja?"

"He liked me. I know he did. Margaret Shanahan said he'd declare himself by the time—"

"Sonja."

She stopped and dropped her arms, letting most of the coat pile on her feet and the floor before them.

"See, it was during the January thaw," she said—quickly, as if to be done with the story. "Papa rode to South Bend to buy a wagon before the prices went up in the spring. He was going to be gone several days, so I stayed at Margaret Shanahan's." She paused . . . and said so softly, "I sneaked over to the smithy, to Papa's workroom, to see Karl."

Thirty-five

*T*he corner workroom in the smithy took shape in Thaddeus' mind—the split-log floor, dirtier at the edges, rough walls lined with rows of blackened hammers, pries, and other odd tools, and barrels of raw metals, waiting for mighty hands to fashion them into nails, chain, horseshoes, and farm implements. There would be a work table, its back edge littered with discards that just might come in handy one day, and its center holding yesterday's project that would get finished today.

"He'd been filling the kerosene lamps," Sonja continued. She shuddered.

She hated the smell of kerosene.

"He . . . started touching me." The urgency in her voice faded into a distance she seemed to follow. "He took liberties and said it was my fault for coming in there and for looking at him the way I did." She shook her head, perfectly bewildered. "I didn't know. I didn't mean to . . ."

She searched for words, and Thaddeus silently begged her not to find them, to not paint him into the picture he didn't want to watch.

"I backed away from him, but he blocked the door. Then

he grabbed my wrist so hard, I thought it would break. I tried to wrench free, but he got so angry. It scared me that he was so angry. Then he twisted my arm behind my back and pushed me to the floor."

On her face. Like an animal. Wouldn't even dignify her with as little respect as it took to face her.

That poor girl with the green eyes . . . this poor girl with the blue ones. Sky blue. Like facets cut from a glorious sky.

Thaddeus' forgiven flesh rose up, entertaining sinful revenge, dreaming of mutilating the man's body, of scattering its pieces for the animals to devour—

"He was so heavy, and there were little rocks digging into my cheek and dirt in my eye." Sonja paused. Admitted in a drone, "I was small and unimportant. But it didn't matter. It was like I wasn't there."

Her voice sounded as if she weren't here now.

"Like it was happening to someone else. I don't think I could move. Maybe I didn't try." She shook her head as if shaking off the distance in her voice. She became matter-of-fact. "I didn't try. I just let him. It was my fault."

"There was nothing you could do."

"No, he just twisted my arm. That's all. Just my arm. I could have—"

"There was nothing you could do. Nothing. He had the control. He overpowered you. Maybe even manipulated the situation so he could get you alone."

And any one of those was rape.

She shook her head in disbelief. "I'm never safe. Any man can hurt me any time he wants." Then, before he could answer that, "I disobeyed Papa by sneaking into the smithy."

Poor judgment? That was the accusation she leveled at herself? Hadn't studied law, but as far as he knew, that wasn't punishable by rape.

"I got away, tonight," she added as if that proved she could have done so in January. "He started to badger me, but I grabbed Papa's coat and ran out the door. I don't think he even followed me."

When Thaddeus started to open his mouth to speak, Sonja said, "I should go back. Will you walk me?"

Silly question. "No. Stay here. Be my wife."

She turned, looking over her shoulder. Her expression was one of confusion. "I can't."

"Why not?"

"You don't want me. You threw me away. You took me to Papa—"

"I was jealous. Crazy with it. Karl was sniffing after you. I could tell that—"

"He didn't come here," she said tiredly, facing forward far enough to give him her profile. "He made it look like we were meeting secretly just to rile you up."

"It worked. What I didn't know was that you had no part in it. You simply ignored him."

"I pretended he didn't exist." She fixed on an obscure spot above the bookcase, the expression in her eyes growing vague. "I got so good at it—at looking through him—sometimes it surprised me when he spoke."

"I thought you were overcompensating for your secret life with him." Thaddeus swallowed, weak with anguish. "Somehow I expect every woman to be like her. Like Amanda."

"I'm not Amanda," Sonja said, quietly. So perceptive. And the tiniest bit of anger flashed a tension in her features—hurt in disguise.

"Forgive me," he said. "Come back. Be my wife."

She stepped away, dangerously close to the door, shaking her hands as if frustrated with whatever dirtied them. "I can't do that. Nothing has changed, don't you see?"

"Everything has changed."

She spun around, arms folded and head rocked to the side in an obvious challenge. "How? What?"

It might have looked easy for her to drop their relationship into a box and close the lid, except she held so still, as though she didn't even dare breathe. That gave her away. Told him to hope, to press forward with the faith that what he sought was there, if he had the persistence to unearth it.

Beyond the door, a wagon and team jangled and thundered down the street at reckless speed.

Not here. Not me. Just a little more time . . .

The racket—someone else's emergency—faded into the night, into silence. With a little sigh, Sonja looked to the coat heaped at his feet as if mentally putting it on.

"Me," Thaddeus said, stopping her. "I'm different."

She stared at him. Waited for an explanation while the lantern burned, shadows danced, and his future balanced on a thread suspended in the few feet—and the chasm—between them. It could wobble, then tumble to either side. Abyss or bliss. One or the other. She held the decision, and he held his breath.

"I've been running, blaming God for the mess I made of my life. Blaming Him for how . . . lonely I was." He looked to where her skirt met the floor. "I didn't think I was lonely. But I was miserable with it. He told me not to marry Amanda. To run the other way. I stopped listening at that point . . . and it just got easier to stay out there by myself . . . then to blame Him for the results. Everything that happened to me, I did to myself." He paused. "Forgive me. I want you back, and I'm ready to be that Christian husband you want."

Hope sparked in her eyes, so blue, then died while he watched. "I can't do that," she said as if this were the saddest truth. A pitiful impasse. "I can't be the Christian wife you want. Not whole. You see?" She looked to the floor between them, though her chin was high. "The only thing I can give you is what we had before, the original arrangement. I'm not capable of . . . a real relationship."

"I won't accept that. It's counterfeit. And there's more in you than that."

"I can't—"

"I can trust you to not be Amanda, Sonja. Why can't you trust me not to be Karl?"

Crystalline eyes turned back. Pierced him. Impaled themselves on him. "It's not that easy," she snapped, except the words burned with regret in their passing. "Besides, you can't want me," she spit.

"Why not?"

"I'm not . . . chaste." It was a whisper, as if the most awful secret.

He wasn't either, and she deserved that much—

Wait a minute. All of this—these months of polite distance—were because she didn't feel worthy? Of him, who'd done some running from his own shame? Except it followed him, because he'd also run from the only One who could reconcile it . . . and give him peace. This Thaddeus understood.

And Sonja couldn't be more wrong.

"Sonja, when I look at you I see—"

"I'm dirty," she whispered.

"You're not dirty. You're the victim of another's cruelty. It wasn't your fault."

She looked away.

"You forgave Karl, Sonja. Forgive yourself."

She looked back and seemed to all but crawl into his eyes as the sound of his voice slid down the walls and fell into the corners. . . .

Suddenly she crumpled in on herself, shoulders curling, then shaking on a sob as she bent and buried her face in her hands. "I can't. It's too hard."

He had her in his arms in less than a breath. She not only let him hold her, but couldn't seem to get close enough, all but crawling into his chest to cry pitiful, soul-shaking sobs that wet his shirt, made him sick with grief, and wore her to a heap leaning into him.

He was stroking her hair, her head tucked safely under his cheek, when she suddenly pulled free and straightened. She cleared her throat and tucked fretfully at her wayward hair, as if she suddenly remembered where she was. As if she'd stayed too long to tea. As if he were a cat to be dusted from her lap. She intended to leave. To actually walk through that door as if there were no reason to do otherwise.

"Stay," he said. Couldn't believe she could consider anything else.

She looked up. Her eyes were a bright blue, contrasted against the irritation of hard crying and fragile skin. Her cheeks were chapped.

"I can't."

"Why not?" He looked deep, desperate to search every corner for the last obstacle, for the stubborn one that hung on, for the "never" that seemed too strong.

Then it nearly knocked him senseless, the way she looked up at him with the caution of a mouse. It was fear, all right, but of him as a man. Simply because of his size and masculinity, the things she'd come to associate with her own helplessness.

No, it couldn't be that simple. Or he was the biggest dolt not to see it.

So much for the diploma behind him.

He shook his head. "You're not afraid of me."

The test—and revelation—was well-placed, for all expression drained from her features. "I beg your pardon?"

Right on the mark, he pressed on. "You think you're

afraid of me, but you're not. You never were." Even though she'd terrified him. "Not even when you didn't know me. I don't know what, but something made you trust me."

"Your eyes."

"Pardon me?"

"I saw compassion in your eyes."

That's what Jackson had said. Silently, Thaddeus begged Sonja to see it now.

"But I'm obviously a very poor judge of character," she added.

He let that pass, unwilling to believe she referred to him. "Do you care for me, Sonja?" he asked, then decided it didn't matter. "I love you. And you know it."

"Don't," she whispered to his shirt.

"That doesn't scare you either. It's what you've longed to hear."

Slowly, carefully, he lifted a hand to the ridiculous twist of hair hanging just over and behind her ear. She let him, though her brows twitched in obvious confusion.

"You see, you don't know what I know." He dug gently for the pins and pulled them free.

She blushed, and her little shoulders lifted and fell with the race of her breathing. Her heart would be beating like a rabbit's. "What do you know?" she asked, captivated by his shirt.

The hair fell loose. He spread it out with both hands, sometimes arranging it and sometimes smoothing a tangle. He slipped the pins into his pocket—a woman's hairpins in the pocket of a man's trousers. This woman's hairpins in his pocket.

"You don't know how you kissed me that first time," he said.

Her brows bunched. "When we got married? That was—"

"That wasn't the first time. That was only the first time you remember."

Now she was visibly perplexed, but it brought her attention from his stupid shirt.

He smoothed the hair from her face with the backs of his fingers. Little strokes that made her blink slowly, made her lean ever so slightly toward him. He kept the arm that wanted to wrap around her at his side—she could step away at any time—but bent slowly to set a kiss on her face, just there, above her temple and where the gleaming hair met creamy skin. He closed his eyes. Oh, the smell of her. The warm, delicious scent of woman and the crisp air they'd walked through to get here.

He placed another kiss and rubbed his cheek against her temple, wallowing in the feel . . . the glory of her.

"That first night you were with the train," he whispered—and she didn't move, with her listening—"I brought you soap and water. You washed your face and cleaned your teeth with my bandanna. Then I combed your hair, Sonja . . . and I kissed you."

She jumped. She stiffened.

He kissed the delicate skin in front of her ear. Then her temple and her cheek, learning her face with his lips. "You gave me a new name that night. And you kissed me back."

"I wouldn't," she hissed. "It's scandalous. I didn't even know you."

"Yes, you did. Better than I knew myself."

He leaned away far enough to see her eyes, which darted about nervously. "You weren't afraid, Sonja."

"I'm afraid now," she admitted begrudgingly.

Always direct. Always frank. And always, always making his heart smile.

"Maybe. Maybe you're simply nervous," he said. "I know I am."

That brought her eyes up to his, with surprise in them—
as if he were made of stone. As if she were supposed to have
no effect on him. As if he knew the way through every entan-
glement and mystery. His heart welled with gratitude, that
she believed him so capable. That she would go to these
unknown places with him, or with no one at all. Ever.

She looked away, to his shirt, eyes wide. "You want to
kiss me, now, don't you?"

If he didn't know her, he would laugh in nervous surprise. She looked up far enough to watch his mouth. He
watched hers . . . and nodded.

She slapped a palm over her stomach. "Ooh."

They would laugh about this someday—provided they
lived through it. Her fear was such a tangible thing. And he
was suturing connections more delicate than skin.

"I'll wait, Sonja. I'll never press you. It's more than the
. . . than the physical. It's you I want. Your heart. I want to
court you, to woo you. We'll take our time."

God help him to go slow. To not devour her at the first
taste.

"Perfect love casts out fear," he added.

"Are you going to heal me with it?" she asked.

"No."

She looked up. Gave him her eyes to fall into.

"You're healing me," he said.

Calm eased into her features. Her breath even settled
into a more gentle rhythm. Her blue eyes watched him.
Studied him. And agreed.

Then her expression shifted in a typically Sonja way. *Well,
are you going to get on with it?* her eyes seemed to say.

Don't rush me, he replied.

Now, who's afraid—the almost imperceptible taunt of a
lifted eyebrow.

With the moment finally here, he glanced at her mouth,

fixing on where he intended to go. Then lowered his head. Just above her lips he stopped, sharing her breath and giving her a chance to change her mind. Her eyes fluttered closed, giving him her answer.

Her mouth was soft and hesitant under his, but there was a measure of curiosity there, and desire in the way she leaned up to receive him. He pressed more firmly and moved his lips, letting himself fall just a little into what she allowed . . . and fought not to lift his arms and squeeze the stuffing out of her.

Sonja's heart fluttered. It threatened to stop altogether. An amazing thing, this kiss. Complete in its giving, in its connecting a woman to her husband . . . but lacking, as if there were more. More to come. More she wanted. The beginning note and the ending chord, all in one and at the same time.

Mysteriously she knew how to do this. That she needed to close her eyes. That she would tip her head one way while he tilted his the other. And how to breathe while her mouth was so engaged.

Yet it was terrifying. What came next? When would be too far to turn back? When would it hurt and smother her—

Except Noble demanded nothing. Didn't even put his arms around her. Only leaned down to kiss her lips. Simply bent to give . . . not take.

And that was what gave her the courage to lift her hand . . . slowly . . . and set it on his shirt, just over his left breast pocket. To let herself feel the solidity of this man under her fingertips. A man's warmth and heartbeat and strength . . . and tenderness, in the way he gently slid his arms around her. Not to take her captive, but to make her precious. To let her learn, so carefully, how to hold and be held.

It wasn't until his lips were buried in her hair that she realized he'd even broken away. That there was a parlor with a fire and a coat heaped at their feet. But that there was also a shoulder pressed to her nose, that he held her delicately in his strength . . . solid planes against her curves . . . and that he was speaking, murmuring words that seemed to rise from a depth. That he was whispering he adored her, that he valued what she gave. That it was his and only his kiss.

Author's Note

According to the figures I uncovered, one in four women in the United States will be sexually assaulted or raped in her lifetime; 84 percent of them will know their attackers—because the men are friends, friends of siblings, friends of the family, or someone they are attracted to. The women aren't "asking for it," and they say no. They just aren't heard, believed, or valued by the men who maneuver and manipulate them into a situation where they will feel powerless. Please relieve them . . . by believing them. No victim ever asks for the crime committed against them . . . or to lose the trust they fight so hard to regain.

On a lighter note, there really was a Russell, Majors, and Waddell freighting company whose bullwhackers were issued Bibles, asked to sign a morality agreement banning foul language, drunkenness, gambling, and cruelty to animals, and were given Sundays off. God has a record of blessing those who honor Him; the company opened the West and made wealthy men of its three owners.

There really is a plaza in Santa Fe that teemed with activity—including children who smoked!

And there really is a Chapel of San Miguel that sits on the threshold of what was the *Barrio de Analco,* the Ward Beyond the River. The oldest church in the United States, it boasted a triple-tiered belfry until a storm blew it over in 1872. That original belfry was perfect for my needs, but it lacked easy access for a heroine with child and her rescuing hero. Adding a winding staircase hung in the balance between historical accuracy and fun scenes; the fun won, and for the price of precision I pay an apology. Weigh that with the fact that everything else about the Chapel, Santa Fe, bullwhacking, and 1858 medicine is as exact as my research could make it. Perfectionist that he is, Noble wouldn't have it any other way.

Sherrie Lord

Dear Reader:

We love to hear from our readers. Your response to the following questions will help us continue publishing the excellent Christian fiction that you enjoy.

1. What most influenced you to buy *Only His Kiss*?
    - ❏ Cover/title
    - ❏ Subject matter
    - ❏ Back cover copy
    - ❏ Author
    - ❏ Recommendation by friend
    - ❏ Recommendation by bookstore sales person

2. How would you rate this book?
    - ❏ Great
    - ❏ Good
    - ❏ Fair
    - ❏ Poor

Comments:

3. What did you like best about this book?
    - ❏ Characters
    - ❏ Plot
    - ❏ Setting
    - ❏ Inspirational theme
    - ❏ Other_____

4. Will you buy more novels in the **Promises** series?
    - ❏ Yes
    - ❏ No

Why?

5. Which do you prefer?
    - ❏ Historical romance
    - ❏ Contemporary romance
    - ❏ No preference

6. How many Christian novels do you buy per year?
    - ❏ Less than 3
    - ❏ 3-6
    - ❏ 7 or more

7. What is your age?
    - ❏ Under 18
    - ❏ 18-24
    - ❏ 25-34
    - ❏ 35-44
    - ❏ 45-54
    - ❏ Over 55

Please return to
ChariotVictor Publishing
Promises Editor
4050 Lee Vance View
Colorado Springs, CO 80918